Aphrodite's Whisper

William Charles Furney

Aphrodite's Whisper

Black Hearts Publishing

www.billfurney.com

Aphrodite's Whisper is a work of fiction. All incidents and dialogue,
and all characters with the exception of some well-known historical
figures, are products of the author's imagination and are not to be
construed as real. Where real-life historical figures appear, the
situations, incidents, and dialogues concerning those persons are
entirely fictional and are not intended to depict actual events or to
change the entirely fictional nature of the work. In all other respects,
any resemblance to actual persons, living or dead, events, or locales
is entirely coincidental.

Cover art: Consuelo Parra
Model: Faestock.deviantart.com
Design Consultant: Meredith Walsh

Second Edition

ISBN: 0-9988921-9-X
ISBN-13: 978-0-9988921-9-1

Table of Contents

"Would you die for her?"
"I do. Every day."

Jessica Shirvington, *Emblaze*

Chapter One

The Storm

Friday, December 11, 1903
Cape Hatteras, North Carolina

With one hand clutching the collar of his slicker tight under his chin and the other grasping the handle of an unlit lantern, the lone surfman trudged through the sand and the darkness, leaning ever forward into a downpour blasted horizontal by the brutal winds of a frigid nor'easter.

As he walked, he listened for the crash of the waves breaking on the beach to guide him. Veering too far right would put him waist-deep in the roiling surf and at risk of being swept out to sea. Too far left, and the powdery sand of the inner beach, turned into the consistency of wet cement by the rain, would make walking impossible. His storm lantern would have provided the light needed to reveal the hard-packed sand in the area between the two extremes, but its wick had long since surrendered to the relentless wind.

The storm's arctic cold had replaced the tempered warmth of the Outer Banks with a freezing rain, turning the five miles of Ethan Roberts' watch-walk into a soaking, miserable test of endurance. Though the surfman's feet throbbed with icy pain, the fear of frostbite drove his pace. At twenty-eight, he was old enough to know the dangers of the cold, but too young to admit it could defeat him. He would do his job to its completion, as expected. The weather be damned.

Reaching the northern-most point of his patrol, he reversed direction and headed back to the warmth and shelter of the station of lifesavers that was his home. The gale blew from behind now, pushing him toward his destination. The wide brim of his oilskin hat diverted most of the rain down the back of his slicker, but the wind blasted spray around his head to soak his bearded face.

Pausing to wipe the water from his eyes, he searched the darkness ahead for the beacon that stood sentinel beside the station. Every seven-and-a-half seconds, the rotating lens of the Cape Hatteras lighthouse sliced its bright beam through the swirling black rain, beckoning the lifesaver back to where his patrol had begun. But it was too early to have thoughts of warmth and comfort. He still had miles to go, and the rain was turning into a mix of icy water and sleet. Suppressing a cold shudder, the surfman dismissed the circumstances of his misery, grasped the slicker's flaps tight beneath his chin again, and resumed the patrol.

Not until he was close enough to see the dim, yellow flash of lantern light shining through the station's windows did he allow himself to think of the glowing wood stove within the clapboard refuge. Once inside, he would use its warmth to thaw his aching flesh before settling under the wool blankets on his bunk. By the time the next lifesaver had left to walk the coastline to look for ships in distress, he would be dry, warm, and asleep.

Ethan stopped in his tracks as a fiery streak of orange and red bolted from the waters of the open ocean and then disappeared into the thick, angry clouds above. A moment later, brilliant white spears of light from the rocket's bursting flare stabbed holes through the stormy blackness. A ship had run aground on the Diamond Shoals! The surfman's thoughts of warmth and sleep vanished as rapidly as the glowing ball fell to the sea. The lives of the foundering ship's crew now rested in the hands of Ethan, the station's other six surfmen, and their ability to row through the churning waters with all the speed their arms could muster.

Sprinting to the station, Ethan darted inside to wake the others. The seasoned rescuers began gearing up without question while Ethan ran back outside to set off a Coston signal on the beach. The ground flare's brilliant light would let the sailors on the shoals know that help was on the way. The race had begun.

As Ethan made his way back to the station, the other six men gathered in the shed where their surfboat waited on its cart. As one, they pushed the cart over the sand on a path hardened by oyster shells and into the surf until its wheels rolled hub-deep beneath the cold December waters. With the boat now floating free, the lifesavers scrambled aboard, paying no heed to the raging surf around them.

Taking his seat at the stern, Station Keeper Ephraim Jenette fought with the steering oar, struggling to keep the bow pointing into the oncoming waves. The huge breakers would hit them broadside if the wind and current forced the boat off a direct heading, turning the rescue attempt into its own disaster.

On his cue, the men thrust their oars into the water, pulling together with all their strength. The surfboat surged forward, plowing through the cresting waves. Each breaker brought gallons of frothing water crashing on top of them, shaking the boat to its frame and every man to the bone.

Into the darkness they rowed, not knowing how far out to sea their quest would take them. Once past the breakers and into the open, the swells became rolling mountains that shifted into canyons of water. The boat slid down the back of one giant surge after another as the oncoming swell that followed rushed up to hurl them atop the next mountain. With each cresting, the keeper scanned the horizon for the distressed ship. Because his was the only seat facing the bow and the open water, it was up to him to spot the distressed vessel.

Sitting in the foremost seat, Ethan bore the brunt of the pounding more than the others. Waves cresting the bow soaked him with seawater, sending ice-cold jolts of agony through his body. Most lifesavers sought any excuse to avoid the bow seat and the pounding it absorbed from the waves. The Hatteras crew, however, never drew lots or took turns at the bow. Ethan was always at the front when bringing the boat to the surf and always first to jump in to take the dreaded bow seat. They did not know why and they never asked.

What they did not know was that Ethan welcomed the constant pounding and numbing cold of the water. The unrelenting assault on his hardened body kept his mind free of any thoughts except the pain of the moment. For a few hours, there would be no memories of Cuba or San Juan

Hill or the smoldering house to haunt him. There would be no agonizing images of his friend Zeb or the twisted face of the Spanish woman – the madre.

Despite resolving never to acknowledge the matter, he understood it was those dark memories that kept him from leaving the isolation of the Outer Banks. If he were lucky, this would be the storm to take away the ghosts of his past. If not, the attempt to save the lives of others would provide a few hours of refuge, a reprieve for which he gave thanks.

Sensing the lethal nor'easter had reached its peak, Ethan wondered whether the keeper could spot their objective through the darkness and rain. The driving wind almost matched their pull on the oars, pushing the little boat back almost as fast as they rowed it forward. If not for the warmth created by their exertions, the cold would have been unbearable. As veteran lifesavers, they were no strangers to storm and danger, but neither Ethan nor the other surfmen of the Hatteras Station had ever encountered such a relentless combination of cold, wind, and rain as this storm.

They would need all their experience and training to survive. Regardless of what befell them, there would be no turning back. The regulations of the Lifesaving Service required them to attempt the rescue despite the weather or the odds of surviving. Each man was bound by oath to attempt a rescue when they were called, even during hurricanes and bitter nor'easters. After all, what good would lifesavers be if they only came out in fair weather?

"Ship ho!" the keeper shouted at last, the wind snatching away his words as they came from his mouth. But the lifesavers did not have to hear their captain's words to know what he was saying. There was but one reason he would be yelling.

Ethan turned around long enough to spot the vessel. Light still shining along its deck meant the men aboard might still be alive. The vastness of the nighttime ocean made it impossible to tell how far away they were. The light could be a single candle or an entire ship on fire.

It didn't matter. They were lifesavers – or surfmen, as the locals called them. They had to believe that the sailors on board the ship were waiting and praying for deliverance. The keeper's call to quicken their strokes interrupted Ethan's thoughts, and he pulled on his oar harder to match the pace of the others.

Chapter Two

Keeper's Choice

The rain had turned to sleet, adding a muffled, staccato beat as the ice bounced off the surfmen's slickers and cork-filled life vests. As the captain of his crew of lifesavers, the keeper knew his men were no longer marking time by minutes but by pain. He had been a crewman once, and he knew they would continue rowing to the point of exhaustion if called on to do so.

Forced to peer into the wind, the frozen water pelted his face without mercy. With one hand on the steering oar and the other protecting his eyes, he stole a glance every few seconds as they closed in on the object of their quest. The ship had snagged a shoal and was being battered by the waves. Its running lights were electrical, their yellow glow revealing sleek, graceful lines. She had two masts with its lowered sails lashed tight to their spars. A smokestack amidships revealed that she also employed steam power.

"For the love of..." the keeper muttered, the wind snatching his words into oblivion. "It looks to be a yacht!"

As if insulted by his declaration, the lights began flickering. But between the flashes, he could read the word APHRODITE painted in bold letters on the ship's bow.

"Look sharp now! There's no telling what kind of sailors there'll be on a gentleman's pleasure boat."

As they approached the foundering ship, the keeper saw four crewmen in a desperate struggle to lower a lifeboat into the rolling sea while two other men sat inside. The keeper leaned into the steering oar, bringing the surfboat about to parallel the bigger vessel. He had to size up the situation before coming closer.

The crew of surfmen could now see the two men in the lifeboat as it swung in wide arcs just above the water. A jammed winch had turned the unsecured lifeboat into a battering ram, unable to move up or down. While those on deck struggled to repair the winch, a man in the lifeboat shrieked useless orders, adding to their panic. Each time the yacht rocked to port, the lifeboat swung out on its retrieval lines. When the yacht rocked back to starboard, the lifeboat crashed against the larger boat's hull. A few more violent swings would either throw the two seamen out of the lifeboat or crush them against the yacht.

A sailor on deck spotted the surfboat and began shouting and pointing. As one, the four men turned away from the winch to yell and wave at the surfmen. The keeper pulled on the steering oar and the surfboat glided closer to the yacht.

As they closed the gap to within a few feet of their goal, a huge swell rolled the yacht into a dangerous tilt toward port. The lifeboat swung out from the reeling yacht and, for a moment, floated on the ocean. The retrieval lines on the small boat's bow and stern fell slack into the water. As the swell passed underneath, the yacht keeled back to its starboard side. The sudden reversal of direction snatched the slack out of the lines. With a double *KA-POW* as loud as gunfire, the ropes snapped the eyebolts securing the lines to the little boat free from their mounts. The lifeboat had launched itself and was now adrift on the sea.

The two men inside were in imminent danger, so the keeper guided the surfboat toward them instead of the yacht. As they closed in on the smaller boat, he saw the sailor shrieking orders was now in a frenzy. Without warning, the sailor sprang from his seat, flinging himself into the surfboat before the surfmen were ready. The sailor lost his balance, turning his wild scramble into a panic-driven lunge. The desperate man crashed into a dazed heap in the surfboat's hull.

"There!" the keeper shouted, pointing to the second sailor hunkered deep in the bow. Two surfmen grabbed the lifeboat's rail, taking care not to let their hands or arms get caught between the grinding boats.

"Give him a hand!" the keeper ordered. "He's not coming out on his own!"

Ethan sprang from his seat, slid across the bumping gunwales on his belly, and crawled to the man wedged in the bow. The sailor felt the surfman's hand on his shoulder and peered up at his rescuer from beneath the brim of his oilskin hat. His eyes reflected the yellow of the yacht's electric lights.

Once, twice, three times the boat lights flickered and then went dark. Before Ethan's eyes could adjust, a brilliant white flash flooded the night accompanied by a massive explosion! The yacht's untended boiler had reached its limit.

The image of Ethan flying across the lifeboat was the last thing the keeper saw in the blinding light. His hand slammed into the deck as his forehead crashed into the bow's cross-member. The surfman fell unconscious across the sailor, pinning him to the deck.

A violent shudder rippled through the *Aphrodite*, breaking her free from the shoal. Wind and waves worked together, pushing the yacht forward and between the two smaller vessels. The lifeboat was now drifting on the yacht's seaward side. The surfboat was on the landward side, pinned against the yacht. The bigger boat was pushing the surfboat beneath its hull.

"Hold on!" the keeper yelled to his men, grabbing the rails himself. The *Aphrodite* kept pushing the smaller surfboat before it.

The four crewmen who remained on the *Aphrodite's* deck screamed in terror as the yacht's deep keel bottomed out on another shoal. The boat came to an abrupt stop, pitching them overboard. Still pressed against the side of the bigger boat, the surfmen fought to free their oars and bring their surfboat about to collect the thrashing sailors. Flames ignited by the explosion were devouring the crippled yacht, illuminating the surrounding sea.

"Hurry!" yelled the keeper. "This light won't last long!"

Heeding his own warning, the keeper pulled a burning plank from the water and managed to re-ignite the running light extinguished by the sleet, rain, and the relentless waves. Thirty minutes passed before they finished pulling the *Aphrodite's* crew from the water. But when the keeper piloted the surfboat to the yacht's seaward side to look for the lifeboat, his heart sank. There no sign of his crewman or the boat. If he'd been able, he knew Ethan would have kept close to the burning yacht to reconnect with the surfboat.

With clenched teeth, the keeper accepted the dark truth. Ethan either lacked oars for the lifeboat, or his injuries prevented him from rowing. And the odds of spotting a drifting lifeboat in the night, even with his running light, were slim. Still, the keeper had never lost a crewman, and he wasn't about to lose one now.

He knew his men were watching, his face illuminated by the boat's lantern. They were waiting, eager for the order to go in search of their brother in harm's way.

"OK, lads!" he shouted above the wind. "Prepare to row. We're headin' south by southwest, before the wind."

"We're with you, cap'n!" a surfman yelled in jubilation. "We'll row this boat all the way to hell and back if we have to."

"Ready the oars!"

"No! You can't stay out here! It's... It's too dangerous! We'll all die!"

All eyes turned toward the source of the shout. The sailor who had scrambled from the lifeboat to save himself stared back at them. The yellow glow from the running light played across his unshaven face. His wild his eyes revealed a man whose sanity was one frayed thread away from breaking. And, judging by his red eyes, the keeper wondered if the man had been drinking.

The disheveled sailor stole a nervous glance at the surfmen sitting around him. The same light amplifying his panicked state twisted the crewmen's scowls into demonic masks of fury, leaving no doubt they didn't appreciate the idea of abandoning their mate.

"Listen to me!" the sailor pleaded, the wind whipping away the small clouds of moisture from his breath. It was clear his concern was for himself, but the keeper could see the desperate wheels turning in his head. "I'm first mate of that there vessel what just sunk, and as such, I'm responsible for these men. They're wet and cold, and if we don't get them back to shore, some may die."

The keeper's face drew tauter. His first duty was to save the lives of others. To turn his back on one of his own was a decision that did not come easy.

"I hate to say it, cap'n, but he's right," the surfman sitting closest to him said. He paused in his efforts to comfort one of the shivering sailors to make his case. "This fellow won't stop shaking. I think he's in shock an' his wet clothes ain't helpin' matters none. I don't think he'll make it if we don't get back soon."

The keeper surveyed the rescued sailors and then the faces of his men. He knew what he had to do, but he didn't want to admit it.

"All right," he said in defeat, hating the order even as he gave it. "Ready the oars! We're heading back to shore."

Shaken by the order, a few of the surfmen cursed to themselves, but they knew their captain had no choice. As the surfboat turned back toward land, the Hatteras keeper thought about Ethan, praying he was still alive. A drifting lifeboat was little match for the tempest blowing about them, and if no one was at the rudder, capsizing would be inevitable. At least in Ethan's case, he would not have to worry about notifying the next of kin. He had come to the Hatteras Station from out west, a strong but empty young man with no family. He never talked about his past and seldom showed interest in anything but his work. The keeper, an excellent judge of men, had always understood that Ethan was trying to make peace with himself – though he had no idea why. Perhaps the peace he was searching for had found him.

Chapter Three

Two Adrift

Though it was registered to Jack Canady, the *Aphrodite* was his daughter's passion. Caelyn had talked him into purchasing the vessel and she had named her. And though she would not yet call herself an expert sailor, she was competent enough to understand the seriousness of her situation.

The wind was pushing the lifeboat south-by-southwest, driving them ever farther from the Hatteras lighthouse and into the darkness. There would be a steady stream of freighters sailing up and down the coast, but even after it turned light, the tiny lifeboat would be hard to spot in the rough waters. Having no food or water, the provision of which was the first mate's responsibility, their chances of survival were almost zero. She had known from the beginning that hiring Ansel Stick was a mistake, but she had had little choice. The *Aphrodite* required a first mate who knew steam engines, and Stick had been the only sailor with such skills available. It was not the first time her impatience had gotten her into trouble.

Prying herself out from under the unconscious lifesaver, Caelyn shifted around as much as she dared in the rolling lifeboat and placed his head in her lap. The boat's shallow decking kept them from having to sit in water, buy they had no protection from the bitter cold and rain. Each swell passing beneath them pitched the boat over on its side so far they came close to capsizing several times. And when she thought their situation couldn't get any worse, a massive wave breached the port rail, soaking them to the bone.

"Zeb!" the lifesaver cried out after the wave hit. "Zeb! Answer me! I'm coming for you! Hold on!"

Rather than a dream, the desperation of his pleas spoke of a dreaded memory, and Caelyn wondered at his torment.

If only the wind would die down a little, she thought in frustration. *I can't do anything to help either of us as long as this keeps up.*

Later in the night, while lost in thoughts of her poor decisions and their chances of surviving, the lifesaver brought her back into the moment with a horrifying scream.

"NOOOOOOO!" he shrieked, his voice so laced with terror it was as if he was seeing the Keres reaching out to claim his soul. Caelyn shivered at the thought and grasped his hands to comfort him. But the unconscious surfman gripped her fingers so hard she cried out in pain and fought to pull her hands free.

Alert now, she realized that the water collecting in the lifeboat was rising fast. The little vessel was half full and would soon sink. Shunting her fear, she began a methodical search about the boat with her hands until she found the bilge pump. Several minutes of steady pushing and pulling on the handle siphoned off enough water to stave off the immediate threat. For the next several hours, she alternated between sheltering the lifesaver's face from the rain and pumping. It was precious little comfort, she knew, but it was far better than doing nothing and feeling like a helpless child.

Though exhausted from exposure and from the pumping, when dawn broke, Caelyn remained undaunted. Once again she left the surfman at the bow, this time to take the seat in the center of the lifeboat. Bracing herself against the cold, she removed her oilskin coat, her wool sweater, and her blouse. In an instant, she slipped back into the sweater and coat. As brief as her nakedness had been, her tolerance was low. Her teeth chattered from shivering, and the rest of the muscles in her body soon followed. For the next few minutes, she couldn't control her limbs. When warmth returned and the trembling subsided, she returned to the bow and spread out the blouse to catch the rain. Again and again she let the rain soak the blouse, then twisted it above her head so that the water ran into her mouth.

"Here," she said to the unconscious lifesaver after letting the blouse soak again. Though doubtful he understood, hearing her own voice helped bolster her confidence. "You must drink this. I don't know how much longer we shall be out here, and I need your help. If you don't wake up soon, I'm afraid it may mean the end of us both...and I'm not ready for that yet. I'll never be ready for that."

A sudden tightening of her throat and welling of tears took her by surprise. She swallowed her fear and turned her attention back to the lifesaver. Though not sure he was taking it in, she continued to twist the water from the blouse onto his lips – until the rain stopped. Nature was taunting her.

"Is that the way of it then, fair Artemis?" she asked aloud, the stress of the moment bringing out the crisp annunciations she had inherited from her British-born mother. Even in the face of death, she turned to her beloved Greek mythology for inspiration and guidance. "Another setback...another chance to prove myself? You don't know me! You don't know me any better than the rest of them! Damn you all! I...WILL...SURVIVE!"

Words that began as defiance turned to rage. But while the anger might keep her warm, she understood it would do nothing to keep her alive. Latching onto the rush that came with the fury, she channeled the energy into finding solutions. It was the way her mind worked when freed from the shackles of those who would limit her.

As she considered and eliminated various possibilities, she realized she had failed to consider the most obvious. She knew Ansel Stick had not supplied the boat with food and water because one of the last orders he had shouted to the crew was to have them brought up from the galley. But a lifeboat should also have non-perishable supplies stored onboard to help castaways!

For the first time since sunrise, she took a careful look around the lifeboat. It was obvious the only places to store survival equipment were the bench seats. Taking a closer look at the one in front of her, she saw that the seats were box containers, their tops serving double duty as places to sit and as hinged lids covering the boxes. Unfastening the latch on the seat closest to the stern, she opened the lid.

Recoiling in deep-seated terror, she tripped backward over the next seat and fell in a heap in the boat's bottom!

17

The lid slammed shut with a sharp *BANG* as she fell, triggering an avalanche of sounds and images from her subconscious she had never experienced before. The shadowy outline of a man, his features unformed and indistinct, wavered before her. His mouth moved as though speaking, but she heard no words. She had no idea from where the voice and the image had risen or what it meant. Was it a forgotten memory, a long-lost dream, or did fatigue conjure it? And then the vision was gone, disappearing as quickly as it had come, trailing into nothingness.

Too spent to move, she stayed in place for several minutes, collecting her breath and piecing together the cause of her hysteria. She hated herself for having such unreasonable fear. For some unfathomable reason, she had always loathed guns.

The thing in the seat-box wasn't even a real gun, she reasoned to herself. *It was a flare gun, mounted to the underside of the lid. It must have been the noise the lid made when it slammed shut that had triggered her strange reaction. But why?*

Clenching her jaw, she pushed the mystery aside, determined to regain control.

Whatever is wrong...it will have to wait. Now is not the time for such foolishness.

Though her hand still trembled, she braced herself, lifted the seat's lid again and peeked inside. Her heart raced as the bulky flare gun came into view. Her face flushed hot and perspiration seeped out on her forehead, but she managed to control her fear for the moment.

It's not a real pistol, she argued to herself. *It's only a device to shoot flares, to signal for help. It could save our lives.*

18

But the thing was close enough in shape and function to an actual weapon that the anxiety grew stronger. Taking a deep breath, she forced herself to reach toward it.

I have to do this. Our lives may depend on it.

The closer her hand moved toward the gun, the harder it shook. She had stopped breathing and teetered on the edge of passing out. At the last moment, realizing that she was about to faint, she closed the lid and sank to her knees in defeat. Her aversion was so strong that she could not overcome it, even in the face of death.

She shook as much from frustration as from the exertion. But as her fear subsided, anger and defiance rushed in to replace it.

If I can't use the flare gun, then I must do something else. I can't...I won't just sit here and let us die.

Unlatching the lifeboat's oars from their stowage clamps along the hull, Caelyn mounted them in the oarlocks on the gunwales and rowed. A woman of slight build, she struggled with the heavy oars at first, accomplishing little more than to splash water. After several awkward attempts, she found her rhythm, propelling the boat a few feet forward with each pull. Though the victory was intoxicating, it was short-lived. Less than an hour later, she stopped. Her small hands, raw with blisters, could no longer grasp the oars.

Their situation was desperate. It mattered little that the wind was dying and the sky was almost clear. Without fresh water, they would not survive long. Exhausted, she rested against the oar handles crossed in an X before her.

How had things gone so wrong? This time yesterday, she had been on her way back to New York, satisfied with the decision she had made. No, it was better than that. Her voyage to Florida had been the answer to a prayer.

Her Aunt Frances in St. Augustine – her mother's twin who had emigrated from England to be closer to her sister – had helped Caelyn work through her concerns and reservations about marriage without making her feel self-conscious about her indecisiveness. She despised being the way she was. It was the trauma of her mother's death that had driven her into a shell as a child. As she grew older, her father's overprotective, obsessive manner had kept her imprisoned behind invisible bars, affording few opportunities to rediscover her true nature. Even her closest girlfriends would be amazed to learn about her secret desires. To travel and study, and to make a positive contribution to her life. As they had grown older and moved on with their lives as adults, she had remained in place, never growing, never breaking from her shell.

Only sailing, and later the *Aphrodite*, stirred her passion. It was acknowledgment of a small facet of her true self, a seed that would sprout and grow if given the chance. And though she believed her father saw it as an indulgence that might threaten his plans, he did not interfere. She wasn't sure why, but often suspected he saw it as the lesser of two evils.

When it came time to leave her aunt, Caelyn was at peace with her decision. As soon as she got back to New York, she would meet with Hunter Winslow and accept his offer of marriage. Having resolved her apprehensions and decided the next steps, she had wasted no time departing St. Augustine. As the *Aphrodite's* foresail had caught the morning breeze and sailed from Matanzas River into the Atlantic, she waved a sad farewell.

"I expect to see you at the wedding," she had called out. But the expression on her aunt's face told her it would not be so. Frances despised Caelyn's father and not even the marriage of her only niece would prompt her to suffer his proximity.

Now, as she retraced the return leg of the voyage in her mind, Caelyn cursed her impatience. The prudent thing would have been to sail during the day and anchor in protected harbors at dusk. But sailing by night meant arriving in New York in half the time. Just after nightfall on the third day, the failing of such logic became obvious.

Though it had rained for most of the afternoon, the bad weather had been little more than a nuisance at first. Neither she nor the crew had any way of knowing that the storm closing on them was the beginning of a full nor'easter. Soon, the hard winds forced them to lower all the sails and switch to steam power. Running sails during a powerful blow could snap a mast, and with the engine to power them, the risk was unnecessary. They would have been better off on the leeward side of a barrier island, but the seas became too rough, too fast to attempt a run through an inlet. The rough seas left them no option but to ride out the storm on the open sea.

The *Aphrodite* had made it to Hatteras Island and the Diamond Shoals a few hours before midnight, guided by the beacon of the cape's unfailing lighthouse. Dressed in a set of crewman's storm gear, Caelyn had stood with her helmsman at the wheel. The *Aphrodite* was her vessel – she would not leave its survival in the hands of others while cowering below deck.

The goal was to make it past the shoals and the relative safety of the northern waters. But as they struggled past the cape's point, the engine had lost power. Drifting toward the shoals and certain death, Caelyn ordered the crew to drop the sea anchor. It was too late. The *Aphrodite's* keel had snagged the sandy bottom of the shoals, bringing them to an abrupt halt. They were stuck in the shallows and the relentless pounding of the waves.

Caelyn could not remember every detail that followed. The one thing she knew for sure was that Ansel Stick was not on deck when she had needed him most. It was not until they began lowering the lifeboat that he appeared from the engine room. Despite her protests, he had forced her to climb aboard and had jumped in behind her.

"Don't worry," he had shouted to the four confused sailors left on deck. "I'll go first to make sure she doesn't drown."

That she needed help, especially from the man Caelyn somehow knew had condemned her sweet *Aphrodite*, made her furious. If not for a quirk of fate, Ansel Stick would have been with her now instead of the lifesaver. Caelyn shuddered at the thought, glancing at the man to reassure herself that he was still alive. If he came to, he might help, or at least keep her company. If he did not regain consciousness soon he might sink into a coma. At worst, she might be trapped on the small boat with a corpse.

By mid-afternoon, Caelyn judged they were four or five miles off Ocracoke Island, drifting with the current. The air was cool, but the sky was clear and the sun warmed her skin. If they removed their storm gear and laid low, out of the wind, their clothes would dry.

As she tugged off the lifesaver's gear, she saw his left wrist was swollen and purple; perhaps broken. The blouse she had used to catch the rain would now serve another purpose. Ripping off the sleeves, Caelyn wrapped his hand and used the rest of the cloth to fashion a sling. She was doing everything possible to increase their chances but what they needed more than anything else was water. Unless someone found them soon, the lifesaver would die from dehydration, and she would not last much longer.

With nothing left she could do, Caelyn studied the lifesaver's face, wondering what manner of man he might be. His dark beard hid the more telling features, but she could tell he was a younger man, about thirty. His skin was tan and weathered, but not yet turned to leather like that of a fisherman. Both his face and hands were lean and sinewy. No surprise for someone whose profession was rowing a glorified rowboat. He wore no rings or chains or jewelry of any kind. She took him to be a man of simple means and simple tastes as befitting his profession. There was nothing remarkable about him except the suggestion of an underlying strength. He had an inner strength as well, she sensed, or was it the imagination of a grown woman too long indulged in the romance of classic tales?

Chiding herself for such childish musings, Caelyn turned her attention to the setting sun and the growing sense of foreboding that came with it. It would be impossible for anyone to spot them at night, and by morning they would be far away from the shipping lanes. There would be no passing ships to spot them.

Placing her face in her hands, she sobbed, cursing the strange aversion that kept her from doing the one simple thing that might save them. But only for a few moments. She may not be stronger than the phobia, but neither was she weak of constitution and determination. The tears shed were seen by no one and the release of pent-up emotion gave her new hope. Settling in next to the fallen lifesaver to share body warmth against the growing cold, Caelyn first prayed to the God of her faith and then to the gods of mythology.

Though she knew the latter were only myths, she always found comfort in their stories.

Chapter Four

The Fisherman and his Mate

The wait had been agonizing for Captain Harry Joyner of Harkers Island. He knew trawling after a storm was futile, but having installed a gas-powered engine in his little fishing boat, he was itching to see what she could do. He had convinced himself that the horsepower generated by his engine would be the difference needed to make a profit.

As soon as the nor'easter passed, he ordered his first mate to prepare to shove off. It was close to noon when the 18-year-old finished filling the gas tank and stowing the lines, but the weather was clearing and Harry would wait no longer. He cranked up the *Henrietta*'s engine, slipped the boat through the channel at Cape Lookout and began puttering up the coast in search of bluefin tuna.

Several hours later, they had trawled half the length of Portsmouth Island with nothing to show for their troubles. But with night coming on the short day, Harry was ready to turn his boat around and head back home.

From the pilot's position atop the *Henrietta*'s cabin, the big waterman looked down at the aft deck surveying the day's catch. He had been right about the power of his new engine. It did make a difference. The day's catch of seaweed was the biggest he had ever pulled from the ocean. Some aspects of nature could not be overcome by technology. It was time to head for home.

But as the *Henrietta* made a wide turn toward home, a small patch of something white in the distance caught his eye. Had the water been rough, the thing would have blended in with the white caps. But it was calm, and the setting sun reflected light off the object as if it were a mirror. Men who made their living off the sea learned to read the ocean's nuances or they paid a heavy price. To Harry, the small splash of white was as obvious as a squall line on the horizon. Something was amiss, and he wanted to know what it was.

Reversing direction, the waterman pointed his trawler toward the curious flotsam. With the nets pulled in and the engine at full throttle, Harry marveled at the way his converted fishing boat flew across the glassy water. A distance that would have taken an hour or more by sail was traversed in minutes, thanks to his new engine. And as they closed the distance, the fisherman saw his instincts were right. About a mile ahead, he saw a small white boat drifting in the sea. A passenger was waving his arms, no doubt frantic to know for sure he had been spotted. Harry let out a long blast on the foghorn.

"Look alive, Danny boy!" he shouted to his first mate. "Looks like we'll be hauling in a catch after all."

As the *Henrietta* came alongside the lifeboat, both Harry and Danny saw the castaway was a woman and that she was not alone. A bearded fellow wearing the clothes and trappings of a surfman lay in the boat's bow, though it was impossible to tell if he was living or dead. Danny grabbed a rope and began setting up a tow line to the lifeboat while Harry climbed aboard to see what they were dealing with.

"Is he sick or injured or dead?" Harry's rough voice boomed, as was its natural state.

"He hit his head," she said, looking up at her rescuer who spoke with a Down East brogue. She had not realized how big the bearded fisherman was until he was standing next to her. "He's been unconscious since last night. I'm not sure he's going to come out of it."

"What about you, missy? Are you OK?"

"Yes, I'll be all right. I'm more concerned about the lifesaver. We need to get him out of this boat and make him more comfortable."

"Yes, he's a surfman, all right," Harry said, befuddled as to how the lifesaver became separated from his crew. "How in blue blazes did you two–"

"Sir!" the slight woman interrupted. "If you don't mind, he needs to be moved. Now. We can converse later."

"Of course, of course," Harry said, knotting his brow. He wasn't used to being ordered about but allowed for circumstance. Whoever the woman was, she had salt, and that impressed the waterman.

With Danny's help, he hoisted the surfman into the *Henrietta*, carried him into the cabin, and laid him on a bench that was attached to the bulkhead. Danny covered him with a wool blanket and applied a damp cloth to his forehead.

Harry kept a curious eye on the woman as she sat on a bench-seat that mirrored the one on the opposite side of the cabin. Removing her storm cap for the first time in two days, she shook her head, allowing a long shock of copper hair to fall across her shoulders. He became transfixed as she ran the fingers of both hands through the tangles, mesmerized by her beauty.

Realizing that he was staring, Harry feared he had compromised his stoic demeanor. Embarrassed, he stole a quick glance at Danny to see if the boy had noticed. If the lad had witnessed his brief loss of composure, there was no doubt he would make sure all their friends back home found out. But he needn't have worried. His young first mate was even more entranced by the woman than he had been.

"Danny. Danny boy!"

The only response the teenager could muster were a few blinks of acknowledgment.

"Go check the engine, lad. Make sure she's not getting low on oil. When you're done with that, start cleaning the seaweed off the deck what came from the nets and then go an' check the line to that lifeboat."

Danny took his time backing out of the cabin, unable to tear his eyes away from the woman. It wasn't until he stumbled and almost fell that he turned to look where he was going.

"Forgive him, ma'am," Harry said, the edges of his gruff voice blunted by his cockney-like accent. "He's only eighteen. A good kid, really. It ain't that he hasn't ever seen a woman before. There's aplenty on Harkers Island, for sure. But, the truth be told, I don't think he's ever seen one with any looks to her. I mean, it's a small island, and you... You're..."

He stopped in mid sentence, realizing too late that his ham-fisted admiration was coming across as something inappropriate. Shifting his enormous frame from side to side, he waited while the woman studied him, as if trying to make up her mind. Adda Lynn Joyner was his mother, and she had raised him with proper manners. The thought that he may have insulted a woman – even if by accident – was a shame he did not want to bear.

"My name is Caelyn Canady," she said, offering her hand and a confident smile. "Thank you for rescuing us. Another day without water would have made our situation extremely difficult."

"Cap'n Harry Joyner, at your service, ma'am," he said, though the way he pronounced it, there was no H in Harry. He continued shaking her hand and staring at her, expecting her to continue. An awkward moment of silence passed before realizing that her comment had been a request rather than a statement.

"Of course, ma'am! Water. You must be parched."

Harry grabbed a tin cup and filled it with water from a metal cask in the cabin's corner.

"Here," he said, handing her the cup. "Have some water I took from my cistern back home. I filter it myself. You know, no bugs nor nothing like that."

She pursed her lips together, perhaps to stifle a smile, he thought. Taking the cup, she kneeled beside the surfman and placed it to his mouth. The surfman's response was reflexive, taking in the water a sip at a time. She waited until he finished before she drank. When she'd emptied the cup, she handed the cup to Harry for more.

Having recovered from his awkward introduction, the waterman watched the woman with a practiced eye. Beneath his simple appearance and manner of speaking, the waterman was a well-read man with a list of accomplishments. It wasn't luck that made him successful enough to afford the *Henrietta's* new engine. It was his ability to learn things through keen observation – like the habits of ocean creatures – and his willingness to try new methods that put him ahead of the other fishermen.

He had known Caelyn Canady but for a few minutes, yet he already knew more about her than the woman could imagine. He could tell from her accent she was from up north. New York City, probably. But there was a hint of British mixed in with it, so he couldn't be sure. She was from high society, a woman used to getting her way. At least she didn't have that damned Yankee air every Southerner recognized as condescension and superiority. But the jury was still out on that one. And it wasn't lost on him that she had attended to the surfman's needs before her own. That was promising.

There was one other thing about her he had noticed right away. She wore no wedding ring. Strange for a society woman who looked to be on the tall side of her twenties. People such as that tended to marry off to each other as if they were medieval princes and princesses, making sure the union would benefit the good of the kingdom. He had always seen them as a very different lot, more interested in out-doing each other than achieving something with their lives.

"Thank you," Caelyn said, handing the cup back. "Where will you be taking us?"

"Well, the closest harbor is on Ocracoke," Harry answered as he readied himself to go topside. "The folks there will tend to his injuries. Besides, there's a Lifesaving Station at the north end of the island. I'm sure his fellow surfmen will be glad to know he's OK. But we better hurry if we're going to make it afore nightfall. I don't want to be crossing the bar of a strange inlet in the dark."

Leaving Caelyn in the cabin, he returned to his position behind the wheel and piloted the *Henrietta* toward Ocracoke. With darkness coming on, he pushed the engine as hard as it would go. He had been to the island many times, but the channel between Ocracoke and Portsmouth Islands was in constant change and dangerous to navigate. On the positive side, the water was calm, and it looked like they would make it in time.

Harry was in deep thought and did not hear Caelyn until she stood next to him. He wondered what caused her to leave the warmth of the cabin.

"Danny volunteered to watch the lifesaver," she said, anticipating his question. "I'm afraid the smell of fish was making me a little nauseous. I had to come out for some fresh air."

"You're welcome to stay, Miss, but it's a mite cold and getting more so every minute."

"I'll be all right," Caelyn said, pulling the blanket she had brought with her tighter. "I'd rather be out here where I can see the ocean and can smell the salt air."

Harry glanced at her from the corner of his eye. She might be pretty and pampered, but she was not timid.

"So, how did you come to be floating around in the middle of the Atlantic, pray tell? The name on your lifeboat says 'Aphrodite.' That would be the name of the boat you were sailing in, I take it?"

"Yes," she said, continuing to stare ahead. The chill of the wind reddening her face. "She was only three months out of dry dock and on the return leg of her maiden voyage. It all seems such a waste."

"What happened to her captain an' crew?"

"I am the captain," she said, her back stiffening at his assumption. "I'm not sure what happened to the crew, but I have to believe that the lifesavers got them back to land safely."

"I hope so," Harry said. "I'd sure hate to be the captain of a ship what lost the crewmen under my command."

Caelyn grew quiet and Harry kicked himself once again for speaking without thinking. From the corner of his eye he saw her turn and lower her head, hiding her face.

"There now, missy," he said, putting his free arm around her shoulder while piloting the boat with the other. The action was effortless, an unconscious manifestation of his protective nature, and a comfort she didn't reject. "I'm sure your crew is all right. Those surfmen, they're brave and well-trained. They saved your crew, you can be sure of it. But tell me, just what did happen out there?"

Taking a deep breath, Caelyn composed herself and told the fisherman everything that had happened from the time she'd left St. Augustine until the moment Harry had blown his foghorn. As she talked, he heard recrimination in her voice, accepting the blame. But when she related the part about Ansel Stick appearing on the deck too late to help, he wondered if she was bearing too much responsibility. By the time she finished, the inlet between the two islands was coming into view and Harry had learned everything he needed to know about Caelyn. Chief among them was the fact she was a very intelligent woman who, for some reason, did not grasp the depth of her own potential.

Turning his attention to the task at hand, he guided the *Henrietta* through the potato patch of choppy water where the outgoing sound waters met the incoming waves. A few minutes later they chugged into Silver Lake, the harbor that provided haven to the boats of Ocracoke. The sun was slipping below the horizon and the chill brought on by the nor'easter lingered in the air. The coming night promised to be a cold one.

As they approached the main wharf, Harry saw Caelyn's eyes widen with amazement at the sight of forty or fifty people converging on the dock. It appeared the entire village was turning out to greet them. The women hung back, chattering with each other, while the men pointed at the *Henrietta*, gesturing with excitement and speaking in loud voices. A strange boat was cause enough for rousing the interest of the islanders, but a trawler powered by a gas engine was an event. The men in the back of the crowd kept pressing forward, trying to get a better look. The jockeying for position continued until three men standing near the edge toppled into the cold water. Not wanting to meet the same fate, the men who now stood at the dock's edge began shoving back against the people behind them. Several of the men began swearing at each other and a couple of half-hearted fights broke out.

"Ha, haaaa! Ocracokers!" Harry laughed. "God love 'em. Half of what they own comes from shipwrecks and the other half comes from the sea. But they're good people. Many is the sailor they've fished out of the ocean after a storm. They'll feed them and nurse them and they'll treat them better than family. But the only thing those castaways leave with is the clothes what's on their backs, because everything that ends up on the beach gets scarfed up by the 'Cokers."

Harry cut the engine off, letting the *Henrietta* glide the last few feet to the wharf. Danny threw the mooring lines to two men who secured the boat to the dock. Eager to inspect

Harry's creation, the crowd pushed forward, blocking exit from the boat.

"Stand back!" Harry shouted. "I've got a surfman on board what's in need of a doctor."

The crowd's mood changed with the swiftness of a gale wind. To the people who struggled to survive the primitive conditions of the Outer Banks, no one was more deserving of respect than lifesavers. Every boy who lived on the coast worth his salt aspired to become one of the iron men who rowed their small surfboats through raging waters to rescue ships and their crews. It was even possible that the injured surfman might be one of their own.

A barrel-chested man with a wind-hewn face and a handlebar mustache stepped up and began barking out orders. Six men jumped aboard the *Henrietta*, disappeared into the cabin, and reemerged a minute later carrying the surfman.

"Take him to the Pamlico Inn," the barrel-chested man ordered in a brogue akin to Harry's. "And be gentle with him. Esra, get word to the Hatteras Inlet Station that we've got an injured surfman here, and he's still alive. There's sure to be somebody looking for him. Maynard, go fetch Miss Ina and tell her to bring her nursing bag. But be sure to tell her it ain't a birthing that needs tending."

As the six men carried Ethan through the crowd, the man who had taken charge turned to Harry and shook his hand.

"Nathaniel Elisha O'Neal the third is my name, friend. But you can call me Nat. Most folks around here do. I'm pretty much what serves as a mayor here in our little village." Pausing, he leaned forward as though to let Harry in on a secret. "But don't go calling me Mister Mayor or anything like that, or folks here will think I'm trying to put on airs."

He winked and laughed at what he considered was humor.

"I'm Harry Joyner and this is Miss Caelyn Canady of New York City. I found her and the surfman drifting in the lifeboat 'bout five miles off Portsmouth. We don't know what his name is or which station he's with. He took a terrible blow to the head and I think his wrist is broke. I figure they would have drifted clear to Cape Fear by now if I hadn't come along."

Harry caught the puzzled look in Caelyn's eye and he smiled to himself. She had told him she had sailed from New York, but she never said it was her home.

"Well, Miss Caelyn Canady of New York City," the mayor said as he took a bow, "I imagine you're a mite hungry an' tired after the ordeal you've been through. I'd be exaggerating if I said there was lots of places to stay on Ocracoke. Truth is, there's only one formal establishment here that lets rooms. The good news is, I'm sure they have one available."

"Thank you, sir. But I'm afraid I won't be able to pay...at least not now," Caelyn replied. "I have no purse and no money."

"Well, we'll just worry about that later," Nat smiled through his well-waxed mustache. "There ain't never been a castaway on Ocracoke left without help before, and we certainly don't aim to start turning folks out now. Especially ones as pretty as you."

Though she was in good hands, Harry had brought Caelyn this far and wasn't about to leave until he saw the thing through. Ordering Danny to stay with the *Henrietta*, he fell in beside Caelyn as Nat guided them through the sandy, narrow lanes. As they walked through the village, their mustachioed guide commented on the shipwrecks off their island and the houses built from their remains. With each word he spoke, a small gray cloud billowed from his mouth like a tiny steam engine.

When they arrived at the inn – a two-story building with a porch running across the front – the inn's keeper was waiting for them at the door.

"Thought you folks might be coming," the rail-thin innkeeper with a shock of graying hair said. "I was just upstairs fixing up a couple of rooms for you. Already got that surfman fella laid out and Miss Ina is tending to him. She says he ought to be OK, but she's gonna clip some of his nails and hair and put them in a hole bored in a live oak tree, just to be safe. I don't believe in that superstition, voodoo stuff myself, but, well, it won't hurt none neither. Come on in the kitchen. My wife's got something warm for you to eat."

A short, round woman named Betty – the physical opposite of her husband – introduced herself as she whirled about the room like a devout dervish. Leaving no doubt the kitchen was her domain, the innkeeper's wife ordered Harry and Caelyn to sit at the table. The well-meaning woman prattled on about this, that, and the other as she placed two bowls of left-over venison stew in front of them, but Caelyn heard almost none of what she said. A full stomach and exhaustion had her nodding even as she attempted to bring the last spoonful of venison to her mouth.

Taking her by the arm, the innkeeper guided her up the stairs to a dimly lit room and closed the door as he left. As she removed her clothes, it occurred to her through the fog of fatigue that she had never gone to bed without something covering her body. Too drained to be concerned with modesty, she blew out the nightstand candle and slipped naked under the sheets and the goose down quilt covering the bed. Sleep came at once.

Chapter Five

The Surfman

Ethan woke to the sounds of excited voices and people moving about outside his window. Before he opened his eyes he knew he wasn't at the lifesaving station. A quick glance about the room gave him no clues. More sounds of people greeting each other and laughing drifted in through the window.

Where the devil am I and what the hell is going on? he wondered.

He attempted to push himself upright, but a sharp pain shot through his wrist and he collapsed back onto the bed. Pinpoints of light danced before his eyes, forcing him to remain still for a moment. Raising his hand to his temple, he discovered soft gauze wrapped about his head.

The Aphrodite! Yes! Details of the rescue began unraveling in his mind's eye. He had been on a lifeboat – with one of the yacht's sailors. He remembered the brilliant light and the explosion and wondered if anyone else had survived. He had to find out if the rest of his crew had made it.

Making slow, deliberate moves, he sat up and glanced around the room for his clothes. Not seeing them, he slid out of bed and looked inside a large armoire in the corner. Inside, he found a pair of someone's heavy khaki pants and a black wool shirt. Though cut for a taller man, they weren't a bad fit.

Unable to find a pair of shoes, he shuffled barefoot from the room and down a hallway. Descending a narrow carpeted stairway, he passed through the empty lobby of what had to be a hotel and into a large dining room. Drained from the exertion, he leaned against a doorjamb to steady himself and looked inside the next room. A plump, middle-aged woman was standing over a stove tending to several steaming pots. A large black-bearded man and a blond-haired boy in his teens sat at a table in the center of the room.

"Where am I?" he asked. "Where's the rest of my crew?"

Harry and Danny turned in time to see the surfman begin sliding to the floor. Jumping from their chairs, they grabbed him by his arms and helped him to a seat at the table.

"Here," the woman said, placing a cup of coffee in front of him. "Drink this. It's guaranteed to put hair on your chest."

Ethan raised the steaming cup to his mouth, blew on it a moment, then took a cautious sip. The familiar taste of chicory mixed with the coffee told him he wasn't far from home.

"I'm Betty Williams," the woman continued. "Most folks around here call me Aunt Betty. My husband Tom and I run this establishment, the Pamlico Inn, here on Ocracoke Island. These gentlemen are Cap'n Harry Joyner and his first mate, Danny Williams, no relation to me, mind you, unless his folks are kin to the Williamses of Martin County.

That's where my folks come from, originally. You're not from those Williams, are you, boy?"

Danny started to answer, but the animated woman resumed talking before he could get the words out.

"We were worried about you last night when they brought you in. But when I looked in on you this morning, I could tell you weren't knocked out any more...just sleeping. We sent a man to the north station to let them know we have you here. We just didn't know what to tell them as far as a name goes. So, what's your name, son?"

"Ethan...Ethan Roberts," he answered, checking himself as he spoke. "Surfman...Ethan Roberts...of the United States Lifesaving Station...Cape Hatteras. And thank you for taking care of me, but...how did I get here? I don't remember anything after the explosion. And what about the rest of my crew?"

"We don't know nothing about your crew yet," she said. "I imagine we'll find out when we hear back from your people at the station. As far as how you got here, well, you can thank your lucky stars for these two. Yes, sir. If it hadn't been for them, you'd still be out there on the ocean with your friend. Be getting a bit hungry, too, I imagine. Yep. You wouldn't be getting ready to dig into some of this good ol' fried fish and spoon bread. No sir."

It wasn't until then that Ethan thought to ask about the crewman from the yacht, the one who had hunkered down in the lifeboat's bow.

"The other man in the boat with me," Ethan asked, "is he OK? Did he make it?"

"The other man is–" Betty began to explain, but Harry cut her off.

"The other man is fine," he said, trying not to sound too obvious. "Yeah, he's fine, 'cept for some blistered hands. Still upstairs, third room on the right. Sleeping, I imagine. Quite an ordeal the two of you went through, but that fella did a pretty good job of keeping you alive."

Never one to pass up a good joke, Harry caught Betty's eye and gave her a wink.

"I'd like to thank him," Ethan said. "I'm not sure what happened. The last thing I remember was jumping into the lifeboat and then...the explosion. I think I recall the sailor looking over me, taking care of me. But..." The surfman shook his head, trying to remember. "There was something about him that doesn't make sense."

"Well, that's probably it," Harry said, stringing Ethan along. "I guess you could say he ain't quite a man...not really."

Picking up on the joke, Danny joined in.

"Yep, definitely not a man. But, not really a boy, neither. But that sailor did do a real good job nursing you, though."

Having caught on, Betty joined the farce as well.

"You know, come to think of it, that sailor sure had some pretty skin for a man," she said. "And the prettiest copper hair I ever did see. Why, it was so pretty, I dare say it would turn a few women jealous."

If Ethan had been himself, he might have picked up on the conspiratorial tone, but his thoughts kept turning back to his crewmates.

"When do you think we'll hear from the north station?"

"Hard to say," Betty said. "I'm sure you know that they've got the only telephone on the island...just like the Hatteras station...and it gets knocked out every time there's a storm."

"Don't know if this means much," Harry said, "but most of the 'Cokers ran off to the beach just a while ago. There's wreckage washing up on the beach, so it's a safe bet that the ship you was trying to rescue broke up. Of course, that doesn't mean anything happened to your crewmates."

"That must have been what woke me up," Ethan said. He paused a moment, contemplating the fate of his fellow surfmen. They weren't his friends, not really. He did not seek to make genuine friends. But they were his crewmates and they had faced death together many times during the past five years.

"Ocracoke," he said at last. "This is Ocracoke? We must have been drifting for a while to end up here."

"We just happened to be in the right place at the right time," Harry said. "Weren't too many other fishing boats out yesterday. I wouldn't have been that far up the coast if it weren't for my new engine. I reckon it was just meant to be. Truth is, I kind of fancy the idea of rescuing a surfman. Seems like fair return for what you folks do."

Ethan averted his eyes and shifted in his chair. Even after five years, he wasn't comfortable with the way people on the Outer Banks revered lifesavers. A need to do noble things wasn't the reason he became a surfman. It was isolation from a world that no longer evoked passion that appealed to him. Ocracoke, even as small as it was, compromised that coveted solitude.

"Missus Williams. If you don't mind, I'd like to clean up a bit. Would it be possible to have some hot water to take to my room?"

"Already thought of that," she replied. "But you don't have to settle for a birdbath. No sir. I've already got a big bucket of hot water ready for the shower outside. Tom's been working on it so it should be ready to go. We don't have much call for showers this time of year. During the fall, the rich hunters that come down from up north pay extra to use it. Truth is, when the regular folks stay here, we let them use it free of charge...if they ain't no hunters around."

"Really, I don't need anything special. I just want–"

"Now, look here young man," she interrupted. "Folks around here will disapprove if I give short shrift to a surfman. You go right on out there and take yourself a shower or elst I'll be so shamed I'll have to shut down and move somewheres else. Now take these and get."

Ethan understood Banker ways well enough to know that she was right. He accepted the towel and washcloth she offered and let the squat woman usher him through the kitchen's back door. A row of huge wax myrtles surrounded the grassy backyard, providing privacy from the outside world. A large storage shed dominated the corner of the lot farthest from the kitchen. Two stalls outfitted with showerheads were built onto the end of the shed facing the inn. The doors started at knee level and stopped about neck high, allowing users to maintain modesty while still being able to see what was going on around them.

This may work well enough for the hunters, but I'll wager there aren't many female guests who use these things, Ethan thought.

"Morning," a voice behind him said. Ethan looked over his shoulder to see a tall wiry man shuffling past him at a fast pace with a bucket of steaming water. "Tom's the name. Betty's husband. I already put the cold water in. This hot water should make the temperature just right."

Ethan waited while Tom climbed a ladder to finish filling the shower's reservoir.

"There's a bar of soap on the shelf," Tom said as he headed back to the kitchen. "If you need any more hot water, just give a holler. Hope you enjoy it."

Hanging the towel on a hook, he stepped inside the stall and closed the door. Being careful not to move too fast, he removed his borrowed clothes and draped them over the half-door. Though the air was crisp and cold, it wakened his dulled senses and cleared his mind. Suppressing a shiver, he pulled the rope above his head. The steamy water fell like summer rain, soothing his aching muscles. Removing the gauze from his head, he pulled the rope again and reveled in the sensation of well-being. It had been many years since anything had given him pleasure. It was surprising, almost frightening, to discover that a spark of something good still glowed within. Picking up the fresh bar of store-bought soap, he lathered his body and pulled the rope again. As the water ran over his body he considered the innkeeper's promise of more hot water and hoped the man was true to his word.

Chapter Six

Reflections

Wakened by odd noises coming from beneath her window, Caelyn wrapped the sheet around herself and rolled out of bed. Raising the shade, she saw the innkeeper preparing an outdoor shower, filling its reservoir with hot water drawn from a steaming vat heated by a wood fire. Then came the surfman, barefoot but oblivious to the cold turf, dressed in ill-fitting clothes, treading gingerly but on his own.

Despite being disappointed she had not awakened early enough to greet him, see him conscious and doing well thrilled her to the core. She was also proud to know that, when both their lives had depended on her actions, she had risen to the occasion, her gun phobia notwithstanding.

Her satisfaction at being the reluctant heroine, however, shifted into a less virtuous sense of being an unintentional voyeur when the surfman entered the shower stall and began removing his clothes. From the second-story vantage point, she could see well down into the shower. And though the proper thing to do when the surfman removed his shirt would have been to lower the shade and turn away, she just couldn't. Sculpted by years of rowing, his well-defined muscles flexed and rippled as he washed. His injuries were forcing him to make deliberate motions, which intensified the masculinity he projected. Caelyn had little experience in such matters, but she knew that, physically, the surfman was not an ordinary man.

He wasn't tall – just under six feet – but his proportions made him appear so. Despite the beard covering his face, his features conveyed a maturity and soberness of thought beyond his years. And while most women would not describe him as handsome, neither was he homely. Whatever he might lack in looks was more than compensated by the confidence with which he carried himself.

Caelyn's face flushed, surprised by the thoughts the naked surfman evoked. She had not even spoken to the man. Any positive traits she attributed to him were nothing but conjecture. He could be an empty-headed simpleton or a self-centered lout. He did not appear to be a particularly warm or outgoing person. Indeed, he wore his reserve like a cape, protecting him from the cold that was human contact.

She turned away from the window, angry at investing her emotions into pointless musings. Hunter Winslow was a fine man from a good New York family. He had gone to the right schools and universities. His father's prestige as a shipping magnate would ensure their status among New York City's upper crust for all their days. What could a simple man of the sea have to offer?

The judgment was harsh and left a bitter taste in her mouth. These were not her beliefs. Such sentiments were echoes of the values her stepmother had drummed into her head as she was growing up. Caelyn had learned at an early age that a person's social status was an important consideration in the Canady household.

A long-forgotten memory of when she was a child of seven angled its way into her mind. She had longed for a friend to play with – something her father refused to allow. The arrival of a new housekeeper who moved into the servant's quarters with her daughter, Annie, had been the answer to her prayers. The two girls were close in age and soon became playmates. One rainy afternoon, Caelyn thought it would be fun to break the monotony by letting her new friend try on her clothes. Dorothy caught them and put a quick end to the fun. Nothing was ever said about the matter, but Caelyn soon discovered that her actions did have consequences.

Upon returning home from a surprise weekend trip to the country, she rushed to the servants' quarters. Instead of finding her friend, she found a new housekeeper – one who had no children. A few days later, Dorothy began her lectures about the importance of status and class.

"There is a plan for you, Caelyn. We must make sure nothing interferes with it. Someday you will understand, and you will thank me."

Glancing back toward the window, she wondered how great the difference between her and the man she had saved might be. Did social status make her a better person than the surfman? The echoes of her childhood indoctrination were more thoroughly woven into the fabric of her being than she realized. Almost every decision, every movement, every thought she had carried the imprint of her parents.

Moving over to the washstand, she picked up its pitcher and filled the basin with water. The reflection in the pool stared back at her in silent judgment as it had a thousand times before. *What is your true heart, Caelyn? What lies in your soul? What kind of person are you, really?* These were questions she thought she had resolved in St. Augustine, but now they returned louder than before. *Do you want to be the woman that Dorothy would have you be?*

Dipping her hands into the basin, the accusing reflection disappeared, but the water burned the raw flesh of her exposed blisters. Ignoring the pain, she splashed her face.

Chapter Seven

Of Virtue and Vendues

Ethan wasted no time drying himself and putting clothes on after the hot water ran out. The shower's warmth had soothed his aching body, but the cool air did not encourage standing around while soaking wet. Returning to the inn, he passed by the check-in desk where Harry and Danny were discussing their food and lodging arrangements with Mr. Williams.

"Has the young sailor come from his room yet?" Ethan asked, fearing that he may have missed a chance to meet his rescuer.

"Nope," Harry said, not giving the innkeeper a chance to reply. "He's still up in his room, sleeping, I imagine. Why don't you go knock on his door and make sure he's OK?"

"I don't know," Ethan hesitated. "If he hasn't gotten up yet, he probably needs the rest. I think I'll wait until he wakes up on his own. But if he comes downstairs, be sure to give me a yell, will you?"

"You're the cap'n," Harry said, hoping to keep his little prank in play.

Nodding his thanks, Ethan climbed the stairs and walked down the second floor's long hallway toward his room. As he passed the sailor's door, he heard movement inside and reconsidered Harry's suggestion. Deciding to take a chance after all, he tapped on the door. No one answered, but the noises inside continued. Ethan had no way of knowing that the sailor inside hadn't heard the knock because she was toweling her hair dry.

Perplexed, but not wanting to be rude, Ethan shrugged and turned to leave. At the same moment, Caelyn's boisterous movements with the towel knocked the porcelain water pitcher onto the floor with a crashing shatter.

"Damn it!" she cursed.

Ethan heard the crash and what sounded like a cry of pain. Fearing the worst, he opened the door and dashed into the room. Instead of a sailor, he saw a woman crouching down on one knee, picking up the broken pieces of porcelain. Though her long copper hair hung around her body, it hid little of her nakedness. The woman looked up at him with eyes of green fire.

"Are you just going to stand there like an idiot?" she said between clenched teeth, maintaining the crouch to keep herself concealed. Keeping her eyes on Ethan, she reached up and grabbed the towel she had left on the washstand.

Ethan was so confused he didn't understand her question. His befuddled mind, still operating under the assumption that he should do something to help, took a step toward the naked woman. Her eyes grew wild with disbelief. As he took a second step, she began wrapping the towel around herself while still crouching.

"Excuse me, sir!" she said as she stood. Her voice was a half-octave away from being a siren. "What do you think you are about?"

Though the towel covered the telling parts of her body, Ethan now understood the truth of her gender. The sailor was very much a woman. Ivory-like skin splashed white above and below the edges of the towel. The wild copper hair framing her face made her piercing glare ominous.

Emotions and thoughts raged within the duped surfman. He was in awe of her beauty. Her near nakedness stirred feelings long lost to indifference. No longer able to draw breath, the room closed in on him. As if from far away a flicker of a thought suggested that retreat would be the best response, but his ability to communicate in any way no longer existed. He parted his lips to speak but his dry mouth refused to make sound.

"I... You... You're not a man!"

Caelyn's eyes widened in disbelief.

"My, aren't you quite the Sherlock," she seethed. "I suppose you have to be very intelligent to be a lifesaver. *Your* intelligence is astounding. Now, if you are quite certain of my gender, I suggest you leave this instant or I shall call for assistance."

Only now did the inappropriateness of the situation dawn on Ethan. Backing up as fast as he could, he tripped over his own feet. The momentum carried him into the hallway where he landed on his backside. Clutching her towel, Caelyn came to the doorway and scowled down at him.

"I can see you are as quick of foot as you are of mind," she said, then slammed the door.

Laughter echoed down the narrow hallway. Upon hearing the pitcher break, Harry and Danny had come upstairs to see what had happened. They had arrived in time to see a red-faced Ethan trip and fall to the floor. The fisherman's prank had borne fruit at last.

Ethan opened his mouth to launch a string of profanities at the two watermen but stopped himself. Harry had duped him! And though he refused to let himself laugh, he couldn't help but see the humor. Half smiling, he crossed his arms over his knees and shook his head.

"I owe you one, cap'n, and I'd advise you to watch your step. I will return the favor."

"I'm sure you will," Harry chuckled. "But you've got to admit, it was a fine farce. Besides, I think you may have gotten the better part of that deal, if you know what I mean. All things considered, some folks might say you owe me a favor."

Extending his hand, Harry helped his new friend up off the floor.

"Well, you're not looking too much the worse for wear, now," Harry said. "If you're up to it, you're welcome to come over to the beach with me and Danny. The vendue master should be about ready for auction. I thought we might find something for the *Henrietta*."

Even if he had money, Ethan thought it unlikely that the vendue would yield anything that he would want, but a walk in the fresh air on the beach seemed a good idea. Returning to his room, he found his uniform and sweater on the bed. And though his boots stood in the corner as well, someone had left a serviceable pair of leather shoes at the foot of the bed, their size, no doubt, matched to the boots. A few minutes later, the uniformed surfman joined the two watermen in front of the hotel.

Leaving the sound side of the island and the village, the three men followed a hard-packed trail through the marsh grass wetlands. Fifteen minutes later they came to the sand dunes that protected the interior of the island. Standing atop the row of dunes closest to the ocean, they could see the inlet a few hundred yards to their right and the miles of beach to their left. About every hundred yards along the shore, for as far as the eye could see, was a pile of wreckage collected by the Ocracokers. Judging by the number of piles, it looked to Ethan as though everyone who lived on the island had turned out to collect the *Aphrodite's* debris.

The government appointed a vendue master, an official who oversaw the auction of shipwreck salvage, to each inhabited island in the Outer Banks. Moving from pile to pile, he would call out bids on the collected materials and rule on final offers. Exceptional pieces were separated from the pile and auctioned individually. The person who had salvaged the materials would take a third of the profit, as would the vendue master. The original owner of the goods would receive the final third.

Most of the debris was wood, a valuable commodity to Outer Bankers. The villagers needed the ship's lumber to build houses and other structures, and buying it at a vendue was cheaper than having it shipped from a lumber mill by boat. If a freighter had wrecked, the vendue piles and the profit would have been much higher.

Other than lumber, an occasional personal item, and the occasional nautical device, today's haul looked to be a meager one for the villagers. Having started at the pile of debris closest to the inlet, the vendue master was working his way up the beach northward. Each scavenger stood by his pile waiting. After the wreckage was sold, the man who had collected the debris left his wife or other family member to stand watch over their collected goods. From time to time, spirited bidding would take place for an exceptional object or high-quality lumber.

As the growing crowd moved up the beach, Ethan, Harry, and Danny left the dunes to follow them up the beach. At the next vendue, a group of twelve Ocracokers stood in a semicircle facing the vendue master who had taken a strategic spot in front of the collected debris. Holding up a winch he had separated from the pile for all to see, the vendue master called for bids. Harry, in need of such tackle for handling his nets, entered the bidding and purchased the tackle for a fair price. When bidding began on the lumber, Ethan lost interest and walked ahead to see what the next pile offered.

As the drone of the vendue master's auction chant faded, the surfman was better able to appreciate the day. Afternoon clouds were moving in, helping to keep the air crisp and invigorating. Some two hundred yards offshore, a squabble of gulls worked the water where a school of Spanish mackerel was chasing smaller fish to the surface. Now that he was alone, his mind was free to wonder about the woman back at the inn.

Given her state of undress he had plenty to remember, but it was her eyes, as green as polished peridot, and her shimmering copper hair that he could not get out of his mind. Both features were striking, but her bright green eyes, blazing with fire, were forever burned into his memory. Even the hard glare she had given him had done nothing to detract from their piercing beauty. But there was more to her eyes than that. Even the brutal glare she had delivered had done nothing to diminish the intelligence that gave them light.

The surfman stopped in his tracks, realizing that for the first time in five years he had gone hours without thinking about Cuba or the war or the madre. That the hiatus was because of the copper-haired woman, there was no doubt. Despite the brevity and awkward circumstance of their meeting, she had somehow managed to penetrate the fortress he had built around himself. The revelation made him uncomfortable.

I only have room in this life for being a surfman, he thought. *And it's one too worthless to thrust upon a woman who correctly deduces that I'm a fool. And, if I'm fortunate, one that is too short for any of it to matter.*

The angry cry of a gull overhead brought Ethan back from his self-deprecating reverie. His mood now devolved into its normal shade of gray, he continued his trek to the next vendue. As he came upon the pile of debris, he found a plump, middle-aged black woman wearing a red bandanna on her head. Sitting on a large black steamer trunk, she watched over her small collection of boards, planks, and timbers. The woman had set aside a few items that might fetch special consideration from the vendue master, but nothing that interested Ethan.

"Care to make a bid when the master comes?" the woman asked, making conversation.

"No thank you, ma'am," Ethan replied, irked at having placed himself in a position where he had to engage in conversation. "There's little I need and nothing here that I could take with me. Besides, I have no money."

She studied him for a minute as though she were trying to remember the face of an old friend.

"You're the surfman they brought in, ain't you?" she asked. "No, no. Don't answer. Of course you are. I knew you was coming here. I sure did. Seen it in a dream two nights ago. Don't know why nor how. It's just a gift, like my mother before and her mother before that. But I knew you was coming. Handsome and strong, a man from the sea. It was all in my dream."

Ethan couldn't help but smile. He had known of such people, even back home in Missouri, but had never encountered one. He neither believed nor disbelieved in their abilities. He had never cared one way or another enough to think about it. It was, he supposed, enough that they believed.

"You met the woman," she said. It wasn't a question. "Pretty, ain't she?"

Ethan's skin prickled despite himself. Anybody who knew about his rescue would know that there was a woman involved – even if he had been the last person to find out. One didn't need to have supernatural powers to connect him with the copper-haired woman.

Motioning him closer, she spoke just loud enough to be heard above the surf.

"Can't tell you everything, child. Don't know everything they is to tell. But I can tell you this. Your future ain't out there," she said, pointing to the ocean. "It's up there. In the sky. But that's a little ways down the road. Right now, you gotta take care of little Miss New York City, 'cause that was in my dream, too."

Stepping back, Ethan took a longer look at her. Was it possible people on the island knew things about the he had rescued he didn't?

Voices from the crowd of bidders and onlookers following the vendue master to her site made them both turn to look down the beach for a moment.

"Listen quick, now child," she said, tugging on his sweater. This here steamer I be setting on is meant for you. You bid on it and don't let no one else take it, you hear? It was all in the dream. Trust me now."

Harry and Danny came to stand on either side of Ethan as the vendue master made notes in his notebook and then began the auctioning. Most of the lumber went to an Ocracoker in the first bidding, boards he would use to add on to his house. A brass lantern missing its glass went next, followed by two coils of hemp rope and a crate of coffee packaged in tins. Having saved the best for last, the vendue master turned to the trunk.

Several people in the crowd whispered to their friends, who nodded in excitement. The unknown contents were much more interesting than the objects they could see. The chest might contain silverware, expensive nautical equipment, or almost anything. The anxious villagers waited to see inside.

Breaking the trunk's latch with a pry bar, the vendue master lifted the lid and the crowd leaned forward. The combined groans from the men announced their disappointment. The top tray of the chest contained several blouses and some accessories. Removal of the top tray revealed more female clothing.

"Well, what do I hear for the whole thing?" the vendue master asked. "If nothing else, it's a pretty good chest."

"I'll give you three dollars for it," a stout man with gray hair said.

"What the heck, Russ," a man in the back piped up, "all your skirts in the wash? You need a new dress for the next dance?"

Everyone laughed and the man's face turned as red as the black woman's bandana. He glared at his tormentor.

"I've got three daughters and a wife that have to be clothed," he countered. "You got a problem with that?"

"Nope," his antagonist replied with a snicker. "Just don't bother saving the last dance for me, all right?"

The crowd laughed again and the man named Russ grew angrier. Before he could think of a face-saving comeback, the vendue master resumed the bidding.

"I hear three dollars! Anyone else?"

The gathering remained silent. The black woman looked at Ethan, waiting to see what he would do. Ethan looked from her to the chest and saw something he had not noticed before. Embroidered upon the lid's silk lining were the initials "C.N.C."

"Harry, what's the name of the woman who was in the boat with me?" Ethan asked.

"Canady. Caelyn Canady." Harry saw the initials. "Hey, you don't think that belongs to her, do you?"

"I got a lot more vendues to go," the master said. "If there are no more bids, the trunk goes to–"

"Five dollars!" Ethan interrupted.

A few members of the gathering laughed to hear another man bidding on a woman's clothes. Others, seeing that it was the surfman, whispered to their neighbor in curiosity.

Ethan sensed everyone's eyes watching him. He felt like a fool. The chest might not be hers. If not, he'd be stuck with it. That the other man, Russ, was only trying to clothe his family made him curse the misguided decision to bid at all.

"I'll give you ten dollars for it." Russ countered. His jaw tightened with determination. The crowd waited with anticipation, enjoying the novelty of two men bidding on female apparel.

"Fifteen!" Ethan said without thinking. Given the circumstances of their first encounter, he doubted the woman would be that grateful even if it was her chest.

Russ pushed some sand around with the toe of his shoe weighing his next move. The value he was looking for was evaporating.

"Seventeen-fifty," he said, not looking up.

"Eighteen dollars," Ethan responded without hesitating. He knew the man had reached his limit.

Russ kicked the sand and shoved his hands in his pockets.

"Shucks, they's summer clothes, anyway. Wouldn't do us no good 'til next spring."

"Anyone else?" the vendue master asked, looking around the crowd. "Sold to the man in surfman's uniform with the beard! That'll be eighteen dollars, lifesaver."

Ethan had realized before the bidding started that he had no money, which made him question his own sanity. Or had the black woman cast a spell upon him?

Catching the look on Ethan's face, Harry knew right away what the problem was.

"Here, surfman," he said, handing Ethan a twenty-dollar bill. "Your IOU is good with me. Just send me the money when you get back to Hatteras."

"Thanks," Ethan said, feeling more foolish than ever. He hated taking a loan from a man he had just met, but he had no choice. He paid the vendue master who gave the black woman her share. Tucking the money under her bandana, the woman turned to Ethan.

"She won't 'preciate it at first, but stick with her. If you don't, there won't be no Kitty Hawk, and that would be the worst tragedy of all."

As she turned to follow the others, Ethan looked at her with uncertainty. Just like before, her words could have meant anything, or nothing at all. Who would ever know?

Chapter Eight

The Superintendent

Searching for something to eat, Caelyn entered the kitchen wearing an old calico dress Betty had provided. Happy to have the company, the innkeeper's wife paused from her chores long enough to round up a few leftovers. As she handed a plate of food to the castaway, the ding of the bell at the front desk announced a new arrival.

Upon entering the reception area, Betty was surprised by a striking man in a well-pressed uniform without stain or blemish. He stood straight and tall with his service hat tucked smartly under his arm. His demeanor spoke of authority and a demand of respect from others.

"Superintendent Samuel Collins, madam," he said, nodding his head in greeting, "Superintendent of the Seventh District, United States Lifesaving Service. I'm looking for Surfman Ethan Roberts. I was told I would find him here."

Though seldom at a loss for words, it was all Betty could do to say her own name as she introduced herself.

"I figured they would be sending somebody down here to check on him," she said. "But the superintendent himself... Why, I had no idea. Can I get you some tea? How about some food? A late dinner? Early supper?"

"Tom!" she shouted over her shoulder, "Go fetch Nat and tell him Superintendent Collins of the Seventh District is here! An' be quick about it."

"Would you like a room?" she continued without missing a beat. "They're clean and we ain't got no bed bugs neither, I guarantee it. Are you going to be staying awhile? If you are, we can–"

"Excuse me, Missus Williams. I'm sorry to interrupt, but this is important." Betty stopped in mid-sentence, not understanding. "Surfman Roberts? Is he here?"

"Oh Lord, yes. I mean, no. I mean, he's staying here but him and Cap'n Joyner and his mate all went to the vendue not a half-hour ago. You just missed them but they'll be back by dark, I'm sure."

"In that case, I accept your offer for a late dinner."

Betty took the superintendent to the kitchen where she introduced him to Caelyn.

"I'm glad to see that you are safe and sound, Miss Canady," he said. Hanging his hat on the back of the chair, he shook her hand and took a seat at the table with her. "I know you have been through quite an ordeal."

They talked for a few minutes before Tom came back with Nat, who gave the superintendent an "official" welcome to Ocracoke. With the formalities completed, Tom leaned against a cabinet close to the table and filled his hand-carved pipe with tobacco. The mayor joined Caelyn and Superintendent Collins at the table while Betty continued to flitter around the kitchen.

"Every six months I travel to all the stations in my district to conduct inspections and check the morale of their crews," the superintendent said. "As chance would have it, I was at the Big Kinnakeet Station just north of Hatteras when the *Aphrodite* ran aground. This morning, I was at the Durants Station when I received word that someone had brought a surfman and a castaway here. I already had official business to conduct out this way, so I decided to advance my schedule and come immediately. I can tell you that news of Surfman Ethan Roberts' survival came as a great relief to his mates at the Hatteras Station, who hold him in the highest regard."

"Ethan Roberts... Ethan Roberts..." Tom mumbled, reflecting on the name as he chewed on the stem of his pipe. "Now that I hear you say it, I swear that name sounds familiar."

"No doubt," Superintendent Collins said. "Just two years ago, he singled-handedly rescued a crew of ten men from a three-masted barkentine."

"Yes!" Tom said, slapping his knee. "That's the fellow I heard about, for sure. And it was the *Priscilla* that went down, right?"

"That's the one, all right," the superintendent continued. "It happened one night when he was on a beach patrol during a big blow. He had almost reached the point where he was about to turn around and head back to his station when he heard sailors calling from the darkness. Their ship had run aground a hundred yards offshore, and the crew was desperate for help."

"Where was the rest of the surfmen?" Betty asked, so captivated by the story that she had paused from her perpetual kitchen chores.

"Because he was more than an hour out from his station. He knew he needed help but it would have taken three hours to go back, rouse his crewmates, and return to the wreck. So instead, he watches the surf for a few minutes and figures out a way he can do it by himself. Every time a wave rolled out, he ran behind it, getting as close to the barkentine as he could, and shouted out instructions to the crew. Then he would race back to shore before a big breaker could get him. One at a time, the sailors jumped into the surf and Surfman Roberts would grab them and help them ashore before the next wave hit. Once one was safe, he would go back and help another and another until he had rescued seven sailors. After doing all that, he went back three more times, climbed on board the ship, and assisted three injured crewmen through the surf. It was one of the damnedest fine acts of heroism...excuse me, ladies...ever recorded."

"A surfman from the north station told me he's not missed a day of work in five years," Tom said, using the pipe's stem to stab at the air for emphasis. "He also said that Ethan always volunteers for the most dangerous duty. The queer thing is, he also said that the man doesn't have a single friend. You know, like a buddy or a chum. Just acquaintances and crewmates. How can that be?"

Caelyn, who had listened to the story with great interest, now leaned in closer to the superintendent so as not to miss a word.

"That's not quite true," the superintendent said. "As I conveyed earlier, he certainly has the respect of his crewmates and every member of the service, for that matter. There's not a one of us who wouldn't put to float with

Surfman Roberts. But it is true he pretty much keeps to his own. That's by his choice, so we respect it."

"Come now, superintendent," Caelyn pushed. She wanted to find a flaw with Ethan, though not sure why. "I spent a day adrift on the ocean with the man. He looked to be very ordinary to me. I admit he was unconscious the whole time…but a hero? There must be something wrong with him if he spends every day with other lifesavers and yet not have any friends."

Superintendent Collins studied her for a moment, wondering what would motivate such a statement.

"Miss Canady," he asked, "how did you first meet Surfman Roberts?"

"On the night of the wreck, of course. He jumped from his boat to ours."

"'Ours?' You mean you were not alone?"

"Well, First Mate Stick…the wretch…was in the lifeboat with me at first. But he panicked and jumped aboard the rescue boat. Surfman Roberts came across and moved to the bow to help me. That's when the explosion occurred."

"In other words, the first time you ever saw Surfman Roberts was when he put his life on the line to rescue you, a total stranger? In fact, his actions were in direct contrast to your first mate's, who was busy trying to save himself. Yet Surfman Roberts, exposed to the same dangers, disregarded his own safety while trying to save you?"

"Well, yes," she replied, aware that everyone was looking at her. She realized how callous her question must have sounded. "I'm sorry. I simply meant that there must be a reason he doesn't have someone he considers to be a friend."

"Indeed, there is a reason," the superintendent said. He paused for a moment to consider his next words.

"I'm a man who detests idle gossip," he said. "And I respect the man's privacy. But given that what I'm about to tell you isn't truly a secret, and given that you saved his life, I guess you've earned the right to know. So I'll tell you what I know if you'll promise not to repeat it."

Caelyn nodded agreement.

"I remember the first day Surfman Roberts came to Kill Devil Hill, about five years ago. I was the station keeper there back then. He came in carrying an enormous duffel bag over his shoulder, looking for the Midgett family. I knew the Midgetts because Zebulon Midgett had been one of my surfmen. Zeb left us in the spring of ninety-eight to join the volunteers and fight Spaniards in Cuba. He was a good man, a kid really, but...he didn't make it back."

The superintendent paused for a moment, surprised that the memory still touched him.

"Anyway, I took Ethan to the Midgett's house and introduced him to Zeb's parents. It turns out that Ethan and Zeb were good friends while they were fighting with the volunteers. Ethan was at San Juan Hill when Zeb got hit by a bullet from a German machine gun. I can remember as clear as day the moment he opened his duffel bag and gave the Midgetts Zeb's possessions and a citation for bravery. Ethan had traveled all the way from Miami where the troop transport ship docked just to deliver those things, and to tell Mister and Missus Midgett that Zeb had died a brave death. The way the Midgetts carried on when he handed them the citation was enough to make any man cry."

"Well, I was so moved by the fine thing he had done, I let him stay at my cabin that night. My natural inclination after having witnessed such a display was to share a few drinks with the man. We drank a bottle of port and then another.

But even when he was drunk, he talked very little. What I do know is that something terrible happened to him in Cuba, and I don't just mean Zeb Midgett's death. Later that night, after we had gone to bed, I heard him shout out something. Then he started crying. He was crying in his sleep, by God. He kept saying something about a 'madre' or some such thing. I couldn't stand that, so I tried to wake him. He opened his eyes and stared at me like he was seeing me for the first time. Then he said, 'Why did she have to die, Colonel? Why did she have to die?' That's when he looked at his hands real peculiar, like there was something wrong with them. After that, he laid back down and went to sleep. Truth is, I don't think he was ever awake. Not really."

"The next day, he never said a word about it. I didn't want to say anything for fear of embarrassing him. Later on, he told me he didn't want to go back to Missouri because he didn't have any family left there. The war was over and he didn't have a job, so I checked around and found out that the Hatteras Station was looking for a new man. A lot of men wanted that job, but the keeper there owed me a favor. I told him that Ethan was a veteran of the war with the Spanish and to let him have the job. The keeper was a patriot and knew the Midgetts, so he gave Ethan a chance. He's been with them ever since."

He stopped for a few seconds to let Caelyn absorb the information before continuing.

"I know that doesn't answer your question but I do know this. Surfman Roberts carries a ghost with him. I don't know what haunts him but I do know it's something that scars him, long and deep. You can't imagine what it's like to be in battle unless you've been there. I guess the point I'm trying to make is that I don't think Ethan has the capacity to make friends now, not like you or me. He lost his best friend in the war and only God knows what else. My guess is, he's afraid to be that close to anyone again."

Nat, Tom, and Betty appeared lost in thought, not remembering nor caring it was Caelyn's question that had prompted the impassioned tale. But the superintendent's focus was on Caelyn and the hint of embarrassment he saw on her face.

Seizing the opportunity to steer the conversation in another direction, the senior surfman began regaling them with stories about other lifesavers and rescues. Though the others hardly noticed when Caelyn backed her chair away from the table, the senior surfman noted her departure to himself but continued without pause, hoping that his words had hit the mark he had been aiming for.

Stepping outside on the front porch, Caelyn took a deep breath. Relief washed over her as if she had been drowning but had somehow managed to break to the surface just in time. The superintendent had no way of knowing that his words had been like a slap in the face, forcing her to question almost everything she thought she knew about herself. Unsettled, she sat on one of the porch's rocking chairs and tried to clear her mind.

Gazing upon the sandy pathway passing before the inn, she wondered at the people of the Outer Banks. It was a beautiful place but so remote. If Ethan was trying to isolate himself, the barrier islands were the place to do it. There were few distractions and few visitors. The people who lived here were too busy seeking the basics of life to care about much else. Everyone shared the same status and there was little pretentiousness. It was the perfect place to be an anonymous soul making the most of life by just trying to survive.

She chastised herself for having judged the surfman unjustly and wondered what tragedy had befallen him during the war. She was still pondering the mystery when a large yellow dog with a troop of puppies in tow came trotting down the path. The bitch was moving fast, tired of the whelps with teeth too sharp for her teats. This was the weaning. They would have to find a way to make it on their own if the dog had no owner. Caelyn pitied them as they disappeared into the brush and hoped that they would somehow make it.

The plight of the puppies made her think about her own coming of age. She had never "weaned" herself from her family. Becoming independent had never been an option. After high school, she considered going to college but her father forbade it.

"Academic endeavors are a waste of time for women," he had said. "What you really need to do is make yourself available and find the right man."

It was a strange comment coming from Jack Canady. It was the first time her father had ever encouraged her to meet men. But his change of tune made more sense when he began introducing her to eligible bachelors he preferred. They were much older and somehow always connected to his business dealings some way or another. She came to understand that, to her father, her marriage had everything to do with economic opportunity and nothing to do with her happiness.

His efforts became more persistent as she approached her mid-twenties but she had stood her ground. He had acted as though they were in a race against an unseen clock. The tension between them increased with each passing day.

It was as if, somehow, her vows would release him from some unspeakable contract. She theorized that this peculiar manifestation of his personality stemmed from his overprotective nature and the growing distance between them since her mother's death. Whatever his underlying motivations were, however, did not matter. If she did not marry soon, there would be a confrontation. And though she dreaded it, she was prepared for the worst.

Then Hunter had come along. Different from the others her father had brought home, he was the fair-haired son of a local businessman and the answer to a prayer. He was well-to-do, tall, handsome, and full of promise. But best of all, he was her age! Their friendship blossomed so quickly she was sure her father suspected it was a trick designed to appease him. But as the relationship continued to grow, everyone became certain that Hunter Winslow was the man who would capture Caelyn's heart. Everyone except Caelyn.

Again, she remembered her conversation with Aunt Frances on the beach. "He truly is the best friend I've ever had." The declaration continued to echo through her mind, fading away until the only word that remained was "friend." It was only at that moment she realized Hunter Winslow was the only male friend her father had allowed her to have. She had no references with which to gauge whether he was a "best" friend. The doubt she was certain she had resolved during her trip to St. Augustine had returned. The emptiness of the revelation joined with the chill of the evening and she shivered.

If only I could talk to Aunt Frances, she thought as she rubbed her arms for warmth. *It's strange to think that neither she nor my parents even know I am still alive. The Aphrodite is just now past due. Father and Dorothy will begin to worry. Unless the telephone lines are working and someone at the Hatteras Station called them, they will think I've perished at sea.*

She smiled despite the morbid thought. For the first time in her life, she was on her own. She had no family, no servants, no friends, no staff or crew to report her actions to her parents. For the next few days, every decision she made would be hers and hers alone.

Again, she shivered. She knew she could be self-reliant, but no one had ever given her the opportunity. The thought was intoxicating and frightening at the same time.

So this is what it feels like to be free. This is what it means to be alive!

Chapter Nine

The Chest

Caelyn was still sitting in the rocking chair when the three men returned. She had wrapped herself in a blanket, unwilling to let the cold drive her inside. Harry and Danny came down the path first, carrying the chest by its end handles. They placed the steamer on the porch at the top of the steps. Harry removed his hat with a flourish and took a sweeping bow.

"To your rescue, fair maiden," he said, enjoying the theatrics. "I believe this chest of feminine treasures belongs to you."

"My steamer! Are my clothes still inside?"

"Not only will you find your belongings intact and complete, I believe you will be happy to know that they even remain dry. Quite a piece of luggage you purchased, I'd say."

"It's the steamer with my summer wear! They may not be very practical but at least I will be wearing my own clothes. How can I ever repay you, Captain Joyner?"

"Don't thank me," Harry replied. Continuing his act, he stepped aside and swept his arm in a broad motion as though introducing an honored guest to a royal court. "My lady, Caelyn Canady, I present to you the most noble and gallant Surfman Ethan Roberts, who is single-handedly responsible for salvaging your chest. It is to him you owe a debt of gratitude, not I."

Ethan stepped forward to stand between Harry and Danny, his demeanor a mix of determination and reluctance. Despite promising to govern his expectations, a rush of excitement threatened to overwhelm his resolve.

Ethan regretted his attempt at chivalry as quickly as Caelyn's expression changed from gratitude to animus. His attempt to repair the damage done at their first meeting was a miserable failure. For the second time that day, his face flushed hot with embarrassment.

"Tell Mister Roberts that I appreciate his thoughtfulness," she said, a different person than she had been moments before. "I suppose you deserve a reward. How much do I owe you?"

"He paid the vendue master eighteen dollars for it," Danny blurted, not understanding that Caelyn was slighting the lifesaver.

"Danny!" Harry snipped, shooting him a hard look.

Ethan froze into silence, bewildered by Caelyn's contempt. Averting his eyes, he turned and began walking toward the harbor.

"Why the hell did you do that?" Harry asked, holding back his rage. "Is that the way people where you're from show their appreciation?"

"I don't need a nursemaid, Captain Joyner. I can take care of myself. Besides, it would not be appropriate to encourage Mister Roberts in any way."

"His name is *Surfman* Roberts. Can't you at least give him that? Or would acknowledging his profession be taking too big of a step toward admitting that he might be worthy of respect...despite having been so shortsighted as to have selected parents with no name or fortune?"

"As I said, I can take care of myself," Caelyn replied, unwilling to relent. "I'm sorry if I insulted Mister... Surfman Roberts. I assure you it was unintentional. But frankly, I do not want to be indebted to him or anyone else. I also told you I pay my debts, and I meant it. Now, if you would be so kind, I'd like to give you the money to take back to him."

Opening the chest, Caelyn pulled on the lining of the lid. The seam, held secure by a row of concealed snaps, gave way to reveal a secret pocket. Feeling inside, she removed a banded stack of bills, pulled out a twenty, and offered it to Harry.

"It's a bit ironic, ain't it?" he said.

"How so?" she asked, though sure she did not want to know the answer.

"If Ethan hadn't bought the chest, you wouldn't have the means to be paying him back.

The waterman looked hard into her eyes, still refusing to take the offered bill.

"When I first picked you up, I thought there might be a little salt to you. But now I'm thinking maybe I was wrong. Maybe you're just as worthless as the rest of them popinjays that roost up there in your fancy birdhouses."

Harry held his stare as Caelyn returned the money to the pouch and closed the lid. Was there a look of hurt in her eyes? He couldn't tell for sure.

Grabbing one of its handles, Caelyn tried to pull the chest inside but only moved it a few inches. Again she tried and again she failed.

"Danny," Harry said, drawing out each word. "Help Miss Canady get her chest upstairs to her room...not that she can't do it herself. You can take my room tonight, I'll stay on the *Henrietta*. Things is a bit too stale around here for me. I need to smell the salt air."

Not waiting for a response, Harry turned and walked down the path in the same direction Ethan had gone. He sensed Caelyn's eyes following him as he walked away, but refused to look back. He wouldn't give her the satisfaction of thinking that somehow, she might not be in the wrong.

But now he had a foul taste in his mouth that needed to be washed out. He buttoned his pea coat against the night chill and walked through the village searching for the landmarks a local had given him. Always one to plan for necessities, he had made a point of finding out who and where the local provider was. Ocracoke was a small village, and the directions had been spot on. Upon finding the specific house, he knocked on the side door. To his surprise, an elderly woman answered, opening the door just enough to peer outside. Her hooked nose and protruding chin made Harry wonder if she might fly off on a broom before he got what he had come for. Looking him up and down, the old woman decided he was all right and opened the door wider.

"Ain't got nothin' but rum," she said without waiting for his question. "And you better be glad I got that."

Harry was the rare seaman who despised rum and did not understand why anyone with a choice would drink the stuff. But if rum was all she had, then rum it would be.

The woman closed the door for a few moments and returned with a bottle of Cuban rum with the label still on it. She handed him the bottle with one hand as she took a swig from a small bottle of her own.

"Bit cold tonight, 'ay," Harry said with a wink.

The old woman looked at her little bottle for a moment, then laughed.

"T'ain't nothin' but a Pepsi-Cola," she said.

Harry looked at her, not understanding.

"It's what they call a soft drink. You know, a caramel, sugar-water kind of thing. Used to be called Brad's Drink, for some reason. Wait, I'll let you try one for yourself.

Again, she disappeared into the shanty and returned with one of the little bottles. Harry took a sip and a smile broke out across his big, bearded face. He swallowed the rest in one big gulp.

"Lord A'mighty, that's some kind a good," he said. "You got any more?"

"You betcha. Got several crates of it."

"Let me have one...crate that is."

"How much do I owe you?" Harry asked when she returned with a sectioned wood crate of twenty-four bottles.

"That'll be a dollar for the rum and three for the cola."

"Three dollars! This stuff costs more than the rum?"

"That's right. I can get rum any time. The cola's hard to come by. Take it or leave it."

The big waterman fished in his pocket and handed her a five-dollar silver certificate. She took the bill and gave him a one-dollar greenback from her apron pocket as change.

Harry laid the bottle of rum lengthwise between the two center rows of Coke and hoisted the whole thing to his shoulder. With his mission accomplished, he said goodnight and followed the winding pathways back to the *Henrietta's* mooring. Sitting at the end of the dock, gazing across the water, was Ethan.

"Was hoping I'd find you here," Harry said with as much cheer as he thought the mood would allow. "Got something that might make you feel a little better, or at least forget for a while."

Harry stepped onto the *Henrietta* and rested the crate on a salt barrel. Ethan followed him on board and sat on the aft deck where he could lean back against the starboard bulwark. Sensing that the surfman wasn't ready to talk, Harry didn't try to engage him in conversation. Instead, he went inside the cabin and commandeered a couple of tin cups. Upon returning, he filled them both and handed one to Ethan.

The surfman took a sip and paused. Having fought in Cuba, he was no stranger to the smooth taste of good rum. Chugging down the rest, he held out his cup for more rum. Harry obliged him and then took a seat on the deck. Together, they sat in silence, staring up at the brilliant display of stars against the crisp winter night, listening to the water lap against the boat's hull.

Every few minutes, Ethan drew a deep breath, exhaled, and then shifted around to get more comfortable. Harry didn't know if the surfman appreciated his company but he knew he was doing the right thing. The lifesaver's past haunted him, and no man should face his demons alone. That something had happened to him in Cuba was clear.

That the copper-haired woman had rattled his self-constructed prison was clear as well.

Why wouldn't she? he wondered. *She is the vision of a goddess, with her long wild hair and her green eyes as clear as Austrian crystal. And the surfman had seen her with no clothes, an occurrence that he wasn't soon likely to forget. Even with clothes on, she was unforgettable, beautiful, feminine, perfect. The harshness of her rejection must have been a real kick in the gut to a man who hadn't said "boo" to a woman in a coon's age.*

"What a strange thing life is," Ethan said, as if reading Harry's mind. "Today was the first time in more than five years I've felt alive...and the person responsible for making me feel this way wouldn't care if I died tomorrow."

Harry waited for Ethan to continue but the surfman drew back into his shell. Harry filled their cups, settled back, and resumed looking at the stars. Taking another swig of rum, he shuddered in disgust.

"Damn bilge water," he spat, breaking the silence. "Pond scum with mullet three-days dead floating in it tastes better than this."

His eyes caught the glint of light reflecting off the glass bottles in the crate where he had left it. Opening one with a pair of plyers, he drank half the cola and placed it next to his cup. A few minutes later, he poured the remainder of the Pepsi in his cup, having forgotten that it was still half full of rum, and took a swallow.

"Hell's bells!" the waterman said. "That ain't half bad! Here, give it a try."

Ethan took the cup and tasted Harry's accidental concoction.

"Hey, that is pretty good," he said, perking up despite his melancholy. "What did you do, mix the cola with the rum?"

"Yeah, how about that? Pepsi-Cola and rum ain't bad. Ain't bad atall!"

Harry fixed them both another drink, then took his seat on the deck, allowing the silence to return. The occasional howl of a dog and trilling of tree frogs were the only sounds interrupting the quiet now. Ethan stood long enough to relieve himself over the *Henrietta's* stern and returned to his seat. They continued drinking rum and cola until they'd emptied the rum bottle.

"Harry," Ethan said at last. "Have you ever been scared?"

The big waterman wasn't sure how to answer. Coming from a man who was both a war veteran and a surfman, it was a strange question. Ethan was struggling with something.

"I'm scared, Harry," the lifesaver continued before the fisherman could answer. Harry breathed a silent sigh of relief. "I'm scared to death. I'm sorry if that makes you think less of me as a man. But God's truth, Harry, I just wish I could be back at Hatteras and get away from this place."

"What is it that's got you scared?" Harry asked, though sure he already knew.

"Her," Ethan said without hesitating. "I'm scared of what she's already done to me...and she hasn't even done anything yet, except make me out to be a huckleberry. All I can think about is her. I can't stand it. I don't want to think about her, but I can't stop the thoughts from coming."

"Tell me something," Harry asked, "when you are out there in the middle of a big blow trying to make your way to a ship, what do you think about?"

"Well, nothing really. I just keep rowing and let the keeper pilot us to where we need to go. If you start thinking about how bad it is, it will drive you crazy."

"Then quit thinking about it and let your keeper take you where you need to go. They ain't no storm like what happens to a man when he falls in love. The difference is, this storm is on the inside. You just gotta ride it out and let nature take her course. Do that, and no matter what happens, you'll do all right in the end. If you try to make it happen when it ain't there, or try to deny it when it is, it's like fighting the sea during a nor'easter...you always lose. You have to go with the wind, at least for a while."

As Ethan considered the advice, Harry played the entire exchange over again in his mind, hoping that his drunken cornpone wisdom made sense. With the rum gone and the air turning ever colder, he decided it was time to turn in. Lighting a lantern, he guided the way below deck where they stretched out on the two sleeping racks that met at the bow.

"Harry," Ethan said as Harry extinguished the wick. "You know, when we go out in the surfboats, we always wear lifejackets."

The waterman smiled despite himself, pleased that Ethan had taken the metaphor seriously.

"Surfman," Harry said, "they ain't no lifejackets where you're headed. This is one trip where you'll sink or swim on your own."

Chapter Ten

An Awakening

Ethan awakened to the predawn noises of fishermen loading their boats and heading out to ocean and sound. Sleep had come in brief interludes between long stretches of fitful introspection and uncertainty. The rum had done nothing to stave his inner turmoil and the pounding in his head quashed any hope of finding sleep again. Being careful not to disturb Harry, he left his bunk and went topside.

Entering the cabin, he lit an oil lamp and began poking through the various storage bins in search of a coffeepot. Opening a drawer in what served as the galley section, he spied a leather pouch rolled up and bound with two strips of flat rawhide. Adorning the outside surface of the pouch were hand-tooled letters spelling out the words "TONSORIAL HYGIENICS." Curious, he unrolled the pouch and lifted its cover flap to find an assortment of shears, combs, and razors. It was an odd thing to find aboard a fishing boat, but Harry did seem to be meticulous about his appearance.

Redirecting his search, Ethan looked in the cabinet beneath the drawer and found a tin washbasin with a shaving cup and soap, but still no coffeepot. As he placed the basin on the counter, he noticed a small square of mirrored glass mounted on the bulkhead. The brightness of the white bandage wrapped around his head stood out in the reflection and he wondered how bad the injury was. Unwrapping the gauze revealed a large bruise with a slight abrasion but no open wound.

No longer concerned about the injury, he studied the reflection gazing back at him in the mirror. The person he saw was as a stranger, someone he had known long ago but forgotten. He touched the whiskers on his cheeks and chin and took a proper look at himself for the first time in years. Beards were a common look with the men of the Lifesaving Service. Having no desire to stand out from the others, Ethan had let his facial hair grow out after joining the crew of the Hatteras Station to blend in. After five years of not giving it a second thought, he now wondered how he would look without the beard.

But why now? he wondered?

The answer came as quickly as he had thought the question. Angry with himself, he returned the pouch to the drawer, located the percolator, and lit a Primus burner. As he filled the little pot with water and coffee, his thoughts wandered back to the copper-haired beauty who had spoken to him with such contempt.

It's a small village, so it's likely our paths will cross again. And what if I do see her? Will she even speak to me?

The sound of the coffee pot beginning to perk and the aroma of dark coffee shifted his mood away from brooding to the somberness of reality.

It doesn't matter. I'll be leaving soon, anyway. My wrist will heal quickly enough and there is no reason to stay. I need to get back to Hatteras and my crewmates. If not tomorrow, then the next day for sure. After that, none of this will matter.

But it did matter. And that it did, disturbed him, because he understood why. He was not the same person he had been two days ago.

Once again, he scratched his chin, feeling the roughness of his beard. He had become detached from the world by choice. It had never bothered him that his personality prevented people from getting close. That was the intent.

As he poured himself a cup of coffee, he tried to imagine how he must look to the woman who had saved his life. The sober self-assessment cast a dark shadow on the truth of what he had become, and then a new thought elbowed its way into his consciousness.

People don't see me as a loner. They see me as a broken man and someone to be pitied. And why should she be any different?

Choosing a life of solitude had been his choice, He accepted the consequences of that decision. Having people look at him with pity, however, had not been part of the bargain. It was a point of view he had never considered.

Instead of making a second cup of coffee, he poured the steaming brew into the tin basin resting beneath the mirror. He could do nothing to erase what had taken place during the past five years or even yesterday, but he could control some things in his life.

"If I'm not willing to face myself," he asked the image in the mirror, "why would anyone else?"

Chapter Eleven

A Twist of Fate

As she went through the contents of her steamer, Caelyn came across an old cameo attached to a worn, black velvet ribbon. It was an inexpensive accessory she had received on her sixteenth birthday, and though it wasn't the most elegant jewelry she owned, she had always appreciated the way it accentuated her cheekbones and had worn it often. Realizing that it was the only piece in her possession at the moment, she tied the ribbon around her neck and continued perusing the trunk's contents.

When done, she retired for the evening in hope of getting a good night's rest. Instead, she found herself lying in bed wide awake, reliving the scene on the porch over and over. As hard as her stepmother had tried to ingrain the concept of social appearances, it surprised Caelyn that the exchange bothered her as much as it did. The man named Ethan was, after all, just a simple lifesaver.

Sleep came at last on restless feet, filling her mind with haunting visions of her life. A dream took her back aboard the lifeboat, adrift on the ocean in the dark of night. But instead of watching over the surfman, she was alone on a dead-calm sea, without even the sound of water lapping against the side of the boat to interrupt the unbearable silence. Without the presence of another human being, the sense of being lost was overwhelming. When she thought she could stand it no more, a small but clear voice drifted through the darkness. The closer the voice came to the boat, the more she believed it belonged to someone she knew.

"Caelyn," a little girl pleaded. "Please, Caelyn. Where are you? I need you. I'm so lonely."

Caelyn tried to answer, but couldn't force her lips to move. Even when the voice came to be right beside the boat, she was incapable of answering. Petrified, Caelyn watched a small white hand emerge from the darkness to clutch the lifeboat's gunwale. As the girl's other hand appeared from the darkness to grip the rail, Caelyn scrambled backwards into the far corner of the boat. She watched in terror as the waif strained to pull herself out of the water. Her head crested the rail, and she looked across the boat at Caelyn. In a blur of motion only possible in dreams, the girl traversed the distance between them. Now sitting on the seat closest to Caelyn, she eyed the terrified woman with an accusatory look, water dripping from her dark, wet hair.

"You said you would play with me, Caelyn. I wanted to come to play with you, but mummy wouldn't let me. She said I could never play with you again...and then she cried. What happened, Caelyn? Why did you make my mummy and I go away? Was it because I found the gun?"

Caelyn bolted upright in her bed. Soaked with perspiration, her nightclothes clung to her body. Looking around to make sure she was still in her room, she took a deep breath. The girl in the water was Annie, the daughter of the servant she had played with so many years ago. But why dream about her now?

The past pulled at Caelyn's memory. Dorothy and her father had given her everything a child might want – except the opportunity to have a friend. A person she could share a secret with. Someone to play with and dream with and to pretend wonderful lives. The servant's daughter was the closest thing to a friend she had ever known while growing up, and now she could not even recall her name. She never believed her stepmother's explanation that the housekeeper was fired for stealing, and she couldn't remember anything involving a gun.

The dream and recollections of her childhood forced her to acknowledge what she had missed living a sheltered childhood. Resentment swelled within and her growing anger made it impossible to sleep. With the dawn beginning to light her window, she gave up trying. Slipping on one of the cotton dresses from her steamer, she pinned up her hair and grabbed a coat Betty had loaned her. Being careful not to wake the others, she let herself out the front door and followed the well-worn path to the beach.

The early morning air was crisp and cold but the day promised to be warmer than the day before. About a mile off the beach, a schooner was following the coastline, headed north under three-quarter sail. The clear air made the vessel appear closer than it was but the breeze was blowing offshore, making it impossible to hear the shipboard sounds of snapping sails and shouts of the sailors. The muted light of morning and the absence of sound made the boat appear as though it were a ghost ship, sailing without purpose or guidance from human hand.

Seeking a dune well back from the water, Caelyn positioned herself to take advantage of the sun's warmth while still being able to look out across the ocean. The brisk air and warm sun combined with the gentle morning hues, lulling her into a mood devoid of thoughts. Her mind registered the movements of the sea oats, the seabirds, and waves without interpretation. Her consciousness floated free, hindered neither by self nor by desire. She had no thoughts of New York, or of marriage, or self-doubts, or yesterday, or tomorrow. She absorbed the beauty and all it offered – an intricate and intimate intertwining of herself and the moment. Caelyn sat that way for a long while, unconcerned with the time. She was seeing the world through fresh eyes. Her only desire was to continue lying against its breast and revel in its glory.

The spell was almost broken when she spotted a man ambling along the beach, lost in thoughts of his own. Instead of annoying her, Caelyn surprisingly found the intrusion enhanced the mood. Being able to observe another person without them realizing it, added to her sense of detachment. She had become a nymph of the island's foliage, blending into the surroundings, able to see without being seen.

His age is hard to guess, but he's not old, she thought. *His hair is dark, though the sun has lightened the tips. He's still too far away to discern his looks, but he appears to have a strong face. Judging by his walk, I'd say that he is a man of confidence but without a destination.*

She paused in her assessment long enough to take pleasure in knowing that the other person was oblivious to her presence. If she remained still, he would never know they were visitors to the same place at the same time. One small move might catch his attention, breaking the spell. It was both pleasing and powerful to know she controlled the outcome, even if it was a trivial matter.

Coming to the top of a small drift of sand, the man stopped and turned to look out across the ocean.

He is looking for something, too, she imagined. *It's odd that two people who know nothing of each other would come to the same place, expecting the ocean to somehow provide answers to our human affairs. If only life was so simple and nature so obliging.*

The man turned to look up the beach, using his hand to shade the rising sun from his eyes. Something in the distance had caught his attention, but the dunes didn't allow her to see what it might be. The stranger dropped to one knee and began clapping his hands. A moment later, a puppy appeared, coming close to the man but hesitant to cross the last few feet between them. Caelyn wondered if it was one of the puppies she had seen following the yellow bitch. Tired of their constant feeding and sharp teeth, the mother had used the rolling dunes to lose some of her whelps, leaving this black one to die or to survive on its own.

The man scratched the puppy's head and pulled something from his pocket for him to eat. The grateful pup wolfed down the scrap and looked at the man, hoping for more. Happy to oblige, the fellow repeated the kindness. The puppy came closer and the man scooped him up. Cradling him in one arm, he scratched the dog's head with his free hand. The act of kindness and gentle manner had not only charmed the sad creature, but Caelyn as well.

Though fascinated by the scene, she was still reluctant to reveal her presence. She continued watching from the distance as the man ran his fingers over the puppy's wiry fur, checking his condition. Finding something, he stopped the search and began walking toward the dunes. A wave of fear passed through Caelyn. He was coming toward her! But the man never looked up, focusing on the dog instead. When he reached the dunes a few yards from her, he turned to face the ocean and sat in the soft sand. Holding the puppy on his lap with his belly up, Caelyn's unwitting performer resumed grooming his new friend.

It was a tender, simple kindness of a sort that Caelyn had never before witnessed. She had never had a pet and had never seen animals as anything other than food or beasts of burden, like the horses that pulled carriages. Despite the tranquility of the moment, a comparison began to form in her mind like a single, annoying mosquito. The idea of Hunter handling an animal in such a manner was unimaginable. Though a good man, he was a proper gentleman who would not have dirtied his hands or allowed animal hair to collect on his clothes. He would also have been astounded by how much the stranger's gentle treatment of the puppy had touched her.

The stark contrast made her recall the doubts she had struggled to resolve. For a moment she could see herself through the eyes of others, and she did not like what she saw. And there it was. The same question that had prompted the visit to her aunt in the first place. Was she making the right decision? It had taken a long time to find a situation that felt comfortable. Too many questions now could reveal a truth she was not sure she wanted to face. The ambiguity was driving her mad.

The serenity of a perfect morning has beguiled me. Has allowing my thoughts to wander unfettered suppressed my ability to reason? The stranger on the dune could well be a simpleton or some sort of lout. Can reality hold up to my silly romantic notions? Enough of this!

With his back turned toward her, the man didn't see Caelyn rise from her vantage point and begin walking toward him. Absorbed in his task and with the soft sand muffling her footsteps, he did not know she was behind him until she spoke.

"Is there something wrong with him?" Caelyn asked. The man's broad back stiffened for a second but he did not turn around to look at her.

"It's the seed ticks," he said. Though his tone was nonchalant, his voice was familiar. "They like the tender skin on his belly. They'll sap every bit of strength from the little fella if they're not removed."

"And what will you do with him, pray tell?"

"I don't know. Maybe a boy in the village would like to have him. Maybe I'll keep him. I think my mates at the station would go for a mascot."

How do I know that voice? she wondered. *And why won't he turn around? He must either be very rude or daft.*

"May I hold him?"

Stepping to his front, she saw his face for the first time. It was as strong and reserved as she had earlier suspected. He may have been in his mid-twenties but it was hard to judge. His color was that of an outdoorsman, tanned and somewhat weathered. A cleft chin gave him character beyond his age and his eyes were as familiar as his voice.

She knew those eyes. They showed pain, wisdom, and compassion. But where had she seen them?

The man held out the black puppy and Caelyn saw the bandage wrapped around his wrist. She looked up to meet his eyes. Her face flushed hot as she took the little dog from his hands. He looked so different without his beard.

What have I gotten myself into? she thought, sensing Ethan's eyes following every move she made. *I don't want this man's attention. But if I did, I wouldn't have worn an old woman's coat and I would have done something with my hair. What a sight I must make. And for the love of God, why do I care?*

"...or maybe he's some sort of a terrier. There are many variations of the breed."

"I don't know much about dogs," she said, hoping she was picking up the conversation correctly, "but I saw the mother yesterday and she looked more like a pointer or perhaps a setter."

"That would make sense. There's a good number of sportsmen who travel here to hunt ducks and geese. There's bound to be a fair number of hunting dogs on the island."

Caelyn eased down on the dune next to him and rested the puppy in her lap. Not sure what to say next, she scratched the dog's head, feeling the awkwardness grow with each passing moment of silence.

"Who was the madre?" she asked without warning, the words spilling from her mouth unbeckoned.

Though slight, the tenseness washing over the surfman was palpable. Caelyn felt as if she was watching the scene play out as though she were a third party, unable to fathom from where such an inappropriate question had sprung.

Though it was impossible to retract her words, she could at least try to explain herself.

"Superintendent Collins came to stay at the inn yesterday and he told us about you." The more she spoke, the more she felt like a drowning woman. "He said that he once heard you call out for someone in your sleep...that you used the Spanish word 'madre.' That means 'mother,' doesn't it? Were you crying for your mother? She wasn't Spanish, was she?"

The surfman lowered his head and she could no longer see his eyes. She watched in silence as he struggled with a question that, she realized, was more poignant than she had intended.

"You've never talked about it, have you? Please don't hate me, Mister Roberts. I'm not very good at making casual conversation. It's just that...well, when we were in the lifeboat and you were unconscious, you called out to your friend, Zeb. Superintendent Collins said that he was your best friend in the war. I don't mean to be presumptuous, but I sense those two things are connected."

She stopped, not sure what to say next. It was clear he didn't want to talk about it.

What was I thinking? One day I insult him and the next I pry into his private life, uninvited. By now he must think that I am a rude, nosey woman who babbles on with no regard for others.

"It is...very difficult," Ethan said, considering each word before speaking. "There is...more evil in the world...than you can imagine."

He stopped, unable to continue. With the sounds of the beach and ocean filling the void between them, Caelyn took a moment to collect her thoughts and resolved to quit making a fool of herself.

During the quiet, the puppy spotted a sand fiddler venturing from its hole. Walking sideways, the crab moved farther and farther from its haven. Jumping from Caelyn's lap, the pup chased after the crab, which shot down a second hole. Baffled by the vanishing act, the little dog circled the hole three times, sniffed at it, then began digging up sand as fast as he could.

"Teach," Ethan declared, breaking the silence at last.

"Teach?" Caelyn asked, glad she'd broken the awkward moment.

"Yeah, like in Edward Teach. You know, Blackbeard the pirate. That's what I'll call him. Teach."

"What made you think of that?"

"Blackbeard had a home here on Ocracoke. The island provided a central location from which he could sail up and down the coast to prey on merchant ships. He knew the channels and used them to escape the authorities...that is, on the rare occasions when they came looking for him. The trouble was, most of the colonials didn't want him captured. His black-market trade was good for the local economy...not to mention that they were more scared of him than they were of the authorities. When they did capture him, they cut off his head and dumped him into the ocean. Ocracokers say that his headless body swam around the boat three times before it sank beneath the water."

"That's what the pup just did," he continued. "He ran around the hole three times, and look, he has the black hair to boot. I think the name suits him."

"You don't believe that, do you?" she asked, wondering if he could be that gullible. "I mean, about the corpse swimming around the boat?"

"Of course not. How would a body without a head be able to see where he was going?"

Caelyn hesitated, trying to make sense of the odd logic.

"You're joking!" she said, chuckling at his dry sense of humor and her own gullibility.

Ethan smiled back at her. There was light in his eyes she had not seen before.

"Well, if I do nothing else right today, at least I got you to smile...even if the joke is on me."

Tired of digging for the fiddler, the puppy pranced back to where they were sitting, undaunted by his defeat. Caelyn picked him up and handed him to Ethan. The surfman gave the puppy the last piece of jerky from his pocket.

"Now that he has a name, I think he should have a collar," she said. Reaching behind her head, she untied the cameo's ribbon and removed it from her neck.

Ethan held Teach while she wrapped the velvet strap around the dog's neck twice to make it fit and tied the ends together. He put the puppy down and they watched him for a few moments to see if he would paw at the collar. When Ethan looked up, their eyes met, and she froze. Though she had never truly seen it before, she recognized the look on his face. And while it might not yet be a full-fledged blaze, the truth of the flame burning within him was undeniable. She had started something that both scared her and made her angry.

Teach yapped, breaking the spell. The curious pup had wandered onto the beach but was now running toward them with his ears laid back and tail tucked between his legs.

Taking refuge behind the surfman, he peered around Ethan's legs, growling as he looked back toward the beach.

Meandering between the dunes coming toward them, a horse walked into view. Then came another and another. Caelyn and Ethan continued watching in silence until seventeen horses in all had passed by.

"It's the Banker ponies," Ethan whispered. "They roam free on the islands but they're tame enough. Trust me."

"They don't belong to anyone?"

"They belong to the island and whoever happens to own it. But nobody claims them. The Ocracokers say they're Spanish horses, descended from the survivors of a Spanish galleon that wrecked here hundreds of years ago. Watch," he said as he came to his feet.

Walking toward the open beach, Ethan made catching sounds with his mouth. Used to receiving handouts from the islanders, the last pony in the herd turned around and came toward the surfman. Having no food left, the surfman reached in his pocket and pretended to pull out an apple. Responding to the come-on, the young mare sniffed at his outstretched hand, searching for the unseen treat. In one swift movement, Ethan grabbed the pony's mane with his uninjured hand and threw his leg over her back. He braced for her reaction, but the pony, ridden before, remained still, waiting to see what he would do.

When nothing happened, Ethan gave Caelyn a smug look, gloating at his cleverness.

"I haven't sat a horse since the war," he said, spreading his arms in triumph.

Feeling her passenger relax, the pony reared up, dumping her would-be rider onto the beach. The mare took off after the herd, leaving Ethan on his back. Seeing him struggle to recover, Caelyn ran to Ethan's side. But it wasn't an injury that kept him down, she discovered. He was laughing too hard to sit up. She frowned at him at first, but couldn't suppress the smile that followed.

"You scared me to death. You might have broken your neck."

"Is that why they called you the 'Rough Riders!'" a gruff voice shouted from down the beach. Ethan and Caelyn turned to see Superintendent Collins and Captain Joyner walking toward them. "It must be pretty rough falling on your backside all the time," Harry said, finishing the joke.

Ethan stood and brushed the sand from his clothes. A look of concern swept across his face. Though irritated that the district superintendent had ruined the moment, Caelyn managed to maintain a smile.

"Superintendent Collins," Ethan said, giving his superior a smart salute. "I heard you were here. I'm sorry, sir. I should have come to see you right away."

"Nonsense, son," the superintended said, returning the salute. "You should be doing exactly what you are doing, recuperating. Umm, that is what you're doing, isn't it?" he asked, cutting a quizzical glance at Caelyn. It was easy to assess the situation.

From the corner or her eye, Caelyn saw Ethan's face turn red, embarrassed at how intimate the situation must have looked, tried to answer.

"Well, sir," he tried to answer. "I... I..."

"Stow it," Harry interrupted. "You think the superintendent can't figure things out for himself? By the way, what happened to your face? I see you found my straight razor."

Ethan rubbed his cheek, visibly relieved Harry had changed the subject.

"I didn't think you'd mind, Harry."

A moment of awkward silence followed.

"I didn't even recognize him at first," Caelyn said, attempting to fill the void.

Again Ethan shifted about, her rescue attempt making him even more self-conscious.

"Well, Surfman Roberts," Collins charged in, trying to bring direction back to the conversation. "Do you think you are well enough to travel?"

"Yes sir!" Though he had answered without hesitation, Caelyn saw his temperament was spiraling downward. "As long as I don't push it, I should be all right."

"Good. I have a special assignment for you. It will be a week or more before you're able to pull an oar, so you won't be of much use to the Hatteras crew. In the meantime, I have something for you to do. As you may know, we've been looking to establish a new station at this end of the island. If everything goes right this afternoon, I will have all the necessary paperwork completed to procure a plot for what will become the Ocracoke Lifesaving Station. If so, I would like you to take those papers to our Kitty Hawk Station. Once he receives them, the Kitty Hawk keeper will have them delivered to the train station in Elizabeth City. After that, you have my permission to take a week off for convalescence."

"Thank you, sir," Ethan said. "There's a supply boat that takes on passengers due in a couple of days. I can–"

"No, that won't do," Superintendent Collins interrupted, shaking his head. "I don't want to wait that long. I want the book on this closed before the new year so we can start on the station as soon as possible. I have secured a local vessel to take you to Kitty Hawk first thing tomorrow morning. You should be there in two days if the wind is good, three at the most."

"Yes, sir," he said, though there was no enthusiasm in his voice. Tomorrow he would be gone, never to see Caelyn again.

"Good, it's settled then," Superintendent Collins said as he pulled his wallet out from inside his coat. "Here's ten dollars. Go buy yourself some clothes. Just be sure to see me at dinner to make certain everything is in place. That gives you the rest of the afternoon to thank the folks at the inn and to say your goodbyes. I'll see you tonight."

The superintendent tipped his hat to Caelyn and turned to leave. He took a few steps, stopped, and turned back around.

"By the way, Miss Canady, I took the liberty of arranging for you to sail with Surfman Roberts to Kitty Hawk as well. From there, it should be a simple matter to get transportation to the train station in Elizabeth City." He paused, choosing his next words carefully. "I thought you would want to be heading back to New York as soon as possible, and Surfman Roberts can act as your escort...at least as far as Kitty Hawk. The United States Lifesaving Service is indebted to you for saving his life. The least we can do is to make sure your trip home is as uneventful as possible. I believe Surfman Roberts will do an acceptable job in making that possible. Do you find these arrangements satisfactory?"

Caelyn was sure she heard a hint of amusement in the superintendent's voice.

"Oh, I think that will be all right. I do appreciate your concern but it is I who am indebted to the Lifesaving Service. After all, Surfman Roberts' intervention likely saved my life. And, I must confess, I feel somewhat responsible for his injury."

"Well then," the superintendent said, pulling his jacket straight at the lapels. "That settles it. I look forward to seeing you both at dinner?"

"It will be my pleasure," Caelyn said, nodding affirmation.

The superintendent began walking back toward the village and Teach gave chase, yapping at his heels. Caelyn took off after the pup, calling his name as she ran.

Ethan looked at Harry who was wearing a broad grin.

"You had something to do with this, didn't you cap'n?"

"Well, I'd be lying if I said I didn't, and Missus Joyner's boy Harry don't lie. I just thought I might try and help things along a tad, if you don't mind. Of course, I'd be more than willing to see if the superintendent would prefer that it be me who escorted Miss Caelyn...if that's what you'd like?"

"Take me where?" Caelyn asked, coming in at the end of the conversation.

"Don't pay any attention to him," Ethan said. "He thinks he's being clever."

Harry laughed and Caelyn saw a gleam in Harry's eyes, pleased with himself. Putting the two former castaways back together must have been his doing. Caelyn wasn't sure where this thing with Ethan was going, but she appreciated Harry's well-meaning efforts.

"Soooo, what do we have here?" Harry asked, looking at the puppy in Caelyn's arms.

"We found him on the beach. Surfman Roberts named him Teach, after the pirate."

"Come here, little fella," Harry said, taking the puppy from Caelyn and holding him up for a closer look. "He's a handsome mutt, for sure. How would you like to come an' live on Cap'n Harry's boat?"

Teach wagged his tail and licked Harry on the face. Ethan and Caelyn laughed at the sight of the small dog taming the big man. They stayed on the beach for a while, playing with the puppy and getting to know one another. It was almost noon before they started back toward the village, taking their time as they admired the beauty of the island.

Harry turned the subject to the next day's trip, giving Ethan pointers on landmarks to look for and potential water hazards. The safest passage for a small vessel would be to sail the western side of the islands. The ocean was unpredictable and too dangerous. Except for an unexpected squall, their biggest concern on the sound would be the risk of running aground.

Caelyn listened to their conversation, trying to follow what Harry said. The nautical and piloting terms were specific in meaning, some of which she had never heard before. The command they held on their subject impressed her. Harry was as much the master of his craft as Ethan was of his. They shared the commonality of the sea, though the way they made their living could not be more different. Their conversation made her realize how little she knew about people beyond her circle, the things they did, the cultures that made them who they were. She loved the newness of it all. Most of all, she loved that she was seeing life through new eyes.

Harry pointed to a bank of clouds moving in from the northwest, their progress pushed on by an increasing wind. As they walked into the village, they saw the Ocracokers preparing for colder weather. The women were bringing clothes off the line and shuttering windows while the men restocked woodpiles, secured nets, and secured their boats. Though the ocean kept the temperatures bearable through most of the winter, the islands were subjected to arctic fronts as much as the mainland.

Stopping at the island's only dry goods store, they picked up a box of soda crackers and a wedge of cheese for lunch. Harry found a shelf stocked with canned peaches and bought all they had. He loved the sweet syrup and always kept a supply on hand when he was fishing. Ethan picked out a pair of blue denim pants, a couple of black cotton shirts, a wool sweater, and a straight razor. Caelyn wanted to purchase some warmer clothes, but except for a dollar she had found in the pocket of her coat, all her money was at the inn. One thing that she could purchase with a dollar was something she wanted desperately. A hairbrush. The one she found was not the prettiest she had ever owned, but it would work fine.

The wind was picking up and Harry, concerned about the *Henrietta*, suggested that they eat lunch on the boat so he could check on her and Danny.

"Well, take a look at that," Harry said as they came to the dock. A sleek new navy vessel was moored on the other side of the dock from the *Henrietta*. As they came closer, they exchanged greetings with a couple of Ocracokers gawking at the boat and the sailors that made her crew.

"You just missed all the excitement," one of the men said, continuing to admire the vessel. "We had a big crowd here a few minutes ago, but everybody else left to get ready for the blow."

"What kind of boat is that?" Harry asked.

"I heard 'em say that it's some kind of new, diesel-powered cutter," the second man said, scratching his chin as he contemplated the ship's design. "She doesn't draw much water, so her hull is shallow enough for the harbor. We see lots of navy ships following the coastline but they don't usually stop here at Ocracoke."

"I wonder what business brought her here?" Caelyn asked. She had no idea how loaded her question was.

"Rumor is it has something to do with setting up some kind of base or station here," the first Ocracoker said, pausing to spit into the water. "The geniuses in Washington keep talking about making the lifesaving service part of the navy."

"Can they do that?" she asked, looking at Ethan.

"Yeah," he said. "They can do it, all right. We're against it but if they decide to make it happen, it will change everything."

"How so?"

"The men who make up the service are local people," Harry said. "They work where their homes are. Becoming a branch of the navy would mean transfers, tours of duty, and extended absences from those homes. The lifesavers don't want any part of that, and it makes for bad blood whenever the men from the two services come together."

Having seen enough, they said goodbye to the two Ocracokers and boarded the *Henrietta*. Caelyn let Teach sniff around the deck while they ate crackers and cheese, occasionally tossing a slice to the puppy. A few feet away, the sailors continued to work on their boat while Ethan and Harry speculated as to what had brought them to Ocracoke. As she started to put the crackers away, Caelyn noticed a sailboat passing through the cut to the harbor. The wind was brisk, pushing the small boat across the water at a fast clip. When he was within a few dozen yards of the dock, the pilot lowered sail and coasted the low-slung boat to a stop behind the *Henrietta*.

"Danny!" Caelyn said.

"It's the boat Superintendent Collins hired on to take you to Kitty Hawk," Harry said as he jumped to the dock to help Danny.

"The superintendent found out that Mister Williams' brother had a boat he wasn't using," Danny said between bites of crackers and cheese. "Turns out his cousin wasn't interested in leaving Ocracoke for any length of time. That's when Harry talked the Super into letting me be pilot. He figured you were less likely to get into trouble that way, what with me knowing the waters hereabouts. And with Mister Roberts' hand being busted and all, he didn't think it would be a good idea to let him sail her by himself."

Ethan and Caelyn looked at the big waterman who made no attempt to hide his grin.

"Why don't you come with us, Harry?" Ethan asked.

"I wish I could, but the fact is I got to get the *Henrietta* back on the open water and make some money. I've got a nephew that can help me out for a few days while Danny's away. I asked Danny if he'd go with you because I'm invested in you, having found you out on the ocean and all. I wouldn't want to be putting the future of that investment in a stranger's hands. I'll sleep a lot better knowing that Danny's with you."

"I appreciate it, Harry," Ethan said, keeping his response low key. Making a big deal over Harry's kindness would have embarrassed the waterman. To people living on the barrier islands, over-praising someone for doing the right thing would be an insult, because doing the right thing was expected.

Harry and Danny spent the rest of the afternoon going over the small boat, making sure the rigging was sound and everything shipshape while Ethan rounded up extra blankets, rope, a spare anchor and an adequate supply of food and water.

"She's a sweet little boat," Harry said as the three men boarded the craft to give her a quick shakedown. "Hard to beat a Carolina skiff when it comes to navigating the sound waters. She's got a wide beam to keep her stable and her mast supports both sail and a jib. And she does well on the open water as long as the weather's not too rough."

Caelyn watched from the dock while the three men experimented with the sailboat. Gradually she became aware that the sailors on the cutter were watching her, and though she tried to ignore them, their comments to each other grew louder and more suggestive. Their behavior reminded her of New York City and some of her more unpleasant experiences. As much as their rude comments bothered her, she resented them most for having reminded her of home.

She was relieved when the skiff returned to dock behind the *Henrietta* again. Danny handled the sail while Ethan manned the rudder, piloting the boat to berth with his good hand. Harry and Danny secured the vessel and began making her ready for the morrow. Still disturbed by the sailors' leering, Caelyn asked Ethan if he would escort her back to the inn. Ethan answered by offering his arm. To Caelyn's relief, he didn't seem to notice her anxiety.

Chapter Twelve

Crossing the Rubicon

It was close to dark when they arrived at the inn. Betty was bustling about preparing the evening meal while Tom added wood to the fire in the dining hall, ensuring the comfort of their dinner guests. When he saw the puppy Caelyn was holding, he smiled.

"Couldn't resist the little fella, could you miss? Well, you let me take 'em. I'll give him a few scraps an' fix a spot for 'em in the shed to keep warm. That's where our dog stays most the time. She's getting a bit old, but she'll keep the pup from crying tonight."

Thanking Tom for his kindness, Ethan and Caelyn went to their rooms to clean up. When he finished washing his face and hands, Ethan went to his window to gaze at the last remnants of sunset and contemplate the day's events. Never in his wildest dreams would he have believed how his life had changed. A morning that had started bleak and dark was turning into the best day of his life. *I may only have the next two days to be with her but it's two more than I thought I would have when I woke up this morning.*

He was still thinking about Caelyn and the moments they had shared on the beach when he heard the front door to the inn open below his window. Looking down, he saw a man he did not recognize step down from the porch and turn to talk to someone. Although it was dark, the interior lights provided enough illumination through the windows for him to recognize the two men who followed – Mayor O'Neal and Superintendent Collins, the latter holding a leather pouch under his arm. The three men shook hands, and the stranger walked away. As the mayor went back into the inn, Superintendent Collins looked around to see if anyone had seen them. Satisfied that no one had observed the encounter, he followed the mayor inside.

Ethan had only a moment to wonder about the exchange before Tom knocked on his door, announcing that dinner was about to be served. Hoping that Caelyn was already in the dining room, the surfman wasted no time going downstairs. Instead of Caelyn, however, he was greeted by the sight of Superintendent Collins talking to a naval officer in a formal white uniform. Ethan realized the officer had to be the cutter's captain, and given that the Pamlico Inn was the island's one true hotel, it made sense he would take a room here.

Choosing not to go closer, Ethan studied the officer from the opposite side of the room. The man's starched and pressed uniform gave him an air of authority, but it couldn't divert attention away from his short stature and round shape. The man barely stood five-and-a-half feet tall and carried extra weight on his slight frame. His thin hair, combed over from one side to the other in a failed attempt to hide his premature balding, made the condition more conspicuous than it would have been otherwise. Standing beside the tall, fit-looking superintendent was like being the punchline to a poor joke.

Ethan was about to approach the two men when Harry dashed through the front door, chased in by a cold, blustering wind. He threw his hat and coat in a chair and joined Ethan at the room's entryway. They nodded to each other and walked to where Superintendent Collins and the navy officer were conversing.

"Captain Sullivan, I'd like to introduce you to Surfman Roberts."

"Ah, yes, the young lifesaver who almost lost his life," the navy man said in a patronizing tone. "The islanders have been all abuzz about your near death, but what else is there to talk about around here? Don't despair, son. Perhaps if you stick to it, you'll get the hang of the lifesaving business in a few years."

The surfman stiffened. The navy officer had chosen the word "son" to establish his superior station, of that Ethan had no doubt.

"Thank you," he said, chewing off the 'sir' that should have gone at the end. "Next time, I'll wait until *after* the ship blows up to rescue the people on board. I'm sure they'll be much more cooperative once they're dead."

Superintendent Collins snorted as he struggled to keep from laughing. Capt. Sullivan's round face turned red.

"And this is Captain Harry Joyner of the *Henrietta*, the man who brought Surfman Roberts and Miss Canady here to Ocracoke."

Sullivan extended his hand and Harry took it into his ample palm.

"Always good to meet a man of the sea," the cutter commander said. "It's seldom I'm afforded an opportunity to interact with the proletariat, especially fishermen."

Harry kept smiling as he tightened his grip on the captain's hand until he heard the muffled popping of finger joints. Sullivan's face contorted in pain as he struggled to keep from screaming.

"Where's Danny?" Ethan asked as the navy captain massaged his bruised hand.

"I left him watching the *Henrietta*. You never know what wharf rats might be skulking about. I'll be taking him one of Missus Williams' sandwiches later."

Sullivan was about to say something but stopped in mid-breath. Following his stunned gaze, the other three men turned to see Caelyn descend from the stairway and enter the room. Dressed in a black summer gown rescued from her steamer, Caelyn's full beauty was apparent for the first time. To compensate for the thin fabric, around her shoulders she wore a black shawl she had borrowed from Betty. Having no pins to do her hair, her copper tresses cascaded around her shoulders. Layered atop the flowing shawl, her hair provided a shimmering backdrop that accented the delicate qualities of her face. The soft light given off by the oil lamps and candle chandelier fell upon her in a way that made her appear as a seraph floating out of the darkness.

"You don't have to tell me who this heavenly creature is," Capt. Sullivan said. In his eagerness to greet her, he almost tripped over his own feet. "This has to be Miss Caelyn Canady. Allow me to introduce myself, my dear." Grasping her hand, he took a stiff bow. "I am Captain Thaddeus Sullivan of the *USS Mayfair*. The island people told me you were beautiful but they simply do not possess the vocabulary to do you justice. Let me say that I have always been a great admirer of your father. If there is anything I can do, anything at all, please let me know."

Caelyn looked at him in awkward silence as everyone waited for her to respond. She was only a little surprised that the list of sycophants seeking to leverage her father's influence was so long it even reached the Outer Banks.

"Thank you," she said, reclaiming her hand from his sweaty grip. "I will certainly keep that in mind."

"That must have been quite an ordeal for you, being stuck out on the ocean. Not knowing whether you might live or die. And having to care for an injured man must have made it all the more difficult. A frail woman like yourself should never have been forced to endure the hardships of survival at sea, especially considering they should have rescued you the very first night."

"I assure you, it wasn't that bad," Caelyn said, glancing at Ethan.

"Tell me," the navy officer continued. "Have you been able to contact your family and, what's your gentleman friend's name...Hunter Winslow, isn't it? He must be going out of his mind with worry by now. You know, everyone in New York is expecting an announcement regarding you two in the near future."

Caelyn was stunned. She did not want Ethan to know about Hunter – not yet. She had wanted to tell him about her presumed fiancée and proposal on her own terms. Now he would think that she had kept it a secret – that she was misleading him.

Her gaze darted back to Ethan, fearing what his face would reveal. But if the surfman had taken umbrage, he was hiding it well.

"Gentlemen," Betty interrupted. "Miss Canady. Please be seated. The evening meal is served."

"Well, my dear, you'll just have to tell me about it over dinner," Capt. Sullivan said without missing a beat. He was so engrossed with impressing Caelyn with his knowledge of New York society, he didn't notice the panicked look on her face.

Leading Caelyn to the table, the portly captain pulled out a chair, seated her, and took the chair next to hers. Sullivan assumed the honor of being Caelyn's escort for the evening. Delighted to have found someone of equal standing, he was not about to let her go.

Caelyn was trapped. The man's graciousness was self-serving and his air of entitlement put her off, but there was no polite way to decline the seat. She found herself beginning to hate the situation almost as much as she was beginning to dislike Thaddeus Sullivan. His incessant chatter about New York and Hunter continued throughout the meal, and each new question seemed designed to push Ethan further away.

"No, I haven't been able to contact Hunter yet."

"Actually, no, we don't know when we'll make an announcement."

"Yes, the article in the paper was correct. Father is hosting a social on Christmas Eve."

"No, I don't know if Hunter will 'pop' the question then."

"Yes, the article did hint that the social will be for that purpose...but the newspaper is seldom right."

110

The questions continued until Caelyn was sure she would strangle the man. Though her answers were short and curt, he never caught the irritation in her voice. Making matters worse, she saw that the more they talked, the more detached the surfman was becoming.

By the time Sullivan's inquisition turned into self-centered droning, Caelyn was openly gazing at Ethan without regard to propriety. His attempt to appear interested in the conversation would have been laughable had it not been for the circumstance. And the cloud cloaking his countenance was like a dark beacon of misery pulling at Caelyn's heart. As he wiped his mouth with a linen napkin, she saw he had come to a decision. But about what?

Pushing his chair back from the table, Ethan stood and gave Betty and Tom a slight bow.

"Mister and Missus Williams," he said, "the meal was excellent. Thank you. Superintendent Collins, I find myself in need of a breath of fresh air to clear my head. Seems I still have a few cobwebs from the blow I took. With your leave, sir?"

"Of course, Surfman Roberts," Collins said with a nod. "Do whatever you need to take care of yourself."

"Poor fellow," Capt. Sullivan said, though his voice bore no empathy. "His injury doesn't look all that serious to me. Anyway, Miss Canady, as I was saying. I seem to recall that your father–"

"I think I could use some fresh air as well," Caelyn said as she stood from the table and started for the door Ethan had exited. "Excuse me."

"What a wonderful idea," Sullivan said as he and the other men stood. "I'll be happy to escort you–"

"No!" Caelyn said without looking back. She knew her actions would invite unwanted speculation, but she no longer cared.

"My word," Capt. Sullivan muttered as he took his seat again. "I wonder what that was about?"

Superintendent Collins glanced at Harry who gave a knowing wink on the sly.

A blast of frigid wind took Caelyn's breath away as she stepped out onto the porch. She pulled the shawl around herself tighter, but the bitter wind cut through it and the thin dress beneath. Ethan stood at the end of the porch, his form illuminated by the light of a lantern inside shining through a window. Leaning against a column and staring out into the darkness, he looked over his shoulder a moment to see who had joined him, then looked away again. Taking a deep breath, Caelyn braced herself against the cold and came to him.

"Ethan," she said, hoping that using his given name for the first time would show the depth of her concern. He did not respond.

"Look at me, damn it," she demanded. The forcefulness of her words took her by surprise.

Caught off guard by her brashness, Ethan gave in and turned to face her. The wind blew Caelyn's hair wildly around her face, turning her honest beauty into bewitching allure.

"I didn't know this was going to happen," she said. "I didn't know I would meet you and it would turn my life upside down."

"I don't–"

"No! Let me finish," she said, raising her voice so that he could hear her above the wind blowing through the trees and brush around them. Her cheeks ached from trying to suppress her shivering. Each word was forced and deliberate. "I don't know what happened today. But I know it was real. And I know you felt it, too. It may mean nothing. In a way, it doesn't matter. But what I do know is that I have to find out. Until now, I've lived my life for everyone but myself. I can't promise you anything...except that I will be honest. If you don't want to take a chance, I understand. But I have to find out what it means. And there's not much time."

She stopped, out of breath, searching Ethan's eyes for a sign that he believed her.

"But Ethan," she said in a quieter voice. "Make no mistake. I do want to know you."

He looked into her eyes for several moments, as though weighing the sincerity in her voice against the abrasive way she had treated him in the beginning. Had she waited too long? Had all of Sullivan's inane talk about Hunter closed the door on her one opportunity to discover her true self?

"Fair enough," he said at last. "But before we go on, you have to promise me one thing. You promise me that, if you ever feel you've made a mistake or no longer wish to interact with me for any reason...you must tell me. I have no expectations and will not fault you or be angry with you. But I will not play the fool and pine after you if you realize this whole thing is just a lark."

Caelyn looked at him with new hope in her heart. She knew she was playing a dangerous game, engaged to one man but captivated by another. And yet she felt no guilt. For the first time in her life, she was doing the right thing for herself. One way or another, the situation with Hunter would soon resolve itself.

"Yes. You have my word."

Her teeth chattered, both from the cold and from the excitement of knowing that she was living life on her own terms. Seeing her discomfort, Ethan pulled her into his arms and she rested her head against his chest. They embraced for a few moments, finding comfort in each other's closeness until the cold became too much to bear.

As they returned to the warmth of the hotel's entryway, Caelyn saw the Williams had cleared the dining room, but their guests still sat at the table. Superintendent Collins and Harry were in deep conversation with Capt. Sullivan.

"Of course, the navy hasn't made any decisions yet, but there is a good possibility that if funding is secured, we will establish a new base," Sullivan said. "In terms of the navy's ability to protect shipping lanes, there would be a lot of advantages to locating that base here, but it is hard to convince a peacetime Congress to foot the bill of such an expenditure."

"So, if it is unlikely they will allocate funding, what do you hope to accomplish while you are here?" Superintendent Collins asked.

"While we don't have the authority to establish a base, I do have permission to sign rights of first refusal with landowners. That way, the navy can hold control over the land, at least until Congress makes a decision. I am set to meet with some locals here with the intent of procuring agreements should I find a suitable location. And I must say, from what I saw when I came into the harbor this morning, I think there is a spot on the north side of Silver Lake that would be perfect."

Even Caelyn realized that, in attempting to demonstrate the importance of his mission, Sullivan was revealing far more information than he should have. Armed with the knowledge that the government was seeking to purchase land, a landowner would stall negotiations, hoping to elevate the value of his property. It could also give a potential uncooperative landowner opportunity to seek ways to thwart making a deal with the government.

She could also sense that Superintendent Collins was interested in the information for his own reasons.

"Would this spot be near the island's south-point?" the superintendent asked.

"Yes! That's it. You know the place? It would give us the perfect site to set up a tower to have good visibility of the ocean. And if we construct docks on the north side of Silver Lake, we would have both a protected harbor and quick access to the ocean. I think it would...serve us..."

Realizing the superintendent was showing more than a casual interest, he let his words trail off without finishing. The navy officer was arrogant and egotistical, but he wasn't stupid.

"Perhaps you have a particular awareness of these two pieces of property?" he asked.

"Oh, not really," the superintendent lied. "As a man of the sea, I have often thought that the point would make an excellent place to build a house. Perhaps when I retire."

"You know, Superintendent Collins," Sullivan said, "I've noticed that there is a gap in the spacing of the lifesaving stations along this part of the coast."

"How so?"

"Well, you have the station at the other end of this island at Hatteras Inlet. And there is another station on the north end of Portsmouth Island, right across Ocracoke Inlet, correct?"

"That's correct."

"It seems apparent to me that if a ship ran aground on this side of Ocracoke Inlet during a rough sea, it would take a long time for the surfmen on Portsmouth Island to row around the rough waters of the inlet to affect a rescue. They would first have to row out to sea, around the rough inlet waters, and then come back to the wreck. The crew at the north end of this island would have to row some fourteen miles to go to the same wreck. Either way, it might be too late for the ship's crew, wouldn't it? But if you had a station, say, near the south-point where I suggested my tower be constructed...well, that would be the answer to your problem, would it not? I mean, from there, you could launch your surfboat directly into the ocean and wouldn't have to navigate through the inlet waters."

"That's an interesting hypothesis," the superintendent deadpanned. "I will have to give that some thought."

"Seriously, sir? I suspect that you already have. But it doesn't matter. If the navy wants it bad enough, we will get preference over the Lifesaving Service."

Sullivan paused to see if the superintendent would respond, but the senior lifesaver refused to take the bait.

"You know," he continued, "in the long run, it won't make any difference. It's my prediction that someday the navy will absorb the Lifesaving Service. So whatever is yours now will someday belong to us, anyway."

"We've heard that before but it's never gotten past the talking stage," Superintendent Collins replied, his voice taking on an edge. "What makes you think it can happen now?"

"Because, it makes little sense to maintain two separate services. The overhead of maintaining the separate command structures alone is justification for consolidation."

116

"But the missions are totally dissimilar," the senior surfman argued. "The navy's job is to secure our coastlines, to protect our nation's interests in foreign seas and to engage our enemies' fleets when we are at war. How could the Lifesaving Service, whose mission it is to rescue ships, freight, and personnel, be an asset to the navy?"

"It's not a question of how it would benefit the navy, sir. It is a question of how it would benefit our nation. And we both know what the answer to that question is."

Superintendent Collins considered his words before replying.

"Perhaps I don't. Why don't you tell us what that might be?"

"Please, Superintendent Collins. Don't tell me you don't think our merchant marines wouldn't be better served if the navy, an organization of trained professionals, was the agency responsible for their rescues."

"We are professionals," the superintendent said. Caelyn tensed at the rising level of aggravation coloring his tone. "To imply that we are not is an insult to all those men of the Lifesaving Service who train hard and risk their lives every day."

"At any rate," Sullivan said in a less combative manner, "I will spend the next few days going over the sites with the owners, after which I will return to Washington with my report and recommendation. By next week, we should have the rights to that location secured for the navy. If you had plans to obtain the site for yourself, well, I'm sorry. But I'm sure you can see, even from your position, that the navy must have priority in such cases."

"Perhaps you are right, captain," the superintendent said as if to dismiss the matter. "There is probably nothing we can do about that location if you are already pursuing the matter. I wish you success on your mission."

Caelyn saw Ethan exchange a look with Harry. Both men seemed surprised that the superintendent was backing down, as was she. But the silence that lingered provided her the opportunity to escape the awkward situation.

"Gentlemen, I have a long day ahead of me tomorrow. I would like to thank you for a most interesting evening and bid you goodnight."

"Indeed," Capt. Sullivan said. He stood from the table and took her hand in his. The other men rose as well. "The pleasure was all ours, I assure you. If I don't see you tomorrow before you leave, please be sure to give my regards to your father."

"Of course," she said, retrieving her hand before he attempted to kiss it. "I assure you I will give him a full account of your...attention."

Nodding to the other men, she caught Ethan's eye just long enough to confirm their pact and ascended the stairs. When she was in her room, she changed into borrowed night clothes and slipped under the covers.

So, the die is cast, she thought as the exchange on the porch with Ethan played over and over again in her head. *Tomorrow, I cross the Rubicon.*

Chapter Thirteen

The Spy

"Well, I imagine Danny will be getting a bit hungry about now," Harry said when Caelyn had left the room. "I'm going to see what Missus Betty has left in the kitchen that I might scavenge and take over to him."

"I guess I will say goodnight as well," Capt. Sullivan said, having no desire to be alone with the two lifesavers. "And as I doubt I will see you in the morning, I hope you will have a safe journey, Surfman Roberts."

"Thank you, sir," Ethan said, surprised by the captain's concern. Perhaps the man wasn't a total scupper hole after all.

Once the captain had left, Superintendent Collins closed the doors to the dining room and retrieved the leather pouch the stranger had delivered earlier from under the chair he had been sitting on.

"Sullivan is only half right," the senior lifesaver said. "In this pouch are documents already signed by the landowners saying that the Lifesaving Service has first right to purchase the property we were just discussing. It also contains an envelope with my orders for Keeper Payne and a hundred dollars in cash to cover expenses. Once you make it to Kitty Hawk, give the envelope and twenty-five dollars to Keeper Payne. He'll give the pouch and the money to one of his men to carry the documents the rest of the way to Washington, posthaste."

"And you want me to continue on to New York with Miss Canady?" Ethan asked.

"That's correct. One man can travel faster than one injured man and a woman. Besides, it wouldn't be appropriate to delay Miss Canady's return home for no good reason. And it's crucial we deliver our paperwork to the federal Procurement Office before Sullivan files his. I have a friend in the Procurement Office who will make sure our papers are processed without delay. Once it becomes a formal agreement approved by the government, *we* have the advantage."

"But, what he said about the navy taking priority over us, isn't that true?"

"The navy certainly has the leverage to take the property from us, but they're not going to want a public dispute with the Lifesaving Service. We have enough congressmen from coastal states supporting us to make sure they know it would become a real battle. The key is, we must get our papers there first. Legally, there is nothing to prevent the owner from signing a similar agreement with Sullivan, but what matters is who has an agreement approved first. Sullivan shouldn't be leaving until the day after tomorrow, at the earliest. If you make it to Kitty Hawk in two days, that will give us plenty of time. Even if our papers arrive in

Washington at the same time he does, my friend will take care of the rest."

After leaving the two lifesavers, Harry waited until Betty had put together a paper bag full of leftovers, paid her, and said goodnight. But as he exited the kitchen, he pulled up short. Hidden in the shadows of the dark hallway leading to the stairway, someone was listening in on the conversation behind the dining room's closed doors. Resisting the urge to confront the spy, Harry stepped back into the kitchen and waited. A few moments later, the person left the hiding place and moved with deliberate stealth to the stairway. Harry's suspicion was confirmed as the faint light illuminated the person's face when he turned to go upstairs.

Once certain that the man had returned to his room, Harry knocked on the dining-room door and entered before anyone could reply.

"I don't know what you folks are talking about, but whatever it is, I think you ought to know that our friend Admiral Portly was listening in on you."

"Damn!" Superintendent Collins exclaimed. "That means he knows what we're trying to do."

"How's that?" Harry asked.

Superintendent Collins looked at Harry and then back at Ethan.

"It's OK, sir," Ethan said. "You can trust Harry. I'm sure of it."

After giving Harry a quick overview, the waterman understood the seriousness of the situation.

"Now that he knows our plan, we have little chance of beating him," the superintendent said. "All he has to do is get an agreement signed first thing tomorrow morning. With his cutter, he'll be back in Washington long before we can deliver our papers."

Harry rubbed his bearded chin for a moment, contemplating the situation.

"How much time did you say you need?" Harry asked.

"Just two days. If the papers are on the train by then, we should be all right."

"I'll take care of it."

"How?" the superintendent asked, raising an eyebrow.

"Begging' your pardon, sir, but I think this is a situation where the less you know, the better...you being an important public official and all."

"I see. I'll take you at your word then."

"Don't worry," Harry said with a wink. "I'll get you your two days, maybe three. No problem."

Chapter Fourteen

Oil and Water

Cold wind blowing across Silver Lake created small waves that slapped against the hulls of the boats moored at the docks. Harry stood in the darkness of an alley a few hundred feet away from the navy cutter. The guard had changed at midnight, confirming his suspicion. Only one sailor was on watch at a time. The crewman, relieved of duty, didn't waste any time getting below deck and out of the wind. Harry waited for another thirty minutes, giving the sailor who had gone below enough time to fall asleep.

Taking a bottle of wine from his inside coat pocket, he pulled the loosened cork out with his teeth and spit it on the ground. Earlier, when the old woman had opened the door to see Harry for the second night in a row, he could see the judgement in her face, pegging him as just another drunken waterman. But tonight, a drunken waterman was what Harry wanted people to see. His request that she go ahead and pull the cork from one of his bottles further solidified this impression.

"Can't even wait until you get back to your boat, can you?" she crackled, handing him two bottles of sweet scuppernong wine. "Be careful you don't fall in the lake, or as sure as simony, you'll die of exposure on this chilly night."

Taking a swig of the wine, Harry swished it around in his mouth and swallowed. Now he was ready. With his cap pulled low and wine bottle in hand, the waterman crossed the road to the dock. He slurred his words as he sang a sea chantey loud enough for the watchman to hear, but not so loud it might wake the sailors sleeping in the cutter. Weaving from side to side, he walked up to the *Henrietta* then stopped just across from where the sailor stood his watch. With his pea coat pulled tight and his back to the wind, the young seaman paid scant interest in Harry. He was much more concerned about staying warm than in the antics of a drunken fisherman.

"Hello, lad," Harry said with a big smile, as though seeing him for the first time. "Care to share a little wine with me? It's my birthday, you know."

The sailor looked at the bottle, trying to decide whether a good stiff drink was worth the risk of a reprimand.

"Aw, come on, lad. There's nobody watching. Besides, it'll warm you up a tad."

"Sure, why not?" the sailor said, giving in. He hopped down from the cutter and came to the middle of the dock. Taking the bottle from Harry, he chugged as much of the wine as he thought he could get away with.

"What do you call this?" he asked, stopping long enough to catch his breath.

"I call it Toobad," Harry said, slurring the words.

"Huh?" the sailor responded. He looked at the label on the bottle and looked back up at the waterman a split-second before Harry's enormous fist slammed into his face. Harry grabbed the bottle from the sailor's hand as he slumped to the dock.

"Yeah, 'too bad' you was the one on watch," he said to the unconscious sailor.

Harry pulled the crewman onto the *Mayfair*'s deck, poured the remaining wine over him, and placed the empty bottle in his hand. He then covered the man with a tarp so that no one would see him and to keep him from dying of exposure.

The rest of his plan was the riskiest. Retrieving a dip-bucket from the *Henrietta*, he scooped up water from the lake and returned to the cutter. Removing the fuel cap, he poured the brackish water into the diesel tank – then repeated the process several more times so the ratio of water to fuel would be sufficient. When done, he removed all signs of his tampering, then returned to the *Henrietta*.

Danny stirred from his sleep as the big waterman crawled into the rack next to him.

"I'm hungry," he said, rubbing his eyes.

Harry handed him the greasy paper bag of food Betty had prepared.

"I didn't miss anything, did I?" Danny asked between bites.

"Nope," Harry said as he wound his Big Ben alarm clock and set the alarm. "Just some sailor got drunk and fell asleep during his watch. I guess it'll be all right, though. I don't reckon anybody would mess with a navy boat, do you?"

Danny thought about it for a second but didn't ask any more questions. He had been with Harry long enough to know that his flippant comments meant the opposite of what they seemed. Plus, it was late, and he was facing a long day come sunrise. He needed to go back to sleep.

Chapter Fifteen

The Terrapin and the Hare

The ringer on Harry's alarm clock had almost run itself down by the time he managed to force his eyes open. A glance at the clock told him it was 5 a.m.

It's too damned early and I'm too damned tired to be getting up. Why is the alarm going off? Then he remembered what he had to do.

After shaking Danny awake, he went topside where the predawn cold, made bitter by a stiff wind, greeted him. If the harbor had been a freshwater port instead of brackish, it would have been a sheet of ice. Feeling pressed for time, he hurried through the sandy lanes to the Pamlico Inn. Letting himself in through the front door, he stole up the stairs to Ethan's room.

"Mission accomplished," Harry whispered to the surfman when he opened his door.

Together they went to Caelyn's room who opened the door before they could knock. As planned, she was packed and ready to depart. Betty had given her an old carpetbag to carry a few personal items, including the clothes and storm gear she had been wearing the night the *Aphrodite* had run aground. As the two men carried her trunk outside, she placed an envelope containing money on the nightstand along with a note thanking Tom and Betty for all their kindness.

Exiting through the inn's back door, she made a quick stop at the shed to pick up Teach. The Williams' old dog opened her eyes and wagged her tail as Caelyn lifted Teach from the warmth of the basket the two mutts shared. Walking as fast as she could, Caelyn caught up to the surfman and the waterman at the dock. Harry glanced at the *Mayfair* as they loaded the steamer onboard the skiff to see if the sailor he had sucker-punched was OK. Curled up against the cutter's bulwark with the tarp pulled tight against him, the seaman was sound asleep, oblivious that the time for waking his relief had long passed.

After stowing everything, Harry gave Danny a sawbuck to cover expenses on his return trip to Harkers Island. Danny boarded the sailboat and hauled up the sail, being careful to make sure it didn't catch the wind.

"Don't worry about running aground," Harry said to Ethan. "Danny will keep you outta trouble. Just let him have his own head and he'll do you right."

Ethan shook Harry's hand, letting his hard grip and steady gaze convey the sentimentalities that men never speak aloud.

"Thanks, Harry, I owe you one," his Missouri accent cracking crisp and clear.

"You owe me nothing, surfman. You just keep on saving the lives of sailors what find themselves in trouble. That'll be thanks enough."

Harry turned to Caelyn. She held out her hand, but he ignored it, giving her a hug instead. His familiarity took her by surprise but she didn't mind. When he ended the embrace, he placed his hands on her arms and looked at her from arm's length.

"He's a fine man," Harry said as he held her gaze. "They ain't many like him. Listen to your heart and your head. Either way, I think you'll get the same answer. All you have to do is be true to yourself and everything else will follow."

Harry saw that his penchant for sage insights no longer took Caelyn by surprise. *She's learned a lot the past few days,* he thought. *I wonder if she has any idea how much she's changed?*

"Thank you, Harry. I hope I will see you again someday."

"As do I, missy, as do I. Now, be off with you afore the wind dies and you have to row all the way to Kitty Hawk."

Caelyn took a seat forward of the mast while Ethan positioned himself aft to help with the sail. Harry untied the mooring lines, tossed them into the boat, and shoved the boat away from the dock with his foot. Danny pulled on the tiller as Ethan let the rope play out a little, allowing the sail to catch the wind. Harry watched them in the dawn's half-light until they had cleared the mouth of the harbor. The little boat's sail billowed large as it filled with icy winter wind, becoming a wisp of white blending with the distant clouds.

The sun was clearing the horizon as Harry finished preparing the *Henrietta* for the return trip to Harkers Island. He was letting the engine warm up when he saw Capt. Sullivan walking down the dock to check on his cutter. The chubby officer looked as over-starched in his duty uniform as he had in his dress uniform. Sullivan stopped short when he saw the sailor curled up under the tarp, wine bottle by his side. His face turned red and he began screaming out orders. The half-dressed sailors scrambled topside to stand at attention in the freezing cold. Still groggy from being concussed and confused, the sailor who had been on watch did not argue when his distraught captain ordered him below deck, confining him to quarters.

Harry knew Sullivan was aware of his presence. While the navy captain's harsh treatment of the crew might have been for his benefit – a demonstration of his iron-fisted authority – Harry somehow knew it was his normal style of leadership. That he was responsible for the hell the sailors would receive made him feel a little guilty, but the waterman took solace knowing his final trick had not yet played out. Sullivan nor his crew would know someone had sabotaged their vessel until they cranked the engine. And after that, it might take a whole day for them to figure out the cause of their problem.

"Hey, admiral," he shouted as he engaged the *Henrietta's* engine. "Don't be too hard on 'em. You know how it is when you've been away from home for a long time. And just to show you there's no hard feelings about last night, here's a little gift for you."

Harry tossed the bottle across the dock in a high arc, allowing the navy officer to make an easy catch. Though he had no idea what the waterman was apologizing for, he tapped the brim of his cap with the neck of the bottle in a salute of appreciation. Harry watched as the captain inspected the bottle's label. Realization spread across the officer's face when he saw that the wine was the same brand as that found next to his crewman. When he looked back up, he saw Harry wearing a big grin.

"Don't think this will change anything," the red-faced captain shouted at Harry as the *Henrietta* chugged away from the dock. "I'll be in Washington by tomorrow night and there's nothing you or your friends can do about it."

That's what you think, Harry said to himself, still laughing at the captain. *That's what you think.*

Chapter Sixteen

The Madre

Keeping to the deeper water, Danny piloted the skiff through the channels along the western side of the barrier island. Caelyn had never seen the sound side of the Outer Banks, and even though she found its rough natural beauty fascinating, its splendor was not enough to make her forget the bitter cold.

Taking a position at the foremost point of the bow, Teach began barking at a blue heron that flew away from one of the many licks of marsh grass and cattails extending into the sound. When he tired of that, he began snapping at the water splashing up on either side of the bow. The game soon lost its appeal, however, when a large spray gave him a good soaking and the three travelers a good laugh. But their laughter turned to shouts when the puppy shook off the water, giving them an icy-cold shower. Having learned his lesson, the little dog found a dry spot next to Caelyn and curled up beside her.

The wind was blowing in an easterly direction, coming cold across the sound at a good twenty knots. Under Danny's skilled hands the skiff flew over the water, requiring few course corrections or adjustments to interrupt the dreamlike feel of their journey. Wrapping herself and Teach in a wool blanket, Caelyn began savoring the sense of adventure enveloping their journey. She watched Ethan when he made an occasional adjustment to the sail to take advantage of the shifting wind or the boat's change in direction.

The way the young waterman and the surfman worked so well together amazed her. Each time Danny called out a change of direction, Ethan made the correct adjustment to the sail. They knew how to use their heads *and* their hands – the surfman sometimes using his forearm for leverage as a substitute for his injured wrist.

In her eyes, they were living as men were meant to live. Using nature to their advantage instead of trying to conquer it. They knew things that more cultured men had forgotten. And they were better people because of it.

By noon they had already passed the rough waters of Hatteras Inlet and were sailing up the western side of Hatteras Island. Ethan and Caelyn ate crackers and cheese left over from the day before. Danny remained at the tiller.

When they reached waters more familiar to Ethan, he took Danny's place at the tiller, giving the young waterman a chance to eat as well. With food in his stomach, Danny decided to catch up on the sleep he had missed by waking so early. Taking Caelyn's seat near the bow, he pulled the blanket around himself and laid down to take a nap. With Ethan at the tiller, Caelyn took a turn at trimming the sail.

Caelyn, an experienced sailor in her own right, enjoyed showing off her skills. She had a natural sense for what to do and when to do it, never making the mistakes of pulling the sail too tight or letting it play too far out. They were sailing in winds that, if she was not paying attention, could snap the mast or blow them over. But more than showing she was capable, the smile on her face revealed how much she was enjoying the challenge and the respect she saw in Ethan's approving gaze.

Caelyn's task became easier when the leading edge of the front passed through and the wind began to lull. Taking advantage of the relative calm, Caelyn tied off the sail's trim line and joined Ethan at the stern. Placing a blanket across their laps, she sat as close to the surfman as she could without appearing to be too forward.

"Is this what it's like for you all the time?" she asked.

"What do you mean?" Ethan asked.

"To have the freedom to go where you please? To do whatever you want to do?"

"Oh. Well, it's hardly like that at all. I have to work, you know. When we're not out on the water, we have to train and make repairs to our equipment. There's always something that needs to be done. It's not like I can just up and walk away any time I'd like."

"I understand that, but you have to admit that your life is your own. You can decide for yourself whether you want to stay a surfman or to try something different. You can sail to anywhere. Visit any place you'd like. My life is a series of expectations and commitments. If I don't go to a certain engagement, people talk and speculate. All of them believe they are self-determined, but they're not. Not really."

Ethan didn't answer right away and Caelyn wondered if she had made a misstep by talking about a world he knew nothing about. His was a life of self-exile and her comments were dragging him back to those things he was trying to escape.

"You know, your life is your own," he said at last. "No one can make you do what you choose not to do. Not really. There may be consequences, sure, but that's what being free means. It means that you suffer...or you celebrate your choices. The important thing is that they are your choices. In the end, no one is responsible for your happiness except you."

It was easy for him, being a man, Caelyn thought. *He could get a job, make his own way. Society frowned on women who did that.*

Then she realized that was his point. The opinions of others mattered only if she accepted their judgments. Choosing to disregard her peers and their views would be true freedom – consequences be damned. It was the same freedom that her aunt had discovered.

Shivering at the thought of the possibilities, she nudged closer to Ethan. If there were people in the world who were not afraid to accept others for what they were, then there must be men who weren't afraid to accept a woman who dared to be different. It would take a strong man. One confident enough to disregard what other men thought.

As Ethan pulled the tiller to adjust course, Caelyn felt the power within his body. Only three days had passed since the *Aphrodite's* wreck. During that time, she had sampled a taste of real freedom and independence. She had also seen firsthand that it was possible for a man to treat a woman as a friend rather than a prize to be put on a pedestal. So much was right about what was happening to her. But there had to be a bad side, and she knew what it was. At some point, she would have to contend with her father. And Hunter.

A sharp clap of thunder rolling off the island interrupted the thought. They both looked to the sky, searching for the dark clouds of a coming storm.

"Where did that come from?" Caelyn asked. "How can there be lightning if there aren't any thunderheads?"

Ethan stood and scanned the horizon. Again, the sound of a distant boom rolled across the water from the nearby island.

"That's because it's not thunder," he said, pointing to the northwest. "There! See that! Over on the other side of the island. It's smoke. That wasn't thunder. That was a Lyle gun. There must be a crew of surfmen up ahead on the ocean side of the island."

"Of course, a Lyle gun," Caelyn said. As a licensed captain, she knew lifesavers used the small cannons to propel rescue lines to stranded ships.

"Danny!" Ethan yelled. "Wake up! We're going ashore."

Ethan swung the skiff starboard, piloting the boat into the marshy bank while Caelyn dropped the sail. Danny tossed the anchor on the embankment, leaving enough line to allow the boat to give with the tide. Another loud boom peeled across the island, this time louder and closer.

"What the heck was that?" a wide-eyed Danny asked. But Ethan had already jumped ashore and was halfway to the sand dunes that fronted the ocean.

The same wave of panic Caelyn had experienced on the lifeboat when she had found the flare gun tried to resurface.

"It's a Lyle gun," she said, still struggling to maintain herself. They both climbed out of the boat and started toward the dunes, trying to catch up to Ethan. Teach jumped from the skiff and chased after them.

With little undergrowth to slow them down, they crossed to the ocean side of the island in minutes. As she crested the dune, Caelyn saw that the surf was a mass of churning white caps, foam, and spray. Dominating the scene before them was a steel freighter that had run aground three hundred yards offshore, its massive hulk leaning toward the ocean. A crew of lifesavers on the beach were gathered around a two-wheeled equipment cart, with all the speed they could muster.

Awed by the enormity of the scene, she watched in silence. Even Danny had never seen a large ship this close to the beach. Being a coastal dweller, he had witnessed a good number of groundings and shipwrecks, but those had been much smaller vessels. This was a huge modern freighter dominating the seascape before them. The ship was so large that it made him wonder how men could build such leviathans. Not knowing what else to do, he stood beside Caelyn atop the dune, watching the surfmen below.

Having reeled in the shot-line and readjusted the gun, the lifesavers fired another round at the rusting steel hulk. Caelyn saw the cannon flash before the sound reached them. The thundering clap rattled her nerves, and the compression wave that followed stripped the air from around her body. Disoriented, she reeled from an onslaught of hazy images reawakened by the invisible assault on her senses. The shadowy forms she had seen before returned – though the faces were still too ill-defined to be recognized. She knew them, she was sure. But it had been long ago. A terrible occurrence had taken place, followed by quick movements and familiar voices and...panic? A man's face loomed before her, twisted and discolored. Grabbing her by the arms, he shook her and yelled about things she couldn't understand nor quite remember.

"Caelyn. Caelyn! Are you all right?"

But this was a familiar voice. One from the present. Its tone led her back to the island and the dune where she now sat.

"Are you all right?" Ethan asked again. "Look at me."

Ethan was kneeling in front of her, holding her head in his hands, forcing her to look at him. Behind him stood the seven surfmen who had been firing the cannon at the freighter, anxious to see if she would come out of her daze.

"My goodness," she said, bewildered by all the attention she was receiving and how she had come to be sitting. Teach shoved his nose under Caelyn's arm and crawled into her lap. "I'm sorry. I'm not sure what happened. I hope I didn't startle you."

Everyone except Ethan chuckled. Her comment was amusing, considering the concern she had created.

"You left us for a few minutes," Ethan said. "Danny called to us when you collapsed and we came running. Has anything like this ever happened before?"

"Not... not quite like this," she replied. "It must have been the cannon. Guns frighten me. It's silly, I know, but..."

"Well then, we'll just have to dispense with any more firing of the cannon," a man of average build and a bushy mustache said. "We don't need to shoot the Lyle gun anymore today, anyway."

"This is Cap'n Midgett, keeper of the Chicamacomico Station and his crew of laggards and mollycoddles," Ethan quipped, glancing over his shoulder. Half of the surfmen laughed at the good-natured insult, while the other half cracked barbs of their own. "Their station is about a mile up the beach from here. They were about ready to set up the hawser and breeches buoy when Danny called."

"The ship!" Caelyn exclaimed, remembering the reason they had come ashore. "Is the crew all right? Can you save her?

Again, the surfmen chuckled. Ethan grinned despite himself.

"What is it?" Caelyn asked, puzzled by their lack of concern and a bit miffed by their laughter.

"The ship," Ethan said with a slight smile. "It's the Cape Ann. A German freighter that ran aground about five years ago. They're just practicing firing the shot-line and setting up the beach apparatus."

"So, there's no emergency? No rescue?"

"No, ma'am," Keeper Midgett said with a wink. "No emergencies here except for the one you created."

"Here come the men from Gull Shoal Station," a surfman in the back of the group said. "And they're hauling their surfboat with them."

Everyone turned to see seven lifesavers coming up from the south. Unlike the small, two-wheeled cart the Chicamacomico surfmen had brought to the site, the Gull Shoal surfboat was on a wagon being pulled and pushed by the station's crew. As they came closer, Caelyn was surprised to see a black man among the crewmen. She had always been told that Southerners barely tolerated blacks. And yet, there he was, working beside the white surfmen as though it was nothing out of the ordinary. Once again, what she had been taught proved untrue.

"Well Pugh, it's about time you got here," Keeper Midgett said as the new keeper and his surfmen arrived. "We've got the shot-line across her bow, but it won't do any good unless we get somebody on board to set up the hawser."

Keeper Pugh was a tall, hefty man with a deep, froggy voice. When he spoke, most people felt a strange urge to clear their throat. When the introductions were done, Ethan explained what had happened to Caelyn and why they had stopped.

"Yes, the Lyle gun," the big keeper said, shaking his head in frustration. "Truth is, we would have been here sooner, but our draft horse pulled-up lame. Thank the Lord it wasn't during a real rescue. I apologize for being late for the exercise."

"Actually, you got here just in time," Keeper Midgett said. "Take your crew on out to the freighter an' we'll practice a few rescues."

While the Gull Shoal crew launched their boat and rowed out to the freighter, the Chicamacomico surfmen set up a tall, X-shaped wood cross called a crotch and anchored it in the sand. After boarding the freighter, the other lifesavers located the shot-line and pulled in the heavier ropes and tackle used to operate the breeches buoy. The breeches buoy was a large lifesaving ring with a pair of oversized pants attached to the bottom. They attached one end of the hawser rope to the cross back on the beach and the other end to the ship's highest elevation. After securing both ends of the ropes, the surfmen took turns acting as stranded sailors. As the Gull Shoal surfmen began sliding down the rope to the beach, two lifesavers in the surfboat ferried some of the Chicamacomico crew to the freighter to take a turn.

Caelyn watched the exercise from the dune with Ethan sitting beside her, fascinated by the process. Forever curious about the way things worked, Danny stood next to the surfmen on the beach to learn everything he could about the apparatus.

"Didn't you say that was a German freighter?" Caelyn asked as the second surfman began his descent.

"That's right," Ethan said. Though he no longer showed outward concern for her episode, she could see that he was keeping a wary eye on her. "She ran aground one night about four years ago. They say she was on her way from New York to South America. The navigator mistook the Bodie Island Lighthouse for the one at Cape Hatteras. We figure he ordered the helmsman to take a southwest heading, as would have been required at the Hatteras Light, and ran aground before they realized their mistake."

"But isn't Cape Ann a funny name for a German freighter? I mean, if it's German, shouldn't it be Kap Anna?"

Ethan glanced at her, impressed that she had noticed what others would have missed.

"There is an interesting story about that," he said, shifting his weight in the sand to get more comfortable. The sun was a couple of hours from setting and the wind was beginning to blow softer but colder. The shouts of the surfmen performing their drills drifted up to their perch overlooking the beach.

"Some folks say she was given an English name to fool American port authorities. The story goes she was carrying a secret shipment of war supplies to a country in South America. It's no secret that ol' Kaiser Wilhelm has been interfering with matters down there for years, trying to disrupt things in hope of taking over land for German expansion. Given what happened in Cuba, that's not hard to believe."

"Anyway," he continued, "the ship caught fire, destroying everything inside before anyone could get on board to see her cargo. Some say the crew torched her on purpose to protect the secret. I guess we'll never know. But there she sits in all her glory. A lasting testament to Germany's expansionist ambitions."

Caelyn sensed his mood darkening and heard a touch of sarcasm in his voice. He was withdrawing again, the same way he had on the beach at Ocracoke.

"What do you mean, given what happened in Cuba? I didn't know that the Germans had anything to do with Cuba."

Caelyn saw the muscles in his jaw clenching and feared that she was about to lose their moment of intimacy.

"You know, Ethan, I have seen you when you were without awareness of the world around you. I have touched you as you slept, and I have watched as the ghosts of your past stalked you in your dreams. I know your heart, your tenderness, your strength. I don't know how, but I know there is more to you than any man I have ever met. I also know that you must confront your memories...or you will never be the person you are meant to be."

She stopped for a few moments, watching him struggle with his inner demons. She sensed he was trying to decide whether to answer or to go back into the shell of his self-imposed exile. Realizing that there can be a fine line between giving in or breaking down, she wondered if the thing he most feared now might be her pity. Brushing back hair that had blown across her eyes, she leaned in closer.

"Trust me," she whispered.

He took a breath to speak and her heart skipped a beat, hoping the wall between them was about to give way.

"It was at San Juan Hill," he said without emotion. He spoke as though narrating an event he had watched from afar. "The Spanish held the high ground. We were taking a pounding. Cannon and rifle fire had killed many of our men. Things were getting desperate. Our company was one of the first to attempt a charge. That was when we learned about the machine guns."

Ethan paused for a moment, struggling with his thoughts. His next words were deliberate, and the pain strained his voice.

"German machine gun fire cut them down...like stalks of wheat...so many men. As we ran up the hill, the German machine guns opened up in a crossfire. We knew the Germans had assigned advisors to the Spanish, but we didn't know they had supplied them with advanced weapons. A few rounds struck the rocks in front of me, spraying fragments in my eyes. I fell to the ground. It saved my life. When my eyes cleared, all I could see were dead and dying American soldiers. Nothing had prepared us for that. Nothing."

"My friend Zeb saw me go down," he continued. "The next thing I know, he's running up the hill, trying to get to me. The machine guns turned toward him. I yelled I was OK. To get down. But he kept coming." Ethan's voice cracked. "He never made it. He took several bullets before falling just a few feet from me. I crawled to him and took him in my arms. He called to his mother." The surfman's voice trailed into a hoarse whisper. "And he was gone."

Caelyn watched the water well in his eyes. A shameless tear rolled down his cheek. He wiped his eyes with the back of his sleeve and then hung his head between his knees.

"I crawled back down the hill dragging Zeb with me. I couldn't bear to leave him. The Spanish didn't fire a shot. I guess they respected what I was trying to do or they were too busy setting up for the next assault to bother. Whatever the reason, it doesn't matter. When I got within a hundred feet of the tree line, an officer came out to help me. It was Colonel Roosevelt himself. We picked Zeb up and together we somehow made it back.

"Colonel Roosevelt kneeled beside Zeb and said a prayer. Then he put his hand on my shoulder and said something I'll never forget. 'The day is not lost. We will take this hill...and America will never forget.' Next, he looked me in the eye and said, 'And we'll jolly well never forget the role the Huns have played here today, will we lad?'"

Caelyn pondered the story, overwhelmed by how brutal the experience had been. *What guilt he must carry, knowing that so many others died while he continues to live,* she thought. *With whom could he share such misery? Who could he talk to that would understand? It's easy to see why he has become a loner, living in a quiet, tragic reality.*

Placing an arm around him, she struggled to find the right words.

"It must have been very hard to carry such pain with you all these years," she said. "To see your best friend die like that. To have seen so much death. Surely, nothing that befalls the rest of your life could be worse than what you have already lived."

Ethan's eyes darted about as if trying to avoid an unfathomable hurt, and she knew she had spoken too soon.

"I... I only wish that were true. Later that day, we charged up the San Juan. I was still crazy over Zeb's death. I didn't care whether I lived or died. God must have been

144

watching over me, because I should have died several times. A group of us overran one of the machine-gun nests. We turned the damned thing on the Spanish command post and that's when the tide of the battle changed."

The surfman paused, steeling himself. Again, he lowered his head so that Caelyn could not see his eyes.

"As our company closed in, I joined the final charge. I was the first one through the door of their headquarters. The room was dark and I couldn't see. A door on the other side of the room flung open and I opened fire. Again and again and again I fired, cursing and screaming, 'This is for Zeb, you bastards! This is for Zeb!' The body fell into the light of the open doorway and I saw it was a woman. I had killed a woman! She was coming to me for protection...not to hurt me."

As he paused to take a deep breath, Teach slid from Caelyn's lap, settled in the sand beside the surfman, and placed his head on his lap. Caelyn remained silent as Ethan began scratching the puppy's head, wondering how it could have been any worse for him.

"The next thing I know, I hear a cry from the room the woman had come from. A little girl, six, maybe seven years old, ran to the woman on the floor. 'Mi madre! Tu mataste a mi madre!' she said. You have killed my mother!' Then a little boy, about three, came to the woman. He kept saying, Diciendo, mamá. Please wake up. When he stopped, he sat next to her then looked up at me as though expecting me to do something."

Caelyn put her arms around him, her cheek resting on his shoulder. She let him sob, saying nothing. Regaining his composure, he continued.

"The Spanish were so confident they could hold the position the officers hadn't bothered sending their families away. We didn't know the women and children were there until it was too late. There were other innocents who were killed by stray fire. Accidents. The thing is, I know I'm the person responsible for murdering that woman. The memory of those two children... God, I'll never forget their faces. So confused and lost. Every day I ask God why, why didn't He let me die with Zeb? Then, maybe those children would still have their mother and they could have laid me to rest without the guilt of their blood on my conscience."

Caelyn took his face in her hands, forcing him to look at her. She did not know where the right words would come from or what they would be, but she was certain that if she didn't speak up now, he might never have another chance to shed the guilt he carried.

"That she died is a tragedy. But what happened to you could have happened to anyone. If any other man had gone into that building first, the outcome would have been the same. I know that this doesn't lessen the pain, but you must think about the greater good you accomplished that day. You know as well as anyone that Spain's General Weyler was not only a butcher of men but of women and children as well. His forces killed thousands of innocent people during Cuba's war for independence. You must think of the Cuban women who can now have their own families because of what you and the rest of our soldiers did. You gave them hope where there was none."

With blank eyes, Ethan looked toward the ocean where the surfmen were wrapping up their drills. A line of pelicans flew above the water between the surf and the freighter, searching for fish to catch. The day was coming to an end and soon there would not be enough light to resume their journey.

Caelyn, too, saw that the surfmen from the two stations were packing their gear and realized that one of their few days together was almost over. As the two crews separated and began walking back toward their respective stations, she wondered what Hunter might be doing at this moment.

It's funny, she thought. *For months, I struggled to determine whether my feelings for him were real. True love. And now, the answer seems so clear, I wonder why it had ever been so difficult.*

Ethan's feelings, however, were a different matter. She couldn't be certain of his feelings toward her, given how she had treated him in the beginning. But they had little time left together to allow things to develop in a natural way. Somehow, she had to find out. And for the sake of her sanity, she had to find out now. Leaning forward, she closed her eyes and brushed her lips against his. She caught his lower lip between hers for an instant and then let go.

Freed from his self-made prison, Ethan allowed long forgotten emotions to rush back into his consciousness. Responding to her soft kiss, he caressed her cheek with the back of his hand. Using the same gentleness she had taken with him, he touched her lips with his, allowing the poignancy of the moment to realize its full potential. Moving his mouth closer to her ear, he whispered his gratitude.

"Thank you. I've never talked about those things before. You don't know what it means to say them out loud. To let them go."

There will be no pawing with this one, Caelyn thought as she nestled closer. *There will be no disregard of my desires or needs. Not with him. His is a different way. But there is so much more I want to say. So much more I need to know.*

Chapter Seventeen

The Fire that Burns

The banging of a loose shutter against the side of the cottage startled Caelyn awake just as dawn was breaking. With a groan, she pulled the covers around herself, intending to go back to sleep, then remembered where she was and what she was going to do. Though she had tried to refuse Keeper Midgett's hospitality, he had insisted on giving up his private quarters. A gust of wind blowing across the barren island banged the shutter a second time, a forewarning that the second leg of their journey would be cold and arduous.

I wonder if he had as much trouble falling asleep as I did, she wondered, noting that the room's stove was already well-stoked and keeping the chill at bay. *There are so many possibilities to consider it's almost impossible to focus on any of them. Still, there is one thing I have to do, and there's no reason I can't start doing it right now.*

After dressing and packing, instead of leaving to look for Ethan at the lifesaving station, she sat at the keeper's secretary and began writing a letter. By the time she finished, the shutter's slapping had become so constant that she did not realize someone was knocking on the door.

"Come in," she said as she folded the stationery.

"Good morning," Ethan said as he came inside. "I didn't want you to wake up to a cold room, so I came in earlier and started the fire."

"Thank you," she said with a smile. "I suspected that the warm stove was your doing. I hope you slept well?"

"I did, thank you," though the tiredness in his eyes said otherwise.

Caelyn repressed a smirk of guilty pleasure, knowing that his sleep had been no more restful than hers.

"I had an idea before I fell asleep last night," she said. "There must be any number of opportunities here for someone with a good idea and a little capital. Perhaps there's a village in need of a good restaurant or hotel. What do you think?"

"Are you sure that's what you want?"

Caelyn could not discern from his tone whether he liked the idea. Splitting the difference, she feigned indignation.

"What, to own a hotel? Why not? You don't think I can manage a business?"

"Well, no. I mean, yes. Of course, I think you can do anything you put your mind to. But it would mean leaving New York, wouldn't it?"

"No," she teased. "Not necessarily. I suppose I could have someone here run it for me. Perhaps you. I could own it and you could manage it for me. How about that?"

The twisted look of confusion on his face was part pitiful, part heart-warming. She would have let him struggle with the deception a while longer, but thought better of it.

"Of course I would have to live here!" she said, smiling. "That's what this letter is about. I've asked my father to notify the bank that I will liquidate my assets. It's my inheritance from my grandmother...a trust fund. It's not a lot, but it will be enough to start a business. It will have to be. Once my family discovers that I am breaking off the relationship with Hunter, I doubt they will be very eager to help me in any way."

There was no tentativeness or hesitation in her voice.

"What about Hunter?" Ethan asked.

"I have to go back to New York to retrieve some of my things and to take care of the financial papers. In my letter, I've asked my father not to say anything to Hunter until I return and can tell him. I at least owe him that much."

"Don't you think that you're taking too much of a chance going back to New York? I mean, it's possible that once you return, you'll realize how much you miss it."

Rising from her chair, Caelyn placed the letter on the writing table and came to where he stood. Gazing into his eyes, she answered the question she had asked herself a thousand times since their kiss.

"To tell you the truth, I've grown quite fond of the scenery here. And I know there's still a lot more to see."

He pulled her close, savoring the feel of her body pressing against his in a way she had never considered possible. The kiss that they had shared yesterday now seemed a long time ago. And though the circumstance for intimacy was ill-timed, she knew she would follow his lead, regardless. He leaned in closer to kiss her but a knock at the door broke the spell. With great reluctance, Caelyn let him go and he opened the door to find Danny with hat in hand.

"Sorry to bother you," the young waterman apologized, realizing that he had interrupted something. "If we're going to make Kitty Hawk before night, we need to make sail soon."

"We're almost ready," Ethan said with obvious regret in his voice. "We just have to thank Keeper Midgett and then we can be on our way. Why don't you take Teach and Caelyn's carpetbag to the skiff and make ready to sail?"

A few minutes later, Caelyn and Ethan entered the station house where the crew's cook served them hot coffee and gave them ham biscuits wrapped in cheesecloth to sustain them for their day of travel. As they were finishing the coffee, Keeper Midgett stepped into the room wearing a worried look.

"The wind's picking up," he said. "Make sure you take it slow, especially when you cross the inlet. It'll be pretty rough."

"Thanks, we'll do that, sir," Ethan said.

"And, Surfman Roberts..." he hesitated, looking for the right words.

"Sir?"

"Be sure to take special care of Miss Canady," he said, recalling her spell on the beach. "We don't want anything happening to her before she gets home. It would reflect badly on the service and it would be a great injustice for her to have endured so much just to fall short of the finish line, so to speak."

Caelyn caught the look in the keeper's eyes and knew that his warning conveyed more than the words might otherwise seem.

"I understand, sir," Ethan said. "I can assure you we won't take any chances."

Keeper Midgett nodded approval and escorted them from the station to where their skiff was waiting. He helped Caelyn board the sailboat and shook hands with Danny and Ethan.

"With this wind, you should make Kitty Hawk before nightfall with no problem," he said. "So be off with you and make sure you don't let your sail get out ahead of you. It's a bit cold to go swimming."

Ethan took the rudder and Caelyn assumed the seat beside him as she had the previous afternoon. Teach curled up beside her, seeking shelter from the biting wind. Danny pushed the boat away from the spit, hopping in as it drifted backward.

A few minutes later, they were well away from the landing and making good time. Taking advantage of the high tide and a steady wind sweeping over their port rail, Danny trimmed the sail tight, making the little skiff sing across the water. With their course set, he moved to the bow seat to look ahead for hazards and shoals that might be in their way.

As they passed the tip of Hatteras Island and sailed into the openness of Oregon Inlet, Caelyn saw a boat to the east, out on the ocean, headed in the same northerly direction. The outline of sails told her that the vessel couldn't be Capt. Sullivan's cutter, but it made her wonder if the navy officer had discovered their treachery yet.

"You know," Ethan said, as if reading her mind, "there probably isn't enough diesel on Ocracoke to run a table lamp. Once they discover we contaminated their fuel, they'll have to run the whole tank through a filter or have more fuel brought to the island. Either way, it will be several days before they're up and running. I'll get to Washington long before Sullivan."

Her concerns allayed, Caelyn settled back and tried to take in the sights as best she could, given the conditions. Continuing to sail northward, they soon reached the sheltered waters between Bodie Island to the east and Roanoke Island to the west. Caelyn knew Roanoke was the island nestled between the Outer Banks and the mainland and said to be the site of the Lost Colony. Makeshift docks dotted the shoreline leading up to the shacks that were appearing more often as they drew closer to their destination.

"That would be Nags Head," Ethan said, pointing toward a scattering of shacks and hovels off their starboard rail. "The better cottages are retreats for more well-to-do folks from out of state. If you're looking to build a hotel, this would be a good place to consider. You've got vacationers in the summer and hunters in the fall, so you might make a go of it."

"How much farther is it to Kitty Hawk?" Caelyn asked, eager to get out of the cold.

"Ten, maybe twelve miles. It shouldn't take too much longer. Be on the lookout for three large sand dunes close together. That will be Kill Devil Hill, which would put us about four miles from the Kitty Hawk Station."

The desolate beauty of the area north of Nags Head appealed to Caelyn. Vegetation was sparse and, at over a hundred feet tall, the huge dune called Jockey's Ridge towered over the landscape. Other sand dunes, built up from years of extreme winds blowing in from the northeast, punctuated the landscape. It was as though the Sahara

Desert had floated across the Atlantic and come to a grinding stop a few miles before reaching the mainland.

Continuing northward, they passed by a few fishing shacks and houses constructed of shipwreck timbers. The barren land held little that would be useful to those who settled on the island. Farming would be almost impossible. Most of the food either had to be shipped in or harvested from the water.

By noon, they had passed the three large dunes Ethan had mentioned. Had it not been for a couple of rickety structures next to them, it would have been hard to gauge their true size. The land was so barren it diminished scale and fooled the eye. The two wooden buildings themselves seemed out of place. They looked more like small barns than houses or shacks, though there was no livestock to be seen or evidence of any life at all.

I can't imagine what their purpose might be, Caelyn wondered. *It's a mystery and will probably remain so. Everything is different here. It's all so wonderfully different.*

The afternoon was half over when they sailed into the protective cove that served Kitty Hawk. Blazoned clouds of brownish-orange streaked across the sky turned red by the setting sun. For Caelyn, the vivid colors heralded a finality to the past few days. She would soon have to face the reality of New York and her family.

But not just yet, she thought as she watched Ethan and Danny square the boat away for the night. *I still have a few more days to enjoy before making that trip but it's going to hurt to leave him.*

For a moment, she considered asking him to come with her, but dismissed the idea as quickly as it came. *It would only make matters with Hunter and father more difficult.*

Besides, this is something I have to do on my own. They have to see that calling off the relationship with Hunter is my decision and mine alone. They have to understand I am my own woman now.

With the boat secured, Ethan and Danny grabbed each end of Caelyn's trunk and began walking into the village. Caelyn followed with Teach tethered to a length of rope from the skiff. Strolling down one side of the sandy thoroughfare, Ethan looked at each building, searching for a particular inn – the same place he had stayed when he had first arrived on the Outer Banks to return Zeb's belongings to his family.

Caelyn soon realized that the openness of the sandy road and the distance between the buildings on either side made the little island settlement seem larger than it was. Besides a scattering of cottages, she saw a general store, a post office, and a weather station. Toward the center of the village stood a large, two-story building, proclaiming itself as the hub of activity by virtue of its size. The aroma of food being cooked gave promise that it might be the place they were looking for. As they came closer, they saw a weathered sign with the words "Lottie Mae's" in fading letters painted over the main door.

"This is it," Ethan said, opening the door for the others. Smelling the food inside, Teach strained against the makeshift leash. Caelyn scooped him up and held him tight in her arms as they went inside.

The inn's interior, in contrast to its bleak exterior, was tastefully decorated and well furnished. Caelyn was surprised such a refined and warm establishment could exist in such barrenness. Despite the inn's modest trappings, its design ensured everything was in balance.

A large counter at the back of the entryway served both the inn and dining areas. To the right was a double doorway providing access to a dining room, and to the left was a wide stairway leading up to the rooms. Attached to the wall that rose with the incline of the stairs hung a wood telephone box with its earpiece hanging on one side and bell crank on the other. A young woman carrying a pitcher of water entered the room from the dining area.

"Oh," she said, surprised to see people waiting in the small lobby. "Do you need a room?"

"Two rooms, actually," Ethan replied. "One for us and one for the lady."

"Just sign the register then and I'll fix you right up," she said. Putting the pitcher down, she went behind the counter and studied a peg board where several room keys hung.

"Sorry, I can't give you rooms right next to each other," she said, deciding which accommodations best matched the travelers. "It wouldn't be proper. But I can get you pretty close. Hope that'll be all right."

Handing the keys to Ethan, she gave him a big smile and a lingering look. Caelyn couldn't help but notice the girl's interest in Ethan but held her jealousy at bay.

It will be interesting to see just how far apart she put us, Caelyn thought.

But while Ethan may not have been affected by the girl's charms, the young waterman was mesmerized. She appeared to be about twenty years old, close to Danny's age. Though she had pinned her sandy-blond hair into a bun, its size gave promise of a long and beautiful mane. Her lips were full and her eyes were pools of indigo. And it was impossible not to notice that, in regard to her chest, she was particularly blessed.

"Your rooms are upstairs to the right," she said, still smiling at Ethan. "Hot baths are fifty cents, and we serve supper at six. There's a small fireplace in each room but it will cost you another fifty cents if you burn the wood. My name is Abbie. Just call me if you need anything."

Ethan and Danny took the lead, carrying the steamer chest up the steps and Caelyn followed. As she reached the top of the stairway, Caelyn looked back over her shoulder. Caelyn wasn't surprised to see Abbie lingering at the foot of the stairs, taking a last look at Ethan. Caelyn smiled despite herself.

I can't blame you, she thought. *But all the same, I'll be keeping my eyes on you.*

Chapter Eighteen

Dragonfly

It was after seven o'clock by the time Caelyn joined Ethan and Danny in the lobby. She had not meant to keep them waiting but the hot bath she had ordered was more relaxing than she had expected. She awakened in the tub to find herself sitting in cold water and already late. The thought of Ethan waiting for her, growing more anxious with each passing minute, had pleased her at first. The thought vanished when she remembered Buxom Abbie and her deep-blue eyes were downstairs as well.

When she descended the stairs with Teach cradled in her arm, she was relieved to see that Ethan was, indeed, still waiting for her and that Abbie was nowhere to be seen.

"I'm sorry for being late," she said. "I hope you're not too upset with me."

"It's all right," Ethan said, perhaps mistaking the relief in her voice as humble regret. He opened one of the double doors leading into the dining area. "I slept for a few minutes myself. Besides, we weren't that hungry yet, anyway."

"Speak for yourself," Danny said under his breath as he followed Caelyn inside.

The steady drone of many different conversations taking place at once greeted them as they entered the dining area. Sitting at the tables spaced around the open room were watermen, surfmen, a few travelers, and a merchant or two – but no women at all. Seeing that the first new arrival was a beautiful woman, everyone in the room turned stone silent.

Caelyn would have smiled if she had not felt so conspicuous. As Danny followed her into the room, the disappointment of her admirers was palpable. When Ethan – a more likely beau – stepped inside, their disappointment turned into defeat.

"Gentlemen!" came a voice from the kitchen doorway. The three newcomers turned to see an agitated, silver-haired woman wearing wire-rimmed glasses. "It's not nice to stare. These folks will think you haven't had any upbringing at all. Now, go back to eating your supper."

Duly chastised, the diners resumed their conversations.

"You folks can sit over there by the window," the woman said, pointing across the room. "Abbie will be here in a minute to get your order. The dog can eat under the table but if he makes a mess...you gotta clean it up." Pushing her glasses back on her nose, she headed off toward the kitchen.

As they navigated their way to the far side of the room, Caelyn noticed two men sitting at the table engaged in an intense conversation while scrutinizing an odd-shaped, foot-long object one of them was holding. Dressed in coats, ties, and white shirts with stiff collars, they stood out among the establishment's more rough-cut patrons. Though it was obvious they weren't Outer Bankers, they were at ease with their surroundings. They weren't strangers to the inn.

"I assume that must have been Lottie Mae," Caelyn said as she led the way.

Not receiving a response, she looked back over her shoulder to make sure Ethan and Danny were following. As she did, the man holding the strange object raised it higher. Caelyn bumped his arm, knocking the thing from his hand. But instead of falling straight down, it glided forward as though a soaring bird, coming to a soft stop on the floor between the tables. The two men jumped from their seats to retrieve the object, almost knocking each other over.

"Pardon me," Caelyn said as the two men inspected the wood and cloth object with the wings of a dragonfly.

"No damage done," said the man who now held the dragonfly. He looked to be in his mid-thirties but his receding hairline made it hard to judge. His subtle accent suggested he was from the Midwest, and the lines of his clean-shaven face spoke of intelligence and earnestness.

"Did you see the way it pitched?" the second man asked. He looked a few years younger than his companion, a few inches shorter, and sported a well-groomed mustache. Judging by his manner, Caelyn imagined he was less serious than his friend, but shared similar characteristics and lineage. "That's what I'm talking about. There has to be more counterweight in the rear. Or perhaps more lift in the front."

"Yes," said the first man, once again fixating on the dragonfly. "I've been thinking...perhaps if we increased the thickness of the wings' leading edges."

Having forgotten about the three newcomers, the two men continued talking as they returned to their meal.

Reaching their table, Caelyn put Teach on the floor to lie at her feet and took a seat next to the window. Ethan took the seat across from her and Danny sat next to him. As they were settling in, Abbie appeared beside the table with a hand-written menu for them to share. Caelyn watched the young woman as she was talking, her attraction to Ethan as obvious now as it had been earlier. Despite her best efforts not to, Caelyn grew more agitated by the girl's blatant flirtations. Almost as frustrating was the fact that Ethan seemed oblivious to her overtures.

Conscious of their surroundings, the three travelers made trifling conversation until Abbie returned. In addition to their order of food, she gave Teach a large bone with enough meat left on it to make a meal, taking time to pet the puppy as he gnawed while cooing soft words to win him over. Caelyn was thankful when the girl finally left them to their meal. Jealousy was an emotion she had never experienced, and realizing it was indeed jealousy fouled her mood.

Feeling the tension and the fatigue of their travels, they ate in silence. The conversation of the two men seated next to them filled the void as they discussed the intricacies of the dragonfly. Though many of the terms they used made little sense, their passion for the thing was undeniable.

None of them noticed the man sitting at a table across the room, staring at Caelyn. He had recognized her the moment she had entered the room. Her distinctive copper hair left no doubt, and he had been in her company for too many weeks to forget her beauty. Fearful of being spotted, he had shifted his position several times, being careful to keep other diners between them so as not to be seen. When he finished eating, he paid his bill and waited. His moment came when Caelyn bent over to pet the dog and he hurried unnoticed through the doorway and out of the building.

Chapter Nineteen

The Telegram

As first mate of the *Aphrodite*, Ansel Stick had been responsible for making sure the boilers maintained proper pressure. But instead of checking the gauges, he had been keeping a firm grip on a bottle of gin. When the boiler's pressure got too low to turn the yacht's screw, he had opened the fuel flow to wide-open, hoping the steam would build back up in time to save them. But the *Aphrodite* ran aground before the pressure came back and he had scrambled topside to save himself. Without the engine running and the release valve locked down, the pressure built until the boiler exploded.

With no one able to argue otherwise, he had told the lifesavers that a faulty valve must have caused the explosion. While that explanation had been enough to appease the surfmen, he was not about to go back and face Jack Canady with such a story. Old man Canady had the canny knack of seeing see right through people. Trying to tell him a lie would have been pointless. Going back to New

York was not an option, so when the rest of the yacht's crew shipped out, he had remained behind. He was not sure what he was going to do. Perhaps he would try his luck in Portsmouth, Virginia, or go south and see which ships might be taking on crew down in Wilmington.

But going back to doing genuine work was a proposition the wiry seaman did not relish. He had gotten used to the easy work of being first mate on a rich woman's pleasure boat. So when Caelyn had walked into the dining room, he knew his luck had changed. Jack Canady would want to know that his little girl was still alive. And if a certain first mate had a hand in making sure she got home safe and sound, it might mean he would overlook the yacht incident.

Stick had not been in Kitty Hawk long but he knew where the telegrapher lived and it only took a couple of minutes to walk to his house and knock on the door.

"What can I help you with?" asked the bespectacled, middle-aged man who answered the door. He had a cloth napkin tucked into the front of his shirt and was clutching a half-eaten leg of chicken.

"Quick!" Stick said. "It's an emergency. I've got to get a message to New York right away. It's a matter of life and death."

"Let's go!" said the telegrapher as they hurried toward the U.S. Weather Bureau Station. Stick followed him, wondering how long it would take the telegrapher – who was still eating chicken – to realize the trick.

"Just go ahead and send what I tell you," Stick said as the operator took his seat in front of the key. "It'll save time," The telegrapher tapped out the letters and words as Stick dictated them.

C CANADY ALIVE AND WELL IN KITTY HAWK STOP MAY BE DETAINED FROM RETURN TO NY BY LOCALS STOP AWAIT YOUR ORDERS STOP A STICK.

"Is that it?" the telegraph operator asked, waiting for the 'life or death' part.

"Yeah, that's it," Stick said, giving him a hard look. "Now, we'll wait until we get an answer."

The telegrapher shrank back in his chair, irritated but unwilling to challenge the rough-looking seaman. He wiped his face with the napkin and wished that he had thought to grab another piece of chicken before leaving home.

Chapter Twenty

Sour Grapes

As soon as they had finished eating, Danny excused himself to go back to the room.

"Got to get a good night's rest," he said as he rose from his seat. "I need to get up early and sail over to Manteo to visit my aunt. I promised my mother I would visit her the next time I got the chance...and you won't be needing me tomorrow."

"Thanks for all your help," Ethan said as he and Caelyn stood as well. "Just don't forget to pick me up on your way back. My surfman mates will be getting real mad at me if I don't hurry up and get back to Hatteras. They'll say I hit my head on purpose to get out of work."

"Don't worry," Danny said as he looked over to where Abbie was waiting on another table. "I'll be coming back as soon as I can. You can believe that."

"I guess I'll be gone by the time you come back," Caelyn said. Saying goodbye to Danny made her realize how little time she had left with Ethan. "Please tell Harry that I'll always be grateful to the both of you."

Danny held out his hand but Caelyn ignored it, choosing to kiss him on the cheek. With his face turning bright red, the young waterman tried to speak but couldn't.

"You take care now, Danny. And who knows, maybe we'll see each other again sooner than you think."

"Yes...ma'am..." he muttered as he walked away, rubbing the spot she had kissed.

Caelyn looked at Ethan and they both laughed, though not loud enough that Danny could hear. Taking their seats again, Caelyn gazed at the surfman for a moment. Now that Danny was gone, she knew what she wanted to talk about but wasn't sure how.

"Can I get you folks anything else?" Abbie asked, interrupting the moment.

Caelyn cringed inside but managed to hide her exasperation.

"Yes," Ethan said, unfazed by the interruption. "Would you bring us a bottle of wine, please?"

Is that a look of disappointment on her face? Caelyn wondered.

"We're not allowed to serve spirits," Abbie said. "Folks around these parts generally frown on consumption."

"Of course," Ethan said. "What was I thinking. What I meant to ask was, would you mind bringing us some of the proprietor's grape juice?"

Abbie smiled at that. Folks who enjoyed a drink once in a while could get what they wanted if they knew how to ask for it. In a community where all the residents saw each other in church every Sunday, certain proprieties had to be maintained. Drinking was permissible as long as you didn't let on that that's what you were doing.

Abbie left the room and returned a minute later with a metal pitcher like the one she had been carrying when they had first seen her.

"I think you'll find these to your liking," she said, leaning over to place two glasses on the table. Then, taking care to lean forward even farther as she set down, she added, "Some men say the grapes around here are the plumpest they've ever seen."

Caelyn saw that the girl's flirtations weren't lost on Ethan this time. Given that her exaggerated bow had given him a grand view of her considerable cleavage it would have been impossible not to notice. Unless he was dead.

"I suspect the men around here have seen the grapes so often they don't think they're all that special," Caelyn said, tiring of the girl's blatant flirtation. Infatuation she could understand. But the young woman's disrespectful fawning in front of her was crossing a line.

"Oh, to the contrary," Abbie said. "Seeing them isn't the same as touching, and I assure you, that's a privilege still being reserved for the right...winemaker."

Satisfied she had stood her ground, the girl retracted her claws and went to another table before Caelyn could reply. But Caelyn knew she had made her point. Abbie wouldn't be a problem – as long as she was still around.

"Were you two really talking about grapes?" Ethan asked with a mischievous smile in his eyes.

"Of course," Caelyn said, both amused and piqued. The surfman's dry sense of humor was a fascinating facet of his personality she had yet to decipher. "What else do you think it could have been about?"

Ethan gave her a genuine smile this time, appreciating the turnabout. Instead of replying, he dodged further banter on the topic by filling their glasses. Caelyn couldn't tell what kind of wine it was, only that it was white, potent, and very sweet. They sat together for a long while, talking about everything that had befallen them and sometimes about nothing in particular. Their words played surrogate to their touches, caressing one another through expressions of desire and dreams, making memories of an affair that had yet to occur. They talked until the room was no longer a stage to anyone other than themselves, all the other actors having long since retired for the evening.

"I hate to break this up but it's past closing time," Lottie Mae said. She had come to stand beside the table without either of them noticing. "I know that's not what you want to hear but believe me, tomorrow's a whole 'nother day."

"What happened to Abbie?" Caelyn asked, trying to sound nonchalant.

"I sent her home an hour ago," Lottie Mae said with a smile. "She seemed a bit agitated. Not sure why. Anyway, you two have been talking longer than you realize and it's time for me to go to bed. We can settle up in the morning if that's all right with you?"

"That'll be fine," Ethan said, though Caelyn sensed a change in his mood.

Saying goodnight to Lottie Mae, they left the dining room and went upstairs. When they came to Caelyn's room, the surfman waited as she put Teach on the floor and unlocked the door. When the latch clicked, Teach nosed his way inside and Caelyn turned to say goodnight. The dim light from the hallway's oil lamps cast a wavering shadow over the surfman's face – now a portrait of inner conflict and

169

desire. She felt his passion and shared it, but was as unsure about the next step as he was. Her breath drew shallow and a carnal warmth passed through her body. She knew that if he kissed her she wouldn't be able to stop, and the thought of what would follow made her heart race faster still.

"I thought you might need these," Lottie Mae interrupted as she came down the hallway carrying three wool blankets. "There's a chill in the air tonight. Of course, you can start a fire if you'd like, but it'll get cold once it goes out."

Caelyn couldn't tell if the older woman realized what she had interrupted, but she could see the disappointment on Ethan's face. They had lost their moment.

"Give one to your friend," the innkeeper said, handing two of the blankets to Ethan. The flustered surfman accepted the blankets and headed toward his room. "And don't be too late getting downstairs in the morning or you'll miss breakfast."

Ethan entered his room, being careful not to wake Danny. Turning her attention back to Caelyn, Lottie Mae handed her the remaining blanket and studied her face for a moment.

"Thank you, Lottie Mae," Caelyn said.

"Please honey, call me 'Mae' if you will," she said as she started back down the hall. Or 'Missus Mae' if you insist. I always hated being called 'Lottie Mae.' Sounds like some yahoo from...I don't know where. But I was meant to be a 'Mae' and that's what I am. The water closet is down the hall, and there'll be hot water in the kitchen in the morning if you want it."

The woman stopped as she came to the head of the stairway and turned to look at Caelyn.

"That's quite a man you have there," she said with a wistful smile.

Caelyn's smile answered the question that Lottie Mae would not ask.

"Yes, he is," she said.

"Don't you let him get away."

"Not on your life."

The older woman nodded approval and disappeared down the stairs.

Chapter Twenty-One

Two out of Three

Ethan stood by the window of his room peering out into the winter darkness, struggling to quiet the tempest that roiled within. Danny was sleeping in the bed closest to the door, undisturbed by the surfman's restlessness. His slow, rhythmic breathing mocked Ethan's churning emotions. Despite his fatigue, the surfman was not sleepy at all. He could not stop thinking about Caelyn, their evening together, and what might have been. One thought kept coming back to him as if it were an echo, but he knew it was a foolish idea and he kept fighting to suppress it.

Hoping some fresh air might help to clear his mind, he raised the window. A frigid wind blasted through the opening and he swiftly closed it again. Now, he was more awake than ever, and the echo returned, even louder than before. What he wanted to do was improper, almost insane. The problem wasn't that someone would see him, there was little chance of that. It was not knowing what would happen once he got there that held him back.

What if I am wrong about all of this? he wondered. *I know her feelings are as strong as mine but this is different. If I insult her, there won't be enough time to fix the damage. But if I don't try now, we may never know. I may never see her again. Our time together is running out.*

A few moments later, Ethan found himself standing in front of Caelyn's door. With his heart pounding, he raised his hand and knocked.

The door opened so quickly it took Ethan by surprise. Caelyn stood before him, her body covered by a white sheet. Her beautiful hair falling around her shoulders like a copper waterfall.

"Come in," Caelyn whispered. And then, with more audacity than she thought she possessed, she asked, "What took you so long?"

Not waiting for a reply, she left him in the doorway to stand by the small fireplace that warmed the room. The dancing flames played across the white sheet and her long copper hair, continually altering her appearance as though she were a creature captured inside a magic lantern. With the sheet clutched tight, she looked down into the crackling embers, too shy to face Ethan.

"When I became old enough to understand what being a woman meant, I made three promises to myself," she said. "I vowed I would not give myself to a man until I knew for certain that I was in love. Second, I had to believe he was totally in love with me. And last, that it would be on the night we married."

Turning away from the fireplace, she met Ethan's gaze. Her lips trembled, belying the confident tone of her voice. The surfman held her gaze, transfixed.

"Two out of three isn't bad, is it?"

Even in the dim light, she could see his face flush. His desire was obvious, yet he remained by the door.

"What's wrong?" she asked, fearful her bravado had been misperceived as the unbridled cravings of an experienced woman.

"You... You are so perfect," he said, as though struggling to understand himself. "I came to you believing that, if you accepted me, what followed would just fall into place. I realize now that everything I do from this point on is the most important thing I will ever do in my life. I don't want to make mistakes. I don't want to be your mistake. I want to be everything that you are to me...and more."

Tears welled in Caelyn's eyes at hearing such a beautiful confession, yet she knew there was more. He was a proud and independent man. Her status would always be an obstacle to their happiness...but only if she allowed it.

The sheet fell away from her body as she raised her hands to cradle his face. He hesitated at first, but the passion of her kiss would not be denied. He pulled her closer, his hard, muscular body pressing against the firmness of her own. Certain that he was now convinced of her sincerity, she stepped back so he could see her in the light's soft glow.

Though he did not take his eyes from hers, Caelyn knew he was drinking in the details of her naked body. She was exposing her physical self the same way he had laid bare his emotions and memories for her – an exchange made in mutual trust. Stepping forward, he placed his hand behind her head, pulling her close again and kissing her softly on the lips. Teasing her, he moved to the soft spot on her neck behind her ear. She trembled as his tender kisses made their way down her neck.

Caelyn somehow knew how he would be with her, and she ached for him all the more because of it. He had the strength to be forceful, but chose to entice rather than conquer. He would derive pleasure, not from the taking, but from the giving.

She, however, had no such inclination. Pulling at the buttons on his shirt, she wished she had the strength to rip the offending garment apart. Her fingers fumbled with them until Ethan, unable to wait any longer, helped her finish. The sensation of her breasts pressing against his hard chest inflamed her passion. Her kisses became rougher as her hands worked to unfasten his trousers – sometimes nipping, sometimes biting muscles too solid to seem real.

More than the physical and emotional desires, she wanted him because, of all the people in all the world, she was the only one he had trusted enough to tell his story. She was the only one who knew why he had become a loner and why he tempted death. Through him, she now understood what truly made life worth living.

But most of all, she wanted Ethan because she loved him. She could not deny that any more than she could deny herself for another second. Surrendering to her more wanton desires, she made it impossible for him to second-guess his decision or the ramifications. Nothing else mattered. Life, as she was now beginning to understand, was too short, too precious, to deny herself – or him.

She trembled again, savoring the touch of his bare skin against hers. To her surprise, the awkwardness she had expected from being unclothed with a man for the first time never came. His response was natural, filled with a desire equaling her own. On the soft cushioning of a down-filled comforter thrown before the fire, she continued to set the pace of their lovemaking. She let herself go, without fear for what it might bring, safe knowing Ethan would forever be her lifesaver in all the ways that mattered.

The fire was a small bank of dying red and yellow flames when their explorations were done. Caelyn had gone from wild abandon to surprise and finally to fulfillment. When their lovemaking came to an end, she turned onto her side, lying with her back pressed against his front, his strong and comforting arm wrapped around her. The muffled sound of waves collapsing on the shore was a gentle reminder of the ocean that had brought them together.

Seeking refuge from the encroaching cold, they slipped into bed and watched the fire dwindle down to glowing embers in silence. The rhythmic sound of Ethan's breathing soon told Caelyn that he was no longer awake. Settling herself into the mattress a little more, she pressed her body closer to his. She remained awake as long as she could, absorbing the feelings of contentment and fulfillment – feelings she had never known.

Who would have believed that a shipwreck could bring a person so much happiness, she wondered. *If only I could make time stop, to remain forever in my surfman's embrace with no fear of what the future might bring.*

176

Chapter Twenty-Two

The Reply

Several hours passed before Ansel Stick received Jack Canady's reply. He watched as the wiry telegraph operator wrote the letters that clicked out in code, barely able to contain himself. When the clicking stopped, the telegrapher tore the page off the pad and handed it to the first mate.

RECEIVED MESSAGE IN NORFOLK STOP KEEP CLOSE EYE ON CAELYN STOP WILL ARRIVE TOMORROW PM STOP LEAVE WORD AT TELEGRAPH OFFICE IF FORCED TO FOLLOW STOP J CANADY

Stick smiled as he read the message. Jack Canady hadn't promised anything, but he was sure to be rewarded. At least he would not have to wait long. Caelyn's father must have already been traveling south to be closer to where his daughter had gone missing. One of his assistants in New

York would have forwarded the message to wherever he was staying.

Stuffing the telegram into his pocket, he started for the door.

"Wait a minute," the telegrapher called as Stick walked out. "That'll be three dollars...and...fifteen cents..." But it was too late. Stick disappeared into the darkness, ignoring the little man behind him.

"Well," the telegrapher said to himself, remembering what the message had said, "I reckon I'll see him tomorrow and get it then."

Chapter Twenty-Three

A Goddess Whispers

Caelyn opened her eyes to the soft hues of the early morning light filling the room. She remained still for a few moments, enjoying the sensation of having Ethan sleeping beside her.

She had never imagined what it would be like to wake up with a man in her bed. She had listened to the girl-talk when she was younger, but such conversations always dwelled on the physical act. The idea it could so totally envelop a person on an emotional level had never been discussed. She had looked forward to the day she would have a physical relationship. At times, she had even longed for it. But with Ethan, it had been more exhilarating and fulfilling than she had ever fantasized it might be. She felt better at this moment than at any other time in her life. And though she understood why, for once in her life, she ceased analyzing her feelings, choosing to immerse herself in them, instead.

To her surprise, the serenity began to stir other feelings. This was her moment, tranquil and uncomplicated, and she wanted to revel in it. Running her fingertips across Ethan's chest, she traced the lines of his well-defined muscles. Ethan twitched as her hand moved down his chest toward his waist, but still he did not waken. The years of rowing had hardened his abdomen into well-defined ripples like those of a Roman statue. Though his body was flawless, he was unaware of his perfection.

As she moved her hand lower, he wakened, but didn't open his eyes. Sensing her intention was intimacy rather than lust, he resisted the temptation to respond. When fully aroused, Caelyn turned over on her side to face away from him, backing into the curve of his body. Ethan shifted to match the contour of hers and pulled her closer. Feeling his hardness pressing against her, Caelyn moved her hips to make sure he would not lose interest. In response, Ethan traced his finger over her ear, along the rise of her cheek, and across her lips.

His gentle touch pushed her across the line between intimacy and desire. She wanted to feel him inside of her again, the physical expression of their emotional bond. Adjusting herself, she helped him to enter from behind, but did not succumb to the desire to let herself go. Their movements were slow, sweet agony. Proceeding at a pace that encouraged appreciation of their joining. Unlike the night before, they did not give in to wild abandon. Their lovemaking was the consummation of the joining of two spirits, and neither of them was in a hurry to break their physical bond. When Ethan's release came, Caelyn held his arm close to her chest to prevent him from withdrawing. They remained embraced for a long while without talking, savoring each other's closeness.

"What have you done to me?" Ethan whispered, breaking the silence. "I've never known anyone like you, and I've never felt anything like this. Seven days ago, the only thing I cared about was when the next call for help might come. Now, I don't care if I ever sit in a surfboat again. How can that be?"

Caelyn smiled, pleased to hear words that echoed her own feelings. She hugged his arm tighter.

"Listen," she said in a hushed whisper. "Do you hear it?"

Ethan stopped breathing and listened as hard as he could, but heard nothing except the distant sound of waves.

"No," Caelyn said, not letting him reply. "Listen with your heart."

Turning over to face him, she stroked the hair on his temple back behind his ear and kissed him.

"There is a story in Greek mythology about Aphrodite, the goddess of love and beauty, who cared so deeply about her children on earth that she wanted to do something special for them. It is said she took great delight in watching them grow up, but was always saddened when they lost their innocence. So, when the time was right, she would come to them during the night to kiss them on their forehead, granting them the gift of love. The next day, the young man or woman would meet another she had kissed, and their union would ensure that there would be more children for her to love.

"But sharing the gift of love was not enough for Aphrodite," Caelyn continued. "She was sad because even her fellow gods did not understand true love or its everlasting power. She had no one with whom to share her joy, nor anyone who understood the happiness she felt at granting love to her children.

"In desperation, she decided to find out if there were any humans on earth who could feel love as deeply as she did. One night, instead of coming to the young men and women to kiss them, she whispered into the darkness as they slept. If any awoke the next morning to fall in love, she would know that they possessed the ability to feel true love.

"The next day she traveled to the four corners of the earth searching for anyone who might have heard her call. Despite her long search, she found no young lovers that day. Disappointed, she was about to give up when she heard a young squire weeping in a faraway glen. Coming to the young man's side, she asked, 'Why are you crying on this most beautiful of days when there is nothing in this world to be sad about?' To which the squire replied, 'I awoke just this morning to discover that I was in love with a young maiden named Brook and that she was in love with me. But by noon the rains came, flooding the river between us. So desperate were we to come together that we both tried to cross the raging waters to reach one another. Alas, Brook slipped on a rock, and I've lost her forever because I couldn't reach her in time.

"Aphrodite was both heartened and saddened by the story. At last, she had found someone who understood love's true essence, but the test had caused the death of one of her beloved children. The story so moved the goddess she brought the young maiden back to life and invited the lovers to live with her as gods. To forever share their story of love and devotion. And from that day forth, the special few who can hear the soft lure of Aphrodite's whisper eventually come to assume their place among the immortals. Allowed to nurture their love. Forever and ever."

Ethan kissed her and looked into her eyes.

"Your strength is subtle, but boundless," he whispered. "Your beauty is undeniable, magnified a thousand times by the goodness of your heart. The story you told is both heart wrenching and joyous. A manifestation of your playfulness and creativity."

She gazed back at him, amazed to discover the love described in poetry and song truly does exist. For the first time in her life, she not only understood declarations of undying love, she understood how a person could willingly give their life for the person they loved. The story was a declaration of her feelings. They were as Aphrodite's chosen, hearing that which others never would.

The sounds of Teach stirring in the corner interrupted her thoughts. With a sigh, she moved to get up but Ethan stopped her. Ignoring her objections, he got out of bed, put on his clothes, and was ready to leave a few moments later. With Teach tucked under his arm, he bent over and kissed her, barely touching her lips.

"Parting is such sweet sorrow that I shall say goodnight till it be morrow," he said, delivering the line as if it were his own.

"It's not mythology," Caelyn said, surprised that her surfman could quote Shakespeare, then realizing she shouldn't have been, she added, "It's better."

Cracking the door, he took a moment to make sure no one was in the hall and then was gone.

Chapter Twenty-Four

Dreams Take Flight

After walking Teach, Ethan stopped by the kitchen where he found Lottie Mae assisting the cook and preparing dishes for guests already in the dining room.

"I'd like a couple of pitchers of hot water to take back to my room," he said.

"TWO pitchers," Mae said in mock surprise. "I saw the lad that was with you leave about an hour ago. You must be especially dirty to need two pitchers."

"Well, if you have to know, I'll be taking one up to the lady," he said with a shy grin.

"Oh..." she said as if she hadn't already figured that out. "Well, aren't you the regular gentleman? And let me guess, you got up early just to walk her dog. It is her dog, isn't it?"

"Indeed, he is. In fact, we're going to the Kitty Hawk Lifesaving Station today and I was hoping I could leave him here if it's not too much trouble."

"Hmmm..." she said, stopping to think for a moment. "That might be possible. There's an empty chicken coop next to the shed. I can put him in there with a blanket and some water. If it rains, we can move him inside the shed. Of course, we'll feed him, too."

"Perfect. Thank you very much."

"Well, don't thank me too much. I love animals but I'm also a businesswoman. I'll charge you...her...and extra ten cents a day for that kind of service."

"A deal at any price," he said, handing her the leash.

Taking the two pitchers the cook had poured for him, Ethan went upstairs and placed one of them beside Caelyn's door. He knew that if he saw her, he would want to stay, but he still had a job to do and no time to waste. After knocking on her door, he hurried to his room before she had time to answer. After washing and shaving, he grabbed the satchel that Superintendent Collins had given him and went to the dining room.

When Caelyn opened her door and saw the hot water, she smiled at the surfman's thoughtfulness and her good fortune. As she washed with the warm water, her thoughts kept returning to Ethan's touch and their love-making. As odd as it seemed, even the soreness between her legs added to her euphoria. It was a lingering reminder she was now a woman in every way and under her own terms. After so many years of lamenting her limited choices and dreading her future, she was transformed. She had shattered the walls of her prison. The possibilities were boundless.

Rather than pin her hair up, she brushed it out and then tied it off with a black ribbon about three-quarters of its length down in the back. Going through her trunk she found the warmest clothes she had left, dressed, and hurried downstairs to find Ethan.

Having taken a table in the dining room where he could keep an eye on the doorway, Caelyn saw Ethan the moment she entered. When their eyes met, his expression changed from anticipation to relief and then to joy. The realization that she could cause him to go through such a shift of emotions both mystified and pleased her. Instead of taking her for granted, he sought reassurance of their union – just as she did.

Joining him at the table, she thanked him for the hot water and asked about Teach. Their conversation was lighthearted, skipping from one topic to another. Each time Ethan made her laugh, the burdens she carried grew lighter. And she delighted at being able to see that her life was changing for the better, even as it was happening.

Among the handful of other patrons in the dining room, Ansel Stick sat at a table across the room, drinking coffee and hiding behind a newspaper. All he had to do was keep track of her for a few hours and he would have his meal ticket. He figured it would be late afternoon or early evening before Jack Canady would make it to the island. As long as Canady's daughter did not take off somewhere, his job would be easy. And unless she left on a boat, it was doubtful that he would lose track of her.

"Time for me to earn my pay," Ethan said after hurrying through their breakfast. "I need to get over to the Kitty Hawk Station so Keeper Payne can deploy a man to Washington as soon as possible."

"May I come with you?" Caelyn asked, not caring if she sounded reluctant for them to be apart.

"Of course," Ethan said with a knowing smile. "I think it's appropriate for the person I'm escorting to New York to hear what the keeper has to say about the next leg of our trip.

Besides, Superintendent Collins ordered me to do everything in my power to make you happy."

"Really?" Caelyn said. "I don't think that's what he said, exactly."

"Well, that's the thing with verbal orders," Ethan said as he stood to leave. "They're often open to interpretation. But if you insist, I can leave you–"

"Not on your life!" Caelyn said, deciding it was time to end their banter. "You're stuck with me for the duration of your mission...no matter how much my presence makes you suffer."

She took Ethan's arm as they exited the inn, walking into a brisk wind and an overcast sky. Caelyn remained close to him as they walked, delighting in his warmth and strength. Not even the cold could diminish the happiness growing inside.

Following them from a distance, Ansel Stick used the buildings and other obstructions along the street to remain undetected. He cursed them for wandering about in the cold and hoped that they would not go far. Pulling his hat down lower on his head, he shoved his hands into his pockets and tried to look casual. When his two marks arrived at the station house and went inside, he found a spot in the shadows of a nearby building where he could hide and stay out of the wind.

Ethan and Caelyn found Keeper Samuel Payne sitting beside a potbellied stove, going over rescue procedures with his crew. With his bushy beard and lean physique, he looked much the same as many other Outer Banks surfmen. Only his snow-white hair set him apart. After introducing himself and Caelyn, Ethan explained the importance of the dispatch and the need to have them delivered to Washington as soon as possible. Grasping the urgency of the situation, Keeper Payne ordered one of his surfmen to hire a waterman to sail Ethan to Elizabeth City without delay. Once there, he was to take the train to Washington and hand-deliver the documents.

"You should be there by noon tomorrow," Keeper Payne said to his crewman. "Mid-afternoon at the latest. Long before the Procurement Office closes. There shouldn't be any problem registering the papers."

"Still, that'll be cutting it close," Ethan said. "But as long as we beat Sullivan, it won't matter. And I don't think there is any way he'll manage to make it there any sooner than Monday. Maybe not even by then."

After explaining that the cutter's fuel tank had somehow become contaminated with water, Ethan told the keeper about their unplanned visit to Chicamacomico, leaving out the part about Caelyn's little spell on the beach. A courtesey she acknowledged by nodding her appreciation with a slight smile.

"I can't blame you for stopping to help your fellow surfmen," the keeper said. "Even though it turned out to be a drill instead of a real rescue, there was no way of knowing that when you stopped. It's a job well done, I would say, Surfman Roberts. Now, I need to ask a favor of you."

"Yes sir?"

"With my crewman gone to deliver the papers, I'm left a bit shorthanded. I've got a crate of Lyle gun charges that need to be hauled over to the Kill Devil Hill Station. I need you to run them out there for me."

"Of course, sir," Ethan said.

His reply had come without hesitation but Caelyn noted a touch of reluctance that escaped the keeper's ears. Ethan, no doubt, would have preferred to spend the rest of the day with her in the inn's warmth.

"Excellent! We've already loaded the buckboard and hitched the horse. You're good to go. All you've got to do is head south on the main road and you can't miss it. It shouldn't take more than a couple of hours. Just stay on the main roadway for about four miles and you'll see the station on your left soon enough. Heck, you can be back in time for lunch if you don't dally."

After helping Caelyn up, Ethan gave the keeper a salute and climbed onto the buckboard to sit beside her. Within a few minutes of leaving the station, they were traveling over a road almost impossible to see because of the waves of windswept sand. Except for an occasional scrubby tree and a few sea oats, the island provided little vegetation to interrupt the wind-swept seascape.

Though it took less than an hour to find the station, the cutting cold made it seem much longer. As they pulled into the lane leading up to the station house and equipment barn, they spotted the three large sand dunes and the two stark shacks they had sailed past the day before. Smoke whipping out of the smokestack atop the station house gave promise that the surfmen were inside. Ethan stopped the buckboard in front of the barn where they stored the lifesaving equipment. Having seen them arrive, a surfman opened the barn door and hurried to greet them.

"Name's Bob Westcott," the Kill Devil Hill lifesaver said as he went to the back of the buckboard. "Thanks for coming out on such a bitter day. We really need these charges. The ones we had got wet during the last storm. We'd have been in a world of hurt if a ship had run aground."

After stowing the crate and stabling the horse, the three hurried inside the station house where four men and a boy sitting around a woodstove greeted them. Surfman Westcott excused himself and went up to the station house tower to take his turn looking out for distressed ships.

Caelyn and Ethan took up spots next to the stove and introduced themselves. The first person they met was John Daniels, a surfman of considerable stature who dominated most of the conversation. Will Dough and Adam Etheridge, two more of the station's lifesavers, also gave the two visitors a warm greeting. All the surfmen were in a casual mood, taking advantage of their station keeper's absence. It was obvious the fourth fellow, dressed in a hawker's suit, wasn't a lifesaver. He introduced himself as a lumber buyer from Roanoke Island.

"I'm Bill Brinkley from Manteo," he said, shaking Ethan's hand and tipping his hat to Caelyn. "Thought I'd come out and see if there was any chance I might make a deal on lumber from the shipwrecks. Once the ships break up, the timber isn't much good for building ships, but it sure does make fine houses. The folks who live in Manteo will pay good money for the boards and beams that come off those wooden ships. And it's cheaper than getting it from a sawmill."

The last member of the group to introduce himself was the teenager. His name was Johnny Moore, a 15-year-old crabber from Nags Head who professed his desire to one day become a lifesaver.

"I came by to see if those two fellas from Ohio might try to fly their machine," Johnny said. "I heard they crashed pretty good last Monday. I don't want to miss it if they crash again, but I reckon it's gonna be too cold today."

"A flying machine?" a skeptical Caelyn asked.

"That's right," Surfman Daniels said, jumping into the conversation. "They've been coming out here for the past four years, all the way from Dayton. The two Wright brothers, that is, Wilbur and Orville. First it was what they call gliders, but now they've got a gas engine attached to the wings. It's the daggonest thing you've ever seen. And they want me to photograph it!"

"But what makes it go through the air?" Ethan asked as he munched on a soda cracker from a tin someone had placed on the table. "I mean, once it's in the air. If the engine turns the wheels, the wheels can't make it go once it leaves the ground."

Surfman Daniels smiled as though he had found a map to Blackbeard's lost treasure. He was taking great pleasure in knowing something that the newcomers didn't.

"Propellers," he said. "The engine don't make the wheels turn. The engine turns two propellers, like two great big fans. The wind from the propellers pushes the flying machine."

Surfmen Dough and Etheridge nodded in agreement. The others sat in silence, impressed by Surfman Daniels' apparent knowledge of the subject.

"Does it really fly?" Ethan asked at last.

"It did Monday, sort of," Daniels replied. "At least it was about to, before it tipped over and crashed."

Everybody began laughing at the contradictory statement. Even Surfman Daniels had to smile, realizing the humor of what he had said. A yell from Surfman Westcott up in the lookout towercut the laughter short .

"It's the signal!" he yelled down from the cupola. "They need some help over at the barn!"

"All right!" Johnny exclaimed. "Looks like we're gonna get to see that thing crash...I mean fly...after all."

Ethan looked at Surfman Daniels.

"Whenever they need help setting the thing up, they hang an old shirt or a towel on the side of the barn as a signal. Come on. If it's like the last time, this'll be something to see!"

The keeper had left Surfman Westcott in charge during his absence, which meant he had no choice but to stay on lookout. It was his job to signal to the others to come back if anything happened to a passing boat or ship. Everyone else put on their coats and hats and began walking over to the two windowless buildings by the three dunes. Surfman Daniels took the opportunity to tell about the two brothers.

"Orville is the one with the mustache, and his brother is Wilbur." Orville's the younger of the two. Wilbur is the one that crashed on Monday. But don't say nothing to him about that. I think he's a little sensitive about it."

When they reached the two shacks, the two newcomers hung back, content to observe while the others went into the larger building to help. When the group of men pushed the flying machine outside, Caelyn and Ethan recognized the brothers as the two men they had seen in the hotel dining room. Except for the caps they now wore, their business attire of coats, shirts with starched collars, and neckties was much the same as they had worn at Lottie Mae's the previous night.

About a dozen feet away from the barn, the brothers were setting up a sixty-foot long track of rail. Its purpose became apparent when the surfmen lifted the flying machine onto the monorail. The sand was too soft to facilitate easy rolling

– making the track necessary to help the machine pick up speed.

The thing itself was beautiful, a much larger version of the model Caelyn had knocked to the floor. It's long wings, covered in tightened cloth, looked like sails billowed by the wind and tipped over on their sides. Its two front wings were a good deal smaller, as were the two vertical wings mounted on the back. When considered all together, they gave the craft balance and symmetry. Even the two sets of propellers complimented its appearance. Mounted halfway between the two main wings and to either side of the craft's center, they told even the casual viewer that this was indeed a machine. It was a machine, however, designed to seek a balance with nature.

The men struggled to keep the medley of wood, wire, and cloth in place as a steady twenty-mile-per hour wind blew down the track. Huddled close together on a small dune behind the track, Ethan and Caelyn watched as the brothers prepared the machine for flight.

After hooking a rope from the machine to the rail to keep it tethered in place, Wilbur grasped one propeller with both hands and pulled down hard. Although the engine was loud enough by itself, the clattering of the transmission chains turning the propellers made the noise deafening. Beginning to shiver from the mix of cold and excitement, Caelyn leaned into Ethan for warmth.

"Do you think it will fly?" she asked.

"By all that's holy, I hope so," Ethan said.

Caught off guard by the excitement in his voice, Caelyn turned to look at him. It was easy to see the machine had captured his imagination. Man had dreamed of flying since the beginning of time. Now, here they were, a handful of people who might be about to witness the fulfillment of that dream.

Off to the side, Orville placed a bulky box camera atop its tripod and pointed it toward the end of the track. He inserted a plate into the back of the camera, pulled out the protective black slide, and handed the rubber bulb that would trigger the shutter to Surfman Daniels.

Returning to the machine, Orville grasped hands with his brother, almost as if he were saying goodbye. With that, he climbed into the pilot's cradle between the two spinning propellers and laid prone on the bottom wing. Grasping the lever that moved the front wings up and down with one hand, he pulled on the restraining rope with the other. The machine ambled down the track into the oncoming wind as Wilbur ran beside it, steadying the wings until its momentum could keep it from tipping over.

As it powered its way to the end of the track, the flyer separated from its carriage and lifted itself into the air. When it was about ten feet high, Orville adjusted the front wings and the craft made a dangerous dive toward the ground. A second adjustment corrected the plunge, and the machine gained altitude again. Everyone on the ground breathed a little easier.

The jerky, erratic movement repeated several more times in rapid succession until the flyer hit the ground hard. Despite the loud engine noise, Caelyn and Ethan heard the sickening sound of wood splintering.

The men dashed to the craft as the engine came to a stop. A quick inspection revealed one of the landing skids was cracked but Orville say they could repair it in short order. Having left Caelyn's side without realizing it, Ethan now stood several feet closer to the track, watching in awe as the men pushed the flyer back to its starting point.

"It didn't go very far," Caelyn said, disappointed.

"It's not the distance," Ethan said. "It's about control. He made it go up and down and up again. Under its own power! The distance will come when he learns how to control it better."

"But they've been doing that with balloons for years," she said, not grasping the significance.

"That's just it. A balloon is filled with hot air. Or hydrogen, if you want to tempt fate. And that makes the balloon lighter than air. But that," he said, pointing to the flyer. "That is heavier than air. Not only did it lift itself off the ground, it flew with a man onboard and a gasoline engine attached. Altogether, I bet it weighs six or seven hundred pounds."

"Just imagine," he said, unable to contain his excitement. "With enough gasoline, he could have flown all the way to Kitty Hawk." As the significance of his own words sank in, his gaze became more distant and his body relaxed. "Hell, with enough gas, he could have flown all the way to Hannibal."

Caelyn stood beside him, clutching his arm with both hands, her cheek resting on his shoulder. She looked off toward the horizon, trying to see what he saw. It was exciting watching the two brothers experiment with their flying machine. Seeing Ethan come alive was more so. For the first time, she was seeing him as a dreamer, and she liked it. The future was calling to him, full of promise and adventure – and she wanted to be a part of it.

After completing the repair, Caelyn and Ethan joined the Wright brothers and their impromptu ground crew as they retreated to the smaller shack. Surfman Daniels introduced the two newcomers to the Wrights as they gathered around the stove to warm up. Ethan watched and listened as the brothers discussed details of Orville's flight. They were leaving nothing to chance, using even the short time by the stove to go over the difficulties of flight control and the technical changes needed to improve performance. They were driven by detail and determined to succeed.

"I hope the photograph will turn out all right," Orville said to Surfman Daniels. The big man kept his eyes focused on the stove as though he had not heard the comment. The two brothers looked at each other and back at the surfman. "You did remember to take the picture, didn't you?"

"I... I don't know. I mean, I'm sure I took a picture, but I can't remember when I took it. I'm sorry, it's just that I got caught up in the whole thing."

Orville and Wilbur looked at each other again. Photographic evidence of man's first flight would be invaluable. Their brief trip through the air was the culmination of years of work and the fulfillment of humanity's oldest dream. But they also understood that the surfmen had always been more than willing to help them. Their efforts had contributed a lot toward their success.

"Don't fret about it, John," Wilbur said, giving the surfman a slap on the back. "I'm sure it will be a fine photograph. Besides, we'll have plenty more opportunities before we're done here."

But almost everyone in the room knew that was a lie. They had precious few photographic plates and there could be only one first flight. If Daniels had failed to trigger the camera's shutter at the right time, the moment was lost forever.

After they had knocked the chill off, everyone went outside and readied the flyer for a second attempt. Now was Wilbur's turn. The older brother climbed onto the wings, positioned himself upon the pilot's cradle and grasped the controls. Standing off to the side, Caelyn and Ethan watched with growing anticipation. Again, the craft ambled down the track with tremendous noise, picking up speed. Once in the air, the flyer went through the same jerky up and down movements it had the first time. Despite Wilbur's erratic piloting, his flight traveled fifty feet farther than Orville's. A third flight followed, with Orville back at the controls, this time traveling three hundred feet from the point the flyer left the track.

Everyone was ecstatic with the success, including the stoic Wright brothers. Their usual reserve gave way to the excitement of seeing years of hard work and experimentation pay off at last.

It was noon when the older Wright slid into the pilot's cradle for his second attempt and the flyer's fourth flight of the day. Ethan watched every move, trying to figure out how the levers controlled the wings and wishing that he could take a try at it. Wilbur released the tether and piloted the craft from the rail. Once again, it darted up and down as it traveled the first three hundred feet.

The older Wright now had a better feel of the controls and the flyer's motions were less severe. The craft flew with perfection for another three hundred feet and showed no signs it would ever stop. As the flyer approached a small knoll of sand, Wilbur adjusted the front wings to gain more altitude. At the same moment, a powerful gust of headwind lofted the machine upward even higher. Trying to compensate, Wilbur yanked the front wing too far downward, driving the craft toward the ground. An instant later, the flyer plowed into the sand, accompanied by the sounds of splintering cross members and ripping cloth. The front wings were destroyed. Caelyn gasped as she watched Wilbur push away from the cradle, struggling to keep himself from falling into a spinning propeller.

Racing to his brother's side, Orville was relieved to find him without serious injury. Despite the damage to their flyer, their spirits soared. Wilbur had flown their machine over a significant distance under its own power to a point as high as the one from which it had started. This had not been a downhill glide. Measuring it, the distance came to eight hundred fifty-two feet, and the flight had lasted fifty-nine seconds. After entering the data into their notes, they took a few pictures of the damaged flyer to complete the record of their efforts. Together, the men carried the machine back to the camp, leaving it outside of its storage shed.

"Do you think you'll be able to repair it?" Caelyn asked.

"Certainly," Orville said, happy to have the company of a woman in their camp for a change. "And when we do, I think I shall fly it all the way to Kitty Hawk and back again!"

Everyone laughed at the audacious statement. Two hours earlier, flight in a heavier-than-air machine had still been a dream. As far as the rest of the world knew, it was still impossible. Now, Orville was talking about flying great distances. To Caelyn, it was like walking into a dream. And if she understood Ethan's expression correctly, for him it was a door opening.

"The two front wings. I can see they make it go up and down. But what makes it turn left and right?" he asked.

The brothers looked at each other, not sure if they should answer. Ethan had no way of knowing that his question touched upon an aspect of flight that had eluded them for years. Some of the most respected names in flight experimentation would make a pact with the devil for the answer to that question.

"The machine!" Johnny yelled, pointing toward the flyer. "The wind's got it!"

Everyone turned to see the flyer lifting from the ground by a powerful gust of wind blowing beneath its wings. Surfman Daniels was the first to reach it, grabbing the rear uprights. But his weight alone was not enough to hold it down. Orville joined him at the rear while Wilbur tried to hold down the front. Before anyone else could grab on, the wind tore the flyer from their hands. Only Surfman Daniels continued to hold on, even as he lifted off the ground. The flying machine tumbled end-over-end with Daniels caught inside of the wing's wire rigging. When it stopped, the big surfman scrambled out from beneath the wreck, shaken, scraped, and bruised, but without serious injury.

The flyer, however, was wrecked beyond repair. With the wing spars splintered and the engine ripped from its mount, there would be no more attempts to fly. Though disappointed with the sudden change of fortune, Orville and Wilbur remained in high spirits. They had collected vital data, confirmed several of their theories, and had plenty of ideas about how to improve their invention. Most of all, the knowledge that they had unlocked the secret of manned flight was overwhelming. They had done it at last!

After carrying the remains of the machine back into the shed, everyone said goodbye to the Wrights and returned to the station house. With the aid of a spyglass, Surfman Westcott had observed the flights from his vantage point in the cupola and was wound as tight as a top by the time they returned. He pumped everyone for more details, which they were all more than willing to provide.

Rather than join in, Ethan retreated to a corner with Caelyn and listened.

"They don't understand," he whispered. "They are speculating about things like how long it might take to get from Washington to New York. Or how a flying machine might be used to spot ships in trouble."

"Aren't those things important?" Caelyn asked.

"Of course. But those things are about function. They are missing the beauty of what this means. Think about it. What would it be like to soar high above the ground, at liberty to go in any direction and to any destination one desired? To see for miles and miles and then go to whatever place looked the most interesting? Any man who could do that would be like an eagle, free to roam the world, unchecked by political borders or physical boundaries."

Caelyn looked at Ethan and saw the same faraway look in his eyes she had seen after the first flight. What she wanted now was to be alone with him and to coax him into talking about it. A fire was burning deep within him and she wanted to share his excitement. She wanted to see what he saw.

When the discussion lulled, Caelyn and Ethan hitched the horse to the buckboard, said goodbye to the others, and started back toward Kitty Hawk. They had traveled about half a mile along the sandy roadway when they came upon the Wright brothers engaged in a spirited discussion as they walked toward town. Accepting Ethan's offer to join them, the two men hopped onto the back of the buckboard. It soon became clear from their conversation that the brothers were going to town to notify their family and the press about the successful flights. When they came to the weather station, the two inventors said goodbye and jumped off the buckboard to seek the telegrapher. Upon returning to the Kitty Hawk Station, Ethan and Caelyn were surprised to find the station's crew already abuzz with talk about the flights.

"I saw it too!" Keeper Payne claimed. "Through my spyglass up in the cupola. Westcott called me on the telephone and told me the Wrights were getting ready to fly their machine. So I kept an eye open over that way. There wasn't much to see from here, just the wings of their machine rising above the sand drifts for a few seconds, and then it would be gone again. But I saw it just as plain as day.

"When Westcott called back after the first flight, I thought he was going to bust a gut," he continued. "I've never seen him so excited. I think a whole fleet of ships could've run aground right in front of his station and he wouldn't have seen a thing except for that flying machine."

The rest of the surfmen laughed at the exaggeration but knew there was an element of truth to it. Everyone involved – both the witnesses and those they had spoken to – understood the significance of the event. The Wright brothers had been coming to their island to conduct experiments for years. And though the Outer Bankers had at first taken them for eccentrics, they soon learned that the two Ohioans were forthright and earnest. Traits the rugged islanders understood and respected. Given their proximity and the assistance they had provided, the surfmen in the area felt connected to the brothers. They had witnessed the Wrights' experiments from the beginning and would talk about them for many years to come.

It was already dark when Caelyn and Ethan left the Kitty Hawkers and headed back to Lottie Mae's. After a brisk walk in the cold night air, they were glad to be back inside the warm inn. Finding a spot by the fireplace in the lobby, Caelyn removed her scarf and coat and handed them to Ethan to hang on a wood peg by the double doorway. Turning to look through the doorway to the dining room, Caelyn gasped.

"Father!" she said, putting her hand to her mouth.

Upon seeing her enter the tavern, Jack Canady had come to the entryway and was now standing in front of her. The well-dressed, distinguished-looking man embraced his daughter. Unlike a lot of older businessmen, Jack Canady was a trim, fit, vigorous man. Despite living in a social circle that celebrated excess, he had managed to refrain from gluttony. With his gray-streaked hair and well-trimmed mustache, he made a striking figure. Caelyn obviously had inherited the more defined aspects of her physical appearance from her father.

"Caelyn!" he exclaimed, holding her at arm's length to take a better look at her. "Thank God...you really are alive! Your stepmother and I had all but given up hope. I even contacted Commodore Davenport in the Navy Department to see if they could mount a search, but he said it was all in the hands of the Lifesaving Service. I was in Norfolk, trying to convince my friends at the naval base to bend a few regulations and take a ship out. Thankfully, I got word you were here before we sailed out. Are you all right, dear?"

"Yes, father, but–"

"Now, don't you worry, darling," he interrupted. "Everything is going to be fine. I have a motor yacht moored nearby, ready to take us back to the mainland and the train station first thing in the morning. We'll be back in New York by Sunday. Dorothy will be so relieved to have you home again."

The walls closed in around Caelyn from every direction, forcing her to face the one man she did not want to see. Not yet. She hadn't prepared for this. It had been her intention to see her father on her terms. Now, everything was turned upside down.

"You look a bit pale, dear," he said. "Haven't these people been feeding you anything? Would you like something to drink?"

A hundred different responses flashed through her mind but she failed to latch onto any of them. The room stopped spinning and closed in around her. Through a fog of crushing anxiety, she saw a man walk up behind her father and realized how ill-conceived her plans had been.

"Caelyn," Hunter said. Though his concern was sincere, his tone was subdued, as though trying not to appear emotional in a room full of strangers. "Caelyn, darling, how are you?"

Though dressed much the same as her father, his clothes were more expensive and more fashionable. If he had sported a mustache, people could have mistaken him to be Jack Canady's son.

Caelyn stood frozen to the floor as her father moved aside. Realizing that she wasn't going to come, Hunter stepped forward, kissed her on the forehead, and embraced her. Caelyn's faced flushed fiery red, knowing Ethan could see everything. But she was helpless to stop it.

Please God, let this be a bad dream, she prayed. *Please, make it all go away.*

"It's so good to see that you're not dead, my love," Hunter said, releasing her from his hug so that he could look into her eyes. "I was beside myself with worry. I'll never let you out of my sight again."

"Come," her father said, putting one arm around Caelyn's shoulder and grasping her arm with the other. "We have a table over here. You must be famished."

"Isn't this place wonderful?" Hunter said, taking her other arm. "It's just so primitive. I bet it was just like this in New York three hundred years ago."

"Wait!" Caelyn said, stopping in her tracks. "There's someone I want you... There's someone you have to meet. Ethan," she called, turning to look back toward the doorway.

A wave of guilt crashed on top of Caelyn's heart when she saw the look of confusion on the surfman's face. Every emotion, every dream, every joy that he embodied seemed to be disappearing down a dark hole. Pulling her arms free, she reached toward Ethan as though he were a drowning man, desperate to pull him back to solid ground.

"Father," she said, taking Ethan's arm in hers. "Hunter. This is Ethan Roberts, the lifesaver who rescued me from the *Aphrodite*. If it were not for him, I might not be alive today."

Too rattled to look at Hunter, she stared at her father instead. He did not respond right away, choosing to analyze the situation first, as she knew he would. Perspiration broke out on his forehead despite the room's low temperature. She waited as his eyes went back and forth between her and Ethan, studying their posture and expressions, and then coming to the correct conclusion. And she knew he knew.

"Bravo!" he exclaimed, grasping Ethan's hand to shake it. "Job well done, lad. How can I ever thank you for saving my daughter?"

Ethan smiled but Caelyn saw there was no joy in his heart. She had unintentionally set him up to be the stooge, the only person who did not know the truth of the situation, and it was breaking her heart.

"Your daughter isn't giving you the entire story, sir," he said, keeping the conversation on the only safe path he could see. "The truth is, she may well have saved my life."

"Petite Caelyn?" he asked. "Saved you, the lifesaver? Pray, tell how that happened, man."

"Caelyn is nothing if not resourceful," Hunter said, coming closer. He was taller than Ethan and his tailored clothes accented his statuesque physique. "I can see how she would be an asset in a life and death situation. But how on earth did you get in a position to rescue the rescuer?"

At last, Caelyn forced herself to look at Hunter. Though he, too, recognized a bond had formed between her and the lifesaver, he was not letting it affect his demeanor.

"I was injured during the rescue," Ethan said. "She took care of me while I was unconscious, and most of all, she didn't panic. You should be proud of your daughter, sir. I don't know many people who could have pulled us through the way she did."

From the corner of her eye, Caelyn caught a subtle but distinct shift in Jack Canady's demeanor. Still holding onto Ethan's arm, her gaze met her father's. Bracing herself to make a stand, she saw something unexpected in his eyes. Fear?

"Well, then, I suppose you two must have struck up quite a friendship these past few days," Jack said. Whatever had rattled him had been shoved aside. "Please, let me buy you dinner. We can all talk and get to know one another."

Caelyn was relieved but still uncomfortable. Though a confrontation hadn't erupted, it still lurked below the suface. She had made her feelings for Ethan obvious, but her father hadn't reacted. That made her nervous.

"Well, Caelyn," Jack asked as they took their seats, "what have you been doing these past six days? Dorothy was about to go mad with worry, not hearing anything for so long. Of course, you know how she can be."

Caelyn had little doubt that her stepmother had given her up for dead the moment she learned she was missing. They had never been close, and if Dorothy had felt anything at all, it would have been the satisfaction of knowing she might not have to share Jack anymore.

But her father's question required an answer, and she knew it would be unwise to admit that she had not attempted to contact them. Rather than make up a story, she ignored the heart of the question.

"It was amazing, father," Caelyn replied, her voice soft, steady, and even. Her eyes betrayed nothing as she related the events of the past few days. The memories were entrenched in the fabric of who she had become, like old friends who would always be there for her.

"You would not believe the places and things I have seen," she continued. "Ocracoke and the wild ponies. The beauty of the islands and the raw power of the tempest. I have seen the best humanity offers in the surfmen who risk their lives for others. And I've seen the way people depend on each other to survive in this wild country. Then, just when there was nothing new left to see, I witnessed a man fly above the ground on wings of cloth."

Realizing how unbelievable it sounded, she paused to collect her thoughts. The extraordinary chain of events had created a stark contrast between the realities of her past and her present. She was a woman reborn, bearing little resemblance to the girl her father and Hunter had known prior to having left New York. To make matters worse, she could see that Hunter and her father not only did not understand what she was talking about, they didn't seem to care. All they wanted was for things to be back the way they were and as soon as possible.

"If you will excuse me, I need to wash my hands," she said without warning. This was not how she had envisioned handling the situation. She needed a moment to figure out a way to regain control.

The three men stood, watched her walk away, and looked at each other again. Jack Canady's amicable demeanor evaporated before his daughter was out of sight.

"Well then, surfman," Jack said as they took their seats again. He placed one arm on the table and leaned forward. "Let's take this opportunity to talk, shall we?"

Ethan steeled himself for what was about to come.

"I won't insult you by offering you money to leave my daughter alone. I can see you are not the type of man who would forgo conviction for material gain. Moreover, unless I miss my guess, you are probably much too in love with her to let a threat of physical harm deter you, either. So, listen to what I have to say carefully, because we have little time."

"Let's just say for a moment," he continued, "Hunter and I walk away from here right now. What do you think would happen? Do you think that the two of you would marry? And then what? Live happily ever after?"

"Jack!" Hunter said. "I'm not about to let–"

"Be silent!" the older man said. "I'll handle this."

"Think about it," he continued to Ethan. "Caelyn owns dresses that cost more than you could earn in a year as a lifesaver. Do you actually believe she would be happy? Maybe it would be all right for a few months, maybe even a year. But eventually, she would look around and realize that there are no banquets to attend, no fundraisers to coordinate, no new fashions to model for her friends. And what if you have a child? Have you thought about that? Do you think Caelyn would stay around very long if she could not provide everything she believes her baby should have? A woman of her background wants to give her child every advantage, to provide all the extras. Can you do that? Will you be able to accept the looks of disdain and frustration she will give you? Will love alone be enough?"

Jack paused, hoping that the surfman would lay his cards on the table.

"I've thought of all those things," Ethan said, though hearing them said aloud gave them new weight. "And everything you said is true...as far as it goes. But your argument is flawed, based on a warped perception. The perception of a father who has always seen his daughter the way he wanted her to be, instead of the person she really is. You've projected traits on her that don't exist. She isn't a shallow debutante with no personal desires or self-determination. She will find happiness in what she accomplishes, not in what she owns."

Jack jumped up, planting his fists on the table. Fire blazed in his eyes.

"This isn't just about me," Ethan said without flinching. "This is about both of us. If Caelyn has enough faith in me to take a chance, I'll be damned if I am going to be the one to betray that faith. And I won't let you decide for her."

Jack Canady's face knotted in anger and frustration but he held his tongue.

"I think you grossly underestimate your daughter and you are absolutely underestimating me," he continued, looking the older man in the eye. "Caelyn and I haven't made plans about the future...marriage or otherwise. But I do know this. Whatever decision she makes, I'll respect it, and I'll respect her. And frankly, sir, for the life of me, I can't understand why you wouldn't want to do the same."

Jack clenched his teeth and his eyes turned black with rage. But again, he held his tongue.

"Then, perhaps there is another way to convince you," he said.

"And what way might that be?" Caelyn asked. No one had noticed her return.

Jack looked down so no one could see his face. When he looked up again, the rage was gone, replaced by a look of embarrassment and remorse.

"I'm a fool," he said, focusing on Caelyn.

"What?" Hunter said. "Surely you will not let this stand?"

"No, it's true," Jack sighed the way one does when accepting a hard-learned fact. I've been a fool. Caelyn, can you forgive me?"

"And you," he continued, turning to Ethan. "You saved my daughter's life, and in return, I have repaid you with insults. It's never been easy for me to admit my mistakes, but even I can see how wrong I have been. I hope you can find it within yourself to excuse the actions of an over-protective father too foolish to admit that his daughter isn't a little girl anymore."

"Of course," Ethan said, the relief he felt because of Jack's sudden change of attitude was obvious but guarded.

Caelyn remained silent, trying to decide whether to believe her father. She had never seen this side of him before. As much as she wanted to accept him at his word, she could not be sure.

"I don't blame you for hesitating," Jack said to his daughter. "I know it's not like me, but the thought of your death greatly affected me. It was the first time I've ever had to consider the possibility of life without you...my only child. And it made me realize what is really important. Please, CC, give me a second chance. All I want is for you to be happy."

It had been many years since her father had called her CC. It was a term of endearment he had given her when, as a young girl, she had discovered that her first and last initials matched. "Daddy, CC is me me. CC is me me," she had kept saying, over and over. That he had used it now, after so many years, touched her more than she would have imagined.

"Yes father, I forgive you," she said, her voice cracking. Despite lingering doubts, her long-held dream that their relationship would return to the way it had been before her mother died was far stronger. And despite the wall that had grown between them since that day, he had never outright lied to her.

In the span of mere minutes, her world had gone from the verge of being torn apart to being better than she dared hope it would be. Not only had she found the love of her life, she had also reclaimed her father. Overcome by the moment, she came to him and they hugged one another.

"Thank you, papa," she said, using a long-abandoned affectionate term of her own.

"And where the hell does that leave me?" Hunter asked.

Caught in the moment's emotion, Caelyn had forgotten about Hunter. It wasn't his fault that her feelings had changed. He had treated her well and had done nothing to deserve being hurt. But she could not deny her feelings, and she would not live a lie.

"Are you saying there will be no engagement," he continued, impatient for an answer. "No wedding? Are you saying that you would rather be with this...this glorified sailor than me?"

Caelyn paused, rallying herself around the person she had become.

"Hunter," she said, taking his hand in hers. "I am sorry. Truly I am. But I don't love you, at least not the way you should love someone you are going to marry. It's not that I wasn't being honest with you before, it's just that I didn't understand myself until these past few days. To marry you now would be unfair to both of us. I didn't want to tell you this way, and I never meant to hurt you. But there it is. I hope you will find it within yourself to forgive me and to believe that I want only the best for you."

The pain Caelyn saw in his eyes surprised her. He had always acquired the things he wanted, and she had been no exception. She knew there were dozens of women in New York who would love to be in her position.

"Caelyn," he said, pulling his hand away. "You are making a big mistake. I won't stand in your way but I hate to see you throw your life away like this. You're not like these people. You have nothing in common with them. I only hope that you will come to your senses before it is too late...for us."

His comment left no doubt as to his love for her. He was leaving the door open for her to come back to him, at least for a while.

"I understand," she said. "Thank you for not making this any more difficult than it already is, but I won't change my mind."

"Well, then," Hunter said, swallowing his pride. "I guess that's it. I hope you'll forgive me if I don't stay and celebrate with you. Now, if you don't mind, I think I'll go back to the yacht and drown my sorrows in a bottle of scotch."

"I hope you know you're getting one hell of a woman," he said to Ethan. "I love her very much."

Ethan nodded in understanding but made no reply. Better to say nothing than to chance saying something that would insult or belittle.

"Good night, sir," Hunter said to Jack as he stood from the table. "I hope we'll be getting an early start tomorrow. I would rather not have to stay here any longer than I have to."

"Certainly," Jack said. "I understand, and...I'm sorry."

Unable to face Caelyn again, he walked away without another word.

"Well," Jack said when Hunter had left, "I guess you two have a lot of planning to do."

"What do you mean, father?" Caelyn asked, though she thought she might know what he was thinking.

"Well, considering how strongly you feel about...things, I suppose you two will want to marry as quickly as possible."

The statement took Caelyn by surprise, though she realized it shouldn't have. Now that her father was presenting it as a logical next step in their relationship, the reality of where they might be heading began to sink in.

"I... I mean... We...haven't even discussed such a thing, father. I guess you could say that we're still getting to know one another."

"Oh. I see," her father replied.

It was only three words but Caelyn understood them for the accusation they represented. Her father's unspoken conclusion was that their attraction may not have the substance to endure.

"I have an opportunity to do something special with my life, father. Not just because of Ethan but also because there is opportunity here. The people who live on these islands accept you for what you are, not for what you own or who you know. This is a place where talent and ability mean more than anything else. And now that I've seen what kind of person I can become, I have to give myself the chance to try. Can you understand that, father?"

Once again, Caelyn saw a tinge of fear flash through her father's eyes. The response made no sense. It didn't fit the context of their conversation. But then, somehow, she knew it had to do with her growing strength.

"All right," he said. "If marriage is not yet in your plans, what will you do next?"

"I want to return to New York. But only long enough to withdraw the money I inherited from Grandmother. After that, I will come back and start my own business. I think there are a lot of people back home who would love to vacation here if they knew there was a hotel that offered the amenities they expect. I truly believe that I can make a future for myself here, and it would be wonderful if I could do it with your support."

Jack mulled over the idea before answering.

"You know," he said at last, "you just might be on to something."

"Yes! I knew you would see it. I think right here at Kitty Hawk would make a great location but there are several other spots in the area worth considering. I can't wait to begin."

"Well," he said, seizing the opening. "If you're that anxious, why don't you come back with me? I know I wasn't very supportive before and this will give me a chance to make it up to you. The bank will move a lot faster if they know I'm pushing things through. We could have everything done by Christmas and you could be on your way back here by the new year. What do you say?"

Now, it was Caelyn's turn to think things through. She had not expected everything to fall into place this quick and she had not planned on leaving Ethan this soon, a thought that left her half wishing that her father had not become repentant.

"Please, Caelyn," her father said. "Let this be my gift to you and Ethan. I'd sincerely want us back on the right track. And this is something you'll have to do anyway, eventually. So, won't you let me help you?"

"Well..." Caelyn hesitated. "What about Hunter?"

"Hunter? Well, I'm sure he will behave himself. His heart is broken but you have to admit, he was the perfect gentleman about the whole thing. Besides, this will give you a chance to smooth things over with him, with my help, of course. He deserves at least that much, don't you think?"

"I guess so," Caelyn said, running out of reasons to say no. "What do you think, Ethan?"

"I don't know," Ethan said, conflicted. "If you wait, you'll have to travel by yourself. I think it would be much safer to go now, with your father. And besides, it will give you both a chance to talk about...things."

Caelyn couldn't help admiring his strength. She knew he did not want to be parted from her any more than she from him. Yet, he had said and done the right things.

"Look, I know that this will be hard for both of you," Jack said, not waiting for his daughter to raise any more objections. "Perhaps you would both feel better if you knew you could talk to each other by telephone, in say...four days from now? There is a telephone in the area, isn't there?"

"Yes, at least two," Ethan replied. "I saw one next to the desk in the lobby and there's one at the lifesaving station."

"Great. That settles it then. I'll give you the number to my office tomorrow before we leave. We'll have to shove off bright and early if we're going to make it to the station in Elizabeth City in time to catch the noon train, so be at the boat by five o'clock.

"Ethan," he continued. "I would greatly appreciate it if you would escort Caelyn to the dock. It will save us time and I know you'll want to wait until the last minute to say your goodbyes."

Ethan and Caelyn nodded agreement. Though the plans had fallen together quickly, there was no need for further discussion.

"Speaking of goodbyes, it's getting a bit late and I need to get some rest before we leave," Jack said. "If you two have no objections, I'm going to call it a night. Besides, I know you have a lot to talk about...just don't make it too late. We have a long day ahead of us."

Caelyn held her breath until her father had passed through the door leading outside. Now that they were alone, she wasn't sure what to say.

"Everything is going to work out fine," Ethan said, taking her hands in his. "He's right, you know? Thanks to the telephone, we can talk at least once a week until you return. You'll be back here before you know it."

As much as she appreciated his words of reassurance, they did nothing to lift her spirits. The more she thought about going home, the more she dreaded it. New York was where the old Caelyn existed, and going back meant having to see and interact with people who would expect her to be the same as when she had left. But most of all, she hated the thought of being separated from her surfman.

"It's just that I don't want anything to ruin this," she said. "I am where I want to be, I mean, as a person. What just happened with father was wonderful, and I'm really thankful that it turned out that way. But...I'm frightened."

"Caelyn," he said. His voice was low, but his words were strong and clear. "Even though I've felt this way since the first moment I saw you, I never thought I'd be able to tell you. But I could wait until next week, or next year, or the next century, and I would still feel the same way."

Sensing what was coming, Caelyn gripped his hands.

"Caelyn, I love you. I suppose there are better places and situations to say something like that, but I can't let you leave tomorrow without telling you how I feel."

Caelyn stared at him in silence, unable to think of the right words to say. She wanted him to understand how much her life had changed and how much of it had been because of him. This moment would never come again, and she wanted her response to somehow convey how much it meant to her.

"I'm sorry," he apologized, misinterpreting her silence. "You don't have to say anything. It's just...I thought it would help if you knew. You don't need to say anything. Really. I just want–"

"What did you say?" Caelyn interrupted.

"I said, I'm sorry. But that's the–"

"No. What did you say before that?"

Caelyn watched as he went back over his words, trying to remember. Then his mouth formed a soft smile.

"I said...I love you."

"Ssshhh," Caelyn whispered, holding a finger to his lips. "Do you hear it?"

Ethan listened to the sounds of the tavern for a moment. Then he smiled again and leaned in closer.

"Yes," he said in a hushed voice. "It's sweet and clear, and it whispers of a love that will last until there are no oceans upon which to sail or stars to guide the sailors at sea. Its life-breath is fidelity, and it rides upon the wings of devotion."

Caelyn gripped his hands tighter, delighted he understood her whimsy.

"It will echo in my heart and soul for the rest of my days," he said. "And if there is a life after this one, it will follow me there. For now that I have heard the whisper of your goddess, I know that my love for you is forever."

Caelyn remained silent, savoring the poetry of his words. The sadness of knowing she would soon have to leave intensifying the tenderness of the moment. Her life had been ordinary. Enough so to know perfect moments like this were rare and she wanted to hold on to this one for as long as she could. Moisure colected in her eyes, threatening to become tears.

Leaning across the table, Ethan cradled Caelyn's face in his hands and kissed her long and deep. It wasn't a proper thing to do in public, but she didn't care.

For the patrons of Lottie Mae's diner, the public display of affection was an entertaining distraction from their winter doldrums. One man clapped his hands in appreciation, then another and another. Whether it was in memory of their own past affairs of the heart or in envy of the surfman's, everyone in the tavern soon joined in the tribute.

With eyes still closed, Caelyn broke the kiss, pushing herself away. Though her face turned warm with embarrassment, she was beyond caring that they were the center of attention. Taking a breath, she opened her eyes again. The only thing she could focus on was Ethan. Again, he pulled her to him, this time to whisper in her ear.

"You saved me from a life that was worse than death," he said. "You have made me feel things I believed I would never feel again. I will wait here for you, but don't take too long, or I shall become like the ships cast upon the shoals. Abandoned forever and broken beyond repair."

This time, it was Caelyn who initiated the kiss. Appearances be damned. With her lips, she sealed the unspoken promise to return as soon as she could and to carry his memory with her every minute she was away. Her kiss spoke of love and fear and memories and promise, and imparted the swirling myriad of feelings she couldn't put into words.

Again, the diners were the appreciative audience, responding with another round of applause and banging on the tables. The boisterous clamor gave Ansel Stick the distraction he needed. Having seen enough, he slipped from the dining room and outside into the darkness.

Chapter Twenty-Five

Sins of the Father

Ansel Stick gloated to himself as he hurried along the sandy pathway to the island's sound side. He was on a lucky streak, for sure. When Caelyn and the surfman had left the station on a buckboard, he feared he would lose them. There was no way he could have kept up on foot. And even if he could, they would have spotted him as he followed on the open beach. But when he heard the keeper say he would see them when they returned, he knew everything would be OK. All he had to do was find a warm place to hunker down and wait.

And tonight had been just as easy. His job had been to stay out of sight but keep his eyes on Caelyn, no matter what happened. When Jack and Hunter left the inn, he stayed, waiting to see whether Ethan and Caelyn would try to slip away. When it became clear they were staying put for the night, it was time to report back to his new boss.

But his luck ended when it came to the weather. Driven by a stiff wind, the bitterness of the night air stole his breath, forcing him to stop for a moment. He drew his coat tight around him and peered into the darkness. And there it was! The moored yacht would have been impossible to find had it not been for a light shining through the cabin's porthole. A few moments later, when he stepped on the dock, his foot slipped on the ice-covered wood and one of his legs plunged into the frigid water. A lucky grab of a mooring line saved him from falling in altogether.

Hearing the splash, Jack rushed out of the cabin and onto the deck. Seeing Stick clinging to the line, he grabbed his arms, pulled him aboard, and took him inside the main cabin.

"Sorry sir," Stick said, shaking from the cold soaking. "I didn't mean to make such a racket. I hope I didn't wake you or Mister Winslow."

"Don't worry about Hunter," Jack said. "He's got so much scotch in him, the dead will wake before he does. Now tell me, what did they do after I left?"

"Well sir, I hate to tell you this but your daughter and that surfman fellow got pretty cozy after you left. They even kissed a couple of times, right in full view of everyone. And she wasn't being shy about it at all. No, sir. You could tell she was really enjoying–"

"Shut up!" Jack snapped. "You'll do well to remember that's my daughter you're talking about. Of course, she wouldn't be here if you were half the sailor you told me you were. What happened out there, on the ocean, anyway?"

"It was the boiler, sir. It had to have a faulty seam or something. It was nothing I done, I swear it."

"Never mind," Jack said, growing impatient. "Short of beating it out of you, I doubt that I'd ever get an honest answer from you if it suited your purpose to lie. It doesn't matter. Just know that I blame you and that I own you now. I own you because if you don't do what I tell you, I'll make sure you never get another job. Ever. Anywhere. Understand?"

"Yes sir," Stick said.

"I'll tell you a little secret," Jack continued. "My daughter won't be coming back here. Not in January. Not ever. You know why?"

"No sir."

"Because, my incompetent sailor friend, there won't be any reason for her to come back."

"But what about the surfman fellow? If she doesn't come back, you know he'll come looking for her."

"No, he won't, Stick. You know why?"

"No sir," he said, though he had a sick feeling he was about to find out and he wasn't going to like it.

"Because, Stick, you're going to stop him."

"Me sir?"

"Yes. I have an idea. It's very simple but I think it will work. After all, how hard can it be to outwit a man who rows a boat for a living?"

Jack looked at the errant sailor and laughed. Stick smiled, though he knew the joke would be on him. If they made a mistake, the Outer Bankers would give them more trouble than they could handle. He also knew that Lifesaving Stations ran all the way to New York and beyond. He might be a jack-leg of a sailor, but even Stick understood the bond the surfmen shared. Their commitment to each other was beyond measure. It was as much a part of their being as breathing air. If Jack Canady's plan – whatever it was – did not work, there would come a reckoning.

Chapter Twenty-Six

End of Dreams

Ethan ordered a roast duck for them to share and they spent the next hour talking about what the future might bring. They held hands, gazing at one another and stealing a quick kiss when they thought no one was watching. When it was time to close, Lottie Mae brought Teach to them, explaining that it was too cold for the puppy to sleep outside. Collecting their coats, they said goodnight and went upstairs.

When they came to Caelyn's door, she let Teach go inside the room first, then turned to Ethan. Taking a quick look to make sure they were alone, he gave her a kiss goodnight.

"Goodnight," he whispered. "I won't be able to sleep tonight but you should try. It will be an early start and a long trip."

"Don't leave," she said, pulling herself closer. "Stay with me tonight."

"I thought that with your father nearby, you might not want to take the chance."

"I don't care," she said, looking into his eyes. "Stay with me."

"Are you sure?

"Ethan," she whispered. "Don't you understand? I love you, too."

Hearing her say the words for the first time stirred both his heart and his desire. Leaving now was impossible. He entered her room and closed the door.

Their lovemaking was slow yet desperate, prolonging their intimacy well into the morning. Keeping their bodies joined in carnal embrace sustained the illusion that the morning would never come. At last, when Caelyn broke their embrace, it was to rest her head on his chest and close her eyes. Though he felt her tears fall warm upon his skin, he said nothing. He understood her pain and words would only make the moment more unbearable for them both.

A few moments later, he felt the steady rise and fall of her chest as she slipped into sleep. But for him, slumber did not come right away. The strange series of events leading up to this moment kept playing through his mind. Never in his wildest dreams had he imagined that his life would change as it had. Less than a week ago, he had resolved to live out the rest of his days as a loner, taking each day as it came. Now, he was looking to the future with anticipation and passion. Just like the wonderful flying machine had done that morning, he began soaring high above the confines of his reality. Going to only God knew where. He was reborn. Beginning life anew. Thanks to a quirk of fate that had brought Caelyn to Cape Hatteras and into his life.

Without warning, a hot wave of dread swept away his euphoria. Perhaps the fairy tale was too good to be true. Precious little good had come to him in his life and none of it had come without tribulation. It wasn't doubt that haunted him, but an honest assessment of what had befallen him through the years.

Suppressing the sense of foreboding, he cleared his thoughts long enough to allow sleep to overtake him. But despite all the reassurances he had given himself, his rest was fitful, haunted by the ghosts of his past. Soon, he began dreaming he was in a surfboat by himself during a storm, once again trying to reach the *Aphrodite*. He kept rowing and rowing, yet never making headway against the gale. He saw Caelyn standing on the deck, calling to him, desperate to be rescued. The harder he tried to row, the slower his arms moved. Her silhouette grew smaller and smaller as the wind kept pushing the yacht toward the open sea, until only her pleading wails remained, begging him to save her.

Chapter Twenty-Seven

The Parting

They held hands as they walked in silence through the darkness to Jack Canady's waiting yacht. Caelyn carried the carpetbag over her shoulder and Ethan carried Teach in his free arm. The air was bitter cold, but as still as the dead. The low rumble of the yacht's engine floated over the cattails and marsh grass to greet them, an unwelcome signal that their time together was almost over.

"Is that all you have?" Jack asked as they stepped into the illumination of the boat's dim electric lights.

"Yes," Caelyn said, stopping short of coming on board. She had made a point of leaving the steamer chest at the inn, a tangible sign of her intention to return.

"Well then," Jack said, stepping down onto the dock to hand Ethan a piece of paper. "Here's the telephone number I promised you. Call us on Monday, say about noontime. I'll have Caelyn standing by."

Ethan placed the folded piece of paper in his shirt pocket.

"As I said yesterday, I really can't thank you enough," Jack said as he shook Ethan's hand. "And don't worry, I'll take good care of her."

Taking the bag from Caelyn, he stepped back aboard the yacht.

"Come dear. Time to move along. The train won't wait for us, you know."

Turning to Ethan, Caelyn gave him a hurried kiss, patted Teach on his head, and then joined her father. A slow goodbye would have been too painful and given her too much time to change her mind.

The quickness of the goodbye disappointed Ethan, but he understood. It had taken all his strength to let her go.

The yacht drifted away from the dock and the chugging of the motor quickened. Caelyn stood in the glow of the lights as the boat pulled away in slow departure, looking back at him with sadness etched on her face. As the boat began to enter the sound waters, Teach whimpered and struggled to jump down. Ethan scratched his head but never took his eyes off Caelyn. With deliberate slowness, she mouthed the words, "I love you."

He remained on the dock even after he could no longer hear the motor, watching the boat's running lights grow smaller. Not until they had disappeared altogether did he force himself to turn away.

"The deed is done," he said with no one to hear but Teach. "Now we shall see if the timber from which this love was made is true."

Placing the puppy on the ground, he began walking along the sandy path back toward the village. The first hints of morning light were chasing away the night, helping to make the pathway easier to see. Teach scampered along behind, keeping up as best he could in the soft sand.

Perhaps I should have been less understanding and asked Caelyn to wait, Ethan thought for the hundredth time. *But waiting would have only prolonged the agony of her departure, and it would have made separating even more difficult.*

An excited bark from Teach interrupted his musing. Spinning around to look back down the pathway, he heard the puppy yelp in agony. Then silence.

Hurrying back the way he had come, Ethan cursed himself for not putting the dog on a leash. The puppy could have encountered any number of dangers. He should have been more cautious.

Coming to a dark hollow between two small drifts of sand, the surfman stopped short. Before him was a small, motionless mound of black fur. Kneeling beside the puppy, he cooed words of concern. Teach lifted his head and tried to stand, but his hindquarters would not move. As he slid his hands under the helpless creature to pick him up, Ethan heard rustling in the tall grass behind him. A blast shattered the still night just as he turned. Lights exploded in his head. The surfman fell face forward to land unconscious beside Teach. Blood began seeping into the white sand.

"Now then, Mister Canady," Ansel Stick said as he straddled Ethan's body to inspect his handiwork. Hanging heavy by his side, he held a revolver, gray smoke curling from its barrel. "That was a plan that worked out just fine. Nice and simple. I'd say this makes us even."

Shoving the pistol into his waistband, he headed down the path toward the village. The mail boat would leave in a couple of hours and he would be on it, the first leg of a roundabout trip that would take him to New York. He had kept to himself while he had stayed on the island, and none of the Outer Bankers could link him to the surfman. Even if he did become a suspect, there was no apparent motive, and once he pitched the revolver into the ocean, there would be no evidence. The only person who would ever know of his crime was Jack Canady. And Stick was the one person who knew that Jack Canady had commissioned the murder, a fact that the wiry first mate figured would keep him employed for many years to come.

After the would-be assassin was gone, Teach rose to stand on his front legs but his hindquarters still would not move. Sensing that life was leaving his master, he struggled to reach the injured surfman, dragging his hind legs with him. Sniffing out the source of blood, he licked the wound until the bleeding stopped, then curled up next to the lifesaver.

Chapter Twenty-Eight

A Boy No More

Danny was more than ready to go back to Kitty Hawk. He spent the previous day listening to stories about his aunt's rheumatoid arthritis, her neighbor's croup, and other ailments suffered by Manteo's older people. He enjoyed visiting his mother's family, but listening to the mundane aspects of home life was a torture he could tolerate for only so long. Making his situation even worse, word about the Wright brothers' flights had swept through the little community like a ship fire. Danny was sure that if he had stayed with Ethan and Caelyn, he would have seen the flying machine himself.

There was another, more personal reason Danny wanted to get back. He had come to admire and respect the Hatteras surfman during the past week. Ethan had proven himself to be of steady temperament and possessed a quiet strength that Danny wanted to emulate. In truth, the surfman embodied everything he wanted to be as a man.

The young waterman could barely remember his father. Solomon Williams had died before Danny turned five. Like most of the people on Harkers Island, Solomon had lived off the ocean and sounds. Sometimes for profit, sometimes to put food on the table. He had gone out in his shad boat one hot September day, never to return. The other watermen suspected a sudden squall had thrown him out of his boat and he had drowned. Others suspected he may have died of a heat stroke and just drifted away. No one knew for sure, and Danny didn't much care anymore. What he did know was that his father was gone, and that he had always missed him.

Danny now saw Ethan as the father he had never known. He was a veteran of the war and a survivor of one of the most dangerous occupations ever conceived. The kind of man any boy would want for a father. But for Danny, the friendship had an even more appealing side. For an eighteen-year-old from Harkers Island, the past week had provided more adventure than he had ever imagined possible. And adventure had a way of following Ethan. It was part of the air about the surfman that set him apart.

As much as Danny respected Harry, the past week had opened his eyes to possibilities that existed in the world beyond his isolated island. He had always admired the men of the Lifesaving Service and now he knew he wanted to be one. If he could hire on with a station close to Ethan, so much the better.

But right now, all Danny could think about was getting over to Kill Devil Hill to see the Wright brothers and their flyer. He had gotten up early, drank a quick cup of coffee with his aunt, hugged her goodbye, and ran the half-mile to his skiff.

An hour later he arrived at the western side of the island close to the village. Mooring his boat to the first dock he could find, he hurried down the path toward Kitty Hawk. Halfway there, he came upon a lifeless figure sprawled across the way – the white sand beside his head turned brown with blood. Though he could not see the man's face, the young waterman saw Teach lying next to him and knew it was Ethan. Fearing the worse, he kneeled next to the surfman, placed two fingers on his friend's neck and found a faint pulse. The surfman wasn't dead yet, but his life was running.

"You stay with him, Teach, you hear," Danny said as he patted the puppy's head. He then noticed an unnatural twist in the dog's spine. Teach tried to stand, but his hind legs failed him again.

"Why?" Danny asked, his heart aching as it never had before. "Why would anybody do this?"

Leaving Teach beside Ethan, he ran toward Kitty Hawk as fast as he could, praying that it was not too late.

Chapter Twenty-Nine

The Junction

"I need to stretch my legs a bit," Jack Canady said when the train pulled into the Norfolk station. "Anyone care to join me?"

"No, thank you," Caelyn said, continuing to peer out of the window. The southern Virginia station was little different from any other and she had no desire to explore. The hollowness in her heart had continued to grow with each mile of track that clacked beneath them. What seemed a positive step in the right direction when she left the Outer Banks had become a marathon of second-guessing.

"It seems a different world now, doesn't it?" Hunter asked, interrupting Caelyn's brooding. Sitting in the seat facing hers, he had watched her mood grow more sullen with each passing minute. "I think I understand why it affected you so. It certainly would satisfy one's yearning to return to the basics of life."

Caelyn continued to stare out of the window without responding. Hunter settled back in his seat again, trying to figure out what he might say to her that would matter.

"You know," he said, breaking the silence again, "if...for some reason things don't work out. I'll still be here for you."

This time, Caelyn turned to look at him, not sure what to say. Was he seeking pity or trying to be nice?

"Oh, don't worry," he said. "I'm not trying to change your mind. But I couldn't live with myself if I didn't at least take one opportunity to tell you that, well, I honestly do love you."

"Hunter," she said as she leaned over to grasp his hands. "I can't tell you how much it means to me to know that. You are a true gentleman."

Though his sentiments were sincere, his love for Caelyn was not the only motivation for his benevolence. If something happened that caused her to change her mind, he could not afford to do anything that would prevent her from coming back. There was, after all, a fortune riding on the possibility.

"Well," Jack said, returning from his visit to the station house. "I'm glad to see you two getting along so well, all things considered. I sincerely hope you will remain friends. You never know what the future may bring."

Caelyn jerked her hands away from Hunter's as if caught in a betrayal, then turned away to resume gazing out the window.

Jack sat next to Hunter as the train pulled out of the station. Recognizing Caelyn's emotional turmoil, he decided to leave well enough alone. *Besides,* he thought, *if Ansel Stick has done his job right, there will be all the time in the world.*

But he couldn't count on Stick to do anything right. He had proven that with the wreck of the *Aphrodite*. That's why Jack had gone in search of a mailbox at the train station to drop his letter to Ethan. All the wheels were set in motion. One way or another, Jack Canady would rid himself of the surfman.

Chapter Thirty

The Letter

Ethan tried to open his eyes but the light made his head pound. Lying still for a moment, he waited to see if the pain would pass. He thought about Caelyn and wondered where she might be.

A memory of kneeling down to pick Teach up and then the blast of gunfire that followed flashed through his mind. His hand went to his forehead. He felt the familiar texture of gauze on his head, revealing another injury. Spurred on by a wave of alarm and anger, he tried to sit up. The room began spinning and he slumped back into the bed's mattress.

"Not so fast there," a gentle voice said. "You've got a pretty good laceration on your head and you've lost a lot of blood. You're not going to want to try going anywhere 'til you get some strength back."

Ethan forced his eyelids open a little, allowing his eyes to adjust to the light. The young woman sitting next to his bed looked familiar.

"I'm Abbie," she said with a smile. "Remember? I work the desk and wait tables downstairs, but Missus Mae asked me to keep an eye on you. Now, if you'll promise to behave yourself, I'll go tell her you're awake. She's going to be real happy."

Closing his eyes, Ethan heard the shuffling of shoes as she hurried down the hall. When he opened them again, he saw Danny, the innkeeper, and Abbie standing next to his bed.

"How you feeling, son?" she asked. "I bet you got a humdinger of a headache. Do you think you're up to eating something?"

Ethan tried to speak, but no words came.

"Hmmm," Lottie Mae said, looking over the surfman. "Can't talk? That's not a good sign. Abbie, did he say anything to you when he woke up?"

"No ma'am. Now that you mention it, he never said a word."

"All right surfman," Lottie Mae said. "Listen up real close. I want you to say something to me. Anything. It don't matter what. I just want you to say the first thing that comes to mind."

Ethan took a deep breath.

"Where...is...Caelyn?"

"Ethan," Danny said, unable to contain himself any longer. "Caelyn went back to New York, remember?"

Ethan struggled for a few moments, trying to remember what had happened. He recalled meeting Caelyn's father – and Hunter – in the tavern. And he remembered watching her boat leave in the icy darkness before dawn. Then there was Teach, injured in the pathway and then the explosion in his head.

"What happened to me?" he asked.

"We don't know for sure," Danny said. "When I came back from Manteo, I found you laying in the middle of the path back to the village. You were almost dead. At first, we thought someone shot you but there wasn't no bullet in you. So, then we thought maybe somebody hit you over the head with something. But there wasn't anything nearby to prove anything one way or the other. What we do know is that you lost so much blood, we thought you were a goner."

"It was a gunshot," Ethan said. "I'm sure of it. But why? Why would anyone try to kill me?"

"Well, it wasn't a thief," Danny said. "You still had your money and belongings, as far as we could tell. Maybe somebody just had it in for you."

"What about Teach? Where is he?"

Danny took off his fisherman's cap and studied it as if it were a puzzle. Not wanting to be the bearer of yet more bad news, he held his tongue.

"I see," Ethan said. "But I have to know...did he go quick?"

"We think Teach saved your life by keeping you from bleeding to death," Danny said. "But there wasn't anything we could do for him. Whoever shot you must've kicked him pretty good, 'cause it broke his back."

The young waterman took a breath, then continued.

"It was the damnedest thing, Ethan. He was perfectly all right except for he couldn't move his back legs. It was pitiful. He wasn't gonna have no kind of life without the use of his hind legs. I... I had to put him down. I'm sorry, Ethan."

"It's all right, Danny. You did the right thing. I'm sure of it."

Everyone remained quiet for a few moments, waiting for the awkwardness to pass.

"Oh, I almost forgot," Danny said, reaching into his pocket. "I thought you might want to have this."

The waterman handed Ethan the cameo with the black velvet ribbon Caelyn had placed around Teach's neck. Staring at the ivory silhouette, he remembered how the piece had highlighted Caelyn's cheeks and how she had handled Teach with such tenderness on that brisk morning back on Ocracoke. Then, in a flitting memory, he saw the sadness in her face when her boat had pulled away from the dock.

"The telephone number! Where's the telephone number?"

"What telephone number?" Danny asked.

"Jack Canady gave me a piece of paper with a number on it before they left. I put it in my shirt pocket. Where is it?"

Danny looked at Lottie Mae, who looked at Abbie.

"Why, yes, now that you mention it, there was a piece of paper with a number on it. I took it out of his shirt when I washed it the other day. I'll go see if I can find it."

Confusion clouded Ethan's face as he watched the young woman leave.

"What did she mean, 'the other day?'" Ethan asked, pushing himself upright. The effort made his head pound and the dizziness returned.

"You've been out of it for three days," Lottie Mae said as she placed a pillow behind his head. "Fact is, you were out of it for so long we weren't sure you'd ever come back."

"Three days," Ethan repeated in disbelief. He spoke with his eyes closed, waiting for his head to clear.

"That's right. Danny told us about you being knocked out on the *Aphrodite's* lifeboat. You've had two major head injuries in a week's time. Doc Watters came by to look at you and said that it might have been better if your attacker had gone ahead and finished the job." She paused for a moment, realizing how crude the comment sounded. "Honestly, he didn't think you were going to come out of it."

Ethan was too preoccupied to notice Lottie Mae's gaff. He was forgetting something. Something important.

"You said three days, right?"

"That's right," Lottie Mae said.

"What's today's date?" he asked, his thinking too scrambled to do the math.

"It's Monday morning, December the twenty-first. Danny found you early Friday and you've been unconscious 'till just now."

Three days! The thought echoed inside Ethan's head. *Caelyn has been gone for three days while I've been in bed, oblivious. Something is supposed to happen today, but what?*

"I found it!" Abbie announced as she came back into the room, waving the paper in the air. "And look, this letter for you came in the morning's mail. Looks like it might be from your lady friend."

"A letter?" Ethan asked.

"She must really miss you to have mailed a letter so quickly," Abbie said. "Here, why don't you read it. It might make you feel better."

Ethan looked at the writing on the envelope and realized that his eyes would not focus well enough to make out the words.

"Please, read it for me," he said, handing the letter back to Abbie.

"Sure," she said, placing the other slip of paper on the nightstand. Being able to do something for the handsome surfman pleased her, even if the letter was from the woman who had put her in her place a few days earlier. Opening the envelope, she unfolded the stationery and began to read.

"Dear Ethan. I know that this will hurt you deeply..." Abbie's voice cracked and her cheerful tone shifted into the cadence of a disbelieving, soulful dirge. "...but I must be honest with you. I have given a great deal of thought about our relationship and I can no longer deny the truth. I do care about you, but I realize we come from two different worlds. As much as I hate to admit it, my father was right. It might be fun for a while but at some point, I would come to resent you. I'm afraid I am too accustomed to the finer things in life to spend the rest of mine with you. I have needs that you will never be able to fulfill. Hunter can provide those things for me, and eventually, I will marry him, as I had always planned to. Please believe me when I say I never intended to hurt you. I hope one day you will find it in your heart to forgive me. Please don't try to find me, as it would only make this more difficult. You have a lot to offer someone of your own station. Someday you will find a woman who will love you, and you will forget all about me. Until then, I wish you the best. Your friend, Caelyn."

Abbie looked at Ethan. The hurt on his face broke her heart.

Ethan turned his head away in a futile attempt to hide his pain. Caelyn's letter had the ring of truth to it but he refused to accept it.

"It's a lie," he said. "Somebody else wrote that letter. Maybe her father wrote it, or maybe he forced her to write it."

Ethan looked at the others for validation but their expressions showed otherwise. Although part of him could not blame them, he refused to believe they were right. They did not know Caelyn the way he did.

"The telephone number," he said, spying the slip of paper on the nightstand. Now, he remembered why today, Monday, was so important. "That's the number for Jack Canady's office. I'm supposed to call her there today at noon. I have to get downstairs to the telephone. Now!"

He slid his legs over the edge of the bed and tried to stand. When he took his first, his knees buckled and crashed to floor. Abbie dashed to his side and helped him back onto the bed.

"I've got to call her," he said. "She's expecting me to call and it will prove that it's all a mistake or a trick. You've got to help me downstairs."

"Right now, you've got to eat something to get your strength back," Lottie Mae said in a tone that did not leave room for argument. "We'll help you get downstairs to the telephone when it's time but, you got to promise not to try that again. All right?"

Realizing that he couldn't make it alone, Ethan nodded in agreement. He would do anything they said as long as he could call Caelyn.

The lifesaver closed his eyes for what only seemed a moment but opened them to see Abbie entering the room with soup that Lottie Mae had prepared. Though her doting went far beyond the caretaking of an attentive nurse, Ethan did not notice. Nor did he notice the growing light of affection in her eyes as she tried to anticipate his every need. When he finished eating, she helped him settle down and turned to leave.

"Wait," he said, grabbing her by the wrist. "Promise you'll wake me if I fall asleep, no later than eleven-thirty. OK?"

"Sure," she promised, though her eyes betrayed her reluctance to do so.

Still, when eleven-thirty arrived, Abbie came to Ethan's room and wakened him as promised. Danny and two Kitty Hawk lifesavers who followed her in placed Ethan in a cane chair and carried him downstairs. Lottie Mae joined them as the surfmen sat the chair next to the wall telephone. Abbie took the receiver out of its cradle, turned the crank on the side of the box a couple of times and got the operator on the line.

"Hey Cindy. This is Abbie. How are you?" There was a pause and then she continued. "Listen, I want to make a long-distance call to New York...yeah...City. Here's the number."

Abbie read the digits off the paper and waited. The strain of being placed in the chair and going down the steps had weakened Ethan but he was running on adrenaline now. He would not have peace of mind until he talked to Caelyn.

"What? Are you positive? Wait a minute, I'll ask."

"Are you sure that this is the number Mister Canady gave you?" she asked Ethan.

Ethan took the paper and looked at it. He had not bothered to look at the number at the dock but the piece of paper looked like the one he remembered.

"Yeah, I think that's it. Why? What's wrong?"

"Hold on," she said, taking the paper from Ethan.

"Cindy," she said into the cone-shaped mouthpiece. "Let's try it one more time, just to make sure. Thanks."

She read off the number again and waited. A moment later, the operator came back with the same answer. Abbie thanked her and hung the earpiece back in its cradle.

"The operator in New York says that number isn't any good," she said, feeling the pain spreading over the surfman's face. "She said that number isn't even a real phone number for listings in New York City."

Succumbing to the truth, Ethan hung his head in defeat. He realized he'd been tricked and could deny it no longer. The physical and emotional fatigue together were too much. He didn't even have the strength to curse her name. Bitterness seeped into the void created by the harsh realization that he was no better than a fool.

"Please, take him back to his room," Lottie Mae said to the surfmen. Judging by the pasty color of his skin, she feared he had exerted himself. "You need more time to get your strength back. Maybe things won't seem so bad after you rest up."

Abbie watched the men carry Ethan back up the stairs. The image of the defeated surfman tore at her heart, but more than that, it made her angry. What type of woman would do such a thing? Shaking her head in disbelief, she came up the stairs behind them, determined to do anything she could to help the surfman recover from both of his wounds.

Chapter Thirty-One

Betrayed

Caelyn was beginning to believe noon would never come. She had spent the morning with her father, going over various legal papers and discussing matters with the bankers. Her inheritance wasn't an enormous fortune, but her grandmother had invested it in several savings accounts, bonds and stocks. Finishing the paperwork would take several more days, but the good start lifted her spirits.

The best part was the way her father had pitched in to help. She was closer to him than she had been in years and it saddened her it had not happened until now, when she was preparing to leave. At least the future held possibilities for them that had not existed before. It was a blessing she would not take for granted.

When the noon hour arrived, she could barely contain herself. She and her father sat in his office waiting for the call to come through. She had a lot of things to tell Ethan, but what she wanted most was to hear his voice – proving that the whole affair had not been a dream.

As the hands on the wall clock moved closer to half-past the hour, her excitement turned into apprehension. Had something happened to him? Was it possible he had forgotten?

As the clock's hands moved closer to one, her apprehension turned to aggravation and then to desperation. She wondered if he might have reconsidered their relationship. Perhaps experienced a change of heart. It wasn't impossible. His life had been difficult and there were a thousand reasons for changing his mind. The second-guessing was driving her mad.

When one o'clock came, she could no longer stand not knowing. Giving in to her doubts, she went to the Strowger telephone on her father's desk, placed the receiver to her ear, and turned the dial on the sunburst faceplate. Something must have happened to Ethan, and she was going to get to the bottom of it.

"What are you doing, dear?" her Jack asked.

"I'm going to find someone down there to talk to and tell me what's going on," she said as she continued her attempts to call up the operator, but the line remained dead.

"Damn!" she said, slamming the receiver onto the hook. "I can't get anyone to answer. Where are they?"

"There now, Caelyn," her father said. "Let me have my secretary try. You just sit down and relax. We'll have someone on the line in just a few minutes."

Jack went to the office door and called to his secretary.

"Missus Stanford...get on the telephone and see if you can reach a place in North Carolina called Lottie Mae's. It's in a little village on the Outer Banks named Kitty Hawk. If you get through, tell them to put a Mister Ethan Roberts on, will you? Thank you."

Her father's calm demeanor helped Caelyn to settle down. Once again, he was stepping in to help when she needed him most.

Jack Canady sat beside his daughter and took her hands in his.

"Everything will work out fine," he said. "You'll see. And no matter what happens, I will be here for you."

A few minutes later, Jack's secretary stepped into the office, holding a notepad. The middle-aged woman looked at Caelyn with a sad, knowing expression, not sure how to begin.

"Well, let's have it," Jack said. "What did you find out?"

"I'm afraid it's not good. I was able to get through to the inn and speak to the innkeeper...Lottie Mae. She told me that Mister Roberts...the surfman, she called him...had gone back to the Hatteras Lifesaving Station. I got through to the station but..."

"Go on," Jack said. "We need to know everything." He grasped Caelyn's hands tighter, letting her know he was there for her.

Caelyn couldn't make any sense of what she had heard thus far, but she knew it was not adding up to be anything good. A hundred possibilities flashed through her mind and her head began to spin.

"Well, I talked to the man in charge of the station. Keeper Jennette. He said that Mister Roberts was there but that he did not want to talk to Caelyn or you. According to Keeper Jennette, Mister Roberts just wanted you to know that he was sorry and that what he did was wrong...but he realized now that he had made a mistake. Then Keeper Jennette asked that we not call back because they need to keep the line open in case of emergencies. And that was it."

Mrs. Stanford looked up from the script Jack had dictated for her to read. Caelyn had covered her face with her hands and was sobbing. Though she did not like being part of the deception, she knew it was for a noble reason. Mr. Canady had explained how the man named Ethan Roberts – a much older man known for preying on emotionally vulnerable women – had taken advantage of his daughter. She had known a man like that once, long ago, and she still hated him. The world was full of men like that, and if she could save poor Caelyn from the misery she had known, who could fault her for that?

"Thank you, Missus Stanford," Jack said, dismissing her. "You did very well."

As she closed the door, she took one last look at Caelyn.

Such a sweet, poor young thing, she thought. *But she'll get over it. We always do. Eventually.*

Chapter Thirty-Two

Haunted

Though his sleep was fitful, Ethan didn't awaken until Abbie announced it was time for the evening meal, a nourishing vegetable stew and toast. If he was ever going to recover, he would have to have food more substantial than soup, and this was a good beginning. After eating, he sat up in bed for a while and listened to the young woman as she talked about her hopes and dreams. She was bright and very mature for her age.

As she continued to talk, he kept thinking of Caelyn and the way she had been the day they had met on the sand dunes after finding Teach. He remembered everything about her appearance in that moment – the color of her clothes, the way the sun shone upon her hair, her cheeks and full lips turned red by the cold. The warm memory, juxtaposed against the harsh reality of her betrayal, was like acid poured on silk, eating away all that was good. He wouldn't be at peace until certain it was Caelyn who wrote the letter and that the false telephone number was her doing, not her father's. He could try to find the telephone number for her home but talk would not satisfy his need to know for sure. He had to see her eyes, and to do that, he would have to go to her.

The food was filling and Abbie's voice was soothing. He let her go on without interrupting, conserving his energy. Tomorrow he would leave for New York and he would need all the strength he could muster.

He fell asleep listening to Abbie's lulling voice. He soon began again the dream that had disturbed him during his last night with Caelyn. This time it started with the *Aphrodite* having already drifted too far away for him to see her.

The distance between them was greater than before, mimicking their new reality. She continued calling to him through the darkness, begging him to come to her. Reaching for the surfboat's oars, he discovered they were gone. He was drifting on the water with no way to move toward her.

Soon, her pleas for help turned into admonishment. "Why?" she kept pleading. "Why have you deserted me?" He tried to answer – to tell her he would never abandon her and that his love was forever – but his voice would not rise above a whisper. Helpless and heartbroken, he listened to her voice drift farther and farther away – until he could no longer hear her at all.

Chapter Thirty-Three

Love Strong

News of the surfman's unkind deed traveled fast. Jack Canady made sure of that. It was by no coincidence that Hunter happened by the Canady's home early that evening to discuss a business matter with Jack. Once they were done, Dorothy Canady was more than happy to have him stay for dinner.

Jack had explained to her how Caelyn had fallen for the Hatteras lifesaver but she could not understand it. In her mind, Hunter Winslow was the perfect match for her stepdaughter and the thought that Caelyn had rejected him was the act of an impetuous girl. Now that the lifesaver was out of the picture, she would do her part to make Caelyn come to her senses. Caelyn, however, was in no mood for company, especially Hunter. But she was too proud to let him know the depth of her pain. She suffered through the meal as best she could, listening to her parents and Hunter making idle conversation about current social events.

How quickly the tables have turned, she thought as she looked at Hunter across the table. *A few days ago, it was you who played the role of a jilted lover. Now, it is my turn.*

Unable to bear the situation any longer, Caelyn excused herself and retreated to the study. Perhaps the warmth of the fireplace would provide comfort in a way her family could not. As she gazed into the flames licking around the logs, she wondered at the cruelness of her fate. She had been so convinced that Ethan's love was real, she never considered the possibility he might be using her.

"How could I have been that wrong?" she said to no one. "Was I so taken by him I saw things that didn't exist? Was I that big of a fool?"

The facts left little doubt as to what the answers were but her heart would not admit the obvious. What they shared was too strong, and there was something about the circumstances that left a seed of uncertainty in her mind.

If only I could talk to him one more time. Then, I would know for sure.

"Nothing like the warmth of a good fire to help one sort things out," Hunter said, interrupting her thoughts. Not waiting for an invitation, he entered the study armed with two snifters of brandy.

"Hunter, I really don't want to–"

"Please," he interrupted. "I didn't come to gloat. I came to commiserate. After all, who would know how you feel right now better than I?"

"Yes...I guess you're right," Caelyn said, feeling guilty at having been ready to dismiss him out of hand.

"Here, take this," he said, handing her a brandy. "It won't necessarily make you feel better but it will make you feel less."

"Thank you," she said, accepting the glass. She took a sip and resumed looking into the fire. Hunter stood silent for a few moments, respecting her sullen mood.

"You know," he said, "when we were on the train and I told you I would be here for you if something happened, I had no idea things would change like they have. And I'm not going to suggest that we pick up right where we left off. But...well, I just want you to know that I meant what I said."

Hunter's gesture moved Caelyn despite her pain. She knew it was not an entirely selfless act, but she believed it was heartfelt.

"That's very kind of you to say," she said with as much warmth as she could summon. "But I won't mislead you. I doubt that I'll be ready to discuss such things for a long time...if ever. However, I promise if I do, you will be the first person I come to."

"Fair enough," Hunter said. "You never know what the future may bring."

That's odd, she thought as she took another sip of brandy. *That's what father said on the train.* But as she continued to observe the twisting ropes of flame wrapping themselves around the logs, she knew that the woman she had become could never settle for a Hunter Winslow. Her heart was forever exiled to the Outer Banks. But Caelyn, the woman she was now, would somehow endure.

Both bolstered by the thought and angry with herself for having wallowed in sadness for so long, she knew the final chapter of their story had yet to be written.

I have been wrong about many things in my life, and I'll be wrong again. But I refuse to believe that I could have been mistaken about Ethan. And I will not believe he does not love me until I hear him say it to my face.

Chapter Thirty-Four

Love Quest

Despite a night of restless sleep, when he awakened, Ethan could tell his strength was returning. Moving with slow deliberation, he helped himself out of bed and made his way down the hall to the water closet. When he returned to his room, he discovered someone had left a pitcher of hot water on the nightstand. Next to the pitcher, cleaned and folded, lay the clothes he had worn the morning of the attack. After bathing and dressing, he descended the stairs, taking a moment to catch his breath at the check-in counter. Upon entering the dining room, he took the table closest to the doorway, unable to take another step.

Abbie saw him and rushed to the table.

"Are you all right?" she asked, then called out to Lottie Mae.

Ethan held up his hand to show that he was OK. The innkeeper arrived a moment later, her brow creased with concern. Danny entered the dining room and, seeing the two women converged at Ethan's table, immediately grasped the situation.

"Have you lost your mind?" Mae asked. "You're not well enough to be getting about on your own. Up 'til yesterday you were near 'bout dead. You've gotta get back upstairs to bed and get some more rest."

"She's right," Danny said, taking a seat next to the surfman. "You look like death warmed over."

Ethan appreciated their concern, but it did nothing to lessen his resolve.

"Missus Mae. Abbie. Danny," he said in his purest Missouri inflection. "Please, don't try to stop me. I have decided to go to New York and nothing will stop me."

"What?" Lottie Mae said. "You can't be serious."

Abbie stared at him in disbelief, her emotions swirling from concern to disappointment to sadness and back again.

"I know I will never be able to thank you enough for what you have done," Ethan continued. "Or you, Danny. All of you are right. But this is something I have to do. I don't mean to be disrespectful, but I won't wait another day longer."

The finality of his words and his manner sent a clear message. His decision was final. Any attempt to talk him out of leaving would be futile.

"Abbie," Lottie Mae said, pushing her glasses up off her nose with a frustrated jab of her forefinger. "Go to the kitchen and find Surfman Roberts some eggs and bacon. I'm going to go fetch a pot of coffee."

In no mood to make small talk, Ethan remained silent even after the innkeeper returned with the coffee and two cups. He sipped the hot beverage, appreciating its warmth and its promise of strength.

"You know, I was just upstairs putting Caelyn's trunk in the attic," Danny said, choosing not to confront Ethan's stubbornness head-on. "It's interesting what she left behind. Considering what some of it's worth, it's hard to believe she doesn't intend to come back for it."

Ethan understood what the waterman was trying to suggest but didn't care. Speculating was pointless.

Seeing that the surfman wasn't going to respond, Danny tried another tack.

"So, you're going to New York," he said, stating it as a matter of fact.

Ethan continued gazing into his coffee cup.

"I always wanted to see New York City. Mind if I go with you?"

The surfman looked at Danny, trying to determine his motive. The young waterman hadn't pressed him, nor was he demanding to go. Even in his obsessive state, Ethan understood he was taking a risk by traveling in his condition.

"That'll do," he answered. "We'll leave as soon as we're done here."

Abbie brought out two plates of scrambled eggs, fried ham, and grits with redeye gravy. Though it was the first proper food he had put in his stomach in three days, he took no pleasure from the meal. But by the time he finished, he was beginning to believe traveling wasn't as crazy as it had seemed before.

At Ethan's request, Abbie went to pack the few things he had and brought them downstairs. Meanwhile, Danny left to get the skiff ready while the surfman paid Lottie Mae for their room and board. Out of habit, he called for Teach but stopped himself. The memory of his puppy and how someone had brutally kicked him tore at his heart. Clenching his fists, he wanted to hit something. But, with nothing close enough to strike, there was no release for his pain and anger.

It just isn't right, he thought as a tear fell from his eye. *Someday I'll find out who did it and he'll pay a heavy price.*

On impulse, he felt for the cameo in his pocket, making sure it was still there.

It's not much, but it was hers, and I'll keep it until I have the opportunity to return it to her...in person.

A favorable wind made the crossing to Elizabeth City a quick one. Danny moored the skiff at a dock reserved for the Lifesaving Service and the two men hurried to the train station as fast as Ethan's condition would allow. No sooner had they purchased tickets and boarded than the departure whistle sounded and the afternoon train lurched forward on its northbound journey.

Ethan found an empty window seat and, exhausted by the morning's travel, rolled his coat into a pillow and placed it between his head and the window. A minute later, he was asleep. Danny took the seat opposite Ethan, keeping an eye on him as the train wound its way through Virginia and Maryland.

It was well into night when Ethan awakened and saw that the train was pulling into Baltimore. As the train chugged through the city, he noticed most of the homes displayed candles in the windows and were decorated with Christmas wreaths and boughs of holly and pine. His preoccupation with finding Caelyn had clouded his sense of time and season. He looked at the young waterman and cursed himself.

"Danny," he said, "I'm sorry. I shouldn't have let you come. You're going to miss Christmas with your family."

"Seems to me I'm the one who asked to come along," Danny said. "Besides, I never would've seen all this if I'd a stayed back home. Heck, I haven't ever been on a train before."

"Just the same," Ethan said, "I could have done this by myself."

"I hear tell these trains have real fine dining cars," Danny said, ignoring the surfman's objection. "Let's go see what it's like. What do you say?"

Ethan let the matter die. They both had made their points.

After taking seats at one of the small tables in the dining car, they looked at the menu and were astonished by the cost of everything. Yielding to his hunger and his growing weakness, Ethan decided they had little choice but to pay the high prices. He still had most of the cash Superintendent Collins had given him, and whatever he spent on this trip to find Caelyn, he would replace with his own money when he returned to Hatteras.

There was little opportunity to eat beef on the islands and Ethan wasn't going to let the opportunity pass. Not long after pulling away from the station, the waiter brought out their steak and eggs, placing their plates on the table. They ate in silence, looking at the houses and buildings pass by as the train continued on its way. A light snow had begun to fall. Philadelphia, New Jersey, and New York lay ahead.

Chapter Thirty-Five

A Boy's Vow

The clock next to Caelyn's bed showed that it was six o'clock in the morning. The day she had been dreading since her return had arrived. Tonight, her parents were hosting their annual Christmas Eve social. This year their guests would arrive expecting to hear a special announcement and – as Captain Sullivan had speculated during their conversation at the Pamlico Inn – the announcement would have been that she and Hunter Winslow were going to wed.

During the evening, it would become clear that no announcement would be forthcoming. People would raise haughty eyebrows and whisper speculations. The hoary guardians of the patrician standard would want to know what had happened and who was to blame. As relative newcomers to wealth, they would blame the Canadys. The vaunted Winslow name, though tarnished, would remain intact.

Caelyn felt bad for her parents but she could not force herself to admit responsibility. *Do I not have the right to make my own choices?* she argued to herself. *Is it my fault that I can't make myself love Hunter?*

The guilt should have been easy to dismiss but Hunter had left the door open for reconciliation. All she had to do was tell him she had come to her senses and everything would be as it had been two weeks earlier. She had the power to spare her parents the humiliation they would suffer and, by marrying Hunter, give them the ultimate key to the societal acceptance they coveted.

Climbing out of bed, she slipped on her robe and went to stand in front of the window of her second-floor bedroom. The pre-dawn sky was overcast and snow was falling. On the street below, a horse-drawn carriage moved past her house, its lanterns casting yellow light upon the fresh snow.

Caelyn recognized the carriage as belonging to Doctor Jennings, making an early morning call, no doubt. The doctor was one of the few neighbors she liked, and though he refused to buy an automobile, the aging doctor was an advocate of technology. During the summer, neighborhood children knew they could get a cool glass of lemonade from Doc Jennings' back porch in exchange for listening to a lecture on modern man's changing condition. Caelyn had always been willing to pay that price, spending many a summer's evening listening to passionate expositions on the future and how much he wished he could be a part of it. He was one of those rare individuals who found wonder in everything and talked about them with such enthusiasm he charmed everyone who came within his presence.

The memory made Caelyn long for the days when her life was less complicated and the wellbeing of others was not dependent on her decisions. Right now, her future was as dark and foreboding as the gloomy winter morning outside her window. Going to Hunter would please her parents to no end, but it would also condemn her to a life without fulfillment. And every time she thought of Hunter, she couldn't help but think of Ethan and wonder what had happened.

The hurt and anxiety wore on Caelyn but she refused to be drawn back into the darkness of depression. Still, her emotions were raw, and the pain was profound. And she had no one to whom she could confide. Feeling more alone than she had ever felt in her life, she took a seat on the chest at the foot of her bed, placed her face in her hands, and sobbed. It was a cleansing cry. A way to release the pain and to purge herself of pity. When she could cry no more, she filled the washstand basin and soaked her face with a wet cloth. Feeling better, she started toward the closet in search of a dress to wear but a knock at her door stopped her.

"Go away," she said, not wanting anyone to know that she had been crying.

A soft, boyish voice answered.

"I can't, ma'am."

"Why not?" Caelyn shot back in irritation.

"Because pop said not to come back to the kitchen until I give you this coffee."

"Wesley?" Caelyn asked. "Is that you?" Wesley was the ten-year-old son of the Canady's butler. Though she felt bad at having snapped at him, she still wished he would leave.

"Yes ma'am. May I come in?"

"Yes, of course," she said, not wanting the boy to get in trouble.

The boy entered the room carrying a cup of coffee on a small silver tray balanced in one hand above his shoulder. Trying his best to look professional, he took great care transferring the tray to the night table beside the bed.

"Thank you, Wesley," Caelyn said. "Tell me, why are you serving this morning?"

"Johnny...I mean, Mister Reese and his wife are both sick, so pop said I needed to come help out. Can you believe it, Miss Canady? I'm going to serve at the party tonight!"

Wesley's enthusiasm made Caelyn smile. He was a bright lad with the potential to rise above his station if given the opportunity. His father, Wesley Bryant Sr., brought him to live in the servant's quarters after his mother passed away giving birth. The closest thing to maternal love Wesley had ever known was Caelyn. Though the servants would come and go, she was the only female in his life who had always been there. But even at ten years of age, he understood the invisible wall between the servant and those who are served. They shared their friendship secretly, to prevent Caelyn's parents from overreacting as they had with Annie, the servant's daughter from years ago.

"Pop has even found a uniform my size, and it looks just like his. I'll be able to see you tonight when Mister Winslow..." Seeing the hurt in Caelyn's face, he stopped in mid-sentence.

"What's the matter?" he asked. Then he saw the redness in her eyes. "You've been crying, haven't you?"

The compassion in the boy's voice made Caelyn feel ashamed at ever having felt sorry for herself. She had been born with every advantage in life and wanted for nothing. Wesley's lot in life, while not hopeless, was almost the complete opposite of her own. And yet, she could never remember seeing him unhappy.

"Wes, I'm afraid I've made a terrible mistake," Caelyn said, giving in to the moment. He was a child, but he was the only person in the house with whom she could confide. "I met a man on the Outer Banks. It's a long story, but I fell in love with him. And though it would seem that he doesn't want me anymore, I refuse to believe it unless I hear him say it. Part of me feels like a fool, and yet another part of me has to know."

Caelyn watched the boy process her dilemma, impressed that he would consider his reply so carefully.

"You know," he said, "pop always says that I'm going to make decisions on my own some day. Hard decisions. And he says that when those times come, I need to remember one thing...never make a choice that will hold me back, because I'll never be happy if I do."

Caelyn knew Wesley was very intelligent, but had never considered he might have inherited his intellect from his father. The senior Wesley, denied opportunities to better his own life, was doing everything he could to save his son from the same fate.

"Your father is a very smart man," Caelyn said. "And I shall heed his advice. Now, you need to run on back downstairs or he will think that you are loafing."

"Yes ma'am," he said, though his eyes showed he didn't want to leave.

"Wes," Caelyn said as he started toward the door. "Thank you. I really do feel better now."

The big smile that spread across the boy's face warmed Caelyn's heart and made her more determined than ever.

Perhaps this won't be such a bad day after all, she thought as he disappeared into the hallway.

For Wesley, the exchange planted a seed that would live in his heart forever. Praise from Caelyn was like gold to a pauper. He spent the rest of the day reliving their exchange over and over. With each recounting, the "man from the Outer Banks" became more reviled and more responsible for Caelyn's heartache and unhappiness. And at the end of each recounting, Wesley made a vow to himself in the chivalrous manner of boys who long to be men.

"One day when I'm grown up, I'm going to find him and make him sorry for what he has done."

Chapter Thirty-Six

Trek of Darkness

It was almost midday on the twenty-fourth when Ethan and Danny arrived in New York City. The station was a sea of people rushing to make their trains on time. The two Outer Bankers picked their way through the crowd until they found a porter willing to pause long enough to recommend an affordable hotel.

After an hour's walk from the station, they arrived at the Englewood Arms. The hotel had once been a prominent destination for travelers but its glory days were long passed. On the upside, it was still a clean place to stay. Judged by Outer Banks standards, it was luxurious beyond imagination.

Dressed in a well-cut suit, the desk clerk who checked them in raised an eyebrow when they indicated they wanted to share a room. Guests who doubled up were yet another sign of how far the Arms had declined. And judging by the looks of the pale-faced man with a bandage wrapped around his head and the roughly clad young man with him, the hotel's caliber of clients was slipping even more.

Upon entering their room, Danny began checking out the amenities, but Ethan threw his pack on the bed and headed back out the door.

"Where're you going?" the young waterman asked.

Ethan turned to look at Danny and leaned against the doorframe. It was all he could do to stand, but he wasn't about to stop.

"It was something Capt. Sullivan said back at Ocracoke. He said that the Canadys were hosting a Christmas Eve party. That's tonight."

"You planning on busting up their party?" Danny asked.

"No," Ethan said. He wasn't sure what he was going to do once he got there, but he had to go.

"What, then?" Danny pushed.

"Tonight's the night that Winslow fellow is supposed to propose to her."

"I see," Danny said. "But I gotta say, you don't look so good. I'm not sure you can make it there on your own, much less make it back."

Instead of answering, Ethan pushed away from the doorframe and stepped into the hall.

"All right then," Danny said, grabbing his hat and coat. "Let's get started."

Ethan gave the waterman a cross look when he caught up but didn't have the strength to argue. Stopping at the front desk, he asked the clerk for directions to Caelyn's neighborhood. Hearing the name, the man furrowed his eyebrows, wondering why such an unlikely pair would be headed to one of the city's nicest areas. But like the good clerk he was, he drew them a map without asking questions and sent them on their way.

On exiting the hotel, the two Outer Bankers discovered that the snow had slowed the city to a standstill. Last-minute Christmas shoppers crowded the sidewalks and negotiating the slippery lanes took great effort. Every step Ethan took robbed him of precious strength. Coming to a trolley station, they boarded a streetcar and rode as far as they could, but the last stop left them far from their destination. Though they tried to hail a Hansom, the driver of the electric cab glowered at the rough-looking pair as he drove on by. Even a cabbie hoping for a last-minute fare before Christmas wouldn't chance to stop for two men who looked more prone to skipping out than paying.

It was long past dark when the exertion of walking along the slippery sidewalks forced Ethan to stop.

"You all right?" Danny asked.

"Yeah...I'll be...OK," Ethan said between labored breaths. Though his body was numb from the cold and his head was pounding, he couldn't stop now. Time was running out. One way or another, he had to find out what had happened to Caelyn and the truth about marrying Hunter. Grasping the collar of his coat, he pulled it tighter and took a deep breath.

"Let's go," he said, forcing himself to resume walking as fast as he could.

Danny fell in beside him, matching his pace.

Chapter Thirty-Seven

Ghosts of Christmas

From the top of the stairway, Caelyn could hear that the party was well underway. Laughter ebbed and flowed as various groups of well-wishers enjoyed good stories or ridiculed those unlucky enough not to be invited. Her father and Dorothy had somehow immersed themselves into entertaining their friends, though they knew that at some point during the evening, the truth would become apparent.

That neither of them badgered her about the situation surprised Caelyn. She was sure her father would try to make her feel guilty or obligated and Dorothy would beg her to change her mind about Hunter. But they never did. It seemed the parents she had always known no longer existed. It was not at all like them to be so understanding.

Taking a deep breath, she forced herself to smile and descended the stairs. As she came into view, the guests grew silent and everyone turned to look. She wore a finely embroidered, full-length white dress with a collar rising under her chin. Although she had pinned her hair up, its lustrous copper color remained undiminished. It was both the blessing and the curse of her life that she was beautiful. Her entry into a room would never go unnoticed.

"Merry Christmas, dear," Jack Canady said as his daughter came to the foot of the stairs. He held out his arm, and she accepted it. "Ladies and gentlemen," he said, addressing the room, "I present to you my beautiful...and eligible...daughter, Miss Caelyn Canady."

The guests laughed at Jack's pointed comment as they rendered polite applause to Caelyn. Dumbfounded by her father's remark, Caelyn responded with a guarded smile and wondered why he had alluded to her marital status. There was little doubt that his comment would build expectations. Was there more going on here than met the eye?

"Maestro," Jack said to the leader of the small ensemble he had hired, "please, something festive, if you will." As the band began to play, the guests resumed their conversations.

"Well," Jack said, turning back to his daughter, "you are quite lovely tonight. If you don't watch out, you just might become engaged despite yourself."

The waggish comment both surprised and confused Caelyn. Her father's playful attitude may have been a noble gesture, but why would he joke about something he knew she would rather not discuss?

"Jack!" a voice called out. Caelyn looked toward the main entryway to see that Hunter Winslow had arrived. Handing his overcoat to the doorman, he gave a cheery wave to his host and motioned for him to come over. Excusing himself, Jack negotiated his way across the banquet room, leaving Caelyn to mingle with the guests on her own.

As her father stepped away, several of the nearby guests moved in to fill the void. Everyone speaking to her wanted to know about her recent adventure and how awful it must have been.

"Did you think you were going to drown?"

"How did you survive the sharks?"

"Is it true the people on the Outer Banks live like peasants?"

"Did you see any Indians?"

"Was there anything to eat besides fish? It's a wonder you didn't starve."

"Did the men leer at you? I've heard that they have no women there."

"I read that two brothers from Ohio flew a machine in the air...can you imagine?"

Caelyn answered each of their questions, feigning interest as best she could. Several times during the evening, she caught Hunter glancing at her as he talked with the other guests. His expression was neither a leer nor a vengeful stare. Hunter, it seemed, was content to let the night unfold, even though their peers would shame him as well. For a moment, she wondered if Hunter might have arranged for an embarrassing turnabout to be committed against her, then dismissed the idea. His compassion toward her had been too sincere to believe he would hurt her that way.

Thus, it went throughout the evening until the midnight hour drew near, the time when most of the guests would begin bidding farewell. Caelyn sensed the restlessness of those who were there to witness a momentous announcement. The clock would soon strike twelve and the guests would realize there would be no announcement. That's when the goodwill would end and the speculation would begin.

Lost in her thoughts about the unpleasantness that was about to begin, Caelyn did not see Hunter winding through the crowd to stand next to her.

"Come," he said with a soft smile as he took her arm. But Caelyn pulled back, uncertain of his intent.

"Trust me," he whispered.

Seeing no mischief in his eyes, she gave in and let him guide her to a bank of huge arched windows that dominated the front of the Canady's mansion. Staking out a spot in front of the center-most window, the guests closed in to form a semi-circle around them.

After handing Caelyn a glass of champagne someone had strategically placed on the window's broad sill, he picked up a second one and lifted it to the crowd. Certain now that she had made a mistake, Caelyn felt the room collapsing in on her. She was trapped.

"In the season's spirit, I would like to say a few words about life, salvation, and new beginnings." Hunter paused for a moment to survey the room, making sure he had everyone's full attention. "As I am sure most of you know, we are very fortunate to have Caelyn with us here tonight. As incredible as it sounds, less than two weeks ago she almost lost her life. A terrible explosion destroyed Caelyn's beloved yacht, the *Aphrodite*, because of circumstances still not fully understood. By the grace of God, she survived.

"But her ordeal did not end there," Hunter Continued. "What many of you may not know is that Caelyn then found herself cast upon the open sea in a lifeboat with few provisions, no way to maneuver, and worse, trapped with an injured man who required her constant attention. Having survived a most horrendous shipwreck, it looked as though our poor Caelyn would perish within sight of land. But a miracle occurred in the form of two fishermen who happened upon her and brought her safely back to land. Though we didn't know it then, Caelyn was safe at last.

"But the story does not end there, ladies and gentlemen. No, indeed, because Caelyn was still far from home. For the next few days she lived with the locals, then traveled by small boat through the backwaters of the Outer Banks until she came to stay at Kitty Hawk. During this time, she had more adventure than most people have in a lifetime. In fact, I know with certainty that her experiences have changed her forever...and that is the 'new beginning' I wanted to speak to you about.

"First, I think we should all give Caelyn a hand for making it back to us alive and unharmed."

Whispers of affirmation mixed with the muffled sounds of gloved hands clapping their appreciation. Caelyn's face turned red at being the center of such attention. Hunter had placed her atop a pedestal she did not deserve. It was the last thing she had expected, yet she still feared his intentions.

"Thank you," Hunter said, quieting the guests. "But, as I said before. This Caelyn. The Caelyn you just welcomed back is not the same Caelyn we knew before her mishap.

The truth is, none of us know the person you now see standing beside me. You don't know her, and neither do I."

Caelyn's face flushed red again, this time from fear. Having allowed herself to be put atop the pedestal, there was nothing she could do now but wait for it to be kicked out from under her.

"No, my friends, this Caelyn is nothing like the person we used to know." Hunter turned to look her in the eyes. "Although she is just as beautiful," he said more softly, "this Caelyn is much wiser and more feeling than the Caelyn I used to know. She sees the world as a much bigger place and understands her own potential within it. Her dreams are bigger and broader and her heart knows no limits. She has been given a second chance, and she does not intend to let it go to waste. And who can blame her?

"That is why I wanted to say in front of you, our friends, that I look forward to getting to know this new Caelyn. For she is more of a woman now than she ever was before. And if she someday decides she loves me, I look forward to standing in front of you again to announce our engagement. In the meantime, I want her to know I love her more now than I did before, and I will be here for her, no matter what."

Moved by Hunter's sincerity, the gathering of friends and family applauded again. It had been a beautiful tribute – almost a proposal – but not quite. Instead of gossiping about an engagement that didn't happen, the guests were talking about the warm welcome home Hunter had given Caelyn and the wonderful things he had said about her. It had been a clever sleight of hand.

Caelyn was stunned. She understood the shrewd maneuver for what it was and appreciated what Hunter had done. He had expressed his feelings for her in a way that allowed both families to save face. He had averted social disaster.

The guests were still applauding as Jack stepped forward to stand beside his daughter.

"Ladies and gentlemen," he said, raising his glass. "A toast to my beautiful daughter in honor of her safe return! If you please..."

Though embarrassed at being the center of attention, Caelyn was relieved everything had turned out well. Raising the glass to her lips, she joined in the toast.

At least it's over, she told herself.

As she sipped from her flute she saw Dorothy's willowy form emerge from the crowd holding something in her hand. A moment later she was standing beside Caelyn, holding the object over her stepdaughter's head.

"Look everyone," Dorothy said with too much glee. "Mistletoe! After such a wonderful evening, I think these two should share a kiss for us, don't you?"

"Yes! Hear, hear!" the guests pleaded.

It was at that moment Caelyn realized it was her parents who had contrived the evening's events. More than an attempt to save face, they were trying to reunite her with Hunter. And though she did not want to kiss him, neither did she want to embarrass him. He didn't deserve that. Her parents, however, were a different matter – one she would deal with later.

Suppressing her anger, she faced Hunter and closed her eyes. Placing his hands on her upper arms, he pulled her closer and kissed her softly. It wasn't a passionate kiss, nor was it long, but Caelyn thought it would never end.

A ripple of approving remarks and fawning comments passed through the gathering. One by one they began to clap until the entire crowd was once again applauding the attractive couple. It was the perfect ending to a beautiful evening.

As the clock in the hall began chiming the midnight hour, the band struck up an upbeat song to match the mood and everyone began talking. A friend put his arm on Hunter's shoulder and led him off in conversation. Her father and step-mother mingled with well-wishers.

Thankful to be left to herself, Caelyn turned away from the revelers to look out the window into the cold winter night. It had been an evening of mixed blessings. Although it was now clear that her parents were still trying to manipulate her into a relationship with Hunter, she couldn't fault them. And Hunter continued to be a gentleman about the matter, showing more sensitivity and patience than she ever thought he would have possessed.

These are all good things, she argued to herself. *But they are nothing compared to what I had...what I thought I had...with Ethan.*

Catching her reflection in the glass, she moved closer to the window. A blanket of snow already covered the grounds as still more of the heavy white flakes continued to fall. Dark, leafless trees juxtaposed against the stark white background gave her home an otherworldly feel. For a moment, she wished she could disappear into the night and the falling snow.

Movement on the other side of the snow-covered road caught her eye. Illuminated by the light of a street lamp, she saw two men walking away from the house and into the darkness. Somehow, they looked familiar, though she wasn't sure why. Then, with a jolt of irrational hope, she realized the two figures reminded her of Ethan and Danny. But forced to concede that such a thing couldn't be possible, the surge of uninvited expectation morphed into an unwanted melancholy.

"Oh, if only it were them," she whispered to herself. The pleasant thought of a surprise reunion made her pain even more unbearable. Placing her forehead against the cool glass, she couldn't stop her eyes from watering. A tear traced down her cheek.

A soft tug on her sleeve pulled her back to the moment. Wiping her eye with the back of her hand, she looked down to see young Wesley Bryant smartly dressed in servant's attire.

"Are you OK, Miss Caelyn? I saw you looking out the window, and I thought maybe you were... Well...you looked sad."

"Thank you, Wesley," she said. She gave the boy a hug, but it was more for herself than him. "I'm all right...really."

Hoping that no one else had seen her, she turned to take one last look out of the window. The two men had disappeared into the falling snow.

"What do you see out there?" Wesley asked, not convinced that she had spoken the truth.

"Nothing," Caelyn sighed. "Nothing but the ghost of Christmases that might have been."

Chapter Thirty-Eight

False Truth

It was after eleven o'clock by the time Ethan and Danny found the magnificent house where Caelyn lived. Ethan's condition had continued to worsen and it appeared as though he would collapse any moment. Several times Danny had stopped and tried to talk his friend into going back, but Ethan would have none of it. Now that they were no longer moving, the cold had become unbearable.

"If there was an announcement I bet we missed it, given how late it is," Danny said through shivering teeth.

Ethan responded with silence, dashing the young waterman's hope Ethan would come to his senses and go back to the hotel. The surfman hadn't traveled all this way just to give up. He would know the truth this night or freeze to death while trying.

After waiting almost an hour, they saw Caelyn and Hunter come to stand in front of one of the great windows comprising the mansion's front elevation. With the downstairs flooded in light, they could see every detail.

Ethan watched in stony silence as Caelyn took center stage with Hunter Winslow. Though the urge to burst into the house and take her away was overwhelming, a small but dying voice of reason held him back. Seeing Caelyn raise a glass in a toast with Hunter, his desire to be with her turned to jealousy. When they kissed, he felt nothing. Beyond Caelyn, there was nothing. Nothing to grasp on to or to believe in, and he only had himself to blame for making it that way.

But, even as he accepted this truth, another emerged. He loved Caelyn more than his own life and he always would. The war's agony and Zeb's death finally let go of its grip on his soul, replaced by lasting pain of a broken heart.

A church in the distance began chiming the midnight hour. Ethan turned without saying a word and walked away. He would subject himself to no more torture. Danny caught up with him but said nothing. Words would mean nothing at this point. Upon the last stroke of the hour, the church bells began clanging out the arrival of Christmas morning. The timeless tune proclaimed its wish unto an oblivious world, "peace on earth, goodwill to men."

The irony of the sentiment caught Ethan off guard, and for a moment, he wondered if he might be wrong. Stopping, he turned to look at the house one last time.

She must have loved me, he thought, *even if it was only for a moment. That has to mean something.*

Chapter Thirty-Nine

The Abyss

For Danny, the return trip to the Englewood was a labor befitting Sisyphus. Already on the brink of collapse, the surfman's broken heart wicked away what little strength remained. Despite his own fatigue, Danny helped Ethan through the snow-covered streets, nearly dragging the stout lifesaver to the next place that provided shelter to rest. The young waterman was certain that had he not been along to help, Ethan would have sat on the curb, never to move again.

Dawn was breaking when they made it to the hotel. After helping Ethan out of his damp, frozen clothes and putting him to bed, Danny laid down and fell asleep as soon as his head hit the pillow. In what seemed like only a few minutes later, a shout from across the room startled the young waterman awake.

"Zeb!" Ethan cried out again. "Answer me! I'm coming for you! Hold on, man!"

Realizing Ethan was having a nightmare, Danny got up and placed another blanket over the surfman. When it seemed Ethan was OK, Danny returned to his bed. But sleep would not come. He spent most of the night listening to the lifesaver thrash about on his bed and calling out to people from his past. But it was Caelyn's name that Danny heard most often, and in the most pitiful way. Danny understood the surfman was exposing a part of himself he would have preferred to keep private. The burden of keeping it private wasn't something he had wanted, but Danny vowed he would never speak of the surfman's moments of weakness to anyone – not even Ethan.

The boy, who was becoming a man, continued to look after his friend for the rest of the day and into the night. When morning broke the next day and Ethan refused to wake up, the young waterman decided it was time to seek help. Then, just as he was walking out the door to go in search of a doctor, Ethan came to.

"Danny!" he called, not sure where he was. "Where are you? I need your help."

Saying a silent prayer of thanks, the young waterman came back inside and helped the lifesaver sit up in his bed. After drinking several glasses of water, Danny gave him an apple and some soda crackers to eat, food he had brought to their room for just this purpose. Famished, the surfman wolfed the snacks down in a matter of seconds.

"More," Ethan said. "I need more food."

Danny returned from the dining room with a tray of soup and sandwiches and was surprised to find the surfman gone. After searching the common areas, he left the hotel and began looking inside the nearby bars and taverns that were so prevalent in the area. When night came and he still hadn't found him, Danny had a new thought – and his heart sank. *Perhaps Ethan had returned to Caelyn's house.*

If so, there was nothing the waterman could do about it, at least not tonight. Returning to the hotel, he hurried to their room hoping Ethan might have returned – but the room was empty – the cold soup and sandwiches uneaten.

Sometime after midnight, someone flung open the door to with a loud BANG! Thinking that someone had broken in, Danny jumped out of bed and grabbed a chair to swing. But the person standing in the doorway, illuminated by the light from the hallway, was Ethan.

"Thank God you're OK," Danny said, putting the chair down.

"God had nothing to do with it," Ethan said, slurring his words. He took a swig from a bottle of bourbon the boy hadn't noticed before.

More than his state of drunkenness, it was the bitterness lacing the surfman's words that disturbed Danny the most. He was all too familiar with the Hyde-like effects alcohol could have on the Jekyll's of the world. The scars on his body from the blows his drunken uncle had once administered were proof.

Retreating to the far corner of the room, he settled to the floor with his back wedged into the crook where the walls met. He knew it would do no good to talk to the surfman while he was drunk. And though grateful no violence had occurred, he was prepared to protect himself if necessary.

As if in answer to a prayer, Ethan collapsed into his bed and was asleep in moments. Relieved, Danny took the bottle from his hand and placed it on the nightstand. Returning to his own bed, he hoped that the day's binge would be enough to purge the surfman's most bitter pain, but he somehow knew there was more to come.

Ethan awakened late in the afternoon of the next day and started where he had left off. After downing the rest of the bourbon Danny had regrettably left on the nightstand, the lifesaver started for the door. The young waterman tried to stop him, to talk to him, but the surfman cursed him and told him to mind his own business. Rather than face another day of waiting alone, Danny followed him and discovered that the surfman had found a seedy tavern down a dark alley that seemed to specialize in cheap booze and a clientele that proved it. He couldn't do anything to help his friend but at least he now knew where to find him.

When Ethan returned from his third night of drinking, Danny knew he had to do something or the surfman was going to kill himself. Working up the courage to use a telephone for the first time in his life, he went to the hotel's lobby and rang up the operator. A few minutes later, she connected him to the lifesaving station on Fire Island and his story came out in a flood of words. At first, the keeper was reluctant to believe the young man who spoke with a curious accent. But when Danny mentioned Superintendent Collins and several of the keepers on the Outer Banks by name, the keeper realized the plea for help was real. Every surfman in the service knew about Ethan Roberts and his heroic rescue of the *Priscilla*'s crew.

Early the next morning brought a knock on the door of their hotel room. Danny hurried to answer and, to his relief, found three Fire Island surfmen had arrived to help. A pungent mix of body odor, vomit, and sour whiskey hit the men as they entered. The room was a disheveled mess of dirty linens, empty bottles, and festering garbage.

Though Danny managed to wake Ethan, it was obvious the Hatteras surfman was still drunk. As he struggled to sit up, the three Fire Island lifesavers couldn't believe that the man they saw had ever been an able-bodied surfman. He was gaunt and pale, and his three-day beard gave him the appearance of an old man. The soiled bandage around his head needed changing – his hair, greasy and matted.

Upon seeing the three surfmen, Ethan became belligerent. Cursing Danny, he threw an empty bottle of whiskey at the Fire Island lifesavers as they closed in. A wild but brief melee followed, ending with the three surfmen pinning Ethan down on his bed. Shocked by the roughness the men had to employ to keep the Hatteras surfman under control, Danny hoped he hadn't made a mistake.

"Give in, man!" the brawny lifesaver in charge said as Ethan struggled to break free. "You won't change anything by killing yourself. If nothing else, think about your mates back at Hatteras. They're depending on you to come back and help them rescue more ships and sailors. From what I've heard, they need you down there. You're not going to let your mates down, now, are you?"

Appealing to Ethan's pride was the only lifeline the Fire Island surfman had to throw to Ethan. It took a minute for the challenge to filter through but his pride won out in the end.

The three days of drinking, food deprivation, and self-pity had taken their toll. He was exhausted and tired of beating himself up over everything that had happened. The idea of taking an oar in hand and losing himself in a rescue had the ring of familiarity that he needed now. Closing his eyes, he took a deep breath and ceased struggling. The surfmen released their hold and stepped back, waiting to see what he would do.

"All right," Ethan said, hanging his head in defeat. "You win. I need to get back to Hatteras. I'm...I'm sorry you had to come here to do this."

"No need to apologize to us," the leader of the Fire Island lifesavers replied. "Surfmen stick together."

"But you do need to thank this one," he continued, nodding toward Danny. "We wouldn't be here if it weren't for him. I think the lad's got the makings of a surfman – if you can find a spot for him."

Ethan nodded in agreement but offered no comment. It would be too easy to say he would help Danny. Given his condition, his word had no standing with these men, and making promises was for men who did not know how to take action.

The three Fire Island surfmen waited for Danny to check out of the hotel and then escorted them to the train station. Waiting until Danny and Ethan were boarding a passenger car to say goodbye, they remained on the platform as the train pulled away just in case Ethan changed his mind. It wasn't until they had traveled beyond the city's tall buildings and crowded streets that Danny breathed easier. Home was hundreds of miles and days away, but at least they were heading in the right direction.

Chapter Forty

Abigale's Heart

"Oh my word!" Lottie Mae said when she saw Ethan. "Look at you...a walking cadaver would have more life...and smell better, too."

"Abbie!" she shouted over her shoulder. "Get a bath ready for Surfman Roberts. I can't have him sleeping in one of our beds smelling like this."

The further south they traveled, the more Danny had feared for Ethan's health. Though cut off from alcohol, the surfman's binging had started a downward spiral that showed no signs of stopping. After making the crossing from Elizabeth City to Kitty Hawk, Danny made a beeline to Lottie Mae's inn.

The moment she saw Ethan, Mae knew he was once again at death's door. The hollowness in his eyes was something she had seen before. It was the look of a dying man who had accepted the inevitable.

Once bathed and settled into a room, Lottie Mae worked every minute, making sure he was eating, drinking, and resting. But, most of all, she made sure there was always someone with him. Having free time to think about his loss would be a dangerous thing. But thankfully, that problem soon resolved itself.

That he had returned without Caelyn was a source of great curiosity and excitement for Abbie. The young woman began coming to his room every chance she could, at first bringing him food the cook prepared and later, bringing food she prepared herself. When he began coming downstairs to eat, she made sure she was always within the sound of his voice, never allowing him to want for anything.

Though Ethan was always pleasant toward her, and even enjoyed her company, he never responded the way she wanted him to. His failure to return her attention, however, did not stop her from telling her many suitors that she was too busy to spend time with them.

"It's not that they aren't nice boys," she told Lottie Mae. "But that's all they are...just boys. I know what it is I want now."

"Abigail," Lottie Mae warned, "be careful you're not setting yourself up for a broken heart. You know and I know that Surfman Roberts is not interested in sparking with you...or anybody else, for that matter. He'll be pining for that lady in New York for a long time."

"Missus Mae," Abbie said with a sigh, "I know Ethan doesn't want me. Yet. He's got too much Caelyn on his mind. But after seeing him and talking with him and getting to know him, well, I know what it is I want in a man. And if it's not him, I won't like it, but I'll be all right. You see, even though he already has half my heart, I'm keeping the other half locked in a box until such time he sees me instead of her. But, now that I know what I know, I'm going to stick with him until there's no hope. And if that happens, then I'll wait until someone comes along that's more like him than not. I won't settle for anything less. Is that such a bad thing?"

Lottie Mae raised an eyebrow, surprised by Abbie's newfound maturity. She understood what the girl was trying to say. Her husband had been a lot like Ethan. Such men were hard to find and even harder to forget.

"No, Abbie, it's not. In fact, that's about the most sensible thing I've ever heard you say. You hold out for what you're looking for, you deserve it. Only, don't be too broken-hearted if this one doesn't work out. You keep a firm grip on the key to that box, you hear?"

Chapter Forty-One

Hell

The light of the January sun shining through the window was muted by the drawn shade, giving everything in Dr. Jennings' study a warm, reddish-brown hue. The effect should have been soothing, but Caelyn couldn't stop fidgeting. She had come to this house many times since she had been a little girl and had never felt uncomfortable.

But this visit was different. She almost hadn't come, it being Saturday and the cause of her visit being of a medical nature. The appropriate thing to do would have been to wait until Monday and visit him at his office – but she couldn't wait that long. She had to know now.

"Well, let's see what we've got here," Dr. Jennings said, ambling back into the room at last.

Though his hair was white, his bushy eyebrows remained the jet black of his youth. Combined with the wire-rimmed glasses sitting atop his large hooked nose, he looked like an owl. He flipped through several papers held in place by a clipboard as he spoke, focusing on none of them.

Eschewing the imposing formal chair behind his cluttered desk, the doctor eased into the matching leather chair next to Caelyn's. Coming to a decision, he placed the clipboard on his desk and looked at her.

"There's no need for me to hide behind props, we've known each other too long for that. And given that we both know why you're really here, I won't beat around the bush. Caelyn...it will take a couple of weeks to know for sure, but based on almost forty years of practice, I'm certain your symptoms are caused by a pregnancy. Now, I know this can't be good news for you, but you've got to believe that things will work out...somehow."

Already having surmised that she was with child did nothing to lessen the blow. The future she faced would not be easy under any circumstances. She was unmarried and pregnant. That the father was not Hunter would make her sin unforgivable. Once everyone discovered the father was a commoner living in the wilds of the Outer Banks, they would scorn, ridicule, and humiliate her. The old-money patricians of New York would point to her condition as proof her family wasn't worthy of acceptance. For Caelyn, such rejection would be an annoyance. For her father – who had worked his entire life to gain entry into their vaunted circle – it would be devastating. That the sordid situation would bring an end to their reconciliation was a certainty. And that, more than anything at the moment, was what hurt Caelyn.

"Come now, my young friend," Dr. Jennings said, patting her hand. "Things will work out. I truly believe that. You know why? Because I know you. You are one of the strongest women I have ever known. You are an intelligent, caring person, and I know you will survive this. You just have to believe in yourself."

The doctor paused for a moment. One of Caelyn's greatest strengths was her capacity to care about others. Making her think about someone other than herself might be the best way to reach her.

"You know," he said in a low, almost conspiratorial voice, "there are people, physicians I know, who can fix problems like this. I could talk to one of them...if you'd like."

Caelyn pondered the question for a minute, trying to grasp his meaning. As it became clear, she became queasy. Abortion was an option she had not considered. Having never seen herself as a person who would become pregnant out of wedlock, she had never given the concept any thought. Nor had she ever given serious thought to whether it was right or wrong. What she did know was that the mental images of the procedure's results made her sick. For that reason alone, she could never allow anyone to invade her body or harm her baby.

"No," she said. The internal strife had left her drained and shaken. "I can't do that. It was my mistake. I will pay the price."

"Good," Dr. Jennings said, relieved that she was still willing to see beyond herself. "I know it will not be easy, but I will help you in every way I can. I think one day you will see that the price you speak of will not be nearly as high as you imagine. You know, good can come from this, if you give it a chance."

Dr. Jennings spent the next half hour going over the things she should expect to happen during the coming weeks, but there were too many thoughts going through Caelyn's mind to focus. When he finished, she promised to come back in four weeks and said goodbye. But rather than go home, she wandered aimlessly through the neighborhood, trying to make sense of things. The more she thought about it, the more she kept coming back to Ethan and his betrayal.

If he had been honest, we would be facing my pregnancy together, she argued to herself. *This could have been the most wonderful time of our lives. Was he misleading me the whole time, or did he change his mind after I left? Then again, did he really change his mind?*

The question became more compelling with each passing moment. After all, she had not spoken to him that day in her father's office. Neither had Miss Stanford, for that matter.

As she thought about it more, she remembered how quick her father had been to support her at Ocracoke. And wasn't it convenient how he had arranged for their telephone call to take place in his office? Had that been part of a bigger plan? Wasn't it funny how Hunter always seemed to show up at the right time and know the right things to say?

Then a new, more sobering thought took hold.

What if Ethan had tried to call me, but hadn't gotten through for some reason? What if he believed it was me? That I had changed MY mind?

Was the idea someone had duped them both plausible, or just a desperate woman's wishful thinking? There was only one way to know for sure. And this time she would do it without the help of her father.

Hurrying home, she rushed to the study and closed the doors. With trembling hands, she picked up the telephone's handset and asked the operator to connect her to the Hatteras Lifesaving Station.

"I'm sorry," the operator said after a few moments. "They're telling me that the line is down. Must have been a storm or something."

"Oh," Caelyn said, her heart sinking. It could take a long time to make repairs, and she was desperate to know the answers to her questions now.

"Operator. See if you can reach a place called Lottie Mae's at Kitty Hawk. That's on a different island than Cape Hatteras. Closer to the mainland. Maybe you can still get through to there."

If there is one person on the Outer Banks who might be able to help me, it will be Lottie Mae, Caelyn thought. *She understood what was going on between us, and if anything had happened to Ethan, she would know.*

Seconds passed like eons but the operator finally came back on the line.

"I'm connecting you to Lottie Mae's," she said. The phone clicked several times, followed by the crackling and whistling sounds of static – and then, a person's voice.

"Hello," Abbie said. She had been working at the front desk when the telephone mounted on the wall by the desk rang.

"This is a call from New York City," the operator said. "Go ahead, please."

"Hello," Abbie said again, gripping the candlestick earpiece harder. "Can I help you?"

"Yes," said the feminine voice through the earpiece. "This is Caelyn Canady in New York. I stayed at your inn for a few days just before Christmas. I'm trying to reach the owner. Is she in?"

Abbie's heart raced faster, realizing her worst fear.

"I'm sorry," she forced herself to say. "Lottie Mae's not here right now. Can I take a message?"

"Abbie?" Caelyn was sure she recognized the young woman's voice. "You remember me, don't you? How are you?"

"Oh, Miss Canady...yes, I'm fine."

"Abbie, I need to get in touch with Surfman Roberts. Do you know where I might reach him? He did go back to the Hatteras Station, didn't he?"

"Actually, no, he didn't," Abbie said. The disappointment on her face would have been pitiful had there been anyone around to see. "The truth is, Surfman Roberts...Ethan...is still here."

"What?" Caelyn gasped. If Ethan was still at Kitty Hawk, everything her father had told her was a lie. "Is he close by? Can you get him to come to the telephone?"

The pause that followed was so long, Caelyn wondered if the call had disconnected.

"I'm sorry," Abbie said at last, her voice crackling with uncertainty. "I don't think that would be appropriate."

That's an odd reply, Caelyn thought. *Something isn't right.*

"I don't understand. Why not, Abbie?"

"Because..." she answered, pausing to gather her courage. She had never told an out and out lie in her life. "Because...he's married."

"Married?" Caelyn asked in disbelief. "Married...to whom?"

Abbie drew in a deep, silent breath.

"To me."

The revelation pierced Caelyn's heart and took her breath away. Too ashamed and hurt to speak, she placed the earpiece back in its cradle. The sliver of hope she had been clinging to, had, in reality, been a vine of poisonous thorns. She could no longer deny the inevitability of her difficult future. A future she would face alone.

"How can this be?" she said aloud. "What could have changed him so quickly? To fall in love with another woman? How could I have been so wrong...about everything?"

Chapter Forty-Two

Puzzle Box

The muted sounds of someone's voice caught Dorothy Canady's ear as she walked past the study. Cracking open the door, she saw her stepdaughter standing by the desk, talking to herself. Had it been anyone else, she would have been concerned. But Caelyn had always seemed peculiar to Dorothy, and nothing her stepdaughter did surprised her anymore.

Dorothy married Jack Canady not long after Caelyn's mother had died. She remembered how much it had bothered her that little Caelyn almost never showed interest in the toys and games that other girls liked. Young Caelyn had spent her time reading, learning about faraway places, and testing her boundaries to see what she could get away with.

Dorothy kept hoping that things would change once her stepdaughter matured. But years went by and nothing changed – until Hunter Winslow had come along. Caelyn's sudden interest in Hunter had been a godsend for Dorothy.

Despite her stepdaughter's total lack of preparation and effort – and being dangerously close to spinster status – she had caught the eye of an eligible bachelor. After years of prodding and cajoling, Caelyn had somehow stumbled onto something right.

Then came the *Aphrodite*. Right from the beginning, she had felt that Caelyn's fascination with that yacht would bring trouble. If Caelyn had not insisted on making that voyage, the absurd affair with the surfman would have never happened. But it had occurred, and it had proven all too embarrassing. Thankfully, Jack had discovered where she was and intervened in time.

But stopping Caelyn from running off to the Outer Banks meant little if they could not figure out a way to reunite her with Hunter. Every step she had taken to push Jack up the social ladder would be meaningless if they could not gain that last vestige of acceptance from New York's elite. If she could only get them back together. Getting Caelyn out of the house would open a pathway to everything she had ever wanted in life.

Catching her stepdaughter at a vulnerable moment might provide the opportunity she needed. Taking a quick breath, she entered the room as though she had no idea anyone was inside.

"Oh, Caelyn, I'm sorry. I didn't realize you were in here."

Instead of replying, Caelyn raised a hand to her forehead in obvious irritation.

"Are you all right?" Dorothy asked, choosing to see the gesture as anguish. "What's wrong, dear?"

Though they had never been close, they had always tolerated one another. Under ordinary circumstances, Dorothy would have taken the hint and left her stepdaughter alone. But this time, she sensed the need to push ahead or lose the opportunity to break through Caelyn's defenses.

"Come, dear," Dorothy said, placing a hand on Caelyn's shoulder. "I know that you've never looked at me as a mother, but I've always tried to be here for you if you needed me. Something has happened, hasn't it?"

Worn down by the day's torrent of bad news, and not having anyone else to confide in, Caelyn gave in.

"I went to visit Doctor Jennings today," she said without looking up. "He told me I am with child."

Dorothy was too stunned to respond. There was no doubt who the father was, a fact that meant there would be no chance of reuniting Caelyn with Hunter. Or would it?

Like a Japanese puzzle box with multiple pieces that must be pressed at the same time to reveal the secret, Dorothy suddenly saw the solution to her lifelong quest. The Winslow family existed in the rarified air of New York City's bluebloods – but their businesses were failing and were losing their wealth. And though Hunter's love for Caelyn was true, marrying a woman with almost unlimited resources was an undeniable part of the attraction. Their mutual needs had been the brew that made the union so perfect. The Winslows would have the Canady's wealth to prop up their business enterprises, while Jack and Dorothy would gain access to the highest rung on the city's social ladder. And now, Hunter had something he could give Caelyn – her child's legitimacy.

"Oh, Caelyn..." Dorothy said. "I am so sorry. You must be sick with worry. You know I will do anything I can for you. Please, dear, tell me all about it."

Dorothy listened to each detail of the visit to Dr. Jennings, making sure she expressed the proper amount of sympathy and concern at the appropriate times. As a woman, she couldn't help but feel sorry for her stepdaughter. She had made a mess of her life and – already taking on the mantle of a protective mother – was desperate to do whatever was necessary to make a good life for her child. But more important, Caelyn had never been this open with her and she wanted to take full advantage of their new relationship. There were more important things at stake than the fate of one bastard child.

"You've certainly endured a lot," Dorothy said when her stepdaughter was done. Given that Caelyn had not included her discovery of Ethan's marriage, her stepmother did not know the full truth of her statement. "But I want you to know that we will be here with you, no matter what."

"We?" Caelyn asked.

"Jack and I, of course. You know we'll have to tell your father."

"Oh, God, I forgot about that. He will hate me now."

"Maybe not," Dorothy said. "Not if you let me break the news to him."

"Do you think so?" Caelyn asked.

"Yes, if you're willing to trust me. I think I can explain it to him in a way he'll understand. I think you'll be surprised at how supportive your father will be. All right?"

"Thank you," Caelyn said, though she both looked and sounded doubtful.

"Now, now, dear," Dorothy said, giving her stepdaughter a hug. "I'll take care of everything...you'll see."

Chapter Forty-Three

False Shepherds

"That son of a bitch should be dead!" Jack Canady said when Dorothy told him about Caelyn's pregnancy.

His wife had no way of knowing that he meant the statement literally. The news of his daughter's condition, combined with having just learned that Ethan still lived, was a one-two punch that left him enraged. He couldn't do anything about the surfman for now, but he could fire Ansel Stick, whom he had put on the payroll after returning to New York. Then, realizing that he couldn't let Stick go because he knew too much, he pounded his fist on the desk in frustration.

"I agree," Dorothy said, placing a calming hand on his fist. "But stop and think about it...this could be an opportunity for us."

"An opportunity? How so?"

"Simple," she said with a wry smile, and then proceeded to explain her thoughts. By the time she was done, Jack

Canady knew his wife was right. His daughter was in an awkward position. She might be more receptive to Hunter if he could be convinced to take Caelyn, despite her condition. He also knew that Dorothy was right about the Winslow's financial misfortunes and he knew what leverage to use to convince Hunter that Caelyn would still make an excellent wife.

Looking at Dorothy, Jack thought about how different she was from Caelyn's mother. *It's strange how things work out sometimes,* he thought. *If Elizabeth had possessed even a little of your ambition and hadn't held on to her damned British scruples so adamantly, perhaps things would not have ended as they had.*

The thought made him remember that a free and independent Caelyn still posed a threat to him. To have her wed a man he could influence and control was the best protection he could hope for, and Hunter was the perfect person for that.

"All right, then," he said, "when should we try to get them back together?"

"As soon as possible. This won't work if he can't convince others the child is his. If they get married right away, it will appear that she had a premature baby."

"In that case, I will meet with Hunter tomorrow. Once I explain how much he stands to gain, I rather suspect he will decide that Caelyn is still worth pursuing. In the meantime, you make sure nothing happens that would cause Caelyn to spoil this."

"Oh, I'll take care of Caelyn," Dorothy said. "She and I are becoming quite friendly these days."

Chapter Forty-Four

A Proposal

Hunter Winslow had always admired Caelyn for her beauty. And he had never doubted that his love for her was sincere or wondered if her family's wealth was part of the attraction. He hadn't had to. He never interpreted the fact she differed from women he considered attractive as a warning sign. It was just the way Quirky Caelyn – as his friends called her – was. Always analyzing things, never adhering to convention, and not caring a whit about keeping up appearances made her stand out in ways beyond her beauty. But her family did have money, and lots of it. More than enough to bring his father's shipping business back to its feet. And as much as it saddened him to have lost her, he considered losing access to her fortune equally unfortunate.

The years of neglecting to invest in modernizing their ships had taken its toll. Now, they were playing catch-up with every other shipping company in North America. They needed more modern freighters to compete, and that required a great deal of capital. Capital that the banks would no longer provide.

Marrying Caelyn would have provided easy access to the funds they needed. And given Caelyn's looks, it wasn't like he would have been making a sacrifice in that regard. But the trip to Kitty Hawk and Caelyn's change of heart had killed that possibility. Or, at least, it had seemed at the time.

When Jack Canady came to him with news of Caelyn's pregnancy, it struck him as sad, but he didn't see what it had to do with him. After all, it wasn't his baby. But nothing had prepared him for the offer Jack made next.

In his pocket, he now carried the answer to all his family's financial problems. It might not be the romantic wedding he had always imagined, but it was a small price to pay for what he was going to receive in exchange. If he married Caelyn, Jack Canady promised to finance any and all investments necessary to rejuvenate his family's shipping business and save him from living the rest of his life as a plebe.

Standing before the Canady's front door awaiting an answer to his knock, he could not believe his good fortune. All he had to do was to convince Caelyn that marrying him was the best thing for them both.

"Good evening, sir," Wesley Bryant the elder said upon opening the door. The butler was surprised to see Hunter carrying a big bouquet of roses. "Mister Canady told me to expect you. May I take your hat and coat?"

"Yes," Hunter said, "and would you please tell Miss Canady that I've come to pay her a visit. Please tell her it is very important I speak to her."

"Yes, right away, sir."

Hunter took inventory of the Canady's home as he waited for Wesley to return. There were many fine sculptures and works of art, and the house itself was worth a fortune. Someday it would all be his, if he played his cards right.

"Miss Canady will see you in the study now, sir," Wesley said, interrupting his thoughts.

He entered the room to find Caelyn sitting close to the same fireplace she had stood next to the night he had eaten dinner with her family. The events of the past few days had taken their toll. She appeared small and lifeless.

"I brought these for you," he said, holding out the flowers. Caelyn continued gazing into the fire, not acknowledging his presence. Hunter placed the flowers on a coffee table and took a seat next to hers.

"Caelyn. I know this will come as a surprise to you, but I know you are... I know about your condition."

Instead of answering, Caelyn's expression went through several changes, revealing surprise, anger, hurt, and disappointment.

"I... I can't believe this," she said at last. "I never would have told Dorothy about being...pregnant had I known she would betray me like this. And to you, of all people!"

"You don't understand, Caelyn. I came here to help you, to–"

"Please, Hunter, go away," she said, cutting him off. "I don't want your pity. And I won't accommodate my stepmother's gossip. I don't know what she is scheming, but I won't be a part of it. Please, just go away."

"Caelyn...you don't understand. I haven't come here to pity you or to gloat over your misfortune. And you need to know that your stepmother just wants–"

"No!" Caelyn said, cutting him off again. "*You* don't understand. I have ruined my life and I continue to put my faith in people who betray me. I know I am a fool, but please leave, and let me keep what little dignity I have left. Can you at least be decent enough to give me that?"

Hunter fell silent, allowing the moment to pass. His one opportunity would be lost before it began if he didn't say the right things. Reaching into his pocket, he pulled out a jewelry box containing the engagement ring he had planned to give her on Christmas Eve. Taking a knee before her, he opened the box.

"Caelyn. I came to ask you for your hand in marriage."

He let the words hang in the air until their full impact permeated the shell surrounding her.

"What?" she asked at last. "No. I don't believe you. This is some kind of cruel joke."

"No," he said, grasping her hand. "It's true. I swear. Caelyn, please listen to me. I don't think you ever realized how deeply I love you. But Dorothy does. And she knew I would want to know about...about what has happened to you. You see, Caelyn, I love you so much I don't care about that. And if marrying you under these circumstances is what it takes to convince you of my sincerity, then so be it. All that matters to me is that you will consent to be my wife. I love you that much."

The crackling of the fire filled the empty spaces of the study, making it appear as if the entire room was ablaze.

"Of all the things that I thought might happen, I never imagined that you would propose to me," Caelyn said. "And despite the suddenness of it all, I fully understand that if I accept your offer, it will solve most of my problems and would give my child a legitimate name."

"Exactly," Hunter said. "I know you. I know you are strong enough to take on the challenges of raising an illegitimate child without a father. But you and I both know that society won't be as understanding. If your child...our child...is going to have any chance at all in the world we live in, that child will have to have a father's name."

"Hunter..." she said, choosing her words carefully. "If I accept your offer...and I'm not saying I will yet...you need to know I don't love you. At least not the way that you want me to. If this arrangement is going to work, we both have to acknowledge that now. I don't believe you want to live a lie and I know I can't. I won't."

"I understand," Hunter said. "I've thought about that as well. I won't pretend that it doesn't hurt. But I believe that once you get to know me, once you see how much I care about you, you will come to love me the same way. I honestly believe that, Caelyn. So much so I'm willing to take a chance to find out.

"Now, what do you say? You have to decide quickly, for reasons I'm sure you understand. If I am to give the child my name, we can't put this decision off for long."

"Give me one day," she said. "Let me think about it for one day and I will give you my answer."

"Of course," Hunter said. "That's more than fair. I will come back this time tomorrow night to hear your answer. And Caelyn, I want you to know that whatever you decide, I will support your decision."

Chapter Forty-Five

Farewell

More than a fortnight had passed since Ethan's return to Kitty Hawk and, now recovered from his wounds, could no longer justify being absent from work. It was hard to say goodbye to his new friends. They had been more than good to him, especially Abbie. But as the recent survivor of a tragic affair, his fear of hurting the young woman was profound. And it was clear the longer he stayed, the more painful it would be for all involved.

Both Lottie Mae and Abbie had accompanied him to the dock and Danny's waiting skiff. After hugging Mae, he turned to look at the young woman, the morning breeze blowing her hair about her face. Abbie's eyes teared as she hugged him goodbye.

"I could have made you forget her," she said, speaking as though they were the only two people on the dock. "I would have been more than enough woman for you...if only you had given me a chance."

Even in his worst moments, Ethan knew Abbie's affection was genuine and unconditional. And though he felt guilty, his departure would cause her heartache, he wanted to leave her with something that would lessen her disappointment. Taking her hand in his, he brought it to his lips and kissed it softly.

"Thank you for trying, Abbie. You are a beautiful woman with a heart as big as the ocean. If it had not been for you, I may well have lost all faith in myself. But you need... You deserve a man who will give all of himself to you. Maybe someday I will be able to think about such things. But it won't be any day soon, and you deserve better than that."

"Ethan," she said as he turned to leave. In a wave of guilt, she considered telling him about the telephone call, but then thought better of it. As much as she hated having lied, she needed to protect him.

I will not be responsible for giving him false hope, she thought as she held his gaze. *And I will not be responsible for giving that witch another chance to hurt him like she did before. He doesn't deserve that. He deserves much better.*

"Yes?" he asked.

"Go with God," she said.

The surfman studied her face, certain she had been about to say something different, but let it go.

When Ethan and Danny shoved off in the skiff, Lottie Mae put her arm around Abbie and the two watched the boat sail away on a bitter winter wind.

"It's a shame," the innkeeper said, "that such a good heart was so badly broken. Because it isn't always true what they say, you know. About how the good die young. I'm afraid this is one good man whose life will be long and filled with misery."

No longer able to contain her feelings, tears streamed down Abbie's cheeks. Lottie Mae hugged her tighter.

"It's sad the way things work out sometimes," she said aloud, though really talking to herself. "Especially when you know the person you're losing is the one you'll never forget."

Chapter Forty-Six

The Brothers Return

Soon after returning to the Hatteras Station, Keeper Jenette offered, and Ethan accepted, the position of First Surfman. But it wasn't ambition that prompted him to take the promotion. Being First Surfman allowed him to influence the hiring of new crew members, an authority he used to bring Danny on board to fill his spot on the roster. Although the process lasted almost eight months, Ethan felt satisfied he'd kept his unspoken promise to the Fire Island surfmen. The young Harkers Island waterman was now a lifesaver.

When Danny arrived at Cape Hatteras to start his new career, Ethan almost didn't recognize him. The boy he had last seen in February had grown to be a man of considerable stature. Danny was now a head taller than Ethan, and once he began rowing, his body took on Herculean proportions. Even among men known for their strength and endurance, Danny stood out. But it wasn't his brawn that soon made him an indispensable member of the Lifesaving Service. It was his aptitude for all things mechanical.

In the winter of '05, the Hatteras Station took receipt of its first surfboat with an engine that ran on naphtha fuel. Although most of the surfmen thought it was an interesting addition to their equipment, few believed it would be powerful enough or reliable enough to use in actual rescues. Danny's experience with the *Henrietta*, however, had taught him a lot about such machines.

Combined with a natural curiosity about how things worked, his willingness to tinker with the engine soon established him as an authority on internal combustion engines. As the Life Saving Service brought more of the new boats online, the more the other stations called on his skills to keep their engines running. When it became clear he no longer had time to be both a surfman and a repairman, Superintendent Collins made him a full-time mechanic, responsible for servicing and repairing all surfboat engines in the district. He sometimes filled in for sick surfmen, but he spent most of his time keeping the new surfboats seaworthy.

While Danny thrived, Ethan's life remained stuck in limbo, somewhere between ambivalence and total dissolution. Though he continued to perform his duties well, he could no longer lose himself in rescues as he once had. While guilt had made for a dark companion prior to meeting Caelyn, the blackness shrouding him since her betrayal gave him nothing but emptiness.

The one thing that managed to capture his interest was news accounts of inventors trying to duplicate the Wright brothers' feat of controlled flight. Though he expected the brothers to be dominating the field, the newspapers had either forgotten their accomplishment or decided that the original reports had been exaggerated. Apart from one

Associated Press article carried in an October edition of the Virginian-Pilot, the two brothers from Ohio seemed to have fallen off the face of the earth. And even though the article described how their craft could stay aloft for an incredible thirty minutes, that was it. No other stories or updates of their progress were to be found anywhere.

Ethan's preoccupation with following news accounts of flying machines was not lost on Danny. Realizing how much the surfman was interested in their successes and failures, the young surfman began asking everyone to send him any reports on the subject they came across. Before long, surfmen up and down the coast were mailing news clips to Danny, who passed them on to his friend.

Ethan was always grateful for the articles and would pore over them for hours. But he seldom discussed what he had read and as soon as he finished analyzing the new stories, he would retreat into his shell again. Despite Danny's attempts to coax him out, Ethan would have none of it. The young surfman came to realize it would take something extraordinary to push Ethan past his pain. But there were few opportunities for new experiences on the Outer Banks, and its remoteness almost guaranteed that it would stay that way. Almost.

The answer Danny was searching for came in the spring of '08. Earlier in the week, the keeper of the Kitty Hawk Station had called him to look at a misfiring surfboat engine. Upon completing the repair, he took the boat for a test run on the island's west-side sound waters. As he approached the dunes off Kill Devil Hill, he saw a flat-bottomed cargo boat offloading crates and other supplies at an old fishing boat landing. His curiosity piqued, Danny made a slow pass by the landing. Conspicuous among the boxes was an odd assembly of wooden spars wrapped tight with cloth and two long, smooth propellers. He couldn't believe his eyes. But when he saw Orville Wright overseeing the operation, he knew it was true. The Wright brothers had returned!

A half-hour later, Danny was back at the Kitty Hawk Lifesaving Station, ringing up Hatteras Station on the telephone.

"Ethan!" Danny shouted through the mouthpiece. "It's the Wright brothers. They're back!"

"Are you sure?"

"I'm as sure as sure can be!"

"Did you talk to them?"

"Well, no. But I saw Orville, and I saw a flying machine."

"Was he flying it?"

"No. The crew of the transport skiff was still taking the parts off their boat. It looked like they were taking the sections to their old camp. Come on and see for yourself. You know they'll be flying that thing as soon as they put it together."

"I can't, not for a couple of days," Ethan said. "But I'll come as soon as I can. Let me know if anything happens."

It was almost three weeks before Ethan found a surfman from another station to cover for him. When he arrived at the Wright brothers' campsite, he saw that someone had replaced the shed that housed their original flyer with a larger one. The sound of hammering coming from within the bay drew him to the open door.

Despite having seen the original flyer, he wasn't prepared for the aeroplane inside. It was bigger and more balanced looking than the previous machine. The brothers' first flyer had tested theories and proved what was possible. The design of this heavier-than-air craft was a statement.

Mankind had mastered flight. Having been silent for four years, the Wright brothers were now preparing to shout to the world that the pretenders must step aside.

"She's a thing of beauty, isn't she, Surfman Roberts?" Mesmerized by the new plane, Ethan didn't realize Orville was standing beside him. "Danny said you might join us. We could sure use your help."

Ethan smiled and shook Orville's hand, pleased that the inventor remembered him.

"You should see this thing fly!" Danny shouted at him from across the shed. He was helping another man with the flyer's engine. "We... I mean, they made their first flight a week ago. And look, there's an extra seat for a passenger."

As he surveyed the new flyer, the feelings that had gripped Ethan four years earlier while watching the first flights returned. This was magic, and the Wright brothers were modern-day wizards. The spell they had cast upon him was deep and everlasting. He knew that somehow, he would one day fly an aeroplane.

"The wind was too strong to fly this morning," Danny said. "We've been waiting for it to calm. I can't wait for you to see this thing fly. You won't believe it!"

But they didn't have to wait long. A few minutes later, Wilbur appeared from outside the shed and announced that the conditions were now suitable for a test flight. As Ethan helped them place the flyer on the launch rail, he noticed several men hiding behind a dune about a quarter mile away. Though it was obvious they were trying to remain unseen, their clumsy attempts to see what was going on kept giving them away. The way they kept popping their heads up above the dune's crest to take a quick peek and then plop down again was comical.

"What's that all about?" Ethan asked, nodding toward the dune.

"Those are our newspaper friends," Orville said with a smirk. "We hope that as long as we pretend not to notice them, they'll stay over there, out of our way."

"They stay at the Tranquil House in Manteo at night and come over here by boat every morning," Danny said. "The surfmen at the Kill Devil Hill Station talk with them by telephone each evening. They tell the reporters when we're up to something and then they tell us what the reporters are doing. We've got newspaper men here from as far away as New York and even London, England."

It struck Ethan that spying on other people was a damnable way to make a living and wondered what sort of person would choose such a profession.

It was almost six o'clock when Wilbur finally took the pilot's seat. Danny helped Charlie Taylor, the Wright brothers' machinist and mechanic, start the engine and Wilbur released the static line. As the aeroplane lifted off the track, Ethan couldn't believe his eyes. Unlike the erratic up-and-down motions of the first flyer, this craft responded to Wilbur's manipulations of the controls with grace and balance. Demonstrating the skills developed through dozens of practice flights in Ohio, Wilbur made a long wide circle around the camp, then landed the machine in the same place he had begun without a flaw.

Nothing had prepared Ethan for how precisely the machine could fly. Both the landing and takeoff had been smooth. The banking turns were graceful, even elegant, and Wilbur had done it all with the slightest effort. Although the flight was less than three minutes, Orville assured Ethan he had made much longer flights, and that even longer ones were to come.

To prove his point, Orville took the controls for the second test run, staying airborne for three and a half minutes. Though not prone to displays of emotion, the brothers couldn't conceal their satisfaction. Also pleased were the reporters who were now running back to the boat that would ferry them to Manteo. Soon, they would fight over who would get first crack at the telegrapher and be first to wire the story to an anxious editor. With darkness approaching, the men wheeled the flyer back into the shed for the night.

When it was time for bed, Ethan turned in with everyone else but found that sleep was impossible. Witnessing the two flights had reawakened his imagination. The image of the graceful aeroplane as it tilted its wings to bank into a turn kept playing in his mind. The memories became so detailed that he began imagining himself flying the machine.

As night turned into morning, Ethan's thoughts turned to Caelyn. With a flash of anguish, he realized that the experience, as great as it was, just wasn't as rewarding as it had been the first time. He longed for someone with whom to share his feelings. And he knew it should be her.

Running his fingertips over the cameo hanging around his neck, he couldn't help but wonder if she was happy. She may have abandoned him and their dreams, but he refused to believe that she could forget him. Then, as he had done a thousand nights before, he said a prayer for her and thanked God for at least giving them one precious week together. It was a ritual created to make peace with his heart. If he didn't blame her for what had happened, one day his pain would fade away. At least long enough to sleep.

But this night was different. The day's events revived her memory stronger than ever. And the realization he would forever link his new obsession with flight to Caelyn was maddening.

The height of his quandary came early that morning after preparing the aeroplane for its first flight of the day. Now confident of their ability to control the air craft, the Wright brothers decided it was time to try flying with an additional rider.

Building an aeroplane that could carry a passenger was more than a good idea. Carrying an observer was one of several mandates stipulated by the army the Wrights had to deliver to win a government contract. Many military tacticians believed aeroplanes would bring an end to war because neither side would be able to move troops and equipment without the other's observation planes seeing what they were doing. If the Wrights delivered an aeroplane capable of carrying an observer, the lucrative contract would be theirs. Winning the contract would also allow the brothers to give up their bicycle business and focus on perfecting the aeroplane and mass producing it. As it stood now, their resources were running out fast. Their hard work needed to pay off financially or their efforts would be for nothing.

After setting the flyer up on the launching rail, Wilbur looked at Charlie, Danny, and Ethan with the closest thing to a smile Ethan would ever see on the stoic brother.

"Well, who's it going to be?" he asked. "I can't take Orville. We can't take the chance of losing both of us at the same time if something were to happen."

Danny and Charlie locked eyes, each one measuring the other as to who was more deserving of the honor. Seizing the moment, Ethan climbed into the observer's seat. Wilbur took the pilot's seat, looking at Ethan with a new appreciation. Like most of the lifesaver's he had met, the surfman had no lack of courage.

Having no choice but to resume their duties as members of the ground crew, Charlie and Danny spun the propellers to start the engine. At the last second, Orville handed the surfman his goggles.

"You might need these!" he said, raising his voice to be heard above the engine noise. "That is, if you dare to open your eyes long enough to see where you're going!"

Ethan grabbed Orville's arm.

"Thank you!" he shouted.

Orville responded with a knowing nod.

Wilbur gave the "all ready" sign and released the static line. The aeroplane lurched forward, and the ground passed beneath them with greater and greater speed. The instant the flyer lifted off the ground, Ethan knew this was where he was meant to be. He felt as if he was returning to something he had been doing his entire life.

A sudden gust of wind forced the flyer into a dive, taking Wilbur by surprise. Rather than take any chances, the senior Wright brother leveled the plane and brought it down for a soft landing in the sand. The entire flight had lasted less than half a minute, but to Ethan, it had been an eternity. The experience overwhelmed his senses. And though he possessed no words to describe his feelings, he knew with absolute certainty he had to fly again.

Wasting no time, the men lifted the flyer back onto the launching rail. Orville took the pilot's seat this time, determined to do better at flying with a passenger on board than his brother. Having tasted the sensation of flight,

Ethan was now a man possessed. He climbed back into the passenger's seat as if he'd claimed the seat for the rest of the day, determined to keep Danny or Charlie from taking a turn.

More at ease this time, Ethan focused on absorbing every detail as the flyer lifted off the ground. He couldn't explain it to himself, but it was amazing how different it was to look down from the aeroplane as compared to looking down from atop the Hatteras Lighthouse. It had something to do with the way the landscape kept moving beneath them, covering distance in a way only birds had known. Until now. And then there was the sense of godliness about the entire experience.

No one will ever be able to truly appreciate His creation, he thought, *until they have seen the Earth from on high.*

As Orville piloted the flyer over a dune, Ethan saw the reporters that gathered daily, their jaws agape in wonder at what they were witnessing. Not knowing what else to do, they rushed about in circles, grabbing each other and pointing up to the flyer as it passed overhead. From the air, they appeared as Lilliputians, amazed and frightened.

For the first time since his encounter with her at the Ocracoke vendue, Ethan remembered the black woman in the bandanna and the words she had spoken. "Your future ain't out there," she had said, pointing toward the ocean. "It's up there. In the sky." How she had known, he didn't care. As he watched the reporters scurrying around below, he knew she was right. Someday he would be a pilot.

Remembering the black woman also reminded him of how he had purchased Caelyn's steamer and what it had led to. As he had the night before, Ethan acknowledged the dark side to his new passion. There was a price to pay for the privilege. For him, it would be the inevitable memories of Caelyn each time he took the controls of an aeroplane.

Shrugging off the thought, Ethan turned his attention to Orville and how he manipulated the controls to make the aeroplane go up and down or left and right. He realized it was harder than it looked, but he knew he could manage it. The Wright brothers had the benefit of experience, making it look easy. On the other hand, he had the advantage of being able to watch someone else do it. By the time Orville pointed the nose of the air craft toward the ground for a landing, Ethan had the fundamentals burned deep into his memory. He had already resolved to "practice" flying by duplicating Orville's movements in his mind over and over again. When the opportunity to pilot an aeroplane did arise, he would be well prepared.

As the flyer's skids scrunched through the sand, Ethan found himself exhilarated but unsatisfied. This flight had lasted just over four minutes. Four minutes didn't satisfy his burning desire to fly. But despite his willingness to go again, it wasn't to be. For the third flight, Wilbur wanted to test the flyer's limits and told the wannabe passengers to stand aside.

Though disappointed, Ethan enjoyed watching the elder brother put the craft through its paces. For seven and a half minutes he flew, completing wide circles and figure eights with ease. In the end, however, the capricious nature of the Outer Banks air got the better of him. Hit by a sudden gust of wind, the aeroplane slammed into the sand, wrapping the older Wright into a bundle of wire and cloth.

Though the damage was significant, Wilbur suffered only a minor cut above his brow and a bruised ego. Of greater concern was the harm done to the flyer. The impact severed the upper wing from the aeroplane's body, requiring several days of repairs. But the brothers were undaunted. The flights had proven they could meet the army's demands. In a few days, they would be back in the air, honing their flying skills in preparation of the demonstration flights scheduled to take place in Washington, D.C.

To Ethan's disappointment, however, the practice flights did not come to pass. The five men were working on the flyer the next day when a Kitty Hawker arrived with a telegram. The Wright brothers' agents in France were calling for them to come overseas without delay. They had reached terms, and a series of successful long-distance flights there would earn them a lucrative European contract for their machine. With the U.S. Army demonstration scheduled for August, the brothers needed to separate. Wilbur would go to France and Orville to Washington. That was it. As quickly as they had come to Kill Devil Hill, they were gone again, taking with them any possibility Ethan could fly in their machine again.

As they said goodbye to one another, Ethan was certain of two things concerning Wilbur and Orville. One was that they would soon stand the world, and indeed, history, on its ear. The other was that if he were ever going to fly, they were the ones who would provide the means to do it. Their invention was the key to a door. To fulfill the promise of flight, it would take men willing to take chances. Ethan was determined to become one of those men.

Chapter Forty-Seven

Life and Deaths

On the evening of August 14, 1904, Caelyn gave birth to a seven-pound-four-ounce baby whom she christened Kathryn Hawkins Winslow. "I selected 'Hawkins'," she told Hunter, "to honor my mother's sister in St. Augustine." But Caelyn had an ulterior motive in choosing the name.

Though he had little interest in the child's christening, Kathryn's birth pleased Hunter. At first. He was honest enough with himself to know a child of either gender would be a constant reminder of Caelyn's affair. But a male child would become the embodiment of the man for whom Caelyn had rejected him. And that would have been impossible to tolerate.

Despite having endured an exhausting delivery, Caelyn insisted on holding the baby right away. While the instinct to mother her newborn child was strong, there was another reason she wanted the baby close to her. She wanted to see whether the baby possessed any of Ethan's traits. Pulling back the swaddling cloth, Caelyn saw fine copper hair covering the newborn's head. The baby looked like her in almost every way. Delicate nose, small ears, and cheeks that promised to one day match her mother's. But there was one exception.

Caelyn traced the slight indentation at the center of the baby's chin with her finger, surprised by the love and satisfaction swelling in her heart. Kathryn responded to her mother's touch with a soft coo.

"A dimpled chin means the devil's within," Caelyn whispered, and then smiled at the absurdity. It would be impossible for a child so beautiful to be anything other than good. For a moment, she wished Ethan could be there to share her joy.

If only you had not been such a fool and married that girl, Caelyn thought. *If only you could know what you have given up.*

Choosing the name "Kathryn Hawkins" had been an easy choice for Caelyn. Though she feared its true meaning was obvious, she couldn't resist paying homage to her daughter's place of conception. Aside from a few raised eyebrows over the odd middle name, however, no one made the connection. When she began calling her daughter "Kitty," everyone thought it was a darling nickname, except for Hunter, who considered it overly cute and too common. Only Caelyn knew that "Kathryn Hawkins" was a name she had contrived to pay tribute to Kitty Hawk, the place of her daughter's conception.

Despite all the positive sentiments and assurances expressed before and after their rushed wedding, the reality of Kathryn's birth soon exposed the couple's arrangement for what it really was – a weak agreement based on false hope and good intentions. Hunter's relief that the baby wasn't a boy was short-lived. Playing father to another man's daughter wasn't what he had imagined it would be. The difference was, instead of the resentment he would have had for a boy, his feeling toward Kathryn was indifference.

The chafing created by the lack of a physical relationship also wore at the fabric of their pact. That Caelyn would succumb to his affections had been a given in Hunter's mind. When he had proposed their arrangement, he believed there was no need to discuss carnal expectations. Once married, he expected her to be a wife in every way. It was her duty.

Caelyn, however, believed the agreement would allow her time to build a true and caring bond before consummating their marriage. It became clear to both of them that the more insistent Hunter became, the less likely it was she would submit to his desires. The impasse left them feeling deceived and resentful toward one another. And as the distance between them grew, the less Hunter felt compelled to invest his emotions into the care and nurturing of another man's child.

Having no desire to force himself on her, Hunter diverted his energies to other matters. He gave up the master bedroom to Caelyn and the baby and took up a suite on the far side of their mansion. The location allowed him to leave and enter the house without her knowledge, an arrangement he used to seek the company of other women without having to explain his whereabouts.

For her part, Caelyn didn't care. In truth, she was relieved Hunter sought the companionship of other women. Doing so guaranteed that he would not be bothering her. Allowing him to be unfaithful without consequence was a small price to pay for being left alone, and all the while she looked forward to the day when she could leave.

There will come a time when I will collect the inheritance left to me by Grandmother, she often told herself. *And when that day comes, I will say goodbye to the hell this house has become, and I will raise Kathryn on my own.*

During the first year, Caelyn endured her suffering in silence, waiting for her time to come. Kathryn, sheltered from the surrounding tension, thrived. When it came time to celebrate her first birthday, Caelyn was relieved that Hunter somehow found it necessary to be out of town.

Summer turned to fall and Caelyn used the momentary tranquility of the beautiful, temperate weather to prepare herself for leaving. On one of the last such days in October, she took a few minutes to be alone on the veranda, immersing herself in Enrico Caruso songs played on the phonograph. Flying on the wings of each passionate note, the tenor's powerful voice carried her away from her worries. She was so lost in the music she didn't realize she had visitors until the sound of a man clearing his throat startled her back to the moment.

Opening her eyes, she was surprised to see that the butler had brought two uniformed policemen onto the veranda.

"I'm sorry to disturb you, madam, but these two officers insisted that they see you right away."

"It's all right," Caelyn said, though annoyed that she had received no warning of their arrival. Seeing the looks of concern on the men's faces, she didn't wait for an introduction. "What is it? Something has happened, hasn't it?"

The senior officer removed his police hat and placed it under his arm. Following his lead, the younger policeman did the same.

"Missus Winslow, I'm Sergeant Enright with NYPD," the officer said, giving her a stiff nod of greeting. "And this is Officer Hodgins. I'm afraid I have some rather bad news for you."

"It's Hunter, isn't it?" she asked, struggling not to sound hopeful. It was a wicked thought, but one she couldn't help thinking.

"No ma'am," Sgt. Enright said. "Missus Winslow, I regret having to tell you this, but your parents were killed in an automobile accident." I hope it will help to know that, according to the reporting officer, your parents didn't suffer."

Caelyn reached inside herself but could find no sadness. Neither her father nor Dorothy had attempted to continue rebuilding a relationship with her after the wedding. The bitter truth that their manipulations had been self-serving was undeniable.

"What happened?" Caelyn asked without emotion.

"From what we understand, they were on their way to the Polo Grounds to see the Giants-Philly game, you know, the World Series. Apparently, the brakes on an ice truck failed and ran into them head-on. They never knew what hit them. Sorry, ma'am."

The only loss she felt was for what might have been had her real mother lived. Steeped in British resolve, Elizabeth Canady had been the grounding influence, keeping her father's success in perspective and always steering them in a direction that best benefited their little family.

After her death, Jack Canady had spent the rest of his life trying to gain access to New York's coterie. He had wanted that acceptance so much that he had even used his daughter as a pawn in pursuing it.

How ironic, Caelyn thought, *that after achieving his goal, an ice truck cut his life short...a vehicle symbolic of the common beginnings he had worked so hard to deny.* It wasn't wishful thinking to believe none of the misfortunes and setbacks would have occurred had her mother lived. But now that her father and Dorothy were gone, she would soon put her own life back on track.

For the next two weeks, Caelyn occupied herself with arranging her parents' funerals, closing their estate, and helping their servants find new positions. Of particular concern was what to do with their butler, his son, and Ansel Stick. At first, she thought she could rid herself of the former first mate who had failed her on the Diamond Shoals. She had never understood why her father had kept him around. He didn't seem to have a real purpose. He just seemed to lurk about in the shadows, doing whatever job or task Jack Canady called on him to perform.

Much to her chagrin, Caelyn discovered she would have to suffer Stick's presence for a while longer. For some reason, Hunter had signed an agreement with her father as part of their financial arrangement guaranteeing Stick a job should anything happen to him. And though it displeased her, Caelyn took solace in knowing she would not be around much longer to care why a bad penny like Stick kept popping back up in her life.

Wesley Bryant, however, was another matter. Money wasn't the issue. It was the perception. Though she had no idea how much she would inherit from her parents, she knew it was millions of dollars. What she really wanted was someone in the house she could trust. As the circumstances of the divorce she was planning developed, she needed someone who knew her. She also wanted to ensure that his son, Wes, would be cared for and have a place to live. For those reasons, she wanted Hunter to believe Bryant's hiring was his idea.

Instead of trying to convince him they needed yet another servant, she took calculated opportunities to subtly make sure he understood the butler's true value. As her father's man, Caelyn advised him, Wesley Bryant had been privy to almost all her father's business dealings that took place in the house. And because of that, he held important information about many of New York's most prominent businessmen. Information that would prove invaluable. It was a lie, but a lie that Hunter couldn't resist.

As much as Caelyn hated using trickery and manipulation, it had become an essential element to her emotional and mental survival. *The need for deception will end soon enough,* she kept telling herself. *Soon, Kitty and I will have all the money we need to live without Hunter. And when that time comes, we will leave New York forever...with or without a divorce.*

When the day to read Jack Canady's will arrived, Caelyn pushed her thoughts about leaving Hunter aside to focus on the business at hand. Despite all the things her father had done, she still loved the part of him she had known as a child. And though she found it hard to feel bad about the death of the man he had become, she grieved for the father she had once believed him to be.

"I'm sorry to have to meet you under these sad circumstances," Edward Dunbar, the firm's estate lawyer said as he welcomed Caelyn and Hunter into his office.

"These things are never easy, but I'm sure you realize your father was a very wealthy man."

Caelyn appreciated his directness. No overdone condolences, no hollow lionizing. *Perhaps,* she hoped, *it is an indication that the formalities will be brief.*

"Please, sit down," the lawyer said, motioning to a couple of stuffed leather chairs. After taking a seat behind his desk, he peered at them over the pair of half-glasses sitting on his nose. "Let's get started, shall we? As I said, Mister Canady was a very wealthy man, and he has generously provided for you. In fact, because Missus Canady perished in the same accident, the entire estate of thirty-two million dollars goes to you, Mister Winslow."

"Thirty-two million..." Hunter repeated in disbelief. I had no idea."

"Of course, that includes the house, business assets, stocks, and bonds...some of which can change in value. But all in all, I'd say that's a pretty accurate sum."

"Thirty-two million dollars," Hunter said again, not believing his good fortune. Thanks to the loans Jack had endorsed, he already had his family's shipping business back on the road to recovery. This windfall would allow him to pay off his loans and make the business even more competitive.

Overwhelmed, Hunter didn't notice Caelyn's face had turned ashen.

"Mister Dunbar," she began, somehow managing to maintain a casual tone, "you specifically said the inheritance goes to Hunter. Didn't you mean to say that it goes to both of us?"

"Actually, no," he said. Though he hadn't hesitated, Caelyn was sure she heard a touch of remorse in his voice.

"The will is quite specific. Everything goes to Mister Winslow. Of course, as his wife, you will never want for anything. I can only assume that your father wanted your money to be handled by the more, shall we say, fiscally competent member of the household."

A burning rage swept away the initial sting of the news. Beneath a pallid visage that betrayed nothing of her inner turmoil, Caelyn fought back a scream of primal anguish. Her father had anticipated her desire to leave Hunter and had written the will accordingly. Without the inheritance, it would be impossible to leave Hunter and still provide for Kathryn. Unless... Having been immersed in settling her parents' affairs, she had forgotten about the money her grandmother had willed to her.

"What about my trust fund?" she asked, grasping for the last straw.

"Oh yes, the trust," Dunbar said, leafing through the pages of the will. "Ah, here it is. It was one of the last changes he made."

Caelyn's heart stopped.

"As trustee, your grandmother gave Mister Canady the prerogative to make adjustments as he saw fit. The document states that last September, Mister Canady specified that if he could no longer perform his trustee duties, Mister Winslow would become trustee and the trust funds would go to your daughter, Kathryn Hawkins Winslow, on her eighteenth birthday.

With hands resting in her lap, Caelyn stared straight ahead as if a statue.

"There's one other thing," Dunbar said, removing his glasses. "Mister Canady specifies in his will that the trust fund will go to Kathryn only if you are still married to Mister

Winslow on her eighteenth birthday. Otherwise, the entire trust passes to Mister Winslow."

Struggling to reclaim focus from the cyclone of conflicting thoughts and emotions, Caelyn sat paralyzed by the brutal ending to all her plans. Hunter, oblivious to the chaos erupting beneath his wife's stilled mien, continued discussing the details of the will with Dunbar.

Why? she kept asking herself. *Why was it so important to him I stay with Hunter? Why was he so determined to keep me from having my own life that he would reach out from the grave to prevent it? And for the next seventeen years, his damnable manipulations will control Kathryn's life as well.*

Now lost in a brume of resentment, betrayal, and anger, she latched onto the one emotion that could save her from falling into complete despair. For the first time in her life, she felt hate.

Chapter Forty-Eight

Partners

Ethan was skeptical when Danny came to him with his idea. They had followed the Wright brothers' progress by subscribing to newspapers in New York, Washington, and Ohio. The information was days old by the time their papers arrived at Cape Hatteras, but the firsthand reports provided details the local papers always left out.

The two surfmen weren't surprised when, in July of '08, they read how Wilbur's series of extended flights in France sent a shock wave through Europe. Nor were they surprised in September when Orville silenced their critics forever by duplicating his brother's feats for the Army in Washington, D.C. By the end of the year, the Wrights commanded the world's attention and their destiny was their own to dictate.

During the whole of '09, Wilbur and Orville continued to set new records and make improvements to their aeroplanes but the rest of the world was catching up. By copying their technology, and sometimes improving it, aviators from other countries began winning some of the competitions that were sprouting up everywhere. Promoters realized that record-breaking aeronautical events and exhibitions attracted crowds of people willing to pay money to watch. While the Wrights took their share of awards, their focus remained where it had always been, with the business of making aeroplanes.

In January 1910, Danny was scanning the latest delivery of newspapers when he came across an article in an Ohio tabloid that struck him as interesting. As the information sank in, an idea took hold that would not let go. Before an hour had passed, the idea had become an obsession that he had to share with Ethan. Danny found his friend in the station's boathouse, checking on some of their equipment. Shoving the newspaper in front of Ethan, he pointed to the headline that announced, "Wrights Break Ground for Aeroplane Factory, Plant to Produce Four Per Month."

"And did you know," Danny said, "that they've already started building aeroplanes in an empty building they took over while their factory is being built? Do you know what that means?"

Ethan's blank look told him he didn't have a clue.

"It means that you an' me are gonna buy our own flyer!" Danny said. "We can buy a Wright flyer and start performing exhibitions! Think about it. I'll take care of the mechanical part and you can fly it. We can win us some of those exhibition prizes, make some big-time money, and see some of the country too!"

Ethan studied the article, saying nothing. After a couple of minutes, he walked to the open doorway of the boathouse to look out across the ocean. Danny stood still, waiting for Ethan's response.

"How would we pay for it?" he asked at last.

"I've got a little money saved up," Danny said. "I've got about five thousand dollars I can put toward it."

"Five thousand dollars!" Ethan said, amazed. "That's a lot of money. How did you get five thousand dollars?"

"I've been saving up for a long time. I've also got some money that my father left when he disappeared. My mother always said that it was mine if I wanted it. I figure that with what we could make at flying exhibitions, I'll be able to pay her back and then some."

Danny hadn't lied. It was true his father had left money in a bank account, though it was less than five hundred dollars. It was also true he had saved most of his earnings through the years, but that amounted to little more than fifteen hundred. It was the source of the rest of the funds that he did not want to own up to, and wouldn't, unless he got pinned in a corner. Fudging was one thing, but lying was a line he wouldn't cross. Still, he knew that if Ethan found out where the other three thousand dollars was coming from, he would never accept it.

"How much do you have?" he asked, quick to change the subject.

Ethan hesitated. To answer the question would be an admission Danny's idea might have merit. Because he had never found anything he wanted to spend his money on, the senior surfman had a fair amount himself.

"Come on, Ethan," Danny pleaded. "You know it's what you've been wanting ever since you flew in that plane at Kill Devil Hill. And I know you've got to have some money saved up somewhere 'cause you never do anything. What do you say?"

The memory of soaring above the dunes was as vivid as if it had happened yesterday. Flying his own aeroplane was a possibility that Ethan couldn't resist.

"Let's do it!" he said with uncharacteristic enthusiasm.

Though it had been Danny's idea, there was no doubt who was the leader of their partnership. Now that he was committed, Ethan threw himself into the business with every fiber of his being. Two days later, they had collected their money, packed their bags, and bid farewell to their fellow lifesavers.

He hadn't thought about it, but it didn't surprise Ethan that saying goodbye came with no remorse or sadness. Except for one glorious week, his existence on the Outer Banks had been a self-imposed banishment from a world he wanted nothing to do with. But life now offered something new and exceptional and he had no reservations about leaving. His time to soar had come at last.

For Danny, leaving his family and friends was bittersweet. Though Harkers Island and the coastal islands would always be his home, he had no qualms about leaving to pursue his life-long dreams. His restless nature compelled him to travel and see different parts of the world. The flying exhibitions would satisfy that longing. But before they could sever ties with the Outer Banks, the two men had to pay a last visit to Kitty Hawk.

They spent their one night at the inn reminiscing with Lottie Mae and Abbie. The innkeeper had aged, hastened by the harshness of living on an island. Abbie, on the other hand, had turned into a beautiful and independent woman in her own right. Lottie Mae depended on her to handle the day-to-day operations of the inn and had adopted Abbie as though a daughter. Abbie was still single and still determined to remain so until the right man came into her life. Having never lost her affection for Ethan, she was always happy to see the Hatteras surfman come for a visit. And though she never threw herself at him, her deep affection was evident to anyone who looked. Their conversation lasted long into the night, each of the four sensing that it was the last time they would see one another.

During their reminiscing, Danny excused himself, promising to return in a few minutes. But instead of going to the water closet, he went up into the attic and located the trunk he had stored away six years earlier. After Ethan was shot, everyone forgot about Caelyn's steamer. And only Danny, Ethan, and Harry Joyner knew about the secret pocket.

Even Danny had forgotten about the cash until the idea of buying a Wright flyer had come to him. It was then he remembered the three thousand dollars tucked away in the liner of Caelyn's trunk, expecting she would return one day to retrieve it. Now, by candlelight, Danny found the hidden money where Caelyn had left it.

It's not really stealing, he told himself as he retrieved the bills and stuffed them into his shirt. *She left the money and never came back to claim it. Besides, using the money to help Ethan become a pilot…she would want that.*

But the rationalization did nothing to appease the tenets of his Baptist upbringing. As he closed the trunk lid, he quit trying to fool himself and accepted whatever punishment God deemed appropriate.

"Lord," he said in silent prayer. "I've lived most of my life honestly I'm asking you to forgive me for this sin, but if I'm going to go to hell for this, then so be it. I don't plan on breaking the other nine commandments nor making a habit of breaking this one. I believe doing this will help to save a good man's life from being a waste. If that's a sin, then deal with me as you see fit, Lord. Besides, if we make a lot of money, I'll pay her back, somehow. I swear. Oh…and Amen."

Returning to the dining room, Danny spent the rest of the night talking about their plans to travel to Dayton and how they were going to make a fortune in exhibitions. Lottie Mae and Abbie could see that Danny had found his calling, and they both hoped that the venture would be the thing that would free Ethan from Caelyn's memory. When the inevitable moment came to say goodnight, the men went upstairs to their room to retire with no one the wiser about the money.

The next morning, Ethan and Danny stood on the porch of Lottie Mae's inn, braving the early February cold to say their goodbyes. When Abbie hugged Ethan she remembered how he had once kissed her hand to say goodbye and how she wished it had been more. On impulse, she threw her arms around his neck and gave him a deep kiss. When she finished, she stepped back to take a last look at him.

"I could have loved you, Ethan Roberts."

Ethan started to speak but she raised her hand to stop him.

"No, don't you say anything. I want to remember you just this way. If you say anything else, you'll spoil it. Now go, before I say something I'll regret."

He paused long enough to show respect for her feelings, turned, and walked with Danny to their waiting boat.

"I should have told you the truth," Abbie whispered to herself. "But you're better off without her. I just know it."

Chapter Forty-Nine

A Spark

As Kathryn grew older, Caelyn discovered her daughter had a predilection for taking chances. She also had a natural curiosity about the world around her and was always more interested in playing boys' games than those of girls. Her tendency for adventure came into direct conflict with Hunter's occasional attempts to push her toward more ladylike pursuits, but Caelyn refused to see her daughter held back from exploring her potential for any reason. Kathryn, she vowed, would be allowed to become her own person.

But while Caelyn managed to maintain a bubble of serenity around Kathryn, she lived in fear that, one day, the façade would fall apart. The gulf between her and Hunter grew wider with each passing week and she knew he could use the truth of Kathryn's birth to hurt either of them at any time. For Kathryn's sake, she never said anything that would cause her daughter to resent Hunter or dislike him. It was a practical decision, made in the hope of making both their lives easier.

It was a perfect Saturday in the spring of 1910 when Caelyn learned the true depth of her daughter's nature. Seeking to escape the oppressive air of the mansion, she packed a picnic basket and drove Kathryn to the country. Sitting on a blanket beneath a majestic oak in the middle of a large clover field, Caelyn watched as Kitty wove a handful of daisies into a white and yellow floral chain.

She was proud of how her daughter was developing, extroverted when she needed to be and smart enough to know when to back off. She was still a few months shy of her sixth birthday, but mature beyond her age. She also had her own mind and was already asking questions for which Caelyn did not always have good answers.

"Mother," she said as she added another link to her chain of daisies, "will I be able to go to college when I grow up?"

"Kitty, sweetheart, you'll be able to accomplish anything you set your mind on," Caelyn said, remembering how her own parents had held her back. "Never let anyone tell you differently. There are people who will say that you aren't supposed to do certain things because you're a girl. Don't ever accept that. You can be better than that. You can be the best there is. But most of all, remember that you can be whatever you want to be."

"I don't think papa cares what I do," Kitty said, latching onto the one subject Caelyn didn't want to discuss. "Do you think he loves me?"

Caelyn tried to hide how much the question hurt. She had always referred to Hunter by name rather than saying "your father." Despite the betrayal she still felt, she would always think of Ethan as Kathryn's father, something

Hunter would never be. Caelyn took a deep breath before attempting a reply.

"Hunter has much work to do," she said. "I'm sure things will be better someday. In the meantime, you know I will always be here for you."

Caelyn thought about how different it would have been...if only.

"One day," she said, pulling her daughter into a hug to keep her from seeing the tears forming in her eyes, "perhaps you will get to know your father in a way you never thought possible. And maybe then, you and I will both be happy beyond our wildest dreams."

She left it at that, holding Kathryn close in her arms, rocking back and forth. Caelyn had shielded her daughter from the hell that had become her life, but she knew it wouldn't be long before she wouldn't be able to sidestep some of Kathryn's questions.

There will come a day when she will realize all is not as it seems to be, and she will demand answers, she told herself. *When that day comes, I must have her prepared for the truth...or she will end up hating us all.*

They sat in the shade of the giant oak for a while, enjoying a gentle breeze and perfect air. Caelyn sang songs with Kathryn, laughing at the way her daughter made up new rhymes to go with old melodies. The beauty of the moment suspended time, allowing Caelyn to forget the disappointments of her life.

From the distance came the steady drone of an engine as it intruded on their seclusion. The noise came from above, moving toward them at a steady pace. Soaring in just a few feet above the treetops on a stack of broad double wings, an aeroplane roared into view of the open field. It sailed over the oak they were sitting under and continued to the other side of the field. Banking to its left in a slow graceful turn, it came back around to pass over them again before disappearing over the trees from where it had come.

"Mother, wasn't that wonderful! Have you ever seen anything like it?"

The tightness in Caelyn's throat kept her from answering. Her thoughts had taken her back to the hill where she and Ethan watched Orville Wright make his first flight. She remembered the look of wonder in Ethan's eyes and how the sight had captured his imagination. She saw the same look in Kathryn's eyes, and she saw how much of Ethan was in her daughter.

"Where did it come from, mother?"

"I believe there is an airfield near the edge of the city," Caelyn said. She had heard that several men in the area had pooled their money and purchased an aeroplane to put on flying exhibitions.

"Oh, mother, I want to fly, too! Can I? You said I can be anything I want to be. I want to be a pilot."

"But don't you think it would be too dangerous?" Caelyn replied with exaggerated alarm.

"Maybe. But it's dangerous for boys, too. I'll be careful, mother. I promise."

"Maybe one day," Caelyn said, feeling trapped between the values she was instilling in her daughter and the reality of the world in which they lived. "If that is what you really want to do, we'll find a way. But not until you get a lot older."

"Missus Winslow!" a voice called from the road. Caelyn turned to see Ansel Stick standing next to one of Hunter's company trucks. He had driven up unnoticed while they had been watching the aeroplane. He cupped his hands around his mouth and called to her again.

"Missus Winslow, your husband is looking for you! He says it's time for you an' missy to be coming on back home now!"

Caelyn still despised Stick. Though he had done nothing to her directly, no matter where she went, he was always just around the corner, watching. She often wondered, if not for his role in losing the *Aphrodite*, would she have seen the small wiry man as a sympathetic figure? But she still resented him for having failed her so miserably, and knew she always would.

Stick, waiting for them at the car, took Kathryn's arm to help her up onto the passenger's seat. As the little girl put her foot on the running board, he placed his free hand on her backside to give her a boost. Seeing the maneuver, Caelyn grabbed Stick by the arm and pulled him to the back of the car.

"Never," she hissed through clenched teeth. "Never let me see you touch my daughter that way again, Mister Stick! Do you understand?"

To her surprise, the wiry man removed his cap and held it in both hands as he stammered an apology.

"Begging your pardon, ma'am! It was an innocent mistake. I swear it. It's the sort of thing I used to do with my own kid."

Caelyn stared at him, stunned.

"You have a child? Where is he?"

"She was a girl, ma'am. And she ain't no more. Her and her mother both died of consumption some fifteen years ago, long before I met you. Her name was Lori, an' she was the apple of my eye, she was. I mourn her to this day."

340

In all the years she had known Stick, Caelyn had never considered the possibility the man might have a family. The revelation forced her to wonder if there might be something more to him. Something she had missed.

Having nothing more to say, Caelyn climbed in behind the steering wheel while Stick went to the front of the auto to turn the crank. When the engine started, she shifted the gear lever and drove away without waiting for Stick to catch up. She didn't like being wrong about people and the exchange left her unsettled. When they reached the paved streets of the city, a revelation popped into her thoughts. An insight that added to her foul mood.

I don't know what I would do if anything ever happened to Kitty, she thought, recalling her suspicion that Stick had been drinking the night the *Aphrodite* had foundered. *I might turn to the bottle, too, if I didn't kill myself.*

"Kitty," she said without thinking. "I love you."

"I love you too, mother." Then, placing a hand on Caelyn's arm, she said, "Don't worry, mother. Everything will be OK, you'll see."

Chapter Fifty

Prey

Caelyn had half hoped Kathryn would forget about the flyer they had seen, but it was not to be. Every day she scoured the newspaper, searching for pictures of aeroplanes and pilots. When she found one, she would cut out the accompanying article and make her mother read it to her. She soon knew more about the machines and the pilots than most adults did.

For Kathryn's sixth birthday, Caelyn purchased a balsa model of an aeroplane that, when properly assembled, would glide like a real plane. Ignoring the rest of her gifts, she coerced her mother into helping her assemble the plane that evening. The next morning, she rushed through breakfast and hurried outside, spending hours tossing the plane about the grounds and chasing it from point to point.

Instead of waning over time, Kathryn's enthusiasm for all things related to aviation continued to grow. A month after her birthday she came running to her mother, waving a page of the newspaper.

"Look!" she said, pointing to a picture that covered a third of the page. "I think there's going to be a flying show here. Please tell me what it says, mother."

Reading the article beneath the photo aloud, they discovered that an "International Aviation Tournament" was to be held at the Belmont Park racetrack on Long Island in October.

"Oh, mother! That means the Wright brothers will be there, and Glenn Curtiss and even the flyers from France. Please, mother, please take me. Can we go, please?"

Doubting Hunter would take them, Caelyn put her off at first. To her surprise, when she got around to mentioning the exhibition, he had already decided to attend. Thanks to the wealth Jack Canady had left him, his family's ailing shipping business was thriving. Diversifying into other areas, like aviation, would ensure they would never fall into financial dire straits again. His theory was that building aeroplanes large enough to carry freight would allow him to combine his business with the expanding aviation industry.

Also, the event would draw tens of thousands of spectators, the perfect venue to show off his new Rolls-Royce automobile. More than an excessive display of wealth, the British-made Silver Ghost was a declaration that the Winslow family had returned to financial prominence. And to complete the statement, Hunter made Ansel Stick his chauffeur, even going to the added expense of having a set of driver's uniforms tailored for the former seaman.

On the first day of the tournament, they arrived early, joining the throng of people who came to observe the opening ceremonies of the nine-day event. Having obtained special access, Hunter led his family onto the field where the pilots had staged their aeroplanes. Together, they wandered about the aviators and crews performing maintenance and making last-minute adjustments. But instead of immersing himself in the spectacle bubbling around them, Hunter focused on finding Glenn Curtiss, founder of the Curtiss Motor Company. Hunter believed Curtiss would be open to his air-shipping ideas because, unlike the Wright brothers, the New Yorker was a true businessman and entrepreneur.

When they found Curtiss, he and his flight team were huddled around a sleek-new flyer, preparing it for competition. The sleek new flyer even impressed Hunter, who knew nothing about aeroplane design. Employing two wing-tip ailerons instead of wing-warping technology, the aircraft would have resembled a huge mobile had it been dangling at the end of a cable.

Not having seen an aircraft up close in six years, the aeroplane's innovative design and configuration fascinated Caelyn. The graceful lines of the first planes were giving way to more functional and durable machines. The observation made her wonder what the other flyers in the competition might look like. Especially the ones built by the Wrights.

Taking a quick look around the field, she spied a group of aviators and mechanics gathered beneath a banner bearing the name WRIGHT COMPANY. Spotting a gentleman wearing a bowler who, from the back, might be Wilbur Wright, Caelyn started toward the group without a second thought. Though the brother-inventors had come a long way in the past seven years, their bond, forged by witnessing one of history's greatest moments, was unbreakable.

Bored with listening to her father discuss business, Kathryn also began looking around the grounds, hoping to spot some of the other aeroplanes the newspapers had promised would be competing. The flyer she wanted to see most, though, was Roland Garros' Demoiselle. Garros was a dashing young aviator from France who had captured the newspapers' attention flying an Alberto Santos-Durmont "damselfly." With a rush of excitement, Kathryn recognized the French tricolors hanging over the doorway of one of the nearby aeroplane sheds, where flight teams stored their planes.

Thrilled at the prospect of seeing something different, she worked her way through the crowd to the shed. Both Caelyn and Hunter thought the other was watching Kathryn, so neither of them realized their daughter was no longer with them. But the little girl's wandering hadn't gone unnoticed.

Cracking open the access door set within the larger, sliding barn door, she peered inside. As her eyes adjusted to the dim light, she felt herself lift from the ground as if by magic and swept inside. She tried to scream but a leather-gloved hand covered her mouth, turning her pleas for help into muffled gasps for air. Frozen with terror, she could do nothing to resist as her abductor whisked her across the open bay. When they reached the corner farthest from the door, she felt herself being thrown to the floor and then flipped over onto her back so hard it knocked the breath out of her.

As she chomped at the air, a sliver of light fell across her abductor's face. All she could see were his eyes, dark, menacing, and obsessed. But she knew those eyes. They belonged to a man she had known and avoided for as long as she could remember. Ansel Stick!

Chapter Fifty-One

The Predator

Always hoping an opportunity would present itself, Stick had been watching Kathryn from the distance. He had been watching her since she was three-years-old. That was when the beauty of her long copper hair and cheekbones became impossible to ignore. She was the most alluring child he had ever seen, and he promised himself he would have her. The same way he had taken Lori, the little girl in the tenement.

That one had been a messy affair, he remembered, his dark eyes stalking Kathryn as she wandered away from her parents. *The girl's mother would still be alive if she hadn't walked in on me before I was done. But not sweet little Lori. She had to die. And the best part is, Winslow's doxy actually believed me when I said she was my daughter.*

As his opportunities to see Kathryn increased over the years, so did his obsession. Catching a glimpse of naked white flesh beneath her skirt or seeing the undergarments she wore beneath thin summer outfits made sheer by the bright sun were like opium to an addict, but more maddening because of the improbability of ever getting a fix. Though the beast inside him howled to be fed, not once during the six-long years since her birth had they left her alone long enough for him to feed. Until now.

That morning, when her parents brought her out to the Rolls, she had looked more perfect than he had ever seen her. It wouldn't be long before she matured past the point where her soft features and innocence were most appealing. The thought kept reverberating in his head like a cannonball rolling around inside a steel drum, driving him to decide that, no matter what, today would be his day.

With the instinct of the predator he was, Ansel Stick had sensed that his moment was at hand when they arrived at Belmont Park. People were everywhere. Confusion and distractions were at every turn. All he needed was an unguarded moment and some distance between Kathryn and her parents.

Now, as he rushed toward the aeroplane shed, he knew he had her. Sweeping the little girl up as she opened the door, he placed a hand over her mouth and carried to the darkest corner of the barn. Pinning her down on the floor, he waited a few moments for his eyes to adjust. As her face became more defined, he drank in her beauty, committing each delicate detail to memory. Unable to restrain himself any longer, he pulled her dress up with his free hand. The sight of her white petticoats and her soft underwear sent mind-shunting waves of lust through his head. Unblemished pale flesh appeared as a field of freshly fallen snow begging to be spoiled.

No longer driven by conscious thought, the long-suppressed beast-thing ruled his actions. With a brutal twist, he tore the panties from her hips and waist. As he fumbled with his trousers, his hand slipped from her mouth. Her terrified scream fed his frenzy. The likelihood of discovery never entering his thoughts. At the same moment, a pilot close to the shed fired up the powerful engine of his racer. The backwash from the aeroplane's propellers swept away any chance of someone hearing her shrill call for help. Ansel Stick's moment had come at last.

Chapter Fifty-Two

Shattered

When they arrived in Dayton, they went to the Wright's interim factory. By a stroke of luck, they arrived while Wilbur was on site to check on plant operations. The inventor, of course, remembered the surfmen and was excited, at least by Wilbur's standards, to learn they were there to purchase an aeroplane. A chagrined Wilbur explained their flyers were so popular it would take three-months to deliver their order, disappointing the surfmen.

"But there may be another way," he said, rubbing his chin. "We have several frames and engines from various configurations we've been experimenting with at the airfield. I'll let you have whatever you want out of that for the price of the materials, if you're game. If Danny here is as handy with machines and tools as I remember, you should be able to construct a cracking good aeroplane and save money to boot."

The experience Ethan and Danny gained constructing their aeroplane far outweighed the time they lost. Charlie Taylor, the Wrights' machinist who befriended Danny at Kill Devil Hill, often came to the "boneyard" to see how they were progressing. Sometimes, he would suggest changes and improvements, and often he would pitch in and lend a hand. The two surfmen were learning more about aeroplane design and dynamics than they ever would have if they had purchased a flyer off the line. By the time they were done, they had established an invaluable knowledge of aeronautical engineering.

Whenever Ethan had time to take a break from helping Danny, he pestered Wilbur to give him flying lessons. The years of keeping up with aviation through the newspapers gave Ethan a solid grasp of the fundamentals. Even Wilbur was surprised by the surfman's rapid progress. It only took a few lessons within a matter of days before he gave Ethan the OK to fly solo.

Both Wrights were on hand the day Ethan took their completed flyer up for the first time. Even as a novice, Ethan knew their flyer was something special. Their aeroplane lifted off the ground faster and responded to the controls quicker than the trainer planes he had flown. Already skilled enough to appreciate the exceptional performance, Ethan put their aeroplane through several difficult maneuvers that had those on the ground wondering if he might have lost his mind.

"He will be a pilot of great skill," Wilbur said to Danny, "if he doesn't kill himself first."

When he landed, the Wrights congratulated both surfmen for their work and welcomed Ethan into the exclusive club of those who could pilot aeroplanes.

"I think we may have made a huge mistake," Orville said as he shook Ethan's hand. "It won't be long before the two of you will be taking a good share of our exhibition money."

Ethan and Danny knew their flyer would be competitive. They also understood that the Wrights interest in exhibitions was less about winning prize money and more about testing their innovations and promoting flying itself. The more people realized flying was possible, the more aeroplanes they would sell. And if people bought planes from other companies, that was all right too, as long as those manufacturers paid royalties on the brothers' patents.

It was an accident of fate Ethan had met the Wright brothers before they became famous. Providence had allowed him and Danny to benefit from the friendship. But if they were going to succeed in aviation, they would have to make it the rest of the way on their own. Thanking the Wrights and Charlie Taylor for all their help, Ethan and Danny hit the exhibition trail.

Success came with their very first event. Entering a competition in Cincinnati, Ethan placed third in a display of aerobatics. The purse gave them a hundred dollars and the affirmation that they were on the right track. Traveling from state to state, they made their mark upon the growing field of aviators as a team to be reckoned with. As Ethan's skills improved, he began consistently taking first- and second-place prizes. His flying ability and Danny's mechanical skills made a winning combination that kept them ahead of the other independents and competitive with the corporate-sponsored pilots. By the time fall arrived, they had made a sizeable sum of money, which they spent making improvements to their aeroplane.

October found Ethan and Danny on their way to Long Island and the International Aviation Tournament, the biggest air competition ever to be held in the United States. Though the prize money was reason enough to make the long trip, the promise of making money from the sale of their flyer added more incentive. The offer for their aeroplane came from the son of a wealthy New York businessman who had heard about the incredible aeroplane the Roberts-Williams team was flying. The young playboy wanted more than a basic aeroplane. Recreational flying was all the rage with his circle of friends and he was dead set on owning a plane that could beat them all.

With aeronautical breakthroughs being made every day, Ethan and Danny knew their flyer had reached its maximum potential. If they were going to continue to be competitive, they would have to invest in a new model. With that aim in mind, they decided the Belmont fly-off was to be the last competition with their custom flyer. They would win as much prize money as they could during the nine-day tournament, then sell the flyer to the New Yorker for a considerable profit.

Eager to prove themselves against the greatest collection of aviators ever assembled, Ethan and Danny got up early on the first day of the competition to prep their flyer. Danny was doing his best to coax more horsepower out of the engine when one of the propeller drive chains broke and tore a hole in the wing. Unable to repair the chain, Ethan went out in search of a new one while Danny stayed behind to patch the hole.

It took more than an hour to find a team willing to help. The camaraderie between the flyers was strong, but the desire to win was stronger. Most of them understood that helping Ethan meant they were contributing to their own defeat. A pair of airmen from Argentina, however, had no such apprehensions. Realizing who Ethan was, they jumped at his request for help. A quick search of their spare parts produced the extra chain Ethan needed. He tried to pay them but they would not hear of it. It was an honor to assist the great aviator, they said, and wished him the best of luck in the competitions.

On the way back to his flyer, Ethan saw one of the new single-winged Blériots with its huge rotary engine. It was a design Ethan and Danny favored for their next purchase and he stopped for a closer look.

Had it not been for his curiosity, Ethan never would have seen the little girl. As he was taking in the details of the French monoplane, a splash of color that he had seen somewhere before caught his eye. Across the field, a little girl, her copper hair flowing over her white dress and shimmering in the sunlight, was peering inside one of the aeroplane sheds. The constant movement of people interrupted his view, and in a blur, she was gone. He resumed his inspection of the Blériot but couldn't shake the feeling something was wrong. Had he seen someone come up behind the girl? He wasn't sure, but for peace of mind, he decided to check on her, anyway.

Just as he reached the barn, a shrill cry came from inside. An instant later, the pilot of the Blériot started the plane's loud rotary engine, drowning the field in a torrent of noise. Opening the door, daylight streaked across the darkened interior. A slight movement from the back of the shed caught his attention. Opening the door wider, the light streaked across the room, falling across the legs of a man lying face down on the floor. Then came another scream!

Now that he was inside, Ethan knew it was a child's desperate cry for help!

The surfman was halfway to the far corner of the barn when the door slammed shut behind him, plunging the shed into darkness. But the last thing he saw burned itself into his consciousness. A man in uniform had the little girl with copper hair pinned beneath him.

Rushing headlong across the dark bay, he ran toward the spot he could no longer see. In a jarring collision of flesh and bone, Ethan knocked the man off the girl. But the blow had been a glancing one that sent him crashing headfirst into the wall. Though he could now see well enough to make out the uniformed man's silhouette, the surfman couldn't move. Seizing the opportunity, the attacker came to his feet with the struggling girl clutched tight in his arms and started toward the door.

When he was but a few steps away from escape, the large barndoor began sliding open. Blinding sunlight flooded the open bay, forcing the would-be abductor to remove his hand from Kathryn's mouth to shade his eyes. With his hand no longer covering her mouth, Kathryn screamed and kicked her legs into the air.

The two Frenchmen who opened the door, though shocked at having interrupted an obvious abduction, didn't hesitate. Crouching, they spread apart and closed in on the uniformed man. In an act of desperation, the man shoved the little girl between the two men and bolted through the doorway. As one of the Frenchmen kneeled to take the girl in his arms, the other sprinted after the attacker, shouting for help.

Darting through the throng of spectators as fast as he could, Ansel Stick looked back to see if the shouting pursuer was gaining on him. As he turned his back around, the last thing he saw were the spinning propellers of the Blériot that had masked Kathryn's cries for help. A pink mist of blood settled over nearby spectators and aviators as several women screamed and others fainted. A moment later, a crowd began gathering around the shredded body, shouting to their friends and pointing to the uniformed cadaver's grotesque remains.

At the sound of the crowd's uproar, Caelyn realized she hadn't seen Kathryn for several minutes. Struggling to suppress her panic, she fell in with the stampeding mass of spectators to find out what had caused such a commotion. When she saw the bloody remains of a chauffeur heaped below the now stilled propellers of the Blériot, she knew it had something to with Kitty. With heart pounding, she scanned the crowd in search of her daughter, but the mass of people converging on the scene made it impossible to see anything. Succumbing to panic, she raced around the field without direction, pushing people aside and screaming out for Kathryn.

"KATHRYN! KITTY! FOR GOD'S SAKE, WHERE ARE YOU!"

"MOTHER!" Kathryn's breaking voice came from behind. Caelyn spun around to see her daughter, dirty and disheveled, being carried in the arms of an unknown aviator.

"Kitty!" she cried, taking her daughter from the Frenchman. "Darling, are you all right?!"

"Mister Stick tried to– He tried to hurt–" she started, but an uncontrollable onslaught of sobbing ended her attempt to answer. Caelyn clutched her closer and looked at the French aviator in search of answers.

The Frenchman tried to explain, augmenting his few words of English with hand gestures and shrugs. Caelyn looked toward the aeroplane shed he pointed to, but only saw the French tricolors. But then the crowd parted for a moment and she saw two men walking away from the shed. A stout, taller man helping another man who seemed to be injured. Something about the shorter man seemed familiar to Caelyn. His hair was wavy with light-colored tips. His form was a lot like Ethan's, but it couldn't be him, could it? The man looked back over his shoulder toward the Blériot and then the meandering crowd blocked her view again.

Hunter grabbed Caelyn by her shoulders and spun her around to face him.

"What happened?" he asked. "Is Kathryn all right?"

"I'm not sure," Caelyn said, hugging Kathryn tighter. She turned to take one last look at the two men but they had disappeared. Turning back to Hunter, she nodded toward the aviator who had returned Kathryn.

"If we're going to find out what happened, you'll have to find someone who can speak French. But don't bother asking your chauffeur. I think you'll find he's lost his tongue."

Chapter Fifty-Three

Exodus

Too dazed to speak, Ethan watched from the darkness as the scene unfolded before him. The confrontation was over in seconds and the girl's rescuers never saw the American. Ethan tried to call out to the French aviator as he carried the girl outside, but the pain that exploded in his head quelled his words.

When the pain subsided, he rose to his feet and shuffled to the doorway. Bracing himself against the jam, he surveyed the excited crowd gathering around the Blériot, trying to figure out what had happened. Through the chaos of people and the dust, Ethan saw the Frenchman with the little girl approach a chicly dressed woman caught in the throes of panic. When the airman handed the copper-haired child to the woman, Ethan saw her face.

Through the swirling dust and the mass of people running about in all directions, the sight of Caelyn unleashed a torrent of memories woven around a mountain of regret. All the feelings he had tried to suppress for seven years came charging back a thousand times stronger than before. He absorbed every contour of her face. Her eyes, her lips, her hair, drinking in her beauty as though a man dying of thirst. Everything with her was as it should be. She was and always would be the most beautiful woman in the world. Standing before him, he could not deny his true feelings. He loved her now as much as he ever had.

Without thinking, he took a step toward her, then stopped in his tracks. The girl in Caelyn's arms must be her daughter! The realization robbed him of his will, leaving him standing out in the open, his face a twisted canvas of pain, confusion, and emptiness. To anyone watching, he must have looked the complete fool. But the surfman could neither think, nor talk, nor move. That which he wanted more than anything in the world stood before him. And yet he could not will himself to walk toward her.

"Ethan? Ethan!" Danny's voice drew the surfman back from oblivion. "Ethan, what's wrong? Are you all right?"

Concerned that his partner had been gone for so long, Danny had come searching for him. The look on Ethan's face was so strange he feared there might be something physically wrong.

"Danny," Ethan said at last. "Help me back to the flyer, OK?"

Now oblivious to the roiling crowd, Danny took his friend's arm and pulled it over his shoulder. As they started back to their plane, Ethan took a last glance in Caelyn's direction. It was only an instant, but he was sure she caught his eye. Then the meandering crowd came between them and the contact was lost.

During the next three days, Ethan never said a word about the incident or attempted to explain what had happened. Too distraught to fly, he missed the first day's events altogether. On the second day, he entered and won an aerobatics contest, surprising Danny as much as it amazed the crowd.

"What the hell are you doing?" Danny asked when Ethan jumped down from the flyer. "We built this plane for speed, not power dives and barrel rolls. Do you have a death wish?"

But the surfman walked past Danny without replying, leaving him to wonder whatever he wanted.

On the third day, the wealthy New Yorker arrived, eager to complete their transaction as soon as possible. Having witnessed the previous day's unbelievable performance, he wanted the plane more than ever, preferably before Ethan crashed it. To Danny's surprise, Ethan took the money, which meant that they couldn't compete in the remaining events.

"So, what do we do now?" Danny asked, no longer able to hide his frustration.

"We do what we planned to do all along," Ethan said. "We just do it seven days sooner."

"Ethan," Danny said, weighing his words. "What happened back there? Back at the aeroplane shed?"

"I saw her, Danny..." his voice cracking. "I saw her. And her daughter. Let's just leave it at that."

The next morning, they packed their belongings and booked passage on an ocean liner sailing to Europe. Like most modern countries, France, Germany, England, Spain, and many others were obsessed with all things aeronautical and competitions were announced almost daily. Though they had advanced their timetable by a couple of weeks, they would stick to their strategy of following the prize money and entering as many competitions as possible.

Standing next to the rail on the deck of their passenger ship, Ethan watched as they sailed past Ellis Island and the Statue of Liberty with eyes that did not see. In his mind, all he could see was Caelyn standing stone-still in the middle of Belmont Field as thousands of spectators flowed around her. The epitome of the "New Woman," she had worn a long-sleeved, white shirtwaist with a simple necktie scarf that matched the color of her hair. Her violet-hewed skirt was drawn tight at the waist by a wide sash with the ends dangling off the hip. And though he did not understand the language of fashion well enough to assign the correct words, the hat she wore had been a wide-brimmed affair with a triplet of feathers demanding the attention of anyone who came near.

Again and again he went over every detail, vowing to never lose the mental photograph that would surely be the last image of her he would ever possess. Eventually, his thoughts turned to the girl, and he wondered if Caelyn had yet discovered that it was he who had saved her daughter. He wondered how that would make her and her husband feel. He had never allowed himself to think about Hunter Winslow, but now he could not help pondering what sort of man he might be.

Hunter Winslow, Ethan said to himself, trying to imagine what Caelyn's life with him was like. He had given her everything. A home, a beautiful daughter, a secure future. As much as he wanted to hate the man, he just couldn't. He only felt envy and loss. *He must have made her happy,* he thought as bitterness filled his heart like a dark bile.

After New York's skyline slipped below the horizon, his gaze turned to the dark water passing by the ship, defined by the dull white wake turned up by the hull. Numbed by the cold, he stared at the briny darkness and the peace it promised. He knew from his lifesaver's training that anyone who fell into the wintertime seawater would die of hypothermia in a matter of minutes. Even if anyone saw him fall overboard, he'd be dead by the time the ship could turn full circle to retrieve him.

"Don't you think you've been out here long enough?" Danny asked, coming to stand next to Ethan at the rail. The surfman's face was ashen from the cold and his hands were shaking. "What do you say we go back to our compartment? I've got something down there that'll warm you up."

The surfman continued staring at the passing water without responding.

"You know," Danny said, sensing the darkness on Ethan's mind, "it's funny, but I never learned how to swim."

Ethan looked at his friend in disbelief.

"It's true," Danny said, straight-faced. "I can't swim a stroke. Every time they gave the swimming test, I got assigned to work on an engine or they canceled it because of weather or a rescue. I'm probably the only lifesaver there ever was who can't swim."

Ethan's stunned expression gave way to a grin, and then to a full smile. The more he thought about it, the funnier it struck him. His smile became a chuckle.

"It's not that funny," Danny said, feigning indignation.

The theatrics layered atop the absurd overpowered even Ethan's dark mood. His chuckle turned into an unbridled laugh. A moment later, they were both laughing so hard the handful of passengers who had ventured outside to view the stars began staring at them.

Chapter Fifty-Four

Undying Whisper

The newspapers reported Ansel Stick's death as an accident, a variation of the facts as arranged by Caelyn. Not wanting Kathryn's name associated with a story about attempted rape, she pulled the two pilots aside and, using what little French she knew, begged them not to say anything to the authorities or the press. Despite the language barrier, they understood a mother's desire to protect her daughter. They also knew that recounting their story to the authorities accurately would not change what had happened to the attacker. To those who had witnessed Ansel Stick's death, it appeared to be a simple but unfortunate accident. Compelled by their nature to help a beautiful woman protect her daughter, the French aviators were happy to oblige.

For Kathryn, the incident had taken place quickly and had not progressed far enough to leave an emotional scar. Her young mind didn't understand Stick's intent nor did she comprehend the danger she had been in. What did haunt her was the image of Stick's bloody body after running into the propeller. For the next several weeks, she seldom strayed out of her mother's sight and the horrible memory faded as time passed. Caelyn thanked God every day for what had not happened to her daughter, and when Kathryn returned to her old self, she added that blessing to her prayers as well.

The day after the attack, she began checking newspapers for accounts of the incident to see how reporters covered it. On the third day, she came across an article reporting that "Aviator Ethan Roberts" had won the tournament's acrobatic flying competition. The sight of his name in print set her blood on fire. It was the answer to the question that had been haunting her night and day. It *was* Ethan she had seen at the airfield.

Not having seen Ethan in the barn, the French pilots could not tell her anything about the pilot she had seen walking away. In telling her story, however, Kathryn said that a man had knocked Stick off of her before the Frenchmen arrived. The article left no doubt in her mind the man she had seen was her surfman. And he was still at the tournament.

Her desire to go back to Belmont Park to seek him out was overwhelming. For six years, she had resisted the temptation to attempt contacting him. She had done everything she could to keep herself from thinking about him. Yet, now that he was close by, she couldn't deny her need to seek him out. She had to find him to say hello, and to ask him...why?

Given the ordeal she had just been through, leaving Kathryn for any length of time wasn't an option. Nor would Caelyn even think about taking her daughter back to

Belmont. If she was going to find Ethan, she would need the help of a third party, a person she could trust.

Chapter Fifty-Five

Knighthood

Wes, as the younger Bryant now referred to himself, had been under Caelyn's spell for as long as he could remember. What he wanted more than anything else in the world was for Caelyn to believe he was better than all the people who had betrayed or abandoned her – especially the surfman who had broken her heart.

He often spent his idle hours reading novels about chivalry and bravery, reinforcing his belief that men of good heart could rise above their station, no matter what the odds. His heroes were legendary figures of literature, Robin Hood, Ivanhoe and William Tell. And he longed to become their twentieth-century counterpart. If only he could find a way.

When Wes saw the newly-born Kathryn for the first time, he expanded his vow of loyalty to include Caelyn's daughter. He watched over her when he could, looking for every opportunity that might let him demonstrate his worthiness.

When Kathryn developed an interest in flying machines, it was he who made the trips to the newsstands in search of articles on the subject. He spent the money he earned helping his father on newspapers and magazines, which he gave to Kathryn. At first, he hadn't bothered reading the news accounts. But the girl's enthusiasm for aeroplanes was infectious and he soon began devouring the articles before passing them on. In his daydreams, he began imagining himself a modern-day knight with an aeroplane for his steed, performing daring aerobatics to demonstrate his courage and to win the adoration of those he loved.

The day Caelyn came home from Belmont with Kathryn clutched in her arms had crushed him. The opportunity he had longed for, to be Caelyn's champion, had come and gone. But instead of being her hero, he had been helping his father polish brass. For the first time in his life he hated the circumstances of his life. But instead of succumbing to self-pity, the lost opportunity reinforced his resolve to make something of himself. To be a man of virtue. He only wished there would be one more chance to become Caelyn's knight in shining armor.

To his amazement, the opportunity came much sooner than he thought possible.

"Wes, I want to ask a special favor of you," Caelyn said when no one else was around. "But you know you don't have to do it if you don't want to, right?"

Wes nodded yes. Saying no never crossed his mind.

"I'll do anything, Miss Caelyn, just tell me what it is."

"Wonderful, just promise me you will never tell anyone what I'm about to ask you to do, ever!"

"Of course not. You have my word." Wes said, his chest filling with pride.

"Good," she said, sealing their pact. "I need you to go to Belmont Park and find a man for me. It's the man who helped save Kathryn. But you can't tell anyone what you're doing or who you're looking for. Do you understand?"

"Yes ma'am, I understand. What's his name?"

"Here," she said, handing him the article she had torn out of the paper. "His name is Ethan Roberts. He is a pilot. I knew him a long time ago when he was a lifesaver on the Outer Banks. Find him and tell him I must talk to him. Tell him that, if he is willing, I will meet him at St. Thomas Church at noon, three days from now. Understand?"

"Yes ma'am," Wes said, trying to conceal his disappointment. "I won't let you down...I swear it."

Wesley couldn't believe his ill fortune. When Caelyn had come to him, it had been as though Guinevere had asked him to be her champion. She had forgotten that day, long ago, when he had come to her room and found her crying. She did not remember telling him it was "a man on the Outer Banks" who had broken her heart. But he did. He had burned it into his memory, as he had the oath to one day repay that man for hurting her. If he were going to keep his word, he would have to put aside his contempt for the lifesaver. At least for now.

Despite his distaste for the task, Wes was determined not to let her down. But his determination changed to frustration when he arrived at Belmont Park. Though he found Ethan's aeroplane right away, he discovered that it no longer belonged to the surfman. The man who had purchased the plane had no idea where Ethan and Danny had gone. Hours later, he found a pilot who thought he remembered Danny saying that they were going to the waterfront. Not knowing what else to do, Wes went to the waterfront where the passenger ships docked. In a frantic rush, he went from pier to pier asking every crewman he saw if they had seen the two men.

After two days of searching, and a sleepless night huddled between cargo containers, he finally found a stevedore who remembered seeing the "famous pilot and another man" boarding an ocean liner bound for Europe. Though he had failed to deliver the message, he at least knew Ethan had left the country.

Upon his return to the Winslow manor, he immediately sought Caelyn to deliver the bad news. Who he found instead was his father. Incensed at his son's unexplained absence, the elder Bryant ordered his son to reveal where he had been. But Wes, determined not to break his vow to Caelyn, refused.

It was the first time he had ever disobeyed his father and it hurt him more than he could have imagined. But he would rather suffer the punishment for being disobedient than tell a lie. Even as his father lashed him twenty times with his belt, Wes would not give in. As painful as the punishment was, he knew it would not last as long as the shame he would feel if he betrayed Caelyn. More important than his honor, however, he understood that his silence was the only thing that prevented Caelyn's ruination.

When done, with the broad leather belt hanging by his side, the senior Bryant assessed his sixteen-year-old son, his face roiling with mixed emotions.

"Wesley. Son. I will never hit you again. I will set you out on the street before I do that again. Please never make me have to make that decision."

"I'm sorry, father. But I gave my word not to tell. And you taught me to keep my word, always."

"I hope it was worth it, son," his father said, his eyes beginning to water.

"The only harm done was to myself," Wes said without malice. "I hope you will forgive me. I meant you no disrespect."

"I hope you will forgive me," his father said. Pausing, he struggled to decipher which of his emotions was the most important, given the circumstances.

"Wes," he said.

"Sir?"

"I'm very proud of you, son."

Wes turned to look his father in the eyes.

"Thank you, sir," he said.

Life can be strange, Wes thought. *If I had not defied him, I might never have heard those words.*

The next morning, Caelyn pulled Wes aside as soon as she had a chance and asked what had happened. With eyes cast down, he told her how he had tracked Ethan as far as the docks but not in time to deliver her message. Knowing that Wesley had suffered at her expense, Caelyn placed her hand under his chin and forced him to look at her.

"Thank you," she said. "I'm sorry your father is angry at you, but I do appreciate what you did...more than words can express."

"It's OK," he said, reveling in the redemption he saw in her eyes. "Everything will be all right. I'm just sorry that I failed you."

"You didn't fail me," she said. "You did far more than I had a right to expect. I can never thank you enough."

Caelyn's words were as a queen's sword, tapping his shoulders in recognition of his faithful service. He had lived up to her expectations and preserved her secret. Not even Ivanhoe could have performed more admirably.

Chapter Fifty-Six

War

Louis Blériot was proud of his aeroplanes. With the single-propeller engine mounted in front of the pilot instead of behind – like those built by the Wright brothers – his planes were setting a standard for performance and safety that pilots were quick to appreciate. Anyone who flew a Wright Flyer lived with the fear that in a crash, the engine would tear away from the frame and crush the pilot sitting in front of it. But Ethan didn't want to own a Blériot because of its reputation for safety. He wanted one because he believed its design offered more speed potential than any other aeroplane.

After arriving in France, Ethan and Danny traveled to Blériot's factory and purchased the latest model to roll off the production line. After flying the monoplane a few times to get a feel for its capabilities, Ethan helped Danny remove the innovative rotary engine and take it apart. Once Danny learned how it worked, he experimented with modifications to make it more powerful.

Three months after their arrival, they entered their first competition with the modified flyer. A regional affair sponsored by Blériot's company, the Frenchman watched with mixed feelings as his pilots kept losing to the Americans. Though happy that a Blériot plane was winning, he knew it was not entirely his aeroplane.

Impressed by their accomplishments, Blériot offered to sponsor Ethan and Danny if they would share their improvements with him. When the two Americans hesitated, he made the offer sweeter. In addition to reimbursing the money they paid for their Blériot flyer, he would let them have one of the first of each of his newest models once production began, if they would share their innovations and allow him to assign an employee to work with them. Their pay would be to keep whatever prize money they won.

The prospect of having a continuous supply of new aeroplanes without the expense of ownership was too good for Ethan and Danny to turn down. No longer would they have to pay entry fees and expenses such as gas, oil, and parts. And much to their surprise, the employee Blériot assigned to travel with them was one of his most capable pilots, Aimé Jacquet. Besides assisting with modifications, Aimé spoke passable English and could act as an interpreter while they traveled about France.

At twenty-seven, Aimé was closer to Danny's age than Ethan's. He was a few inches shorter than the Missouri surfman and slight of build. His pitch-black Vandyke gave him a devilish appearance, which he used to great effect. Calling himself "Le Petit Diable," he had become a crowd favorite at exhibitions, especially with the female spectators. Conceit aside, Aimé was as full of life as he was of himself, and the three men became fast friends.

Though the French pilot liked Ethan, the surfman's quiet demeanor was a riddle that kept Aimé off balance. More often than not, Ethan responded to his pranks and jokes with indifference. Danny, on the other hand, thought everything Aimé said was hilarious. Because of his good nature and down-home gullibility, Danny soon became the target of Aimé's practical jokes. From having bolts switched that wouldn't fit to having the edge of his razor filed off, Danny never knew what was going to happen next.

One day, Aimé convinced Danny that the French had invented a special paint for aeroplanes to reduce wind resistance. Because the paint was clear when it dried, it was called "invisible paint." He let the story ferment for a few days before casually asking Danny to go into town to purchase two gallons of invisible paint. After half a day of collecting peculiar looks and smiles from the merchants, Danny realized Aimé had pulled another joke on him. Seeing the look of exasperation on Danny's face when he returned to the aérodrome, Ethan paused to see what would happen next.

"You crazy Frenchman!" Danny yelled as he stormed into the hangar. "You made me look like a fool. You wait. One day I'm gonna get you back."

"Why, whatever do you mean, monsieur?" Aimé shrugged, feigning innocence.

"The words you told me to say...you had me telling people I wanted paint to make myself invisible! You made me look like an idiot."

"Contraire, Danee, mon amie. For Ethan and moi, you have been invisible all day, no?"

Danny's face changed from anger to confusion to understanding and then to embarrassment. Seeing the rapid-fire succession of facial expressions, Ethan began laughing. A sheepish grin crossed Danny's face, and they all laughed. With Danny's good nature, there was no danger of creating resentment. The incident cemented their bond and the ongoing rivalry to out-prank each other cultivated a comradery that stuck with them wherever they traveled.

It didn't take long for Aimé to understand why Louis Blériot had invested so much in the two Americans. Ethan's piloting skills were second to no one's, as were Danny's mechanical instincts. It soon became clear that it was their friendship that was the real secret to their success. They spoke to each other in half sentences, each one knowing what the other was going to say before finishing the thought.

But the two Americans weren't the only ones with special skills. They soon discovered that Aimé had the ability to aggravate their opponents with biting taunts and veiled insults. When added to the mix, the three men soon became the most envied – and hated – team on the exhibition circuit.

By the end of their first year together, Ethan had become an accomplished stunt flyer. Always able to find the edge of their capabilities, he pushed new aeroplanes to the limit, trying ever more complicated and daring maneuvers. The crowds would watch in awe and show their appreciation by showering him with flowers as he walked by the grandstands.

Stunt flying, however, soon began to bore Ethan. To him, performing aerobatics was little better than being a circus performer. The soul of aviation was in setting records for speed and distance. He believed it was through these competitions that flight would realize its true potential. It frustrated Ethan that most of the world had come to believe that airships were the future of air travel. Conventional wisdom said that aeroplanes were nice for thrill seekers and entertainment, but zeppelins and dirigibles could transport many people and goods. They were the practical side of powered flight.

At the beginning of the 1912 exhibition season, Ethan announced he would no longer fly stunts, choosing instead to focus on the speed and endurance competitions. For Aimé, Ethan's decision was an opportunity. The slight Frenchman was all too happy to be the sole stunt pilot of the team, soon proving himself to be as capable as his American partner. But the thing Aimé liked most about aerobatic flying was the adoration female spectators showered on the flying dare-devils.

Reversing the tradition spectators had begun with Ethan, Aimé began dropping a single rose into the crowd after completing his aerial acrobatics. It soon became understood that the pilot would reward the woman who caught the rose and returned it to him with a kiss. While it was great showmanship, it also served to further antagonize the other pilots.

Freed from having to do double duty, Ethan began to dominate the speed and distance competitions. Thanks to Danny's improvements to their aeroplanes, they always had an advantage over the other competitors. As long as everything held together mechanically, Ethan almost always won or placed, adding yet more prize money to their savings.

As the competitions took them into other countries, the ability to speak other languages became a necessity. Under Aimé's tutelage, Ethan became conversant in French and could speak essential words of Spanish and Italian. Danny, on the other hand, became proficient in all three tongues and picked up a little German, Portuguese, and Dutch as well. Born in the humble surroundings of an isolated backwater like Harkers Island, the world's offerings fascinated Danny. Immersing himself into the cultural crosscurrents of their travels, he lost most of his Southern accent and acquired a discerning taste for food, wine, and art. And though he was his own man, he never developed a desire to strike out on his own. He knew that the quiet surfman from Missouri was the rock he could count on for an honest opinion and a clear perspective. They shared a purpose and Danny never felt a need to prove himself as a lone operator.

For Ethan, life became a series of competitions, races, and records. Going farther and faster was the Holy Grail that, once obtained, was pursued again. He had no interests or distractions other than the never-ending effort to be the best and to keep pushing the envelope. His one shortcoming, as far as Danny and Aimé were concerned, was his refusal to compete in Germany.

He took great pleasure in beating the Huns, as he always called them, but had no desire to go to their country. The memories of Zeb and the machine guns at San Juan Hill left him with no tolerance for Germany or its people. Though he knew such intolerance was overkill, he just couldn't find it himself to care.

As much as Danny would have relished seeing Germany, he accepted Ethan's boycott. If his friend and partner did not want to go there, then they would find other competitions. Aimé, however, pleaded with Ethan to go. The Germans were among the best competitors, they offered some of the biggest purses, and the fräuleins were very susceptible to the French ways of romance. But Ethan refused to give in, even when Aimé threatened to go it alone.

"The Germans have nothing I want," he told the Frenchman. "I have no desire to go to their country or to spend a single minute with them. If you want to go, I wish you well, and I mean that. But short of them dropping a bomb on my doorstep, there's nothing that will ever get me to change my mind."

Dejected, Aimé moped around for a few days but didn't follow through on his threat. While he was a top competitor and a showman in his own right, he knew he would lose his advantage without Danny's mechanical genius. Just as important, he understood that together, they were special, and he didn't have the heart to be the le ravageur of their team.

Because of their dominance over the other pilots and planes, other aeroplane manufacturers began employing Blériot's innovations. By 1914, most manufacturers were building their planes with the engine mounted in the front, the lateral controls placed at the rear, and the fuselage enclosing the pilot. Only the vainglorious Wrights, too proud to adopt the innovations of others, clung to the old designs even as their planes continued to lose on every aeronautical front.

An exhibition in late June brought the three aviators to Dijon. The day had been a long one, consumed by the many preparations necessary to ready their planes. As a reward to themselves, they took in a late dinner at one of the city's more popular bistros. A refreshing breeze was chasing the day's heat away, so they requested an outside table. While Aimé excused himself, Danny ordered a bottle of his favorite chardonnay. Ethan and Danny had almost finished their first glass when Aimé returned from inside the restaurant, his face dark and foreboding.

"What's wrong, Aimé?" Ethan asked.

"A Serbian nationalist has assassinated Ferdinand, the Archduke of Austria, and his wife."

The two Americans looked at him without comprehending. Neither Danny nor Ethan had concerned themselves with European politics enough to grasp the significance of Aimé's announcement. Realizing his friends didn't understand, he took a seat, downed his wine, and looked at them with sadness.

"The Austrians will want restitution from the Serbians. If they do not comply, Austria will declare war. Russia, England, Italy, and France are treaty-bound to aid the Serbians, just as the Bulgarians, Germans, Hungarians and Turks are committed to helping the Austrians."

Aimé's tone left no doubt it was a serious matter, but Ethan and Danny still didn't understand.

"France will be treaty-bound to fight the Germans and Austrians...here!" Aimé said with wide-armed gesticulations. "All of Europe will be at war! No place will be safe from destruction."

The Frenchman poured himself more wine and stared at the glass as though looking into a crystal ball of darkness. Now that they understood the significance of the news, Ethan and Danny contemplated the repercussions in silence. Though Danny had never seen war, he understood such a conflict would destroy much of the wonderful culture he had come to appreciate. He had found his paradise, and he didn't want to see it brought to an end. Everywhere they traveled, he met interesting and likable people and appreciated their differences. Born in a country as vast as America and at peace with its neighbors, he was unable to fathom Europe's long-lived rivalries.

Ethan had known war, and his thoughts took him back to Cuba and San Juan Hill. To him, armed conflict meant the deaths of innocent people, misery beyond comprehension, and the diminishment of humanity itself. He knew enough about France and Germany's military to know that a battle between the two would have catastrophic consequences. As a European military power, France was second only to Germany. It would be up to the French to make sure that Kaiser Wilhelm's army did not open the door to Western Europe, allowing the certain annihilation of their allies. But as much as he liked Aimé and France, he had no desire to take part in combat again.

It's not my fight, even if I had the desire, Ethan thought, lecturing himself. *Leave it to the younger men. They have the blessing of ignorance.*

"It is the end of the competitions," Aimé said. "The army will need pilots to fly aeroplanes to spot the enemies' troops. I am a pilot, and my sweet France calls to me. I can do nothing but go to her aid."

Ethan held his gaze on Aimé, who paused to reflect on his words. A sadness swept over the Frenchman's face. Focusing on his two friends again, he raised his glass in toast.

"Gentlemen, this will undoubtedly be our last competition together. Here is to our friendship. May it last forever, and may we survive the war to fly together again!"

Chapter Fifty-Seven

Das Poltergeist

Always the showman, Aimé took the threat of war as an opportunity to make dramatic statements and moving toasts of undying friendship. In contrast, Ethan hung on to the possibility that the Serbians would come to terms with Austria and avert a conflict. Less than a month later, Serbia dashed that hope when it refused to concede all of Austria's demands and began mobilizing its army. Three days later, Austria declared war and all of Europe prepared for the coming conflict. Germany declared war on Russia on the first day of August.

That afternoon, Ethan and Danny met Aimé at his Blériot to say goodbye. He was leaving to volunteer his services and his aeroplane to the French army.

"I will be the eyes in the sky that spot our enemy and find the path to victory," he yelled above the noise of his engine. Giving them a farewell salute, he flew off toward Paris and the growing mass of French troops.

The Germans invaded Luxembourg the next morning. That afternoon, German calvary crossed the border at Joncherey and attacked a French militia. Two days later, Belgium and Great Britain joined the fray. The Great War had begun.

As the fighting escalated, Ethan knew it was time to return their aeroplane to Louis Blériot. There would be no more competitions and the army would use their plane in the war effort. Once the war was over, they could purchase a new aeroplane to resume competition flying. But the question Ethan and Danny hadn't answered yet was, what would they do in the meantime?

"Maybe there is some other way we can help," Danny said as he prepared their plane for its last flight. His frustration at Ethan's unwillingness to consider fighting for the French had grown with each passing day.

"Like what?" Ethan asked. "You want to join the Aeronautique and spot troop movements from the air like Aimé?"

"What would be wrong with that?" Danny fired back. "It's not like we'd be on the ground shooting people. Or wouldn't that be safe enough for you?"

A flash of anger blazed through Ethan's eyes, then vanished as quickly as it had appeared. A sadness passed over him and he looked at the ground with the burden of knowledge weighing heavy on his shoulders.

"Is that what you think this is about?" Ethan said. "You think I don't want to go to war because I'm scared? As many times as we faced the teeth of a nor'easter together? As many times as you've seen me jockey a flyer past the edge of its limits? You think I'm scared?"

Danny couldn't find his voice. Questioning the surfman's bravery was by far the stupidest thing he had ever done.

"The truth is, yes, I'm scared. And you should be too, if you've got any sense."

Meeting Danny's gaze, he struggled to find the right words to make his young friend understand.

"I'm scared of losing Aimé. I'm scared of losing you. Sure, flying reconnaissance isn't bad now, but wait. They'll figure out a way to shoot at each other in the sky. And the dying up there won't be any better than it is on the ground. I've seen it, Danny. Any glory to be found in war is far outweighed by the death and destruction. People might remember you as a hero, but you'll only remember the friends who died."

"But if everyone felt that way, who would stop the Germans?" Danny asked. "Who would stop them from destroying everything? Who would stop them from killing everybody in France we've ever cared about? And then, what would become of America? Damn it, Ethan, somebody's got to stop them."

Danny's words stung. How could life be good for anybody if no one will stand for what was right? But did this war even have a right side? Other than his hatred of the Germans, little differentiated one side from the other. The alliances and treaties were complicated and arbitrary. It was impossible to understand who was fighting for what. Ethan knew there were things he would fight for, but he wasn't sure this was it.

"I don't know, Danny," Ethan said, shaking his head. "Maybe you're right. There's nothing back in the U.S. for me, anyway. Maybe there is some way we can help. But there's one thing. I won't kill people. I've done that before and I never want to do it again. Understand?"

"Of course," Danny said. "I know it's...different for you. I respect that. Let's just see how it goes. If the right thing comes along, we'll know it."

When the flyer was ready, they returned to Louis Blériot's airfield to bid farewell to the friends they had made. Most of the pilots were about to leave or had already left to join Aimé in Paris. The engineers talked about new designs they were considering to make their aeroplanes more suited for war.

When Blériot heard that the two Americans had returned, he rushed from his office and out to the airfield to greet them.

"I am so glad that you are here," the Frenchman said. "I have been thinking about what you might do, now that there is the war. Unless, of course, you are planning to return to America?"

Blériot's eyes sparkled with excitement when Ethan said they had no intentions of leaving.

"The commander of the Service Aeronautique is in need of experienced pilots to provide instruction to new pilots. I proposed you go as a team...Ethan to provide instructions to the pilots while Danny teaches the mechanics. The instructors you replace will be free to fly for France where they can do the most good. Please, messieurs, France will be indebted to you."

Ethan and Danny reported for duty the next day, intent on working with as many squadrons as possible before the fighting became too intense. But time was a luxury they could no longer afford. Less than a week had passed when news came that Brussels had fallen. By mid-August, the German lines had moved well into the interior of Belgium.

The Kaiser's army was advancing and the people of Paris knew their city was but days away from becoming a battleground. Desperate to protect the heart and soul of their country, the French rallied to Belgium, prepared to sacrifice everything they had to stop the German juggernaut.

It was at Charleroi and Namur that Aimé gave his most memorable performances. After becoming a member of the Air Service, he painted a red rose on the side of his Blériot and flew observation missions over German-held territory. Ground fire hit his aeroplane as he crossed the front lines at Charleroi, damaging the controls. Though able to limp back into Belgian territory, he crashed the plane during landing, destroying it. An ambulance took him to the field hospital, where they treated him for a concussion, a broken nose, and three broken ribs.

While lying on his infirmary bed the next day, news came that the German forces were massing outside of Namur, just forty kilometers away. Before the Allied High Command could order a counterattack, they had to determine the Germans' exact position. Refusing to sit by with France's existence hanging in the balance, Aimé left his hospital bed and returned to the airfield. Not waiting to be granted clearance, he climbed into the first aeroplane he came to, ordered a technician to spin the propeller, and took off toward the front.

He knew the Germans were gathering for a major push, but the number of soldiers and equipment he spotted from his plane still surprised him. The enemy far outnumbered the Belgian and French armies. Many lives would be lost if the Allies attacked head-on. The enemy would cripple their hastily assembled army beyond repair. After that, the only thing standing between Paris and a siege was a two-day march.

Aimé pushed his flyer farther behind enemy lines, taking in as much about the German forces as he could. When he banked his plane to head back, two aeroplanes from the northeast closed in. Not until the planes swooped down from above and pulled beside him did he realize the trap. The German aeroplanes were two-seaters, one in front for the pilot and one in the rear for an observer armed with a mounted machine gun. As the planes pulled up on either side, the gunners caught him in a crossfire. A screaming cacophony of bullets ripped away pieces of cloth and wood. His engine began pouring heavy smoke. Armed with nothing but a pistol, Aimé's only defense was to flee. Forcing the plane into a steep dive, he managed to put distance between himself and the Germans. But the faster he flew, the faster the flames around the engine grew. He was caught in a race between his disintegrating aeroplane and the safety of the Allied lines.

As he flew into Belgium-held territory, Aimé hoped the enemy pilots would break off and head back home. But the Germans knew the pilot of the French plane possessed information about their forces and were determined to stop him at all costs.

His plane now a ball of fire, Aimé climbed out of the cockpit and steadied himself on the wing. Spotting a haystack in the field below, he threw himself from the burning aeroplane. Given a choice between burning to death or taking an insane chance at saving himself, Aimé did not hesitate. And it almost worked.

Missing the haystack by mere inches, he crashed face-first into the rain-soaked sod of the hay field. When he came around, a young Belgian Army medic had turned him onto his back. Aimé could tell by the young man's expression and the gripping pain deep within his chest that he would not make it. Summoning his strength, he told the medic to stop his efforts and to listen.

"You must get word to General Lanrezac," he whispered. "The Germans have far superior numbers and lie in wait. If he advances, our army will be lost. At all costs, you must tell him that I, Aimé Jacquet, have said this!"

He paused for a moment, looking to make sure the medic understood. He drew in another breath, grimacing with pain, satisfied the message would be delivered.

"Tell me...that was a hell of a show, no?" As he stared into the openness of the sky he so loved, he let out a final gasp.

The medic kissed Aimé on the forehead, then closed his medical bag. He had done what he could for the Frenchman, but the pilot had been beyond medical treatment. In six months, the medic would become so callused to death and human disfigurement that he would brush off a dying man's last request as one more among many. But today, death and last requests still held meaning for him. It was up to him to make sure the Frenchman had not died in vain.

As he worked his way through the columns of soldiers going one way and refuge-seeking civilians running all about, resistance met him at every level. Guards challenged him at crossings while untested junior officers – anxious to show their ability to command – questioned him as though he was a spy. But every time he said the words "Aimé Jacquet," the barriers gave way as though he had spoken a magic command.

"He gave me important news about the enemy," he pleaded each time. "We must not let his death be in vain."

Though it had taken almost six hours, at last, the young medic stood before General Lanrezac, repeating Aimé's words.

The general raised an eyebrow and glanced at his advisors, who did not disguise their concern. With a simple, "merci," Lanrezac dismissed the medic. The Belgian would never know that the information he delivered confirmed the general's worst fears. Instead of committing all his forces to an offensive, the French commander held back the bulk of his troops. When the Germans took Namur, the Belgians blamed the beleaguered general for being too hesitant. But as the Germans continued their advance toward Paris, it was clear he had made the right decision. Had the Germans decimated the French ranks at Namur, they would have taken Paris and all of France.

The news of Aimé's death spread throughout the network of pilots like the blaze that had consumed his biplane. Ethan and Danny were with a French squadron on the outskirts of Paris when they learned their friend had died. Though Danny refused to believe it at first, when the truth could no longer be denied, he sat on an empty crate with his head in his hands so no one would see his tears.

Ethan's reaction was very different. Enraged by the death of another close friend, he could no longer separate the political causes of the conflict from the personal assault he felt the war – and the Germans – had thrust upon him. The evil advance had to be stopped. He would make a difference the best way he knew how.

Not noticing Ethan's departure, Danny was surprised to hear loud banging from inside their assigned hangar. Curious, he went inside and found the surfman working on a new Morane-Saulnier, a single-winged racer that the French had converted into a fighter.

"Give me a hand," Ethan said. He was standing in the pilot's seat, working on the cockpit's cowl.

Climbing the maintenance ladder to stand beside Ethan at the cowl, Danny saw what Ethan was attempting to do. The surfman had taken one of the infantry's Hotchkiss machine guns and mounted it in front of the cockpit. The machine gun was pointing right into the arc of the propeller.

"Have you lost your mind?" Danny asked. "A few bursts of rounds will chop the blades down to nubs," Danny said.

"The way I figure it," Ethan said, "for every twenty-five bullets fired, eighteen will make it through."

"What about the other seven?" Danny asked.

"That's what I need you to work on. There are some steel plates in the back of the hangar. I need you to figure out a way to attach the plates to the blades where the bullets will hit, then we'll be in business."

"I see," Danny said, beginning to see the method in his madness. "But won't the bullets ricochet?"

"Sure, but they can't bounce straight back. Anyway, I'm willing to take my chances."

"You mean, take it up for a test fire?"

"No," Ethan said as he continued working with the gun. "It's got to be tested under combat conditions. You don't think I'd let somebody else try this first, do you?"

The surfman realized Danny was staring at him now, and he understood why. It was a complete reversal of the stance he had taken before. Though seldom compelled to explain his actions, Ethan felt he owed one to his friend, at least this one time.

"Look," he said, "it's just a matter of hours before the Germans will be knocking at the gates of Paris. This idea I have, I know it will work. And in knowing that, it would be a crime to keep it to myself. I would be allowing good men to die for no good reason. Besides, it's the least I can do for Aimé."

By the end of the day, both Mons and Le Cateau had fallen. Every Parisian of able body was preparing to fight against the onset of modern siege engines. Observation planes from both sides flew unimpeded, gathering information about each other's forces and movements. As the aggressors, the Germans were most in need of the intelligence. Every piece of information the flyers brought back added to the German's growing advantage. Ethan and Danny continued to work on the machine gun arrangement until well past midnight, refusing to quit until they were sure it would function correctly.

With only a few hours of sleep, they rolled the Morane-Saulnier onto the airfield at dawn. A thin blanket of fog covered the countryside and dew clung to the grass runway, making it appear as if it were a long, wide strip of silver. The two Americans were making the final adjustments to their invention just as the sun began cresting the treetops at the end of the field.

Ethan strapped himself into the seat of the cockpit, the seatbelt being another one of Danny's alterations, removed the cameo from around his neck and tied it to the instrument panel. If he was going to die, the cameo would be the last thing he saw.

Danny spun the propeller and the powerful engine roared to life. Ethan taxied the plane down the runway, lifted off the ground and into the sky. Once above the ground fog, he turned the plane toward the northeast and the last known location of the Kaiser's First Army.

As he flew on toward the enemy he took the Morane-Saulnier as high as it could go. He knew, from years of exhibition flying, that soaring above his adversaries and swooping down on them as fast as possible would provide an advantage. The enemy's reconnaissance planes would be flying only as high as necessary to avoid ground fire.

His plane had just reached its apex when he spotted the first targets. Far below and to his left, he spotted two planes with German markings headed toward Paris. Banking his Morane, he began a dive to give him the extra speed necessary to catch up to the Germans.

Neither of the two Albatros pilots nor their observers expected an attack from above and behind. Ethan swooped into the rear of the trailing plane and brought his gun to bear on the two-man crew before they understood what was happening. Holding his breath, he squeezed the trigger of his machine gun. Sparks flew from the steel plates mounted on the blades, but most of the bullets made it through. When he released pressure on the trigger, he saw the German biplane burst into flames and pitch forward into a steep dive.

The observer on the second Albatros stared at the French monoplane in disbelief. He had just witnessed something never before seen – one aeroplane shooting down another with direct, line-of-sight weapons fire!

Rather than bringing his own gun to bear on Ethan, the observer was yelling at his pilot in desperation, trying to get him to understand what had happened. Maneuvering his plane behind the remaining Albatros, Ethan fired his machine gun a second time. The staccato blasts of the

Hotchkiss streaked fire across the dark blue sky and the German pilot slumped down in his seat. Like his wingman before him, the Albatros pitched its nose toward the earth, spinning out of control. After the biplane crashed, Ethan brought his Morane-Saulnier closer to the ground for a better look at his dark deeds. Dropping speed as much as he dared, he tossed a single rose toward the burning wreckage as he flew by.

"That's for you, Aimé," he said with a silent prayer.

Turning back toward enemy territory, Ethan put a fresh, 24-round strip of ammo in the machine gun, then gave the propeller a quick look. Any damage to the blades wasn't affecting the plane's performance. He still had a half-tank of fuel, and plenty more enemy aeroplanes remained to be shot down.

Swept up in a revenge-fueled euphoria, the former Rough Rider now saw his actions as restitution for the people and the years he had lost. The Germans had brought too much suffering into his life. Atonement would come on the lithesome wings of a Morane-Saulnier and the fiery sting of a Hotchkiss machine gun. Spotting a single German biplane coming toward him, Ethan lined up for a head-on run.

The German pilot was stunned. As he pulled up and away to avoid a collision, Ethan rolled his plane and came up behind the banking flyer. His bullets ripped through the underside of the plane, damaging the control cables to the rudder and elevator. The German pilot attempted to jump out, but his gyrating aeroplane spun him out before he was ready. The tail of the whirling craft hit the man as he tumbled backward out of the cockpit. Ethan flew downward long enough to see the man and his biplane hit the ground.

Once again, Ethan had become the surfman, rowing his boat into treacherous waters, not knowing what dangers he would encounter. But this time he had the ability to fight back, giving him a sense of control that he never had as a lifesaver. Banking the plane back to the aerodrome, he spotted another lone Albatros in the distance. A few minutes later, the unfortunate German pilot joined the fate of Ethan's previous opponents.

The downward spiral of the burning Albatros reminded Ethan of the Lumière brothers' silent picture shows he had seen in Paris. His engine drowned out the sounds of the German plane as it shattered into pieces, turning the whole dark business into an unreal, almost poetic ending. The rage inside him died as quickly as the flames rose from the broken plane below. And he began to understand what he had done. Once the saver of lives, he had again become a taker of lives.

Ground observers who witnessed Ethan's aerial conquests had telephoned the command in Paris, which in turn, notified the squadron. When he taxied the Morane-Saulnier up to the aerodrome, Danny and every man in the squadron were waiting for him. The French pilots congratulated the American and begged him to tell how he had done it. When he showed them the machine gun and the metal plates on the propeller blades, they rushed off to do the same to their aeroplanes.

The two Americans spent the next few days helping the other airmen mount machine guns on their planes and metal plates on their propellers. While grateful for the help, what they wanted to know most was, when would Ethan return to the air to duplicate his feat?

"I'm sorry, my friends," Ethan told the pilots who had gathered around. "I will make your planes better. I will teach you how to fly better than the Germans. But I will not kill anymore."

"But you helped save our beautiful Paris," a young lieutenant named Marc Huffer said in disbelief. "The city is yours. All of France is yours. Your legend will only continue to grow if you go back in the air to fight Germans."

Ethan wiped his hands with a rag and walked away. The lieutenant looked at him in disbelief.

"Monsieur, please! What did I say?"

Ethan stopped, trying to decide whether an explanation would be worth the effort.

"Lieutenant Huffer," he said as he turned around. "How many men have you killed?"

"Why...none, yet. But now that I have this machine gun, I–"

"Lieutenant," Ethan interrupted. "Between Cuba and this damned war, I've now killed seventeen men. As a surfman, I saved the lives of at least twenty-three people by myself. More with the help of others. If God's keeping score, I figure I'm at least six lives ahead of the game right now, and frankly, I'd like to keep it that way."

"Monsieur Roberts, I am sorry. I only thought–"

"Lieutenant Huffer," Ethan interrupted again.

"Oui, monsieur?"

"Lieutenant Huffer, take your plane up and shoot down as many of the enemy as you can. See what it's like to cause death. To kill. See what it is like to know that you've ended another man's life. Then come back and ask me that question. If you still want to. Comprendre?"

"Oui," he said, but Ethan was already walking toward the next plane in need of a machine gun. Huffer looked at his feet and back toward Danny.

"Don't take it personal," Danny said as he patted the lieutenant on the back. "Too many bad things have happened to him these past few days."

"How can that be?" Huffer asked. "Is he not a hero?"

"Not to his way of thinking. Look, he spent a lot of years rescuing people as a lifesaver. The last thing he wants to do is kill people. It goes against everything he's tried to do with his life."

"Oui, a lifesaver. Is that what he meant by 'surfman?'"

"Yeah," Danny said. "And that's another thing that's bothering him."

"I do not understand."

"We saw an article in the paper the other day. Wasn't much, just a few lines. Too much other stuff about the war to put a lot in a little newspaper. But there was enough to find out that the U.S. is doing away with the Lifesaving Service. It won't be long before there aren't any more surfmen. And that doesn't sit well with Ethan."

"How can they do that?" Huffer asked in disbelief. Even he knew the lifesavers performed a vital service, because the American surfmen had rescued many French sailors.

"Well, they're not doing away with it altogether. But they might as well be. They're going to make it part of the armed services. Call it the Coast Guard or something like that. It doesn't matter. It won't be the same. Trouble is, it's just one more thing in Ethan's life that started out good but has changed into something he doesn't want. Life keeps dealing him a bad hand and he can't do anything about it."

"I see," Huffer said, though still not sure. "It does not matter. He will always be a hero to France."

Though loath to kill again, Ethan believed he could do more than just train pilots. Spurred on by Aimé's memory, he began taking the aeroplanes Danny modified out on shakedown flights to make sure they worked properly. He soon discovered that once in the air, no one could stop him from venturing beyond the front lines to peek at the enemy forces. Nor did the French wing commanders mind looking the other way whenever they needed Ethan to fly reconnaissance missions over German territory.

Because he was a civilian and a citizen of a nonaligned country, the French Command never formally acknowledged that Ethan was performing a military role. As far as the outside world was concerned, Ethan's job was to provide instruction and to field test new aeroplanes. The arrangement made it possible for the American to fly recon missions against the Central Powers forces without having to join the military. It was the only arrangement Ethan would work under. The French were more than happy to oblige, as long as the surfman continued spotting German troop movements and teaching what he knew to their pilots.

The Germans soon came to know Ethan too well. His ability to cross enemy lines, gather information, and avoid fighters became legendary. Jagdstaffel commanders came to realize that he was a renegade with no permanent assignment, traveling from Allied aerodrome to aerodrome. They also knew he could pilot any aircraft in the Allies' arsenal. French SPADs, British Sopwiths, or even new planes with names they didn't know yet. The one constant was that he always flew the fastest, most capable plane in the sky.

In tribute to his exploits, the German pilots had taken to calling him Das Poltergeist. In addition to his ability to disappear from one theater and reappear in another, he could also slip away from their fighters, never giving them a chance to engage him in aerial combat.

Just as it had been during their competition days, Ethan's skill at avoiding the enemy was attributable to Danny's ability to make any plane fly better and faster. While other pilots were obsessed with maneuverability, Ethan knew that the secret to survival was speed.

"The enemy cannot kill you if they cannot catch you," he told his students.

Because of his reputation, most of Ethan's trainees were quick to adopt his tactics. Veteran pilots, however, continued to believe aerial acrobatics was the best approach. The dispute became personal one day while Ethan and Danny were drinking in the Officers' Canteen at Rembercourt. Seated close by was a group of veteran pilots that included Charles Nungesser. Nungesser was one of France's fastest-rising aces and had come to the aerodrome to visit his friend and fellow pilot Francois Coli. When their discussion turned to aerial combat and tactics, Coli told his friend that he now believed speed was better than maneuverability. Nungesser laughed at him. As Coli became more adamant, Nungesser became annoyed and indignant. Soon the two men were shouting at each other.

At first, the argument amused Ethan, but he soon grew concerned that it was getting out of hand. Given Nungesser's agitated state, he knew that anything he said would fall on deaf ears. Yet, having seen too many good pilots go down because they had attempted to out-maneuver their attackers instead of outrunning them, he had to do something.

Quickly jotting down a note on a napkin, Ethan stood from the table and motioned for Danny to follow him. As they passed by Nungesser, the surfman dropped the note on his table and continued out the canteen's door. As the bewildered French ace read the note his expression changed to one of surprise.

In aerial combat, speed ALWAYS wins over agility! Watch the three Hun balloons over the Marne. I'll be back in an hour. Yours truly.

E. Roberts.

Nungesser showed the note to Coli, who smiled. He did not know what Ethan was going to do, but he was well acquainted with the American's capabilities. Observation balloons were almost impossible to shoot down. Guarded by a protective curtain of aeroplanes and well-armed with machine guns, many good men had died trying to shoot them down.

A few moments later, the two Frenchmen heard the roar of a plane engine as it approached the canteen. They jumped from their seats and rushed to the door in time to see Ethan fly over in a new Nieuport 17. With its new, synchronized Vickers machine gun, Le Prieur rockets, and Danny's modifications, it was the fastest, most advanced plane Ethan had ever flown.

By now, the rest of the pilots in the canteen had come outside to join the two Frenchmen. They watched in surprise as Ethan flew westward, away from the front lines.

"What is he doing?" Nungesser asked. "He is going the wrong way."

"He's gaining altitude," Danny said as he rejoined the men. "In a few minutes, you will see him swing back toward the southeast."

"That will take him over the enemy lines but he will be too far south to attack the balloons," Nungesser declared.

"That's the way it seems to you," Danny said. "And that's the way it appears to the Germans. Just keep watching. It will all make sense in a few minutes."

When the Nieuport reached its maximum height, Ethan brought it around to head north, back toward the three observation balloons. As the surfman flew closer to the balloons, Nungesser realized what Ethan was trying to do. He flew toward them from the south, lining them up in a row so he could attack all three balloons in succession.

Spotting the single French plane, two Fokkers left their patrol and started climbing toward Ethan. When he saw the German planes, Ethan brought the nose of his Nieuport down and dove straight at the Fokkers. Pushing his joystick to the left, Ethan showed the enemy pilots he was breaking off his attack. The Germans opened fire and Ethan changed course again, popping back into his original flight path toward the balloons and the oncoming Fokkers. The German pilots were shocked to see the French plane flying toward them. Both pilots forced their biplanes down to avoid a head-on collision. At the same time, Ethan executed a barrel roll and passed over them, unharmed.

The two German planes began swinging around to give pursuit but Ethan was already out of range. Seeing that their first line of defense had failed, several more German planes left the balloons to intercept the American. But they had waited too long.

Holding the dive as long as he could, Ethan launched two rockets and pulled up to angle his plane toward the second balloon. Although the first Le Prieur rocket missed, the second one hit the outside edge. The balloon's skin peeled away in a sheet of flame as fire moved from the initial contact point to envelop the entire craft. Trusting in their parachutes, the crew wasted no time jumping overboard to save themselves.

The men at the canteen cheered but Nungesser made a frantic wave of his hand to stop them. Ethan was still within the teeth of the German defenses and closing in on the second balloon. The surfman fired two more rockets. Another cheer went up as the giant bag of gas turned into flames and smoke.

Ethan felt the heat from the exploding balloon blast by him as the violent turbulence buffeted his plane about. Having completed the arc of his dive, he leveled his plane and bore down on the final balloon looming in front of him. The observers brought their machine guns to bear on him and filled the sky with bullets. The sound of metal punching through fabric told Ethan that his plane was hit, but there wasn't time to assess the damage. Seven German aeroplanes were chasing him and several more were waiting on the other side of the balloon.

The lighter-than-air ship in front of him loomed larger and larger, filling his field of view. Waiting until it was impossible to miss, Ethan fired his last two rockets. A wave of hot air lifted his plane up through a billowing, giant black cloud of smoke and flames. The scorching heat was so intense, he feared it would ignite the Nieuport any second. Flying blind, he struggled to keep control and prayed that he would make it. As he emerged from the ball of smoke, he saw two more Fokkers flying toward him on a collision course. He had exited the blast cloud so close to his adversaries that neither of them had time to fire their guns. Reacting with a skill developed over years of competition flying, Ethan rolled his plane to pass sideways between the two Fokkers.

The enormous crowd now assembled outside of the canteen roared when they saw Ethan burst from the smoke and slip between the two fighters. Some pointed toward the sky, while others danced in circles. The white cloth of the parachutes used by the balloons' observers filled the sky. Even Nungesser had to cheer at what he had witnessed. The American was single-handedly shaming the entire German Luftstreitkrafte.

After passing between the two Fokkers, Ethan banked his plane to head west on a direct path to Allied territory. He pointed the nose of his Nieuport down and, using the altitude he had left, went into a dive to pick up more speed. Looking over his shoulder, he saw more than a dozen enemy planes closing in.

A quick check of the throttle confirmed that his engine was at full speed. Straining to look over the edge of his cockpit, Ethan saw heavy black smoke pouring from underneath the Nieuport's engine. He was losing speed, and the Allied lines were still two kilometers away. Looking back, he saw that the swarm of German fighters was gaining on him. With his engine sputtering and his plane clipping the treetops, Ethan knew he would never make it back to the aerodrome. His only hope was to cross the trench lines and land before the German fighters caught up with him.

As he cleared a grove of trees, the openness of the battlefield appeared before him. His low approach caught the German troops in the trenches below off guard. Only a few soldiers reacted quick enough to shoot at the Nieuport as it passed overhead.

Hearing the gunfire, the French soldiers in the opposing trench rushed to see if the Germans were attacking. Instead of an assault, they saw Ethan's smoking Nieuport sputter over the no-man's-land between the two armies.

Passing the halfway point, Ethan looked back to see the German fighters scream past the tree line and over the German trenches. Three planes at the lead of the pack opened fire as one. Bullets whizzed all around him. Splinters flew from wood spars. Shredded sections of wing cloth flapped violently in the wind. With the French line still a hundred meters away, death was certain. Ripping Caelyn's cameo from the panel, he clutched it in his fist and prayed.

Below, he saw the French soldiers rise as one and begin cheering like madmen. An instant later, Nungesser and five other fighters roared over their heads. Obsessed with getting the man who had flamed their balloons, the German pilots had not seen the six Allied planes rushing toward them. Forced to defend themselves, the enemy pilots broke away from Ethan and engaged the French in a ferocious battle.

After landing his plane behind friendly lines, Ethan watched Nungesser and the other fighters battle the Germans. Once the element of surprise had passed, it appeared the Germans would overwhelm Nungesser's smaller force. But just then, another wave of French planes led by Coli swooped down from above the Germans, once again catching them off guard. Of the eleven German planes that had come after Ethan, nine were destroyed. The French lost two.

When Nungesser, Coli, and their men returned to the aerodrome, they converged on the canteen to celebrate their victory. Catching a ride with a field ambulance, Ethan arrived after the celebration was already well underway. Upon his arrival, the French pilots gave him and Danny a table in the middle of the canteen and gathered around. The Frenchmen made one toast after another, never allowing the Americans to pay for their drinks.

Later in the evening, Ethan had to yield to nature's call and excused himself to find the latrine. While he was gone, a young French pilot, new to the squadron, worked his way to Danny's table. Gathering his courage, he cleared his throat and asked the mechanic a question he had been waiting all night to ask.

"Please, monsieur," he said, leaning over the table. "Tell me what it is that makes your friend such a superb pilot?"

The room grew quiet. It was a question every flyer in the squadron wanted to know the answer to.

One side of Danny's mouth curled into a knowing smile.

"It takes a combination of things," he said, leaning back in his chair and spreading his arms. "First, you must have the greatest aeroplane mechanic in the world."

Though they all laughed, they understood the advantage Danny's skills gave Ethan. No plane was better than its mechanic. The young Frenchman, however, aspiring to become an ace as quick as possible, remained serious.

"I will work to make sure my mechanic is as good as any in France," he said in earnest.

Even though dulled by alcohol, Danny could see the young pilot's passion. Beginning to understand that the Frenchman would follow his advice to the letter, Danny chose his next words with care.

"The next thing you must have is great strength. Aeroplanes respond to Ethan so sweetly because he is strong enough to pull and push levers under great loads. He has an unnatural strength because of the years he spent rowing a surfboat for the Lifesaving Service. It will be very difficult for you to ever match his power."

"Perhaps," the young pilot said, though his expression betrayed his disbelief. "But I will train like no man has trained before. I will match his strength or it will be the last thing I ever do."

"Perhaps, indeed," Danny said, again noting his determination.

"The last thing..." he said, taking a long pause, "you must no longer care whether you live or die. Because, if you fear for your life, you will make a mistake on the side of caution and you will be killed."

Danny saw his words struck the young Frenchman hard. He might be desperate to become a great ace but few men could ignore the specter of death. Confronted by a truth he had not expected, the novice pilot left to consider his mortality.

Nungesser, who had been sitting across the table from Danny, broke the silence.

"Tell me, why is it that Ethan does not care whether he lives or dies?"

Danny shifted in his seat. He did not want to talk about Ethan's personal life. He tried to answer Nungesser without betraying Ethan's confidence.

"He was...is...in love with a woman he cannot forget. He met her while trying to rescue her from the sea, and she rescued him from his own despair. He watched her as she accepted the proposal of another man...and his spirit died."

"I know it may sound cliché," he continued, "but theirs was a different love. At least it was for him. He believed she was a very special person and, truly, I think she was. I should know, for I loved her myself, in my own way. But, for Ethan, there will never be another woman. For him, death would be a blessing. At least then he would stop wishing for something he knows can never be."

Nungesser paused to consider Danny's revelation. Almost every man experienced a love he would never forget. Those who were fortunate married the woman and settled down. Those who weren't so lucky usually healed their broken hearts over time. But few things could compete with lost love, and no relationship could compare to an affair made perfect by the passage of time.

"It is sad that he is unable to forget this woman," Nungesser said, attempting to be philosophical. "But the world needs people who feel so strongly about such things, if for no other reason than to remind the rest of us that such love can exist."

Chapter Fifty-Eight

Home Fires

Six months after the Belmont air show, Wes was making one of his regular visits to the newsstand for Kathryn when he came across a new magazine titled *Aeronautics International*. Its feature article focused on a pair of American aviators sponsored by the Blériot Company who were taking Europe by storm. Spotting the name "Ethan Roberts," Wes realized he had discovered the whereabouts of Caelyn's missing pilot.

He hurried back to the Winslow estate and found Caelyn in the parlor with Kathryn, practicing on the piano. Seeing the newspapers and magazines, Kathryn begged her mother for a break. Though she refused at first, Caelyn relented when she saw the urgent look on Wes' face. When Wesley was sure Kathryn was absorbed in the other papers, he gave Caelyn the Aeronautics magazine.

"I think you might want to take a look at this," he said, handing her the magazine. "The article on page twenty-three about an aviator from the Outer Banks is particularly interesting."

Caelyn took the periodical and put it away until she was sure Hunter wasn't in the house. When the first opportunity came, she pored over the words about Ethan and Danny. She marveled at how they were thriving in foreign lands and becoming recognized as the best duo in aviation. Their lives were exciting and fulfilling. But despite having come so far since his days as a lifesaver, Ethan still lived his life on the edge.

Could it somehow be that he is still trying to prove something to me? The thought was more hope than question and its implication reminded her how deeply she still loved her surfman.

During the next several weeks, she re-read the article every chance she got. The information made her hungry for more, and thanks to Wes, she was not disappointed. Providing Caelyn with news accounts of Ethan's exploits was a task the butler's son took on without being asked.

"Tell me," she said one day as he handed her the latest editions of *The Times* and *Le Figaro,* both of which featured articles about Ethan, "why do you hate him so?"

Though surprised by the question, he tried not to show it.

"Is it that obvious?" he asked.

"No. You hide it well. But it's there all the same. It's always been there."

"He hurt you and I cannot forgive him for that."

"I see," she said, trying to remember when she would have told him about Ethan's betrayal.

"It was the Christmas Eve that Mister Winslow was supposed to propose to you," he said as if reading her mind. "I was very young then, but I understood. It wasn't until the

Belmont event that I figured out who he was. And yes, I hate him for what he did to you. You are so..."

Caelyn stared at him as if seeing him for the first time. The brave young boy she had befriended had become a man. There was no need for him to finish his confession. She understood, now.

"Why bring me stories about him, then?"

"Because, as much as I hate him, I hate Mister Winslow. Hunter. Far more. The man named Ethan Roberts hurt you but one time. For some reason, reading about him gives you joy where you otherwise would have none. And I revel in being the person who makes that possible. Hunter, on the other hand, hurts you and Kathryn a thousand times a day. And for that, I wish he was dead."

His bold confession was both moving and unsettling. If she wasn't careful, Wes' reverence could become yet another burden she would have to bear.

"You know about Hunter's...disaffection?" It was a stupid question, spoken in haste to fill the uncomfortable silence. It was impossible to not know about the infidelities and his disinterest in Kathryn. What Wes didn't know and she could never tell him was that she was willing to ignore his unfaithfulness as long as he continued to leave her and Kathryn alone.

"Everyone knows," Wes said, immediately regretting his bluntness. "He is not a discreet man. And he has become something evil."

She knew he spoke the truth. Whispered tales among their coterie spoke of infidelities that were beginning to take on a more aberrant character. The stories of his escapades were so notorious that Caelyn's self-imposed indifference had given way to concerns for Kathryn's safety.

"Missus Winslow," Wes said, placing a reassuring hand on her arm. "Caelyn. If you ever need help for anything, come to me. I would do anything for you and Kitty."

She looked at him for a moment, trying to determine the extent to which he might go to keep such a promise. And in her heart, she knew. She could see it in his eyes.

"Thank you. We are truly blessed to have such a knight as you to call on, Wesley.

She could see her words of praise pleased him beyond measure, though she would never understand how much.

That she might one day need Wes' help took on greater relevance after the war began. As a neutral country, the U.S. supplied raw materials and food supplies to both sides, and the Winslow shipping business thrived as never before. Killing in Europe meant profits in America, and Hunter was in the right business to make more money than anyone. And the more the business profited, the less Hunter needed to oversee day-to-day operations.

Freed from the fetters of work, he immersed himself into the city's darker forms of entertainment more than ever. After late-night forays, he slept most of the day away, answering to no one's schedule but his own. When he did rise, he made the calls necessary to address the few business matters demanding his attention, then drank until it was time for the clubs to open.

Shortly before Kathryn's twelfth birthday, Caelyn realized that the unspoken compromise of her marriage had become untenable. Kitty wakened her in the middle of the night complaining of a stomachache. Having no remedies upstairs, Caelyn left Kathryn lying on her bed while she went to the kitchen in search of fennel or gingerroot to make tea. As she passed by the door to the library, she heard the muted sound of music playing on the Victrola and voices coming from within. She cracked the door open and peered inside. Hunter and two men she had never seen before were dancing with several women in various stages of undress. Too intoxicated to realize they were being watched, the debauchers continued to cavort about the room. Terrified, Caelyn pulled the door to and hurried away.

She made it halfway up the stairway before, her head swimming, she had to stop and sit down. She could no longer ignore the years of denial. Her relationship with Hunter had become a sick, twisted arrangement without even the pretense of respect on his part. And now, not even their house was safe from his depravations.

Collecting herself as best she could, Caelyn went back to her room and locked the door. Thankful that Kathryn had fallen asleep, she laid down beside her and placed a protective arm around her. For the rest of the night she lay that way, wide awake, listening for sounds of anyone venturing upstairs.

That Hunter was now bringing women into their house nauseated her, but it was the drunken men being there that bothered her most. *Should one wander about the house and stumble upon Kathryn's room...* She shuddered at horrible thoughts flitting through her imagination. *Hunter has compromised Kathryn's safety, and I will not allow that to stand!*

The next day, Caelyn hired carpenters to make a doorway connecting her room to Kathryn's. She also had a locksmith install deadbolt locks on both of the hallway doors that gave entry to their bedrooms. If they were forced to lock the hallway doors, they would still be able to move safely between bedrooms. It was a good first step, but Caelyn knew she couldn't put all her faith into a simple set of locks. Locks could be broken.

The next step of her plan would be the hardest. Though it meant she would have to confront her most profound fear, she knew it had to be done. It also required Wes' help.

The purchase of a handgun required a permit. Even if she could find a merchant willing to sell a pistol to a woman, it was almost a certainty that Hunter would discover the legal paperwork required to make the purchase. As she had so many times during the six years since the Belmont Park air show, she once again turned to Wes.

Now that he was a man, he could go out of state and purchase a gun with no one raising an eyebrow. But for the first time in his life, Wes was reluctant to help Caelyn. He did not like the idea of having a weapon close enough for Hunter to get his hands on, and at first, he could not believe there was a need for one. When Caelyn told him about the men Hunter had brought into their house, he changed his mind. But on one condition.

"Only if you learn to shoot it properly," he said. "You can't go to all the trouble of buying a handgun but then not know how to use it if you ever need to protect yourself."

"I don't know," Caelyn said. She didn't want to shoot the thing, she just wanted to have it close by if she ever needed it. "It can't be that hard, can it?"

"Look, you have to learn how to load it, how to turn the safety off and on, how to aim it, how to fire it. You have to learn how to do all of that, not just for your safety, but for Kitty's, as well. Right?"

"Yes, I guess so," she admitted, though she dreaded the idea. "But only if you go with me."

"Of course," Wes promised. "But Caelyn, understand. What I really want is for you to leave. To go away forever, before something bad happens. I'll help you. I don't have much money, but you can have it all if it would get you away from...him."

"Oh, Wes," she said, reaching over to grasp his hand. "I wish to God I could. But I can't. Not yet. If I can just hold on for six more years, Kitty will, at last, have access to my trust. Her trust."

"You know," Wes said, his face drawn tight with frustration, "money isn't everything. You are a smart and capable woman. You could find a way to provide. I know you could. And I would be honored to help."

Caelyn placed her hand on his cheek and looked him in the eyes.

"I know you would, my sweet Wesley. But I can't, for Kitty's sake. I will suffer a hundred hells if it means giving her the freedom to live her own life. I refuse to condemn her to the possibility of a fate such as mine. I will die before I let that happen."

Wes sighed, conceding defeat.

Soon after purchasing the revolver, they drove out to the county with Kathryn in search of a safe place to practice. After making a few queries at a small country store, they found a farmer who, for a small fee, let them use a secluded field off the main road. As they parked the car and walked out into the open field, Caelyn became silent. The moment she had been dreading had almost arrived.

I should have told him, she thought, as Wes set up a line of tin cans they had brought for targets. *I should tell him now. But maybe it won't be so bad this time. Maybe, now that I've had time to prepare myself, I'll be OK.*

When Wes began unzipping the leather carrying case, Caelyn's face flushed, and she broke into a cold sweat.

Stay calm! Caelyn screamed to herself. *It's just a damn piece of metal!*

"Here it is," Wes said, holding the revolver up for Caelyn and Kathryn to see for the first time. "What do you think?"

Caelyn's throat constricted as though someone was grasping her neck, cutting off her air. The surrounding field seemed to collapse onto itself and she fell to the ground. Wes rushed to her side, but it wasn't his face she saw peering at her as if through a fog. It was the face of a man only a little older than Wes. His arm hung heavy by his side, weighted down by the gun grasped in his hand. It was someone she had known long ago. Someone she almost recognized. With his free hand, he slapped her face and called her name.

"Caelyn. Caelyn! Do you hear me?" He slapped her again, harder this time. "Caelyn!"

She forced her eyes open, but the man in her vision was gone.

"Caelyn," Wes said as he patted her cheeks. "Are you all right?"

"Yes... I think so," she answered, confused that it was Wesley she saw. "What happened?"

"You fainted, I think," an anxious Kitty said. "Mother, are you sure you're all right? You're not sick, are you?"

"No," Caelyn said, beginning to gather herself. "It's the gun. I should have told you. I just thought that...well, after so many years, I thought I would be able to suppress it this time."

"This time?" Wes asked.

Taking a deep breath, Caelyn told them about her lifelong aversion to guns and how she had suffered similar spells after losing the *Aphrodite*. When she was done, Wes turned to where he had left the gun and, using his body to shield it from Caelyn's view, returned it to its case.

"There," he said. "I guess we won't ever try that again."

"No!" Caelyn said. Her tone was almost desperate. "You've got to teach Kitty how to use it."

"What? I'm not going to teach an eleven-year-old girl how to shoot a gun."

"I'm almost twelve," Kathryn said. "Don't they teach boys to shoot when they are twelve?"

"Yes, you will," Caelyn said, speaking to Wes. "If I can't fire that thing, then she'll have to, because you won't be there to help. Do you understand?"

"Well, yes, I guess. But—"

"Kitty," Caelyn interrupted. She grasped her daughter by the shoulders and looked her in the eyes. "Kitty, do you think you can do it?"

"Yes, I can," she said without hesitation. "If Wes helps me. It doesn't look that hard. But what about you?"

"I'll be OK. Look, I'll watch you from the car, right over there. I'll be fine. Really."

Despite all the times she had experienced the irrational, debilitating fear, she believed in her heart that should she ever be in a situation where shooting a gun would save Kitty's life, she would. But her rational self knew she couldn't count on an unproven belief to protect her child. And if she couldn't protect Kitty, then Kitty would learn to protect herself.

Though he only possessed a rudimentary knowledge of shooting, Wes had read a lot of guides on the subject and was well-prepared. Together, he and Kathryn taught themselves how to hold and fire the weapon with confidence.

Even from a distance, Caelyn could see that the business of shooting did not intimidate her daughter at all and that she showed a natural skill. By the end of the first day's practice, Kathryn was hitting the targets more consistently than Wes.

Over time, watching them practice and compete against each other became a joy. As long as it was from a distance. With few other distractions in her life, she looked forward to their excursions with great anticipation. Once a week, they would leave the oppressive environment of the Winslow manor for the fresh air and sunshine that were the side benefit of their new hobby. Once again, when things had looked the darkest, she had stumbled on to a way to maintain her sanity and a sense of control over her life. Of course, it wasn't the answer that she wanted. But it would do for now.

As Caelyn watched her daughter grow more confident, she was both heartened and saddened at the same time. She knew that, if she had to, Kitty could defend herself. But Caelyn also realized that if her daughter was ever forced to use that skill, it would be within her own home. This brutal reality intensified her loathing for Hunter. The internal battle to temper her rage was constant and draining.

When summer passed, Kathryn returned to the routine of school, leaving Caelyn and Wes to continue their forays to the country alone. Wes enjoyed the long days they shared, but like the season that was changing, so was he. He had already determined the next step in his life but he did not know how to tell Caelyn.

The opportunity presented itself during one of his daily trips to the newsstand. "American Pilot Flames Three Balloons!" the headlines proclaimed from the newspapers hanging all around the stand. A quick perusal of the article revealed an American pilot in France had single-handedly destroyed three German observation balloons from his airplane, as the journalists now referred to the flying machines. Reading on, Wes wasn't surprised to discover that the pilot who had accomplished the incredible feat was none other than Ethan Roberts.

Paying the vendor for the paper, he hurried back to the Winslow manor to find Caelyn. Kathryn was still at school and Hunter was out doing things better left unknown. Standing in the open foyer, he called out to Caelyn, but she didn't answer. He was certain she was in the house, and he had a good idea where she might be.

After ascending the wide, winding stairway to the third floor, he opened the door that led up to the attic. Realizing that he was about to violate Caelyn's solitude, he entered the musty room with deference.

He spotted her right away, sitting with her back against the frame of a dormer window, allowing the light to fall upon the pages of a large book that lay open on her lap. The scrapbook contained all the articles and pictures of Ethan she had collected over the years. Its yellow pages were worn from the countless times she had turned them.

Caelyn heard the squeak of a board and stiffened, but didn't turn to look. She knew it had to be Wesley. Anyone else would have blundered into the room.

"I worry that one day, he will catch you up here," Wes said. "I hate to think what would happen to the scrapbook, not to mention you, if he found out."

Gently closing the book, Caelyn held it close to her heart and rested her chin on its thick edge to gaze out the window.

"I often wonder if he's happy," she said. Still immersed in a melancholy born from perusing her scrapbook, her vulnerabilities surfaced unbidden. "Do you think he still loves his wife?"

"I doubt it," Wes said, being careful to choose the right words. "I can only tell you that no man who has loved you could ever love another woman the same."

Caelyn smiled, appreciating his thinly veiled flattery. She cherished Wesley for everything he had done over the years. Without his help and confidences, she would have never made it this far. Being forthright with his feelings, however, was not his way. It concerned her that his entendre might be the precursor to a confession she was not sure she could handle without hurting his feelings.

"When I find him, I will tell him about your scrapbook," Wes said, ending the awkward silence.

Caelyn jolted, guessing what he meant. It was a moment she had hoped would never come.

"I have joined the army," he continued, not forcing her to ask the question. "The United States will enter the war soon, I'm sure of it. Somehow, I will find him. He needs to know. And you need to know that he knows."

Caelyn sat still, trying to sort the myriad of emotions swirling within her. She could not bear the thought of his leaving, and worse, subjecting himself to the dangers of the battlefield. Most of all, she knew his leaving would devastate Kitty.

"Wesley..." Caelyn stopped before she could start. She had no idea what to say. No matter what happened next, it would be something bad.

"No! Please, don't try to stop me," Wes said, sure she was about to. "I've already signed up. There's nothing that can be done to change it. I'll be leaving for training camp before the end of the week."

Defeated, Caelyn wished for the boy who had consoled her in her room that Christmas so many years ago. *He was as brave then as he is now,* she said to herself. *If only there was just a little cowardice in him.*

"You have to be the one to tell Kitty," she said, unable to face him. "You know she will be heartbroken."

"Yes, I know, and I truly am sorry for that. I won't tell her tonight. I couldn't bear to stay around after she finds out and it would be cruel to her. I will tell her the morning I leave, I promise."

Wes lowered his eyes.

"Before I leave, I want you to know this. If anything ever happens to you or Kathryn... If you need me for any reason, contact me. Get word to me, somehow. I will find a way back to help you. I swear it!"

Caelyn's first thoughts had centered on Wesley's wellbeing. Only now did she realize that his absence created concerns for her own safety and that of Kathryn's. For the first time, she understood how much she depended on him. But she cared too much for this young man, who now stood so tall and strong before her, to be a cross that he must bear. He had to be free in both mind and spirit to leave without guilt.

"I can take care of myself, you know that," she said. "And I can take care of Kitty as well. My prayers will be with you. God knows you will need them if America enters the war. Please, don't worry about us. Just make sure you come back alive."

Settling next to her on the broad window sill, Wes placed his arm around Caelyn. Accepting his corporal refuge, she rested her head against his shoulder, savoring a long-denied moment of feeling safe. For the first time in many years, her thoughts turned to her beloved Greek mythology. Wes' promise to find Ethan was as a thread of fate woven by the Moirai goddesses, giving her one last chance to know happiness. Or at least completion.

"Wesley," she said, gazing through the window, "thank you for being my Hermes."

Chapter Fifty-Nine

Bitter Wine

Almost nothing about the terrain he walked resembled Hannibal, but the countryside still reminded him of his boyhood home. The stream beside him was a poor substitute for the powerful waters of the Mississippi. The woods were too well groomed to be the wilds of Missouri. It may have been the snow that crunched beneath his cavalry boots or the icy January wind that blew in his face. Or it may have been his youth calling to him, reaching through the death and destruction of the past four years to remind him of the promise his life once held. Whatever the cause, he reveled in the sensation, thankful for its embrace. The horror of war made any diversion welcome.

Coming upon a large chestnut tree, he sat with his back against the trunk to watch the stream flow before him. Pulling the cork from the bottle of Bordeaux, he let the memories come as they might. As he sipped the wine, he tried to recall everything in his life that had been good in the hope that it would provide balance to what his life had become.

He was halfway through the bottle when a young woman on the far side of the stream emerged from the woods, interrupting his thoughts. She ran into the clearing, then ducked behind a tree to look back down the path. A moment later, a young man stepped into the clearing. As he came upon her hiding place, the woman jumped from behind the tree and shouted, attempting to scare her pursuer. Laughing, they embraced and kissed with unrestrained passion. Then, a dog dashed out from the brush toward the two lovers and nipped at the man's heel. The young couple laughed again, and the man threw a stick for the dog to chase. Kissing once more, they turned and continued down the path until they were out of sight, never knowing that there had been a witness to their perfect intimacy.

Alone again, Ethan's thoughts returned to Ocracoke and the day he had found Teach. Fifteen years had passed, yet he still remembered the smell of the salt air and the chill of that December morning. He remembered how Caelyn had come to where he sat, not realizing who he was. He could still see the effect of the sun behind her, highlighting her beautiful copper hair, and the thrill of feeling her touch for the first time.

Now, except for the life or death moments encountered on reconnaissance missions, he seldom felt anything at all. War had changed him – again. Seeing the young lovers walking hand-in-hand forced him to see his life for what it had become.

Perhaps what the other pilots say is true, he argued to himself. *Maybe fate put me here for a reason, to fight and kill*

Germans. *But, if being a purveyor of death is to be my legacy, is there really any reason to live?*

Finishing the bottle, he threw it into the water and watched it float downstream. The power of the wine and the serenity of the woods worked away at Ethan's defenses. Thoughts which he seldom allowed to the surface poured through unabated. Caelyn was the only thing in his life that had ever made a difference. Even beyond flying, the one thing that had kept him going these many years was the hope that they might somehow have another day.

The bottle, growing smaller with distance, was a metaphor for his life. To be as the couple he had seen across the stream was what he had wanted. Their reality forced him to face his truth. Holding onto the hope of reuniting with Caelyn had been a fool's dream. Without that hope, even as slight as it had been, his life had no purpose. Fifteen years had passed in the blink of an eye. Living the next fifteen years in the same fashion was unacceptable.

Once the fighting was over, he would have nothing. Flying competitions would never appeal to him the way they once had. The war had taken that away from him as well. The more he pondered the dilemma, the more it seemed his French friends were right.

"You can take Richthofen," the pilots kept saying. "We know you can. He has downed more than seventy planes. But you could have downed twice that many if you had chosen to fight. Please Monsieur Roberts, for the sake of all those who will die if Richthofen remains unstopped. Please reconsider your reluctance to engage in battle."

If I try and fail...I will still succeed, he argued to himself. *If my flying is not superior to that of Manfred von Richthofen's, I won't have to worry about the future. And if I do best Richthofen...*

The thought held no relevance for him, so he let it pass. Now that he had made his decision, his life had a purpose. Even if only for a while.

Every day for the next month, Ethan took his plane across the German lines in search of Richthofen and the Flying Circus, as his Jasta was known. The surfman no longer pretended to be an observer. When he flew, he flew for one reason – to find the German Fokker with red markings that Richthofen flew. It was the duel the pilots of both armies had spoiled for since Richthofen had made a name for himself. It was also the battle the French command was quietly trying to ensure would happen before Ethan's time ran out.

Since first arriving in France, the American commanders had made Ethan's civilian status an issue. Having spent years training at West Point, the American officers considered it a joke that the Allies' most respected pilot was a civilian. They demanded the maverick aviator join a service or lose access to planes of war.

When the French failed to act, the American intimated that, if Yankee fighter planes were to continue providing support to La République's soldiers to the degree necessary to protect them, they must ground Ethan as soon as possible.

France's Service Aeronautique agreed to the request, assuring the American generals the order prohibiting Ethan from flying was already being drafted. Once they processed all the paperwork, he would be grounded until such time that he took a commission.

In truth, the French knew Ethan would never join his country's air force or anyone else's. And though the commanders of the Service Aeronautique did not give a damn about what the Americans wanted, they had enough savoir-faire to know they had to be placated. Far more important to them was the impending duel between das Poltergeist and le Petit Rouge, as the French called Richthofen. Victory by their beloved Ghost Pilot would bring a much-needed boost to the Allies' morale. Thus began a succession of "clerical errors and logistical blunders" that kept the orders to ground Ethan in limbo. The question became whether the patience of the American commanders would run out before the anticipated dogfight between the two legends came to be.

Ethan's search for Richthofen continued through February without success. Observers sighted Germany's hero pilot several times that winter, but he hadn't recorded an aerial victory since September. Allied intelligence discovered that the Germans were using Richthofen to bolster the spirits of their countrymen in a series of public appearances. They had also learned he was experiencing excruciating headaches, the result of a head wound suffered the previous summer.

But Ethan knew it was only a matter of time before the flying baron would return to battle. The war's momentum was turning against the Central Powers and Germany could not afford to keep its best pilot on the ground. And because they shared a love for aeronautical excellence, he understood Richthofen. Resisting the call to fly was irresistible. He would return again and again until the war was over. Or until he was dead.

The arrival of March marked the freiherr's return to the skies and his string of victories resumed, downing nine more planes in three weeks. And though Ethan continued his pursuit, he couldn't put himself in the same air space at the same time. The futility of his efforts began wearing on his patience. He had always been a private person, but now he cloaked himself with an edginess that made him unapproachable.

Even Danny, his long-time friend and partner, was not immune to the surfman's outbursts. No longer able to see anything beyond his obsession, Ethan was pushing Danny too far. A combination of events at the end of March set the stage for a confrontation that, if allowed to materialize, would test their friendship as never before.

At the end of a long day of fruitless sorties, Ethan taxied his Nieuport into the hangar they used as their base of operations. Danny, who always came out to help after a mission, was nowhere in sight. Having no other choice, Ethan began the post-flight maintenance by himself, his anger growing with each passing minute. Danny's unexplained absence was inexcusable, and Ethan's building anger was a spring wound too tight.

He was working on the engine when the door to the hanger opened. Ethan took a deep breath, preparing to give his partner a dressing down he would never forget. But instead of Danny's, it was another familiar voice that greeted him. Ethan turned to see Marc Huffer, now wearing the rank of major, who had to come to greet him. Though still in his twenties, the war had aged him since Ethan had last seen him. The war had transformed the eager young pilot, who once pleaded with Ethan to fight Germans, into a war-weary veteran now commanding Ethan and Danny's squadron.

For Ethan, a visit by Huffer usually meant he was about to be subjected to yet another plea to join Aeronautique. As usual, he would promise to consider the offer, though they both knew he would not. It was a game for which Ethan had less and less patience, but one he had to continue if he wanted to keep flying.

"How was the hunting, Monsieur Roberts?" Huffer asked as Ethan stepped out from under the engine.

"There was a glorious battle, but I lost," Ethan replied with no humor. Of the many French squadron commanders he had come to know, Huffer was one of the few he liked. Today, however, he was in no mood for friendly chit-chat.

"But you are still alive," Huffer responded, feigning astonishment.

"No," Ethan said, softening his tone. "Actually, I died a heroic death. One that should warrant a poem or a song, I hope."

"Ah, and now I see the real reason the Germans call you 'The Ghost,'" Huffer bantered back. He offered Ethan a cigarette, but the American declined.

"So, what's the deadline for deciding this time?" Ethan asked. "A week? Three days?"

"I'm afraid I have some bad news," Huffer said, a signal to Ethan this meeting would not be business as usual. "They have replaced me as squadron commander."

"What?" Ethan said, surprised for once. Besides being likable, Huffer was the most competent commander he had known.

"In truth, my orders say that I am on a special assignment to provide aid, advice, and support to the new commander...a temporary duty if you will...to wet nurse an American colonel who has taken over the Escadrille."

"I don't believe it," Ethan said.

"Nor did I when I got the orders this morning. But it is true. They are giving this aerodrome and my squadron to the American. We are to learn from him, and he is to learn from us. It is all part of a grand scheme by Allied Command to help our countries work better with one another."

Ethan pondered the information for a minute trying to grasp the full ramifications.

"Well, I really hate that they gave you such a lousy assignment," he said. "I just hope he doesn't bother me or Danny. Otherwise, I guess it won't make a whole lot of difference one way or the other."

Huffer would have smiled at Ethan's bravado if he didn't have another bomb to drop.

"I am afraid that is the real reason I am here, Monsieur Roberts. The Colonel has grounded you. I have been ordered to tell you that all military aircraft are now off limits. I am truly sorry."

Ethan's body stiffened and his jaw muscles flexed as he clenched his teeth. That an untested American officer on a cross-training assignment would be the one to ground him was unacceptable. He had given too much of himself to the war to be shut out by a Johnny-come-lately.

"Who the hell does this son of a bitch think he is?" Ethan swore. Turning on his heels, he charged off toward the hut that served as headquarters, leaving Huffer where he stood.

"Ethan, my friend, wait! There is more!" But Huffer's plea was futile.

Storming into the command hut, Ethan brushed past the duty officer and rushed to the entrance of Huffer's office. Ignoring the duty officer's commands to halt, he threw the door open with a bang. A short, thin man wearing a U.S.

Army colonel's uniform sat in Huffer's chair with his back to Ethan. Disregarding the noisy entrance, the man continued gazing out the window.

"My name is Ethan Roberts, the man you have wrongly grounded. Apparently, you were not informed that I am working under legal contract with the French government. I demand that you rescind your order immediately or I will take my complaint to the highest French authorities."

The duty officer rushed up behind Ethan, his face flushed with anger. He was about to grab the intruder when Major Huffer tapped him on the shoulder and shook his head, no. The young officer took a step back, waiting to see what the new American commander wanted him to do.

Rather than respond to Ethan's outburst, the colonel allowed the silence to draw heavy over the room. He had waited fifteen years for this moment and he wasn't about to rush the delicious ending.

Ethan studied the colonel's thin face, realizing he knew the man from somewhere. But the officer continued to stare at him in silence, allowing Ethan time to search his memory. The more he stared, the more sure he was that he knew this man. It was a face that belonged to someone from his past, yet the details were wrong. And it wasn't just the face, there was something about the uniform as well.

And then it came to him.

"Captain Sullivan," he said in disbelief. The navy officer who had tried to secure property at Ocracoke had lost so much weight he was almost unrecognizable. Having lost most of his hair, his pate was now shaved bald. His once padded flesh had wasted away into a corpse-like version of its former self. His features were gaunt, the skin pulled tight against his facial bones.

"So, you do remember. Excellent! I have waited a long, long time for this moment. It would not be nearly as satisfying if you didn't remember me."

Ethan said nothing. There had to be more but he would not give the former navy captain the pleasure of asking.

"Thanks to you and your friends, my career with the navy was ruined," he said. "Having my boat sabotaged. Not delivering the papers to Washington on time. Your handiwork made me a failure. Oh, sure, I could have kept my commission. But it was clear I would never get a good assignment or an opportunity to redeem my service record. I only stayed long enough to arrange a transfer to the Army, and then only after securing an assignment to an air wing. I knew aviation was the one field that would give me a chance to renew my career, and thanks to the war, it has! But it took a hell of a long time to rise to this rank. If my navy career hadn't been sidetracked, I would be an admiral by now. And I have you to blame for that."

The pitch of Sullivan's voice grew higher with each word, taking great delight in his long-awaited revenge. Thinking more clearly than he had in months, Ethan realized that responding in anger would play into the colonel's hands. Sullivan was a petty man, but he wasn't stupid. The warning bells in his head were ringing like mad.

"That's a sad story, captain," Ethan said, using Sullivan's navy rank on purpose. "But that changes nothing as far as I'm concerned. I still have a contract with the French government, and legally, you can't stop me from flying. So, unless there's something else you've got to say, I suggest you rescind your order. Immediately!"

Sullivan cocked his bald head back and laughed.

"Of course, my surfman friend! Please, go fly. Do whatever you want. I don't care. The order to ground you was just to get you in my office."

The warning bells ceased ringing. Whatever the danger was, it was too late.

"Oh, but before you leave, I'm afraid I have some more bad news for you." Sullivan paused, striving to make Ethan as uncomfortable as possible. "As it turns out, your mechanic friend...Danny, I believe his name is...does not have a contract. Of course, I was surprised to find an American citizen of age right here at our very own aerodrome. As badly as we need troops in the field, I used my power as acting commander to have him conscripted into the army, where he can do his patriotic duty. I hope his absence won't hinder you in any way."

Far beyond a grudge, the depth of Sullivan's hatred was now clear. Danny worked for Ethan, not the French government. It was a fact that had never been an issue. But now Sullivan was making them pay for the oversight.

Ethan clenched his jaw, struggling to keep his anger in check. He had always been willing to take his chances with whatever fate might throw at him. It had never occurred to him that someone might use Danny to make him suffer. He not only failed to be there for Danny when he needed him most, but he was also responsible for Danny's removal. Sullivan was evil and dangerous. Ethan realized he could not make any more mistakes.

"All right, Sullivan," he said with as much calm as he could muster. "You win. What is it you really want?"

"Why, isn't it obvious, Mister Roberts? I want you to become an officer and fly airplanes in combat. If I can get you to do that, I will make a lot of American brass very happy. And if you shoot down Richthofen, they"ll finally give me the promotion I deserve. It's just that simple, Mister Roberts."

"OK," Ethan said without hesitating. He didn't care if it did cut against his grain. Danny was much more important than his vow not to serve in the military. "I will go to the French Air Service Command and ask–"

"Oh no, Mister Roberts," Sullivan interrupted, shaking his head. "That will not do. The French have been more than willing to accommodate your private little war with no regard for military decorum. I want you with the American forces...that way I can keep an eye on you. And more important, I can make your life miserable for as long as the war lasts."

"It would seem that you have considered every possibility," Major Huffer said, stepping into the conversation to give Ethan time to think. "You have presented Monsieur Roberts with a proposal impossible to refuse. Can he not have time to consider his options?"

"But of course, Major," Sullivan said, relishing having the upper hand. "Please, Mister Roberts, there's no need to make any rash decisions. I'll give you until, let's say, 0800 tomorrow to make up your mind."

Ethan clenched his fist in rage, but held himself in check. There had to be a way to thwart Sullivan's plan. Both he and Danny had many friends in France who would intercede on their behalf. Even if it took a few days, he was sure that he could get Danny back. But he wouldn't be able to accomplish anything standing in Sullivan's office.

"I'll be back," Ethan said as he turned to leave the room. The remark was purposely vague, not indicating whether he would return the next morning or not.

"By the way, Mister Roberts," Sullivan interjected one more time. "Did I tell you they assigned your friend to a unit in the Somme region?"

Ethan froze. The German spring offensive was building up to be one of the war's biggest battles. The years of fighting from the trenches had both sides of the conflict desperate for a decisive victory. Amassing all their forces into one great army, the Central Powers were moving across France at a frightening rate, taking new territory each day. Thousands of men on both sides were dying. Without the benefit of training, Danny would have little chance of surviving as a front-line soldier. It was the final cut of Sullivan's vile scheme. Ethan would have to join or be risking Danny's death.

Ethan left the room without looking back, the sound of Sullivan's laughter mocking him. Huffer caught up to Ethan and walked with him to the officers canteen in silence. When they entered the room, the raucous laughter and conversations fell to a whisper, then stopped altogether. The entire aerodrome was aware of what had happened to Danny and everyone wanted to know what the surfman would do next.

"Go back to what you were doing," Huffer ordered. "There is nothing we can do about Monsieur Williams until tomorrow. That is all there is to say for now."

The men resumed their conversations in hushed tones as the French major guided Ethan to a table in the far corner of the canteen. Huffer ordered a bottle of Cognac and turned to Ethan.

"This is a night for slow spirits and contemplation," he said. Near the end of their second glass, Huffer tried to boost his friend's mood.

"The war will not last much longer, I'm sure of it," he said. "Once the fighting is done, you will can return to civilian life. Colonel Sullivan will become but a terrible memory. But you, my friend, you will long be remembered as a hero of France. You will be able to do anything you wish. Of this, I am certain!"

Ethan stared into his glass before speaking, weighing the series of disappointments and failures that were his existence.

"I have no life of my own," Ethan said, "I never have. The only thing I've ever wanted was–" He stopped in mid-sentence. Caelyn was the only thing he had ever wanted, but he had no desire to discuss his broken heart with Danny's life at stake. Finishing the distilled wine in his snifter, he poured himself another. The most important thing now was to help Danny. He could not afford to let his personal failings interfere.

"I think Colonel Sullivan has underestimated your value to the cohesion of the Allied effort," Huffer offered. "If it becomes known that you are doing this against your will, the French people will rally to–"

"Excuse me," a voice interrupted. "Sorry to bother you, but are you Ethan Roberts?"

The two veterans looked up to see a tall American army officer standing next to their table. His well-defined face was fixed with determination. His youthful veneer betrayed a lack of experience. It was obvious to both Huffer and Ethan that the man had not yet seen battle. Noting the young officer's air service insignia, Ethan assumed the American was a newly assigned pilot, seeking Ethan's advice on how to fly in combat.

"Yes, this is Monsieur Roberts," Huffer's said. "But he is busy now and does not want to be bothered. Perhaps he can help you tomorrow. Now, go away, lieutenant."

The newcomer's back stiffened and his face turned dark. Taking a deep breath, he tried again.

"My name is Lieutenant Wes Bryant," he said, fixing his eyes on Ethan. "I am a personal friend of Missus Caelyn Winslow. I think you may know her better as Caelyn Canady. May I talk to you for a minute, sir?"

Ethan's eyes turned black, and he stared at the young officer in disbelief. The room closed in around him. Had Sullivan manipulated one last injury?

"Lieutenant, I said be gone with you," Huffer said. "It has been a long day and there's nothing you need that can't–"

He stopped in mid-sentence, an involuntary response to Ethan's crushing grip on his forearm.

"Sit down," Ethan rasped, his eyes boring into those of the newcomer. "Tell me what you have to say and make it good. But let me tell you this. If you're playing some kind of game at Sullivan's behest, leave now, or be prepared to die with that skinny bastard. I'll not be having you invoke her name as part of some sick attempt to pay us back for a petty incident that happened fifteen years ago."

Wes knotted his brow, not understanding why Ethan spoke as he did.

"I assure you I'm telling the truth," Wes said, declining to take a seat. "And, having arrived just this morning, I can tell you honestly that I have spoken to Colonel Sullivan only once, when I reported for duty. Now, do you want to hear what I have to say or not?"

Ethan studied the young man for a few seconds longer, then gestured for him to sit at the table.

"I could use a drink," Wes said without deference to his superiors.

Ethan and Huffer looked at each other, wondering if the man was overly confident or just stupid. Tired of the posturing and mental maneuvering, Ethan gestured his OK. He wanted to hear what this "personal friend" of Caelyn had to say. Huffer grabbed a glass from the next table and filled it for the lieutenant. Wes took a swallow and looked at Ethan.

"What I have to tell you is very personal. Perhaps it would be better if the major left us alone for a few minutes."

"Major Huffer is a friend of mine," Ethan said, still suspicious of the lieutenant's motives. "If you are here to speak the truth, there is nothing you can say that can't be said in front of him."

"As you wish," Wes said. He reached inside of his jacket to retrieve a slip of stiff paper from the inner pocket and placed it in front of Ethan with no explanation.

Before him, in well-defined contrasts of black and white, was a photograph of Caelyn. But it wasn't Caelyn. She appeared almost the same as he remembered her, but younger. Her dark hair flowed down over her shoulders in a youthful style, and her eyes revealed the sharp mind that had won his heart. Yet, as he studied the picture closer, he saw things that just weren't right. The hair was too wavy, and she had a slight cleft in her chin that Caelyn didn't. *What kind of game is he playing?* Ethan wondered.

"It looks like Caelyn, but it's not," he said. "Who is this?"

"You're right," the cocky lieutenant replied. "It's not Caelyn. I took this picture about six months ago. The girl's name is Kathryn Hawkins Winslow, Caelyn's daughter…and yours."

434

The taut lines on Ethan's face disappeared and his eyes narrowed as he stared at the man in shocked disbelief. Seeing no answers to his unspoken accusations, he looked back at the picture. The teenaged girl in the photograph had to be Caelyn's daughter. She looked too much like her mother not to be. But could she really be his daughter, as well? In all the years of wondering what might have been, he had never considered the possibility that Caelyn might have become pregnant. Yet, the more he looked at the photograph, the more he believed it might be true. A thousand questions swirled through his mind.

Why didn't she tell me? How could she have kept it a secret? Surely, she would have known she was pregnant when she married Hunter Winslow? Had she told Kathryn who her real father was?

"I don't understand why," Wes said, the sting of resentment lacing his words, "but you know Caelyn still loves you, don't you?"

The words were razors, cutting through Ethan's life-hardened mantle and into his heart. The possibility that he might have a daughter and that Caelyn still cared about him pulled his emotions in a thousand different directions. But it all kept boiling down to one question.

Why?

Wes remained silent as Ethan stared at the picture of Kathryn, deep-rooted hatred darkening his eyes. When he could no longer contain himself, he rose to his feet and leaned over the table.

"Tell me, you bastard, why did you desert Caelyn?"

"What?" Ethan asked? The statement was so absurd, he wasn't sure he heard correctly.

"You know what I'm talking about, you son of a bitch." Wes seethed.

"Now see here, lieutenant!" Huffer said, coming out of his seat. "You can't talk to him that way. I'll not tolerate such insolence and disrespect from a junior officer, regardless of what army you serve."

"It's all right," Ethan said, motioning for the Frenchman to sit down. "He thinks he knows something and I want to know what it is."

"You were supposed to call her but you never did," Wes said, letting years of built-up hatred stain his words. "But breaking her heart wasn't enough. You wanted to destroy her spirit as well."

"What?" Ethan said, confused by the wild accusations. "I did call her...or at least I tried. The number her father gave me was false. I even traveled to her home to find her, but–"

"Liar!" Wes pounded his fist on the table, then stuck an accusing finger in Ethan's face. "And what did your wife say when you told her you were leaving to search for another woman?"

Ethan sat in his chair, staring at the lieutenant as though the man had lost his mind. Then, slowly, a look of understanding spread across his face.

Having vented his anger without provoking a response, the young lieutenant's rage waned.

"Tell me, friend, just who is it I am supposed to have married?"

"I'm not sure," Wes said. Conscious of the many eyes about the canteen staring at him, he took his seat again. "Caelyn told me but it was a long time ago. I think it was...a woman named Abbie? Yes, I think that's it. Abbie."

Ethan closed his eyes. The revelation was overwhelming. In the blink of an eye, everything had fallen into place. Almost.

"And how did Caelyn find out about this supposed marriage to Abbie?" Ethan asked.

"Because she called the inn where Abbie worked, and...she told...Caelyn..." Beginning to grasp the truth of the matter, his words trailed off,

"Lieutenant," Huffer said, "even I know Ethan has never been married. It would seem that all three of you are the victims of a jilted lover's jealousy."

"Not jilted," Ethan said. "We were never lovers. I think for Abbie it was an attempt to keep the door open, so to speak. Maybe an effort to protect me. But the result was the same."

"Oh, my God," Wes said, realizing how Abbie's actions had caused a domino effect of profound misery and misplaced blame. "I... I'm sorry. How can I ever apologize for my rudeness and accusations? I have wrongly blamed you for...everything. How can I ever repay you?"

"You don't owe me anything," Ethan said. "Just tell me about her."

"Of course," Wes said. "What do you want to know?"

"Everything," Ethan said, filling their glasses again. "But most of all, I want to know why she married Hunter Winslow."

Taking a deep breath, Wes explained how Hunter had traded giving Kathryn his name for Jack Canady's fortune. He told every detail he could remember, and with each additional fact, it became more apparent how cruel fate had been to Caelyn and her surfman.

The revelations left Ethan speechless and reeling. His surprise turned to concern when Wes told him about

Hunter's moral decline and the parties he held in their home. When Ethan learned how Caelyn had been compelled to purchase a handgun for their protection, he began shaking with anger and regret.

If only I had known, he thought. *I could have been with them, protecting them the way a true husband and father should.*

"Wes, how do you know Kathryn is my daughter?" Ethan asked. "I mean, how do you know for certain?"

Wes shrugged and took a moment to sip his Cognac.

"Everyone knew," he said. "Or, at least, all the servants knew. But Caelyn told me the entire story one day while Kitty was at school."

Ethan raised his eyes in question when he heard the new name.

"Yes!" Wes said, only now understanding the relevance. "Kathryn's nickname is Kitty. And, if you recall, I told you her middle name is Hawkins. Kitty Hawk...see? Now you can appreciate just how much you've meant to Caelyn all these years."

No longer able to look at Wes, Ethan rested his elbows on the table and placed his hands over his face to prevent the two men from seeing his eyes.

"Our lives would have been so different, if only I had known."

"Forgive me if I speak...as you say...out of turn," Huffer said, "but perhaps it is not too late. Si Dieu le veut, the war will be over soon and..."

He stopped and spread his arms, allowing Ethan to imagine the possibilities on his own.

"He's right," Wes said. "Though I said it in anger, what I told you earlier is true. Caelyn still loves you. She keeps a

438

scrapbook with every article ever written about you and looks through it every time Hunter leaves. And the way she loves her mythology, once she learns that you never betrayed her, she will see you as the long-suffering Odysseus returning to Ithaca at last. There is no greater gift you could give her than yourself."

"Yes, mon amie, you must go to her. A hero of the war returning from France to his true love after so many years. It has the makings of epic romance, no?"

Ethan, now a man reborn, continued talking with the major and the young lieutenant until it was time for the canteen to close. Even then, Ethan didn't want to let Wes go. But he knew his new friend was facing an early start. His squadron had assigned him his first airplane and he was scheduled to demonstrate his competency in the morning. The two men agreed to meet in the canteen after sundown the next day and pick up where they had left off.

"Thank you," Ethan said as he shook Wes' hand in the light streaming through the hangar door where Ethan was quartered. "I appreciate what you have done."

Wes held up his hand to stop him from saying more.

"The only thing you owe me is a promise. The promise that you will return to Caelyn as quickly as possible and take her away from New York and Hunter Winslow. No matter what it takes."

Ethan's eyes widened, and he issued a guttural curse through clenched teeth.

"Damn it! I can't go back. Not yet. I can't leave Danny here."

He and Huffer explained what had happened and why Ethan was being coerced to join the army. Ethan wouldn't be able to do anything until they got Danny back to safety.

And unless a miracle occurred before eight, Ethan was forced to stay in Europe until his commission expired or the war ended. The long-troubled loner from Missouri understood the irony of the situation. At any time during the past fifteen years, he had been free to do whatever he wanted. Yet, on the very day he learned the truth about Caelyn, another man was making him bend to his will. He had often felt that he wasn't meant to live his life as his own. Now he knew it was true.

"Do not give up hope yet, Monsieur Roberts," Huffer said. "There is not a Frenchman at any level of the military who will not help you once I tell them your tragic tale. In the meantime, do what you can to rescue Danny from Somme. We will take care of the rest."

Though he appreciated Huffer's pledge, Ethan knew the romantic image the French had of themselves would do little to overcome the glacier pace of military bureaucracy. As the thought passed through his mind, a dark premonition settled in to take its place. He was sure he would never return to Caelyn. It was his fate.

I have known happiness only once in my life, he argued to himself. *And even then, it only lasted for a week. Why should I expect that to change now?*

He had no idea what was about to befall him, but he was sure the ending was already written. And if that was true, he reasoned to himself, then it didn't matter what he did now. Somehow, the upside-down logic gave him a sense of control. If it did not matter what he did, why not do whatever he wanted? The outcome would be the same, regardless.

At peace with his decision, Ethan assured Huffer and Wes that he would be all right and bid them goodnight. When he returned to his room, however, he knew he wouldn't be able to sleep. Between his burning desire to go to Caelyn and the frustration of not being able to help Danny, it was pointless to try. Instead, he sat at the wobbly field desk in the corner of his room and began writing.

His first letter was to Caelyn. The words flowed from his pen with an ease he did not think he possessed. He spoke of love and devotion, as well as the emptiness he had known without her. He lamented the time they had lost and wondered if they might yet share the remainder of their lives. He also made a promise that, should they ever see one another again, he would defy heaven and hell before he allowed anything or anyone to come between them. When he was done, he neatly folded the pages and tucked them into an envelope.

The next letter was to Kathryn, the daughter he had not known existed until now. Her letter was as difficult to write as Caelyn's had been easy. He wanted to be sure every word he put to paper conveyed the depth of his feelings. He wanted her to understand his sadness he felt at never having known one another. He also wanted her to realize she was the child of two people who loved each other more than words could convey. But most of all, he wanted her to believe that he loved her, even though he had never known her.

Ethan looked at Kathryn's picture again and smiled to himself. There she was in all her beauty, proof that his life had not been a total waste. He struggled with the letter for several hours until fatigue became stronger than his emotions. He fell asleep with his head resting on the desk, the last few lines of Kathryn's letter left unfinished.

Chapter Sixty

Icarus Falls

"**M**onsieur Roberts! Ethan! Wake up! Hurry! It is Lieutenant Bryant. He is in grave danger!"

The sounds of Major Huffer's voice and pounding on the door sifted through the miasma of Ethan's exhaustion and addled dreams. It had been less than an hour since he had fallen asleep. His confused brain failed to grasp the meaning of the noise and was incapable of coaxing his body to respond.

"Please, Ethan, you must open the door! Quickly! There is no time to lose."

Ethan rubbed his face, pushed away from the desk, and then lumbered across the room to release the door's catch.

"Colonel Sullivan has sent Lieutenant Bryant on a mission that is certain to be his death!" Huffer said. "He is flying toward the German lines now. In a reconnaissance plane. Without fighter support!"

"What?" Ethan asked, sure that he had misunderstood.

"It is true, Ethan. Someone in the canteen must have told Sullivan that you and Lieutenant Bryant shared drinks last night. I do not know. But they ordered Bryant to make a recon flight first thing this morning. The only person with him is a new enlisted man riding in the Salmson as the observer and gunner."

"You have to alert the squadron and go after him!" Ethan said, beginning to understand. "Now!"

"But we cannot! Sullivan ordered the arrest of anyone attempting to go up. There are some of us who would go anyway but Sullivan has posted guards on the field and will not let us near the planes."

Ethan peered over Huffer's shoulder to confirm that the Nieuport was still there. He had refueled the plane after bringing it inside the hangar. The machine guns remained fully loaded and ready because he hadn't fired them. All they had to do was start the engine and open the hangar door.

"Help me wheel her around," Ethan said as he started toward the plane.

"Ethan!" Huffer exclaimed, bringing the American to a stop. "Do you not understand, my friend? That must be what he wants. Sullivan wants you to go after Bryant because he knows you will have to go far into enemy territory, alone. He wants you to die."

Ethan turned to face Huffer.

"I know. But the kid won't have a chance without somebody to help him. He doesn't even understand the danger he's in. If I catch him before it's too late, I can force him to turn around. Then, I'll come back to take care of Sullivan."

"But what about Danny? It will be 0800 in less than an hour. There is little chance that you will make it back in time."

"Yeah, I know. It's not much of a choice, is it? If I stay here, Wes is sure to die. If I go after him, Danny might die. One thing is certain. Danny will have a better chance than that kid will. And besides, if something happens to me, you'll still be here to help Danny."

"And what about you, monsieur? What are your chances?"

"The same as they've always been, Major. No more, no less."

The tautness in Huffer's face and body waned as he realized he couldn't change Ethan's mind.

"You are a brave man, Monsieur Roberts."

"No," Ethan said, shaking his head. "Not really. At heart, I'm still just a surfman. Saving lives is what I do best. It's the only thing I've ever done that was worth a damn."

Leaving it at that, Ethan picked up the plane's tail section and struggled to pivot it around. Huffer came and helped him point the plane at the hangar door.

When they were done, Ethan returned to his room and grabbed his service pistol and flight jacket. Seeing the letter to Kathryn on the desk, he folded it up and stuffed it in the envelope with Caelyn's. Pulling on the jacket, he tucked the envelope into the inside pocket and returned to the hangar bay. He then climbed into the cockpit, removed the cameo from around his neck and – as he had a thousand times before – tied it to the knobs of the instrument panel where he could see it at all times.

Giving Huffer the ready sign, the French officer spun the propeller. As the engine roared to life, Huffer sprinted to the hangar door and pushed it open. Ethan bumped the throttle and taxied the plane outside.

The French soldiers guarding the fighters on the field saw the Nieuport rolling toward the runway, but did not give chase. With nothing to stop him, Ethan lined his airplane up with the runway and opened the throttle. A few seconds later he was in the air, headed east on the course Huffer told him that Wes had taken. If he pushed it, and if the lieutenant was flying at cruising speed, he might catch the young American pilot before he was too far across the line.

From the other side of the field, standing at the window in his office, Sullivan smiled as he watched Ethan's plane fade into the distance.

"Ahhh, revenge can be so sweet," he said aloud as he pulled the cork from a bottle of scuppernong wine. It was the bottle that the big waterman Harry Joyner had tossed to him as the *Henrietta* pulled away from the dock at Ocracoke. "Goodbye, Surfman Roberts. May you rot in hell."

As Ethan continued flying eastward, he realized there was almost nothing working in the lieutenant's favor. The clear sky meant that he was heading toward the rising sun. Enemy planes coming from the east would be impossible to see. Even the clouds had forsaken him, as there were none in the sky to hide in if attacked. The farther Ethan pushed his plane upward, the more his hatred for Sullivan grew. The colonel may as well have put a gun to Wes' head and pulled the trigger himself. His actions amounted to premeditated murder. Ethan promised himself that, if he survived, he would see that Sullivan got the punishment he deserved, whether it be through military court or his own hand.

The battle-scarred terrain of France passed below him, bearing witness to the travesty that was already being called the War to End All Wars. Having seen the death and destruction firsthand, Ethan hoped that the sentiment was true. Considering what he had experienced the past four years, however, he saw the words as an empty promise. Even now he could see large puffs of smoke on the ground, a telltale sign that German artillery was being brought to bear on an Allied position. When the bombing stopped, a wave of soldiers would advance on the position to push closer to Paris.

Had the artillery fire not caught his eye, Ethan would have never spotted the reconnaissance plane. From his altitude, the airplane was a small dark shape that stood out against the soft pillows of smoke created to screen troop movements. It had to be Wes Bryant. No other Allied planes would be flying eastward this early in the morning, and no Central Powers planes would be flying that close to their own artillery. Ethan drew-in a deep breath of frigid air and changed his heading toward the plane while maintaining altitude. He didn't want to give up that advantage until he could fly close enough to intercept the young American.

As Wes' Salmson passed over the artillery line, Ethan spotted another plane farther east flying toward it. Though relieved that it was only a single plane, it also concerned him. Why were no other German fighters joining the hunt? Was the enemy flyer also a reconnaissance plane? Or perhaps a German pilot was taking his fighter up for a shakedown flight? Whatever the reason, Ethan knew that once the two planes engaged, the Jasta would scramble their fighters and take to the air in case Wes was the lead plane of a major attack. If he didn't intercept Wes within the next few minutes, all hope would be lost.

Turning his plane into a dive, Ethan saw the German Fokker triplane fire a burst of rounds into the lieutenant's Salmson. The Fokker then swooped around to attack from behind. Even with an inexperienced crew, the reconnaissance plane made a formidable opponent against a single fighter. In addition to the pilot's machine gun, the observer wielded twin machine guns, making it a dangerous adversary. Well aware of this, the seasoned German pilot attempted to maneuver under Wes so he could shoot at the plane's defenseless underbelly.

But the American was having none of it. Though he was a novice at combat, he was a pilot of considerable skill. Each time the German made a move, the American maneuvered his plane to give his gunner a chance to fire. Still, the odds were against them. It was only a matter of time before the superior speed and agility of the fighter would get the better of the slower, less nimble Salmson.

With his engine shrieking in his ears from the high-speed dive, Ethan closed in on the unsuspecting German. Just as the Fokker came into his line of fire, the enemy plane vaulted upward into the brilliant blue sky. Painted in crimson, Ethan recognized the triplane he was hunting as the one Manfred Von Richthofen flew.

Cursing the circumstances that had at last brought him into the same airspace as the vaunted German ace, he took solace in the fact that he had stumbled on le Petit Rouge while flying without wing support. Even as the thought completed itself, Ethan realized how foolish it was. Richthofen would never fly without a wingman. He was using himself as bait!

Ethan didn't have to look in his mirror to know that a second German fighter was closing in behind him. His only chance was to use the speed of his dive to pull into a loop that would bring him full circle and behind the plane that was chasing him.

Pulling on the control stick with all his strength, the sudden change of direction pushed him hard against the back of his seat. The Nieuport shuddered, followed by a horrendous ripping of wood and fabric. The control stick gyrated in his hands and the plane broke out of the loop, leaving Ethan disoriented and exposed.

Glancing down, he saw sky where he should have seen a wing. The extreme pressure created by the maneuver had torn his plane apart. Danny knew the Nieuport had this weakness and had always taken measures to make sure it never happened with Ethan's planes. But Danny hadn't been there this time.

With the momentum gone, Ethan struggled to bring his plane in line with Richthofen's, hoping that he might get one last chance to fire. But as he brought the damaged Nieuport to bear on the red Fokker, a hailstorm of bullets ripped through his cockpit from behind. Richthofen's wingman had sprung the trap. Ethan felt a sharp burning fire in his back and his left arm was a shattered, useless mess. Smoke began billowing from the engine as his wounded plane started to freefall.

With one arm, Ethan pulled on the control stick with all the strength he had left. The plane leveled out just as it plowed into the ground, tearing the wheels off the undercarriage. When the Nieuport's propeller snagged the ground, the plane flipped over on its nose, landing upside-down on top of the surfman.

Ethan knew he was done. Broken and bleeding, he lay tangled in the crushed cockpit, his plane burning around him. Black smoke filled the air, and the smells of burning oil, gas, and wood filled his lungs. Though Ethan knew his life was seeping away, he refused to let go. It wasn't in him to just give up, even when faced with the inevitable. With the last few moments of his life, he thought of Caelyn, cursing fate for not allowing them to have a second chance. He also thought of Kathryn, the beautiful young woman who was his daughter, whom he would never get to know.

If only I could have told them how much I love them, he thought. *Now they will never know. I even failed to do that right.*

His vision cleared, and he saw Caelyn's cameo – the only tangible proof of their affair – still dangling from a shattered section of the gauge panel. Pushing back the pain racking his body, he stretched as far as he could and freed the keepsake from the panel. Clutching the cameo tight against his chest, he thought back to that day Caelyn had placed it around Teach's neck.

If only I had known.

The crackling of the fire about to engulf him kept Ethan from hearing the aging French woman as she approached the wreckage. Having refused to leave the farm that had been her lifelong home despite the advancing forces, she had seen the plane crash. Peering through the debris, she gasped. The pilot was still breathing! With the strength of a woman who had worked hard all her life, she grabbed the collar of his jacket and pulled him to safety. Removing his goggles and leather helmet, she rested his head on her lap.

Ethan was glad the woman had come. He didn't want to die alone. After all the years of living a solitary life, he wanted to feel the touch of another human being. As if reading his mind, the woman caressed the hair on his temple and whispered to him in French.

Ethan cast his gaze to his now unclenched fist, hoping she would see the cameo. Having caught his glance, she saw the object half hidden by his bloody hand. She unraveled the cameo's leather strips from his fingers and held it up so he could see. With his last remaining breath, he looked into her eyes and said, "Please...tell her I love her."

Then he was gone.

The woman cried for him, though she didn't know who he was. To her, he embodied all the misery the war had brought, so she cried for herself, too. But, most of all, it broke her heart that she could not tell anyone what his last words were. In his waning moments, Ethan had spoken in English, a language she did not understand.

She was still holding him when Wes and his observer found them next to the debris. The last burst of fire from the Nieuport's machine gun had not damaged Richthofen's plane, but it had forced the German ace to break off his pursuit of the Salmson for a few moments. Wes watched helplessly as the Nieuport fell from the sky. He didn't have to see the pilot to know it was Ethan. Shrugging off the instinct to save himself, he knew he had to land, even if it meant becoming a prisoner of war. For Caelyn's sake, he had to know if Ethan had survived. To live the rest of her life not knowing would have been the cruelest of fates, and she had suffered enough.

After taxiing his plane as close to the burning Nieuport as he dared, Wes rushed to the French woman and could tell by her expression he was too late. Removing his helmet and goggles, he dropped to one knee to look at the surfman he had once loathed. Now he understood why Caelyn loved him so much. He was a brave and selfless man who had given his life trying to save a person he barely knew. Adding to his anguish, Wes realized he wouldn't be with Caelyn when she learned of his death. It was a broken promise, and it would torment him for the rest of his life.

Placing his hand on Ethan's forehead, he prayed.

"If not for his wing, he would have downed me," said a man behind him with a thick German accent.

Startled, Wes came to his feet and turned to see Manfred Von Richthofen. His blond hair and piercing blue eyes stood in sharp contrast to his black leather jacket. A white scarf dangled from his neck and was in front of the jacket, its well-frayed ends buffeted by a slight breeze.

"Yah, I could have strafed you and your plane," he said, anticipating Wes' question. "But I had to find out why you landed when you could have easily escaped."

Resigned to whatever fate Richthofen might have in store for him, Wes answered the flying legend with more calm than he would have imagined possible.

"His name is Ethan Roberts. You would know him as das Poltergeist. He was a soldier, a surfman, a pilot of incredible ability, and a man of true heart and boundless love. He was the bravest of the brave...and someone murdered him.

Richthofen raised an eyebrow, giving the American lieutenant permission to tell his story. Wes described Colonel Sullivan's treachery, having sent him on a suicide mission for the sole purpose of luring Ethan into enemy territory. The more Wes talked, the more Richthofen's body tics betrayed his growing anger.

"Oberst Sullivan's actions are an insult to chivalry and to pilots," the German said when Wes finished. "His jealousy and hatred have sacrificed the Allies' most renowned pilot.

You learn that, though we are enemies, the pilots on both sides share an unspoken bond. Treachery perpetrated on one of us is an assault upon us all. Sullivan must be punished."

Wes collected Ethan's personal items, wrapped him in a blanket, and carried him to the French woman's cottage. The young American pilot and his observer then mounted their Salmson and, with Richthofen and his wingman acting as escorts, flew back toward French territory. Soldiers and pilots on both sides of the trenches watched in disbelief as the unlikely trio of planes flew toward the west. When they approached the French aerodrome, Richthofen and his wingman veered off and, with a wave of his wings, headed back to German-occupied territory.

Upon his return, Richthofen gathered the pilots of the Flying Circus and traveled to the farmhouse, where they buried Ethan with full military honors. He then wrote a report of the incident and had it sent via special courier to the French and American commanders over the Escadrille and Colonel Sullivan.

Colonel Sullivan was livid when he saw the Salmson, escorted by two German fighters, returning to his field. He ordered the French fighter pilots to give chase but none of the aviators made a move toward their planes. Their refusal to obey enraged Sullivan even more, and in the midst of a fit, he ordered the soldiers to arrest them all. By now, however, even the soldiers recognized that the American colonel was out of control. Sullivan continued to rant as they all walked away, leaving him standing in the middle of the airstrip. The next day, the American military authorities came and escorted him away.

Upon resuming command of the Escadrille, Major Huffer's first action was to ask the Americans to find Danny and have him returned. It did not take long for Ethan's story to become known among the people of France. Ethan was one of their heroes, and Danny was his partner. The cry for Danny's return became so loud and incessant that the Americans had no choice but to give him an honorable discharge and let him go where he wished.

Having nowhere else to go, Danny returned to the aerodrome and continued to help the French with their airplanes. The day of his return, Major Huffer came to Danny's room in the hangar to welcome him back. Danny was polite, but withdrawn.

"I have something for you, mon amie," Huffer said, handing Danny a small wood crate. "We collected the personal items in Ethan's room and those that Lieutenant Bryant brought back from the crash site and placed them in here. You are the only family I know of...so I thought you should have them."

Only then did Danny accept the reality of his friend's death. He had always assumed that when the war was over, they would go back to traveling around the world and fly in exhibitions. Now, as he held the box containing the handful of things that had belonged to Ethan, he realized his life would never be the same.

The depression overwhelmed Danny to the point he was incapable of performing routine maintenance. Each morning, he stood outside the hangar to watch the French pilots take off, flying their planes toward the German lines. And each time, it reminded him he had not been there when Ethan needed him most.

Toward the end of May, the Germans pushed the French back across the Aisne and captured Soissons. The aerodrome was in danger of falling to Central Powers forces. The French pilots pushed their planes to the limit, flying non-stop from dusk till dawn. On the second morning of June, Danny rose early, as he always did, to help the French ground crews. Next came the battle-weary pilots who climbed into their cockpits and, once again, flew off in search of the enemy. As he was walking back to the hangar to work on an ailing Nieuport, Danny heard a distant whistle followed by a muffled pop. Had any of the ground crew had infantry experience, they would have known those sounds meant danger. But the relative safety of aerodrome duty hadn't prepared them for the silent death making its way toward them on a gentle breeze.

Danny was already in the hangar when the thin wisp of smoke came across the runway. Then came the sweet smell of almonds, a pleasant contrast to the harsh odors of gasoline, grease, and oil permeating the hangar. A moment later, his hand began shaking and the wrench he grasped fell to the floor. When his legs began shaking, he realized too late what had happened. Crashing to his knees, his body pitched forward, coming to rest face down in the oil-soaked sawdust on the hangar's floor. For a few terrifying seconds before losing the ability to reason, he understood that the smell had been nerve gas.

Had he been outside, he would have received a full dose of the gas and would have died moments later, like those on the airfield had done. They were the lucky ones.

Chapter Sixty-One

The Letters

Caelyn stood at the window of the receiving room in Winslow manor watching the rain come down in relentless waves. For four years since Ethan's death, she often came here, hoping the newspapers, Wes, and the emptiness in her heart were wrong. A part of her refused to accept Ethan's death, choosing instead to believe that he might yet one day walk up to this house she hated and take her away.

The rain brought with it the last deep chill of the winter, making the Winslow house almost too cold to bear. Beginning to shiver, Caelyn called to Mr. Bryant and asked him to build a fire in her bedroom's fireplace. The aging butler informed her that the firewood was wet and it would take a while to start. "Perhaps Missus Winslow would like to take advantage of the fire already burning in the library," he suggested.

As much as she hated the room where Hunter held his parties, the chill made her consider the possibility – but only for a moment. She would rather freeze to death than be in that room by herself.

"Have Missus Pesci heat the leftover bisque from last night and bring it to my room instead," she said.

Mr. Bryant shuffled to the kitchen while Caelyn resumed her vigil by the window. She had not given up on reality, but the news about Ethan had pushed her close to the edge. Hope was the only thing that kept her from letting go – even if it was false hope. The memory of Ethan held more promise than anything her present life offered. Even Kathryn would soon be gone, leaving Caelyn with nothing but memories. She was dreading her daughter's departure because that would be the day she would have to face her future alone.

Caelyn was so lost in thought, she didn't notice a tall, broad-shouldered man ambling up the street until he was but a few feet hundred feet away. He wore a black large-brimmed hat that diverted the water down the back of his slicker and kept his head down to prevent the driving rain from hitting him in the face. The design prioritized function over fashion, something a seaman might wear. The bearded man looked so out of place, Caelyn wondered if he was lost.

Stopping at the end of the long walkway leading to her door, he looked up to stare at the house through the waves of rain whipping by his face. Under his arm, he carried a large object covered with an oilcloth to protect it from the rain. Satisfied that this wasn't the house he was looking for, he turned away and continued down the street.

As the man disappeared into the relentless rain, Caelyn saw herself in his dark form. A person alone, in a place he did not belong. Looking for something that might not exist. Carrying a burden, yet sheltering it from harm. She had no idea what he was looking for but prayed he would find it.

She stood by the window for a few minutes more, unable to contrive a reason to leave. The weather matched the darkness of her mood. She found herself trapped at the bottom of a deep, dismal pit. Soon, she would have to decide whether to claw her way back to the light or let the darkness engulf her forever.

"The soup is ready, madam." Mr. Bryant announced, interrupting her thoughts.

"Oh, thank you. Take it upstairs, please. I'll be there in a moment."

Watching the elder Bryant as he began negotiating the stairs with his tray, Caelyn wondered when Wes would come by to see them again. He had done well as a businessman. But he was much different since the war, much more reserved. He had written to her while still in France, telling her how Sullivan had manipulated Ethan's death, and how the French had forced him to relinquish command of Major Huffer's squadron.

Both Wes and Major Huffer testified against Sullivan during his Court Martial. The military court found him guilty of issuing an unlawful order and abusing his authority by jeopardizing the lives of men under his command. The military court stripped him of his rank and sentenced him to twenty years in prison.

Since returning home, Wes had asked his father to come live with him on many occasions, but the senior Bryant always declined. "Who'd be here to keep an eye on Missus Winslow?" he would say.

Not wanting to rush the aging butler, she waited in the foyer as he made his way up the stairs. When he reached the top, she followed, but a loud knock at the door stopped her. The three hard raps resonated through the receiving room, announcing the new arrival as a person with a purpose. Caelyn could not imagine who would be visiting in such weather, but with Mr. Bryant already upstairs, she went to the door and opened it herself.

Before her stood the man she had seen walking down the street a few minutes earlier, his enormous frame filling the doorway. With his face hidden in the hat's shadow and his body covered by the dark rain slicker, he was the embodiment of the Grim Reaper.

"Well, missy, are you going to invite me in, or are you gonna make me stand outside in this blow till I catch pneumonia?"

Caelyn opened the door wider, allowing the light to fall full upon the man's face.

"Harry? Captain Harry Joyner...is that really you?" Caelyn asked in a whisper.

"Well, it sure ain't Cap'n Ahab," Harry said, waiting for her to let him in. But Caelyn stood frozen in the doorway, unable to believe her eyes.

"Well, what's it gonna be? I ain't getting any younger here."

"Of course, of course! Please, come in! I'm sorry, it's just... I can't believe it's you! It's been so long, Harry."

The aging waterman turned sideways so he could pass through the doorway with the object he carried. With his free hand, he removed his oilskin hat to reveal a head of snow-white hair that matched his beard. Except for a few more wrinkles on his face and the color of his hair, he was still the Harry Joyner she remembered from Ocracoke Island and the *Henrietta*. Of all the people in the world that she knew, the last person she had expected to see was the Harkers Island waterman who had rescued her and Ethan from the *Aphrodite's* lifeboat.

"I thought I'd never find this place," he said, wiping the water from his face. "My eyes ain't what they used to be and the rain don't help. I couldn't read the number on your house the first time I came by. Say, you wouldn't have something to warm an old man's bones, would you?"

"Please, come into the library," she said, remembering the fire. "Mister Bryant!" she called up to the top of the stairs. "Bring the soup down to the library for Captain Joyner if you would, please."

"What about your husband?" Harry asked. "Is he here?"

"No," Caelyn said. Though she wondered why that might be a concern, she didn't ask. "He took Kitty to the university to meet the president and some trustees. He wants her to go to school there, but–"

"Good!" he said, cutting her off. "What I got's not for him. Just you."

Leading the way through the room's double doors, Caelyn cleared the top of a tea table next to a settee. Harry rested the box on the table and removed his storm gear.

"You're as beautiful as the first day I saw you almost twenty years ago," he said. "Now I remember why the surfman was so taken by you."

"Thank you," she said, not knowing what else to say. It had been a long time since she'd received a compliment from someone who mattered.

Mr. Bryant arrived with the soup, placing the tray on a small table separating two wingback chairs facing the fire. He took Harry's storm gear and closed the doors behind him as he left the room. Harry moved over to the fireplace to warm his hands.

"It's wonderful to see you, Harry," she said, taking one of the seats by the hearth. Harry remained by the fire, looking at a collection of framed photographs of Caelyn, Kathryn, and Hunter on the mantel. Reminders of a better day. "It's been so long and I've thought about you so many times since Ethan's... Since the war. But why are you here? It must be something serious to have persuaded you to come all this way."

"Bad news and unfinished business, unfortunately," he said, taking the seat beside her. "It's Danny. He finally passed. About two weeks ago, now. His mother hasn't spoken but once since. Then again, she ain't been right since they brought him home. I feel right sorry for her. But it's a blessing, all things considered."

"I understand," Caelyn said. "Wes told me what happened with the nerve gas and how he was after."

"Whatever he told you wasn't the half of it. I won't give you the details but, he was hardly human after those bastards gassed him. It would have been worse if it hadn't been for good-hearted Frenchies like Huffer and Nungesser. They raised the money to have Danny brought home. It was their last tribute to the sacrifices the two surfmen made for their country during the war. They even went as far as to provide Danny with a soldier's pension that was mailed to his mother each month."

Caelyn's eyes teared, and she felt her throat tighten as she remembered the love-struck teenager who had helped Harry rescue her. Danny deserved a better ending.

"It was nice of you to come all this way to tell me in person," she said, barely able to speak. "It must have been hard for you as well."

"To be honest, that's only the short of it," he said. "I didn't come here just to tell you about Danny. There's more."

Caelyn looked at the old waterman, surprised that there could be a greater purpose for his visit. After almost twenty years, there was little from their past that would have carried over to the present.

"When Ethan died, the French gave all of his personal belongings to Danny. But Danny wasn't supposed to keep them. As it turns out, Ethan had wanted all of his things sent to you if he died. But Danny was...wounded...before he shipped them to you."

Caelyn's thoughts flashed to the package Harry had placed on the tea table.

"When they brought Danny and his belongings to his mother, it included a box with Ethan's name on it. I guess she put it under Danny's bed, expecting to get back to it in a few days. And there it stayed until poor Danny passed.

"The day after we put him to rest, she was cleaning up his room when she came across the box again. Not knowing what else to do, she asked me if I would take it. When I opened the box, there was a note on top in Danny's hand that said, 'Ship to Caelyn Winslow.' Considering all the time that's passed, I figured the best thing to do would be to bring it here myself. And that's why I came."

Caelyn said nothing, allowing time for the information to sink in. Wes had told her about the night before Ethan's death. How happy he had been to learn she still cared for him. How he had sworn to come back to her and Kitty. Knowing these things made it all the harder to accept his death. Now, the box was a chance to have one last moment with the only man she had ever loved. It was almost too much to bear.

"I'm sorry, missy," Harry said, misconstruing Caelyn's silence. "This was a mistake. I shouldn't have bothered you."

"No!" she said, grasping his arm. "I'm the one who's sorry. It's just that...you have no idea what a wonderful thing you've given me. I can't thank you enough."

Though obviously he wasn't convinced she was all right, she breathed a sigh of relief when he settled back into the chair.

"You must think I'm crazy," Caelyn said. "And rude. I've completely forgotten my manners. Why don't I look at what's in the box while you eat? Please."

"Are you sure?" he asked, looking deep into her eyes in search of answers to unspoken questions.

"Of course. Please, go ahead. To be honest, I'd feel better going through Ethan's things knowing you're here. In case I need someone. You know?"

"Sure I do," he said, grasping her hand and placing it between his huge palms. "Take your time. I'll be right here if you need me."

"Thank you," she said, trying not to sound too anxious. She moved across the room to sit on the settee next to the tea table.

Removing the oilcloth, she saw a box made of thin, rough-cut wood. A simple crate once used to ship rations or some other military staple. But Caelyn knew its humble appearance belied the treasures she would find inside. Unfastening the metal clasps that kept the box sealed, she removed the top with shaking hands.

Tears rolled down her cheeks and fell onto the glass cover of a felt-lined tray, showcasing all the medals Ethan had been awarded during the war and his years with the Lifesaving Service. But the keepsake that had brought on the tears with a single glance, fixed prominently in the center of all his medals, was the cameo she had placed around a puppy's neck on a chilly December morning long ago.

Sliding off the glass cover that held the pieces in place, she removed the cameo from its section of the tray and held it in her hands. As she studied the nicked and worn relief, she realized it was stained with Ethan's blood and began to sob.

When she stopped, she felt a warmth growing inside she hadn't known for many years. The memory of the *Aphrodite* came back as a whisper, luring her spirit from a darkness that had all but consumed her soul. Long forgotten memories of Ocracoke and the *Henrietta* and the Diamond Shoals came rushing back. For the next few minutes, it was as if she had gone back in time, filled with the serenity of their backwater travels and the thrill of watching the flight at Kill Devil Hill. Each recollection forcing her to remember the passion she had suppressed for so long.

Then came the memories of the way Ethan had held her and made love to her. The emotional walls that had become her self-imposed prison crumbled. Cursing herself for having let pity consume her, she began to rise above her misery. Filled with a confidence she hadn't known for many years, Caelyn returned the cameo to its place, lifted the tray from the box, and set it to the side.

Most of the items were personal. Several silk aviator scarves, a pair of leather gloves, Ethan's flight helmet and his leather jacket. Caelyn lifted each item from the box and placed them on the table, feeling closer to Ethan with each object she touched. She held one of the scarves to her face, convinced his scent still lingered. Next, she removed his jacket and saw the brown spots from blood and the holes in the back from where bullets had struck. Realizing how much he must have suffered, she clutched it tight against her chest and cried again. Composing herself, she folded the jacket and laid it next to the other items.

One item remained at the bottom of the box, the light too dim to make out its form. Reaching inside, she grasped the object, surprised by its heft compared to its size. As she brought it out of the darkness of the crate, her heart stopped! The room closed in around her. She tried to breathe but her lungs would not draw air. Paralyzed with fear, her fingers refused to release the dark-gray service pistol!

"NO!" she gasped.

The haunting image of the familiar man flashed into her consciousness. Summoning all her will, she relaxed her fingers, and the weapon fell onto the table next to the box. Consumed by panic, she backpedaled blindly until she slammed into Harry. Spinning around, she tried to focus on his face, fighting off the phantom she could not remember.

"What's wrong?" Harry asked, grasping her shoulders.

The waterman's firm voice pulled her back. The ghostly images retreated to the darkness from which they had come.

"Please, hold me," she said.

Harry put his arms around her and pulled her close.

Caelyn remained in the sanctuary of his embrace for a few minutes, her head resting on his chest. He was as a father to her, strong, protective, understanding. A rock to cling to in a sea of confusion.

Harry helped her settle back onto the settee and poured a glass of water from the pitcher she had moved to the tea table's bottom shelf. As she sipped from the glass, the gray-bearded waterman covered the pistol with Ethan's jacket.

"You know," he said, "most pilots carried a handgun during the war. It's only natural they boxed it up with the rest of his things. It's likely Danny didn't even know it was in there."

"I'm sure you're right," she said, taking another sip of water. Her gaze fell upon the collection of medals in the display case.

"What happened?" he asked, pulling at his beard.

"I'm not sure. It's a phobia. Something about guns I don't understand. But let's not talk about that. It doesn't help. And I'd rather talk about Ethan."

"You know," she continued, nodding toward the curio box, "it's just not right, Harry. He gave so much. Saved so many lives. And all there is to show for it are a handful of medals and a few items of clothing. That's not the sum of his life. He was so much more than that."

"You're right," he said, sitting beside her. "But that box there. That's not the whole kettle of fish, now is it?"

"What do you mean?"

"You have a daughter, don't you? You and him?"

"How... How did you know?"

"I didn't...'til just now." He smiled and nodded toward the picture of Kathryn on the mantel. "But I suspected. It may be a small cleft, but it's a big clue, given you don't have one, and neither does the fella in that picture over there."

Caelyn shook her head, chastising herself.

"Oh, Harry. I underestimated you again, just like I did back then. I'm such a fool and you are the smartest man I've ever known."

"You'd have a hard time convincing Missus Joyner of that," Harry laughed. "She thinks I'm so dumb I'd have trouble pouring water out of a boot even if there was a hole in the toe."

Caelyn realized she hadn't bothered to ask the waterman how he was and what had happened in his life. For the next hour, they talked about the Outer Banks, how much the Lifesaving Service had changed since becoming the Coast Guard, and how far airplanes had progressed since the Wrights' first flight. Caelyn felt the breath of new life with each old story they told and all too soon, the time came for Harry to leave.

Caelyn hung on Harry's arm as they left the library, her cheek resting on his shoulder. When they reached the door, she gave him a kiss on the cheek.

"Thank you, Captain Harry Joyner. You came to my rescue...again. I can never repay you."

"Yes, you can," he said. "Your daughter. Make sure she knows who her father was. An' make sure you tell her about Danny and ol' Harry. That'll be payment enough."

"That's the least I can do. Perhaps someday we'll both come to Harkers Island and you can tell her yourself. I would love that."

"As would I, missy. As would I."

But they both knew it would never come to be.

"Goodbye Harry, and may God bless you."

"He already did, missy!" Harry boomed, returning to his flamboyant manner of old. "Getting kissed by a woman as beautiful as you...what more could a man what looks like me ask for?"

Caelyn remained in the doorway for a few minutes, watching as he walked down the street, slogging through the puddles left by the rain as if they didn't exist. When his big form disappeared around a corner, she closed the door and returned to the library. Though she knew the gun still lay beneath the jacket, she couldn't resist taking a closer look at the leather garment. Grasping it and then averting her eyes so as not to see the pistol, she picked it up and held it close.

The leather was thick, the inside lined with fur. Being a pilot, he must have worn it almost every day, a necessity for enduring the cold of altitude. Now, it was a spiritual link to the man she had loved. On impulse, she slipped her arms into the sleeves and pulled it tight around her body. She reveled in its warmth and its connection to Ethan's life. There was strength in his jacket, and it passed its strength onto her.

When she could indulge herself no longer, Caelyn slid out of the jacket and draped it over her arm. As she did, a thick envelope fell from its inner pocket and onto the floor. Reaching down to retrieve it, she saw her name written across the front in a bold handwriting. She shivered.

Averting her gaze, she laid the jacket over the tea table, once again concealing the gun. With trembling fingers, she opened the unsealed flap of the envelope and removed the wispy slips of airmail paper. Shuffling through the pages, she saw there were two letters, one addressed to Kitty and one to her. She skimmed over the text, consuming the intimate feelings Ethan had written for the girl he had just learned was his daughter. His words conveyed deep regret at having missed the chance to be a father and the desire to make up for his absence. And, though his words spoke of promise and opportunity for her, Caelyn sensed he did not see such hopeful things for himself. This was a letter that not only said hello, it also said goodbye.

Caelyn would have cried, but for all the tears she had already shed. As she began unfolding the yellowing pages of the letter meant for her, she could barely draw breath. Rather than take a chance on being overwhelmed, she sat in one of the wingback chairs beside the fire before proceeding.

My Dearest Caelyn,

Do you have any idea how much I love you? Still? After all these years?

Neither distance nor time has done anything to diminish the image of you I carry with me. Scarcely a day or an hour or a moment has passed that I was not thinking of you. I would be the first to admit that my love for you has been an obsession, but I have never had a choice in the matter. From the first moment I saw you, I knew there would never be another woman for me. While I feel as though I have died a hundred deaths, the memories of your touch and your kiss burn brightly within my heart. I could not break your hold on me even if I wanted to. You have always been and always will be, my one true love.

And now, young Lt. Bryant has told me you still share the love we found on the Outer Banks. He has told me of your false marriage, your long-endured misery, and your refusal to give up on life. When I think of how I have indulged myself in self-pity all these years while you have suffered so, I feel nothing but shame. Your strength has always been an inspiration to me and was so much a part of why I fell in love with you. I wish I could have been equally strong so that you might have more pride in me. But I promise I will try to do better to make myself worthy of your affection.

Lt. Bryant has also told me of our daughter, Kathryn Hawkins. I fear I may have compromised my masculinity, but when he showed me a picture of our daughter, I could not stop the tears which came to my eyes. But I will not apologize for tears of joy, for joy is something I have not known these past fifteen years. Not only is she as beautiful as her mother, Bryant tells me she is just as strong and quick of mind.

Oh, how I wish I could have held her when she was born. I would have been a good father, of that I am sure. But I take comfort knowing that you were always there for her, sheltering her from harm, teaching her to be her own person. I would give everything I own and concede any success ever attributed to me if I could see her, to talk to her, but for just one moment. I have written a letter to tell her these things and I hope you will give it to her when you feel she is ready. When you do, please tell her I, her true father, could not be more proud or have more love for her.

I would like, someday, to tell her these things myself, just as I hope I will someday be able to hold you in my arms again. But this war is an evil thing and I fear my purpose is nearly done. Perhaps I am wrong, for I truly do not want to die. And if I am wrong, then you should know that by the time you read this, I will be on my way back to you. And please believe, one way or another, I will take you and Kitty away from this profane creature who stole you and stole our life together.

But if I am right, you must hold on to this one thought. If there is a heaven, and because of you, I believe there is, I will be waiting for you there. The love I have for you is greater than this life, and even God will not deny us our time together but for so long.

As I close and prepare myself for the unknown to follow, I find comfort in a prayer that we used to say during my days as a lifesaver. I hope you will find comfort in it as well. It goes like this...

Caelyn's throat tightened as she read the prayer. Her eyes watered to the point she struggled to finish. It was a simple prayer, composed by men whose only wish was to survive the next storm. Yet, the words were so profound and filled with comfort, it was as though Ethan had come to hold her in his arms.

Embraced by a peacefulness she could not have imagined possible, she finished reading the last few lines.

Please forgive me for my inadequacy with words. It is, I'm afraid, the shortcoming of a man who has seen too much war and gone too long without hope of a better day. But even if I had command over all the words that exist in human language, I could not adequately express the feelings I have for you. Therefore, I will leave you with this simple thought, and hope it will suffice.

Caelyn, I love you...

...as I always will,

Ethan

Warm tears flowed down Caelyn's cheeks and she fought to keep herself from sobbing. Ethan's words had revived her spirit and touched a place in her heart she thought had been long dead. He could not have imagined the impact his letter would have when he wrote it.

How could he have known that, once again, he would be the lifesaver?

The doors to the library flung open with a crash, shattering the quiet! Kathryn stormed into the room, her face red and twisted with anger. Caelyn had been so lost in introspection and remembrances she hadn't heard Hunter's car.

"I won't do it, mother!" Kitty said, tromping into the middle of the room. She yanked off the bandeau, holding up her hair, freeing the long locks of copper that rivaled Caelyn's. "I won't. I don't care what he says."

Though startled, Caelyn had the presence of mind to slip the envelope back into the pocket of the jacket where it rested on the tea table.

"You'll do what I say!" Hunter said, storming into the room behind her. "You heard what Vice Chairman Forde said. None of the schools accept women. Not even the Arts. Just accept it and be done with it."

It was a new twist on an old argument, one Caelyn despised. Although Hunter had never said no to the idea of Kathryn going to school, he had made it clear he wasn't in favor of it.

Not wanting the servants to hear them arguing, Caelyn closed the doors. Hunter went to the liquor cabinet, poured three-fingers of Canadian whiskey, and downed it. Pouring another glass, this time all the way to the top, he turned to face the two women. His face was fiery red. His growing anger morphing his eyes into black pools of resolve.

"It was all a ruse," Kathryn said, placing her hands on her hips. "His well-rehearsed trustee stooges did everything except slam the door in my face."

"What about Barnard?" Caelyn asked, hoping to diffuse the quarrel.

"A lesser school created to appease men who fear that women might be better scholars? You know how I feel about that. It's not right, and I won't lend credence to the farce by pretending a degree from there somehow equals one from the men's college. Besides, father has another plan he thinks would suit me better."

"Another plan?" Caelyn asked, though she feared she already knew.

"Alan McCarthy," Hunter said, taking a long pull on his whiskey.

Caelyn shuddered inside. Hunter was turning the argument into a runaway train that would take them all to hell if she couldn't find a way to stop it.

"Alan is a fine young man from a fine family," Hunter continued. "He would make you a good husband. I have known his father all my life, and it would be a marriage befitting the status of both our houses. Besides, it would be good for business."

"I... I have no desire to see that, that Alan McCarthy boy," Kathryn stammered, humiliated. "I'm not a medieval princess to be bartered...in...in some loveless marriage of state. I don't like him. He's an idiot! Mother, please, tell him."

But Caelyn, overcome by the truth that it was her own marriage of convenience now compromising Kathryn's future, was unable to find her voice.

It's happening again, she thought. *Like it did with me.*

"You know," Hunter said, oblivious to Caelyn's torpor. Though his face still burned red, he spoke with unnerving calmness. "I've put up with your disrespect for far too long. Now, you'll do as I say, or I'll put you out on the street with nothing and be glad to be rid of you."

He paused and lifted the glass to his mouth, this time taking the time to savor its aroma and taste before swallowing.

"This is the only time I will say this," he continued in the same measured cadence as before. "You will not go to college. You will see Mister Alan McCarthy. You will accept his proposal for marriage, should he so offer it. And then you will marry him. Or you will pack your bags and leave...right now."

Though Kathryn was only a few feet away, Caelyn felt as if she was standing on the bank of a river watching her daughter being swept over a waterfall.

Kathryn's back stiffened and her expression transformed from disbelief to defiance. With a confidence that belied her youth, she walked up to Hunter and looked him in the eyes.

"So," she said, the corner of her mouth turning up into a sneer, "what if I tell Mister McCarthy that I'm not really your daughter? That would pretty much be the end of that, wouldn't it?"

The façade of calm Hunter had contrived disappeared in an instant. Caelyn could tell by his eyes that Kathryn had gone too far and that she knew it too. Undaunted, she continued.

"If I reveal the truth, then everyone will know you married mother for her father's money. And once everyone knows that, your status will be nothing. Compromised for all time. No matter where you go, people will see you and whisper, 'Look, there goes the big shipping tycoon who would be broke if not for his wife and her millions. Always acting like the self-made man. But he wasn't even man enough to father his own child!'"

Hunter's response was so quick and unexpected, Kathryn had no time to dodge the blow. The back of his hand struck her face with such force, blood flowed from split lips. She staggered back a step, then fell to the floor on her backside.

Downing the remainder of the whiskey, Hunter threw the glass into the hearth and came toward her.

Despite her shock, Kathryn stared at Hunter in defiance. Even when he raised his arm to hit her again, she resisted the urge to cover her face, as if challenging him to do his worst.

"STOP!" Caelyn screamed, finding her voice at last. "For the love of God, Hunter, stop!"

The plea filtered through Hunter's rage and he hesitated, though his arm remained poised to strike. Kathryn wiped the blood from her mouth with the back of her hand, her eyes still locked on Hunter's.

"Tell me, my pretend father. Do you hate me because I remind you of what mother was before you killed her spirit, or do you hate me because you know a better man was my real father?"

Swinging as hard as he could, he struck Kathryn in the face with his fist. She crumpled into a heap, struggling to remain conscious.

"If you EVER tell anyone, I will KILL you," Hunter seethed. Grabbing Kathryn by her blouse, he pulled her limp body halfway up off the floor. "I've given you and your damned mother everything! EVERYTHING! And this is how you would repay me?"

He raised his arm to strike another blow.

"STOP!!!" Caelyn screamed again.

But Hunter was a crazed man, oblivious to her pleas. He hit Kathryn with the back of his hand and then slapped her again. The blood flowing from her facial wounds splattered through the air.

Caelyn watched in horror, unable to speak. Kathryn was unconscious. Hunter would kill her unless someone stopped him. As he raised his arm to strike again, Caelyn averted her eyes. As the sickening sound of the blow resounded across the room, her gaze fell upon Ethan's jacket.

Summoning her courage, Caelyn slid her hand beneath the jacket. When her fingers touched the cold hard steel of the pistol, all the strength drained from her body. Bracing herself, she grasped the weapon and pulled it into the open.

"No..." she whispered, her head swimming. "Please, God, not now!"

But the fog rushed in as it always had before, bringing with it the swirl of shadows and half-formed images that appeared when she was near a gun. Again, she saw the familiar man with pistol in hand hanging by his side. Smoke drifting from the end of the barrel as he stood over a woman's lifeless body.

"Caelyn," he called to her. "Caelyn, look at me! You must never tell anyone about this. Do you understand? CC...do you understand?"

An all-consuming chill swept through her body, followed by a rush of dark memories. Caelyn saw herself as a five-year-old and the man standing before her. Smoking gun grasped in his hand hanging by his side – was her father! She saw him as a young man, before he had grown a mustache. But it was him. There was no doubt. Jack Canady was the only person who had ever called her CC. And as her memory reconstructed the image of a lifeless body at his feet, she at long-last remembered it was he who had murdered her mother.

The revelation opened a floodgate of still more repressed memories. The arguing, the abuse, the threats. Horrible things that a little girl could not understand. She remembered her mother, furious, packing their suitcases and her father storming in, swearing and yelling hurtful words. When she refused to listen, he pulled a gun from his pocket. But instead of cowering, her mother had laughed at him and said that he wasn't man enough to shoot her.

That had been her downfall. She had said the one thing Jack Canady, a man filled with doubts about his masculinity and worth, could not forgive. Then came the roar of the gunshot and the sight of her beautiful mother falling to the floor.

It all made sense. Why her aunt instinctively hated her father. Why he had manipulated her life to keep her under his control. Her unnatural fear of guns. Why she had suppressed the memory for so long.

"CC, if you ever tell anyone, I will kill you!" he had yelled, shaking her by the shoulders. "Do you understand? I will kill you, do you hear? I will kill you!"

And then he had slapped her so hard he knocked her unconscious.

The slap from her memory melded with the sound of Hunter striking Kathryn yet again.

"I'll kill you!" Hunter screamed. "If you ever tell anyone, I will kill you! Do you understand!"

"Father," Caelyn said, no longer seeing her husband.

The tone of Caelyn's voice and her strange reference to him as "father" pierced Hunter's rage. It was a tone he had never heard her use before, and it told him that something was terribly wrong. He forced himself to turn and face her.

"Caelyn...put the gun down," Hunter pleaded, his voice laced with disbelief. "You know you can't shoot me. Please, I'll do anything you want. I'm sorry. I made a mistake. I'll let Kitty go to college. Please, just put the gun down."

The haze created by the tsunami of memories was clearing now. As her father's form dissolved and became Hunter again, she knew the situation had changed. Since he was no longer hitting Kathryn, shooting him would be cold-blooded murder.

"I hate you," she said, as if stating her distaste for humid weather – and squeezed the trigger.

With the blast still ringing in her ears, Caelyn assessed what she had done. Yes, it had been murder but, once people saw Kathryn's face, no one would question that she had killed him to save her daughter's life. And she wasn't going to tell the authorities otherwise.

Looking at Hunter's body lying next to Kathryn's, his blood seeping into the carpet, she felt no remorse. The only thing that mattered was that Kathryn would never have to fear Hunter again. Laying the gun on top of Ethan's flight jacket, she hurried to her daughter's side.

"Kitty, are you all right? Talk to me, dear."

Kathryn jumped in response to her mother's voice and her eyes fluttered.

"Mother? What happened? Where's Hunter?"

"He's dead," Caelyn replied without emotion. "But don't worry about that now, we have to take care of you."

"Are you sure, mother? Are you sure he's dead?"

"Oh, yes dear. I'm quite sure. Come now, let me help you to the couch."

Once Kathryn was comfortable, Caelyn prepared an ice pack and held it to her daughter's blackened eyes and swollen cheeks. Next, she called the police station to report what had happened and advised them to bring medical assistance or they would have to take her statement at the hospital.

"I'm sorry, mother," Kathryn apologized when Caelyn returned to her side. "You've killed him and it's my fault. I shouldn't have defied him."

"Oh Kitty, my dear, sweet daughter. Don't be sorry. It's not your fault. The truth is, I couldn't be more proud of you. The way you stood up to him would have made–" Caelyn cut herself off, realizing her slip.

"...my father proud?" Kitty finished.

"Yes," Caelyn said. "How did you find out? How do you know Hunter wasn't your father?"

"I guess I've always known," she said. "But I think I really began to understand it the day Ansel Stick ran into the propeller. It was only for a second, but I saw the look in your eyes when you watched the man who saved me walk away. You were different to father...to Hunter after that. Every time I saw the way you looked at him when he wasn't watching, I knew. I knew you didn't love him, and I knew he couldn't be my father.

"But it was Wes who told me for certain. When he returned from the war, I forced him to tell me. Of course, he tried not to, but I was unrelenting. You know he could never deny me anything."

"Now, it's my turn to say I'm sorry," Caelyn said. "If there was some way I could change things, to go back in time, everything would be so different."

"It's all right, mother," Kitty said. "I know it wasn't your fault. Wes explained that to me, as well. But please, tell me about him. I have to know who my real father was, in your words."

"In due time," Caelyn said, reluctant to tell the story of their love while the pungent odors of blood, death, and spent gunpowder hung heavy in the air. "Right now, I'm afraid–"

"No mother! Now, please, before the police come. Who knows what will happen after that. Five minutes is all I ask."

Searching for a place to begin, Caelyn's thoughts wandered back to the time she had sat in the kitchen at the Pamlico Inn, listening to Superintendent Collins talk about Ethan and his exploits. She remembered the respect in his eyes and the admiration in his voice as he told them about Zeb Midgett and what they had endured in Cuba. She wanted to tell her daughter everything, every detail. But what could she say in just five minutes that would matter?

"As you know, his name was Ethan Roberts," she began. "He was a surfman of the Hatteras Lifesaving Station and later he became a pilot. He was like no man I had ever known before or have ever known since. I loved him with all my heart and I still do. He saved my life...and he saved yours."

Caelyn paused to look at the handgun sitting atop Ethan's jacket and smiled despite the morbid setting.

Somehow, Clotho, Lachesis, and Atropos had conspired to deliver the instrument of their salvation at the exact moment it was needed.

"And now...he has saved us again."

Chapter Sixty-Two

Return to Ocracoke

Except for a few personal items, Caelyn had sold almost everything in Winslow Manor. She had gotten rid of it all, leaving the great three-story mansion an empty shell awaiting the arrival of whoever would follow.

She had wanted to leave after Hunter's death but her attorney advised against it. After the grand jury ruled Hunter's death as justified, she had to postpone the move again, this time because of illness. At first, she thought her ailment was nothing but exhaustion taking its toll, but the sickness did not pass. After several weeks with no improvement, she decided it was time to see a doctor.

"I'm sorry Caelyn, but...you have a cancer," he said, his tone devoid of hope. "It's breast cancer, and quite progressed, I'm afraid. We could perform surgery but your chances of surviving would be thin at best. And it might only give you a few more months. I'm very sorry."

The thought of dying did not bother her as much as the unfairness of it all. Why, just when she had become free, was her life to end? It was as if Hunter had planned a final vengeance, scheming to deny her happiness even after his death. She wished she could cry but her anger would not allow it.

That evening, when she felt she could talk without betraying herself, she placed a long-distance call to Boulder. She wanted to talk to Kathryn, not to inform her about the cancer, but for the joy of hearing about her daughter's new life at the university. As she told stories about her classes and friends, Caelyn inwardly rejoiced at how well she was adapting to her new surroundings. Kathryn had matured a great deal since Caelyn had enrolled her without her knowledge.

"But why Colorado?" Kathryn had asked. "It's so far away and you still need me here."

"Because I've been looking into it. The university there has been accepting women as students since their beginning. Not just for appearances, but because they believe young women should have access to a higher education. It's perfect for you. Colorado is a state with independent, open-minded people. A place where a person with your potential has a real chance to grow."

"But what about you? I can't leave you here, in this house, by yourself."

"Don't worry about me. I'll be fine. Besides, I'll have closed this place and moved before you come home for Christmas. The thing that's most important now is that you get away from here. And, considering everything that's happened, the farther the better."

It was late when Caelyn said goodbye and hung up the phone. Emotionally and physically drained, she skipped her customary cup of tea and went straight to bed. But even when sleep came, it offered little refuge. Several times during the night she dreamed she had died, but instead of Ethan coming to greet her in death, it was Hunter. Each time the dream occurred, she woke herself shouting "NO!" at Hunter's ghost.

The episode left her angry and her faith shaken. All her life she had held on to the belief that there would be a better day, if not in this life, then in the next. Now, when she needed her faith most, she was having doubts. If only she could talk to Ethan, even for just a minute, she would be all right. It was a ridiculous thought, but she could not stop herself from thinking it.

Caelyn felt little better the next morning and stayed in bed for a long time, trying to rally the energy to put her clothes on and finish the business of moving. As her thoughts drifted in the grayness between sleep and wakefulness, Hunter appeared again, smiling as if to mock her naiveté and helplessness.

Caelyn came wide awake, both disturbed and angry with herself. The dream was a warning. A warning about giving up and waiting for death would be a victory for Hunter. She had endured too much to let him win, and now was not the time to give up on herself. She wasn't sure what she could do, but whatever it was, it would be under her terms. In the meantime, she would finish closing the estate as planned and make the most of what life she had left.

After dressing, Caelyn brought several suitcases into the room and began packing the clothes she would need for the next few weeks. Having reached the point where it was necessary to vacate the house, she had reserved a suite at The Plaza where she would stay until she decided on a permanent residence. As she removed the last dress from the closet, she saw the crate in the corner where she had stored it months earlier.

Fate, perhaps? she wondered as she pulled the wood box from the closet. *It's not the same as being able to talk to Ethan, but if taking a last look at his personal items is the best I can do, then I will settle for that.*

Removing the lid, she took out his jacket and drew it around her like a cape. Its weight on her shoulders provided comfort she had not felt in many years, a tranquility that reminded her of the wonderful letters Ethan had written. Removing the envelope from the inside pocket where she had returned it, she began to re-read the words that had touched her heart.

Though the words were the same, the circumstances of her life had changed since she had first read them. Ethan's unwavering certainty that somehow, all things will be made right in the end, was like a message in a bottle. For the first time in weeks, she allowed herself to breathe and to think beyond her misery. At last, she knew what to do with the little time she had left.

During the next few hours, Caelyn finished packing the suitcases, then penned a short missive to Kitty. She placed the note into an envelope with Ethan's letter to Kathryn and addressed it to her daughter's residence hall in Boulder. Caelyn had not had time to show Kitty the letters after the shooting, and she had forgotten about them during the investigation and hearing that followed.

After loading her suitcases into the car and locking the mansion's doors for the last time, she dropped the envelope off at the post office. If her calculations were right, it would take four or five days for the mail to reach Colorado. It would take at least another two or three days for Kathryn to travel back to the East Coast. More than enough time for what she had planned.

The farther south she drove, the more comfortable she was with her decision. The act of leaving New York for the first time in twenty years lifted her spirits more than she had imagined possible. New York was death. North Carolina was life. And as she drove the car over the bridge connecting Manteo to the Outer Banks, she knew she was returning to the place she had been reborn.

The drive to Nags Head had taken two days. Another day and a ferry ride across Oregon Inlet got her to Cape Hatteras. On the morning of the fourth day, she left her car in Hatteras Village and boarded the mail boat to Ocracoke.

As the little craft chugged into Silver Lake, she let the memories rush in to greet her. From the deck of the mail boat, she noticed there were a few new houses and businesses but there was far more old than new. The little village of Ocracoke was almost the same as it had been twenty years earlier.

Leaving her bags at the dock, she began walking through the village in search of a place to stay. Discovering that fire had destroyed the Pamlico Inn some years earlier, she headed toward a new hotel that a villager assured was "just a hop and a skip away." Resuming her walk to the hotel, she noticed a small boat in front of a shop. Filled to the rails with various seashells and driftwood, a sign attached to its side proclaimed, **"Scotch Bonnets – $2 Each – 2 for $5."** Caelyn laughed to herself and continued on.

When she found the hotel, she checked in and asked the innkeeper to have her bags brought up from the dock. They arrived just after she had finished freshening up from the trip. The teenage boy who brought them stared at the dollar she tipped him in disbelief. It was an enormous sum for such a simple task.

"If there's anything you need," the boy said in his Down East brogue. "Anything at all. You call on me, Billy Garrish. I'll do you right, for sure."

She unpacked her clothes and settled in to stay for a while, though she had no idea how long it would end up being. With the evening meal still a few hours away, Caelyn decided to visit the site where the Pamlico Inn had stood. As she walked back toward the lake, her eyes were once again drawn to the small boat filled with shells and driftwood. Something about the little vessel was familiar. Though its dried-out wood and flaking paint betrayed years of neglect, the boat didn't appear to be beyond repair.

Looking closer, she saw something under the flaking paint that made her stop in her tracks. *It can't be,* she thought. *It just can't be!*

Hurrying across the road to the boat, she picked up an oyster shell and used its sharp edge to scrape off the larger flakes of paint. As each letter appeared, she saw her intuition had been correct. Written across the stern in bold block letters was the word APHRODITE. The old vessel, now reduced to a display for cheap trinkets, was the lifeboat from the *Aphrodite.* The boat that had carried her and Ethan to safety.

Caelyn was so engrossed in her discovery that she didn't see the old shopkeeper walk up until he spoke.

"What can I do for you today, ma'am?" he asked. "They's some real pretty bonnets in there. They'd make splendid gifts for the folks back home."

"How much?" Caelyn asked without looking up.

"Well, the regular conchs are a dollar apiece. But I can make you a deal if you want to buy more than one."

"No," Caelyn said. "How much for the boat?"

The question took the old man by surprise.

"Whatcha gonna do with a whole bunch of seashells and driftwood?" he asked, misunderstanding Caelyn's intent.

"You can keep the shells and driftwood. I want the boat. How much will you sell it for? I'll give you a hundred dollars for it."

"Well gee, I don't know, ma'am," he said, scratching his head. "What would I do with all my shells?"

"How about two hundred dollars?" Caelyn said, growing impatient. She knew the shopkeeper would be able to buy five or six new boats for that much money and was in no mood to haggle.

"Lady, for two hundred dollars, you can have the boat and everything in it!"

"No, all I want is the boat...and the name of someone who can repair it."

"Well, I reckon that would be Tyler Ballance. He lives 'bout a quarter-mile that-a-way," he said, nodding toward the sound side of the island. "He's got a pretty good wood shop and he lives right on the water. Just follow the road here and look for a white house with a white picket fence. If you go too far, you'll be walking in water."

Chapter Sixty-Three

Life Boat

Tyler Ballance was like most of the men who lived on Ocracoke – the easygoing sort who spoke with an economy of words. He came out on the porch after Caelyn knocked on his door, a Pall Mall hanging from the corner of his mouth. He appeared to be in his mid-forties, though it was hard to tell because of his weathered skin, dried out from long hours spent in the sun while on the water. After wiping his hand on the bib coveralls, he offered it to Caelyn. Believing the waterman would be impressed by a woman who knew how to shake hands properly, she gripped extra hard.

"Evening, ma'am," he said as he looked her over. "How can I help you?"

"I was told that you are a fair carpenter. Is that true?"

"No ma'am, not really. I'm a craftsman. A boatwright, if you will. Carpenters build houses an' such. I lovingly create works of art that float on the water."

Caelyn smiled despite herself. If nothing else, Tyler Ballance was a man who took pride in his work.

"I've just purchased the boat that sits on the main road, the one with the seashells in it. Are you familiar with it?"

"Yes ma'am. Of course. You can't hardly get from one place to another around here without walkin' right past it."

"Would you be willing to repair it for me? Make it seaworthy again? For a fair price, of course."

"Well," he said as he scratched his chin, trying to visualize the boat in his mind's eye. "It's been settin' on the ground a good while now, so it's gonna need some new planking on her bottom. May be in need of a new keel, too. And she's somewhat dried out, so she'll need some work to seal the joints. And paint. Lots of paint. But I imagine it could be done, all right."

"How long would it take?" Caelyn asked, becoming excited about her good fortune.

"Well, let's see. If I worked on her every night after fishing, two, maybe three weeks."

Caelyn thought about the letter she had sent to Kathryn. Two weeks would be too long.

"How much would it cost?"

"Oh, let's say...a hundred and fifty dollars?" He said, raising one eyebrow as if watching to see if she would balk. "Plus the cost of the materials, of course."

"And how much do you make when you go fishing?" she asked, ignoring his obvious price gouging.

"About twenty dollars, thirty if'n it's a good day. Why you wanna know?"

"What if I gave you a thousand dollars to cover your losses for not fishing and you worked on the boat full time? How long would it take you to repair the boat?"

"Ma'am," he said, unable to restrain the excitement in his voice. "For a thousand dollars, I'll have her done in three days."

"Good, then it's a deal," she said, shaking his hand again. "And Mister Ballance, when you paint her, use the original colors. It shouldn't be difficult. You can see the old colors under the newer coat of paint that's flaking off."

"Yes ma'am. That'll be no problem."

"And find a motor to mount on the transom. I don't care how much more it costs. I'll want to take it out as soon as you're done."

"Yes ma'am," he said, not believing his sudden good fortune. "Anything you say. You're the boss!"

Chapter Sixty-Four

Kathryn's Father

Kathryn recognized her mother's handwriting on the envelope waiting at the dorm for her when she returned from classes. She removed the pages and saw a sheet of new stationery folded over several older, yellowed sheets. She unfolded the first page and read the message Caelyn had written before leaving New York.

Dear Kitty,

I'm afraid I have some rather bad news. The doctors have discovered I have a cancer that cannot be cured. Forgive me for not calling to tell you, but my reasons for doing it this way will soon become clear. Meanwhile, please do not worry about me. I have very little pain and, thus far, I retain my strength.

Kitty, I want you to know how proud I am of you. You have become the woman I always wanted to be. Your life is so free and so fulfilled. If I accomplished one thing in my life, it was giving you the chance to be your own person. You have done that and much, much more. You have your father's spirit, and I know he would be very proud of you as well. I only wish that he could have lived long enough to see you as the woman you've become, but I take comfort in knowing that there will be another day for us all.

I do have one bit of good news that may help you during this trying time. Enclosed, you will find a letter written to you by your father. I meant to give this to you earlier, but with the hearing and so much going on, I never found the right moment. I discovered this letter and one written to me inside the jacket that was in the box Capt. Joyner brought to our house. After talking with Wes, it is apparent Ethan wrote the letters the night before he was killed and never had a chance to mail them.

I know how much you love hearing stories about your father and how much you wish you could have known him and talked to him. Now your dream has come true, at least in a small way. These are his words, written in his hand, just for you. I know it's not much, but I think this letter will give you the chance to know him in a way the stories never could.

In closing, I want you to know I will not be home for Christmas. Please, do not be upset. I know it is hard for you to understand, but I have to face this thing my own way. Don't worry about me, I will be all right. In fact, I've never felt better. It's just that, before I die, I have to go back to Ocracoke where it all began. I hope you will understand. May God bless you and keep you safe for all your days.

Love,

Mother

Refusing to believe her mother's news, Kathryn read the letter several times to make sure she understood everything correctly. Especially the last paragraph. *Why would mother travel to such a remote place to spend her final days? Who will take care of her? Why doesn't she want to be with me during such a difficult time? None of it makes sense.*

Putting questions about her mother aside for the moment, she unfolded the old stationery bearing her father's last words and, with shaking hands, began to read.

Dear Miss Kathryn Hawkins Roberts.

You cannot imagine how many times I have said that name these past few hours. It is such a beautiful name, so full of strength and purpose. Forgive me for indulging myself in assigning you the "Roberts" surname. You see, I have never had a daughter before, and saying it that way makes it seem so much more real. There are so many things I want to say to you. Where do I begin?

The one thing I want you to know, above all else, is how much I love your mother. I hope she has told you about me, and I hope she recalls our time together with the same affection I do. I have only known happiness once in my life, and that was the time I spent with her.

You should probably know I am just an ordinary person who has accomplished little of any real meaning in life. But I have tried to be an honest man and have always tried to treat others with respect. I have many regrets concerning my life, but none greater than the fact that I was not able to be a father to you. Lt. Bryant told me your childhood has not been terribly happy, but that you were never mistreated. I feel responsible for your unfortunate situation and I hope you understand that, if I had known that you were my daughter, there is nothing on earth that could have kept me away from you. It is a cruel fate that allowed this knowledge to come to me so late in life and while I am so far away. But, if I should be so fortunate as to survive this terrible war, I will do everything within my power to find you and your mother and somehow make things right. This I swear to you by the God your mother loves so dearly.

The most surprising thing I have learned is that we have actually met, or almost did. The terrible thing that happened to you that day at Belmont, when you were just a little girl, is something no child should have to endure. But I thank God that he put me there at the same moment in time as you. Of course, I did not know it then, but that was my one chance to be a father, and I thank the good Lord that I did not fail you.

Lt. Bryant has also told me of your love for air planes. Has your mother ever told you of the day we watched the Wright brothers fly their plane at Kill Devil Hill? It is a wonderful story, and I cannot help but wonder if I somehow passed the fascination for flight on to you that day. You may have heard that I have done a little flying myself these past few years. I have no doubts you will make an excellent pilot, and who knows, maybe one day we will fly together, father and daughter.

It does not surprise me at all that you are driven to do the unconventional, it is a trait you share with your mother. I knew from the very first moment I saw her she was unlike any other woman I had ever known. It was her spirit that drew me out of

Kathryn sat silent for a few moments, contemplating the letter and wondering why her father hadn't finished it. Her mother's life would have been much different if it hadn't been for the *Aphrodite* and a journey of personal discovery that had begun on a remote island many years ago.

Ocracoke! That was it, Kathryn realized. *It had to be. Her mother wasn't going to the Outer Banks to reminisce. She was going back to the place where it had all begun...to die.*

Rushing to the dorm's receiving room, she seized the house telephone and dialed the long-distance operator. She had to stop her mother before it was too late. The doctors may have missed something. There might be a chance. There were a thousand reasons, but most of all, she was not ready to let her mother go.

"Operator. Give me Ocracoke, North Carolina. No, no, no! O-CRA-COKE. It's an island on the Outer Banks. What? I don't care. Anybody. Try the sheriff."

Kathryn waited as the operator searched for a number.

"There's no sheriff's department? Jesus! Well, what is there?"

Another moment of silence followed.

"Yes, the Coast Guard Station will do. Try that."

Kathryn listened as the operator dialed the number but no one answered.

"No calls can get through? The lines must be down? How can that be?" she said, then slammed the phone's handset back in its cradle.

Rushing to her dorm room, she began packing her suitcase. If she couldn't reach her mother by telephone, then she would have to go to Ocracoke. She knew it would take at least three days to reach Elizabeth City by train and another to travel to the island. But she wasn't going to sit around waiting for the phone lines to be repaired. She would stop her mother and they would face this thing together.

Chapter Sixty-Five

Ruth

Caelyn pulled her coat tighter as she walked toward Tyler Ballance's house. The wind from the previous night's storm, now only a breeze, had left freezing temperatures in its wake, chilling her to the bone. And though the storm had been strong enough to knock down a few limbs, it hadn't been as bad as the nor'easter that had blown through three nights earlier, leaving them without power or telephone service.

When she arrived at the Ballance cottage, she ignored the front door and continued to the workshop behind the house. It had taken the fisherman-boatwright a few days longer than he had expected to make the repairs, but now the work was done. Caelyn stood in the doorway, admiring the results of his labor. The lifeboat looked as she remembered it, including the bold black lettering proclaiming it had once belonged to the *Aphrodite*.

"Well, what do you think?" the Ocracoker asked as he walked into the shop behind her. "I don't know why you wanted this ol' boat fixed up so bad, but I can tell you, right now, she's as seaworthy as anything on the island."

"She's beautiful, Mister Ballance," Caelyn said, impressed. "She looks the same as she did twenty years ago. You have done an outstanding job."

"No thanks necessary, ma'am. You've paid me four times more than what this thing is worth. That's thanks aplenty."

"What about the motor, Mister Ballance? Is it working yet?"

"It was when I checked her out last night. It's only a ten horsepower, mind you. But it's small enough I think you'll be able to crank it by yourself with no problem."

"Tell me, Mister Ballance," Caelyn said, stepping out of the shed to look up at the sky, "how soon do you think I might take her out on the water? This weather seems pretty bad."

"Well, it has been," he said, joining her outside. "I wouldn't have any trouble taking her out but I wouldn't advise a woman to. Especially one that don't know the waters. But, I'll tell you, when this front is done passing through, things are gonna get real still. Tomorrow morning, the water will be as smooth as glass. Take my word for it."

"That would be perfect. If you will put her in the water, I'd like to come over at first light. Take her out fishing."

"Sure. That'll be no problem at all. The water's at a good temperature right now. There ought to be a plenty to catch. In fact, I think I'll head out after you do. You can't keep a fisherman away from the water but for so long, you know."

When she left the waterman's house, Caelyn followed a path that meandered through the marsh grass and dunes to the beach. Large waves generated from the storm crashed on the shore, propelling long trailers of water and sea foam almost to the line of dunes. Sitting on one of the higher mounds of sand as she had years before, she tried to recall everything, just as it had been that December morning. She remembered how she had watched Ethan happen upon Teach, coaxing him to eat from his hand. She remembered how hesitant the surfman had been to talk to her, and how they had laughed together when he fell off the Banker pony. But most of all, she remembered their long, yet tentative, first kiss. Her boldness had been so out of character. And yet, his response so respectful. It was, she knew now, the moment she had fallen in love with him.

Caelyn looked out over the ocean, still able to see the black clouds in the distance moving eastward. A bolt of lightning flashed from the clouds to the waters below. Tears ran down her cheeks, despite having promised herself she wouldn't cry.

"Be patient, my darling," she whispered. "I'm coming."

"Don't you worry, child, he'll be there awaiting," came a thick voice behind her.

Startled, Caelyn turned to see a black woman wearing a red bandanna. Her face showed few wrinkles, but her gray hair suggested that she was older than she appeared.

"Who are you?" Caelyn asked.

"Some folks calls me Ruth, but that ain't no matter. What's important is that I'm here."

"But...why are you here?"

"Don't know, exactly. I had a dream last night, and it told me I needed to come here before you go to be with your surfman."

"How do you know about that?" Caelyn asked. Her skin tingling as if a thousand ants were crawling over her body. She hadn't told anyone about her plans.

"Ha, ha," the old woman crackled. "I told you, it came to me in a dream. I don't know hows it happens, but it does. So, here I am."

"What else did your dream tell you?" Caelyn asked, testing the woman.

"Well, I don't know everything, but I do know that your daughter will be here tomorrow. What's her name, Kitty?"

The pronouncement was almost too much for Caelyn. How could the woman know her daughter's name? But more important, if Kathryn was coming to Ocracoke, it might interfere with her plans.

"They's one other thing," the woman added. "I think you have something to give me."

Caelyn thought for a moment, then realized what she must be talking about. It was all so strange, but somehow it made sense. The woman had come to her for a reason.

"Why, yes," Caelyn said. "I do have something to give you."

Chapter Sixty-Six

Crossing the Bar

Rising early the next morning, Caelyn dressed, slipped on Ethan's leather flight jacket, and left the hotel. A grin tilted the corners of her mouth as she practically skipped with down the path. The dawn air was chilly but there was no wind. The day promised to be as beautiful as the boatwright had predicted. She was more at peace with herself than she had been in many years. It was going to be a beautiful day.

When she arrived at his dock, the waterman noted her good mood and greeted her with a cheery "hello." The "Aphrodite" was sitting in the water as he had promised, gassed and ready to go.

"Here's your check, Mister Ballance," she said, jumping into the boat. "I think you'll find it adequate."

Tyler looked at the check but didn't understand the numbers on it. Caelyn had written the amount to be paid as five thousand dollars.

"Merry Christmas, Mister Ballance," Caelyn said as she pulled on the motor's starter cord. "Go buy your wife a nice present. And make sure you tell her you love her."

"Thank you," he said, glancing back and forth from the check to her.

"Just remember, Mister Ballance, there is nothing greater than love," she said as she removed the lines holding the lifeboat to his little dock.

"Wait!" he called out over the noise of the engine. "I forgot to give you a life jacket!"

"Not necessary, Mister Ballance! I'm off to find Thanatos!"

She waved at him as she powered the boat away from the dock and into the sound waters. Tyler Ballance waved back at the strange woman, wondering what the hell she had meant.

As Caelyn piloted the boat toward the inlet, the memories of the trip she had made in the Carolina skiff with Ethan and Danny rushed back to her. The salt air filled her lungs, and the wind created by the boat's motion blew in her face, reminding her how wonderful their two-day sail to Kitty Hawk had been.

"This was the life I was supposed to have lived," she said aloud as she passed through the inlet and into the ocean waters. "This place was supposed to be my destiny...and so it shall now be."

The little motor pushed the boat northwestwards along the coast toward Cape Hatteras and the Diamond Shoals. Almost two hours had passed before she saw the white tower with the black spiral that told her she was approaching the Hatteras Lighthouse. When the lighthouse aligned due west of the boat, Caelyn turned the bow toward the east and the open sea. As she changed heading, she spotted an airplane passing in front of the lighthouse, turning to follow the southeasterly lay of the Outer Banks' lower islands. *A good sign,* she thought as the plane grew smaller with distance. *The future and the past, coming together as one.*

When she reached the area where she imagined the *Aphrodite* had run aground, she cut the engine and let the boat drift. It was impossible to be certain, but it didn't matter. It was close enough. Bowing her head, Caelyn began reciting the surfman's prayer she had memorized from Ethan's letter.

"Into your hands I place my life, a humble surfman filled with strife.

"Guide me now to your most forlorn, through the tempest and the storm.

"Help me find lost souls at sea, and let them see your strength through me.

"An' when I make it 'cross the bar, I'll tell the world how great thou are."

The warming air was creating a stiff breeze. Waves were forming that rocked the boat from side to side. Pulling the jacket tighter, she stood and took a long look at the lighthouse.

"Forgive me, God, for I know what it is I do," she said. "But you have already taken my life. All that is left is my soul. I have given so much of myself to you these many years, and I tire of waiting. I must be with Ethan now. If that is a sin, then damn me for all time. As long as it is with him."

The wind grew stronger and the boat's canting from side to side grew more pronounced. Caelyn looked at the water and knew that the time had come. But she hesitated. Despite her bravado and determination, it was harder than she'd imagined it would be. Her faith told her what she was about to do was a sin, and she could not shake the feeling that God was watching her.

What Caelyn didn't know was that days before, a thousand miles away, a powerful storm in the middle of the ocean had already decided her fate. Its gale-force winds created large swells that began a slow journey toward the east coast of North America. In a few moments, it would complete its long trek across the ocean to crash on the beach sprawled before the Hatteras Lighthouse. But not before it passed beneath the *Aphrodite's* lifeboat.

Standing with her back to the ocean, Caelyn didn't see the first of the swells as it approached. And then, the struggle to rationalize her actions became pointless. As the rolling mound of water passed beneath the little boat, it rocked from one side to the other, pitching Caelyn into the cold, salty water.

She struggled to save herself at first. But water saturating the jacket and its fur lining weighed her down. When she understood she couldn't save herself, she chose to believe God had intervened. Doing what she might not have been able to.

Come, my dear Ethan, she said in her mind as the darkness closed around her. *Come to me as you did so long ago. We belong together. Forever.*

With no one to pilot her, the wind pushed the empty lifeboat along until its hull snagged one of the same shoals that had brought an end to its namesake many years before. A moment later, a huge wave struck the craft broadside, flipping it over. With its white hull pointing toward the heavens, another wave crashed down, snapping it in two. The steady succession of waves breaking on the shoal continued to pound the wooden boat until nothing but pieces remained.

Chapter Sixty-Seven

Kathryn, Daughter of Caelyn

It was dark when Kathryn arrived in Elizabeth City. After three long days of traveling by train, a hundred miles of sound waters still lay between her and her destination. After finding a hotel, she tried calling the island again but was told that the lines were still down. She was about to ask the clerk for the names and telephone numbers of local watermen who might sail her to Ocracoke when she saw a handbill posted on a wall littered with other notices.

"Crop Dusting and Aerial Surveys." the leaflet proclaimed. **"Reasonable Rates!"**

"Please, please be available," Kathryn pleaded as she dialed the number printed on the handbill. The phone rang nine times before a man with a deep country twang answered.

"Sure, I can take ya," he said, agreeing to pick her up at the hotel at first light. "Just make sure you dress warm, 'cause it gets real cold up there in an open cockpit."

By midmorning of the next day, the crop duster pilot had flown them to the ocean, where he banked the plane southward to follow the coastline. It was perfect flying weather, and though she could see the faint remnants of a storm moving off to the east, the air was calm and clear. During the next two hours, they flew past Kitty Hawk and the lighthouses at Bodie and Hatteras islands.

Spying an old two story building behind the Hatteras lighthouse, she wondered if it was the lifesaving station that had once housed her father and his crewmates. At the same moment, an unexpected calm swept over her. The cape's point and the shoals beyond drew her attention. Somehow, she knew her mother was no longer with her. And though it defied reason, she felt at peace with what her mother had done.

It was just past noon when the biplane touched down on the grass landing strip paralleling the shoreline outside Ocracoke Village. Kathryn walked into the hamlet and, upon asking the first person she came across, discovered that her mother was staying at a small hotel nearby.

"Yes ma'am," the teenage boy said. "Everybody's seen the Yankee lady who bought the shell boat and is paying Mister Balance to fix up. She's staying at the hotel just around the bend. I work there sometimes, run errands for folks. She's treated me real nice, and she's a real good tipper, too."

A short walk later, the innkeeper greeted Kathryn with a friendly "hello" as she entered the small hotel.

"Nope," he said, perusing the register. "Sorry. There ain't no 'Caelyn Winslow' staying here. But, now ain't this a coincidence? There's a woman with the same first name, but her last name is 'Roberts.'"

"It's the same woman," Kathryn said with a dry smile, pleased that even till the last, her mother had no qualms about sticking a symbolic finger in the eye of convention. "'Roberts' is the name she has taken since a change in her marital status."

"I see," the innkeeper said, though it was clear he didn't.

"Is she here?" Kathryn asked, already knowing the answer.

"No ma'am. Sorry. She went out first thing this morning, headed toward Tyler Ballance's place, just like usual. Kinda surprised she ain't back yet, though."

A few minutes later, Kathryn found the little white house with a picket fence and found the part-time boatwright, part-time fisherman, working in his shed.

When she asked if he had seen her mother, Caelyn Roberts, he smiled and shook her hand.

"She's your mother! A wonderful lady, that's for sure. I never met a woman like her before. Can't say enough good things about her. Why, she's practically made me rich with one job."

The waterman continued, telling Kathryn about the lifeboat and what a good job he had done rebuilding her. She could see that, not only was he proud of his work, he was also smitten by her mother's charm.

"But where's the boat now?" she asked when he paused to take a breath.

"Oh, she took it out first thing this morning to go fishing," Tyler said. "But I don't think she's coming back today."

"Why is that?"

"She said she was going to go see some fella named Thanatos. There ain't nobody around here with that name. I reckon there might be some folks on Hatteras with that name. But not here."

Kathryn smiled to herself despite the dark meaning behind the boatwright's unwitting revelation. As a child, her bedtime stories had always been about Greek gods, goddesses, their ill-fated interactions with humans, and their own failings. She knew who Thanatos was, and she knew her mother would not be returning. Caelyn Roberts had accomplished what she had wanted, to reunite with her surfman. The only thing left for Kathryn now was to say goodbye.

It was almost sunset by the time she made it to the beach. She had decided to stay on Ocracoke and explore for a few days, hoping she might begin to learn what it was about the Outer Banks that so captivated her mother. But tonight, she had to be near the ocean.

As she stood looking out over the waves crashing on the beach, she wondered where her future would take her. Having seen the promise of her mother's life wasted, she vowed to live hers in a way that would make both their lives meaningful.

But what will I do after college? she wondered. *I have all the money I'll ever need, but I must have a purpose. Otherwise, her suffering will all have been for nothing.*

"Whatcha looking out there for?" came a female voice from behind her. Kathryn turned around to see a black woman with a red bandanna covering her graying hair. "Your future ain't out there, child," she said, nodding toward the ocean. Then, pointing overhead, "It's up there. In the sky. But that's a little ways down the road."

"Who are you?" Kathryn asked.

"A friend," the black woman replied. "I knew your father and your mother, too. I was right about them, and I'm right about you."

"You knew my mother?" Kathryn asked, not sure whether to believe the odd woman.

"Yes, child, I knew your mother. I spoke to her just last night, I did. Right here on this very beach. She asked me to give you these."

The black woman reached into her apron pocket, then held out her hand to reveal an old envelope with Caelyn's name written across the front and a cameo attached to a leather strap.

"Your mother wanted you to have these. This here is a letter your father wrote to her, and this cameo belonged to her. But he kept it for years so he would never forget her."

"Thank you," Kathryn said, realizing that the woman had to be telling the truth. Her mother would have never given such personal items to a stranger.

"She didn't say much when she gave them to me. She just wanted me to tell you that she loves you and to read the letter. She said it will make you feel better."

Kathryn's eyes began to tear as she read her father's words of undying love. It was only a glimpse of what they had shared, but it helped her understand why her mother had accepted death. Dying was not the end of her life, but the beginning of her eternity with Ethan.

Looking up from the letter, Kathryn started to ask if her mother had said anything else, but the woman had already disappeared into the long shadows of the dunes, leaving Kathryn to grieve in private.

Taking in the orange and caramel-colored hues of the day's last light, Kathryn reflected upon the poetry of what her mother had done. Almost from the beginning, she had known her time with Ethan was borrowed, and would have to be returned too soon. She could have despised fate. She could have sought to denigrate Ethan's memory because she couldn't be with him. But her devotion to the quiet surfman never waned. It was a love so strong even the capricious gods of mythology could understand. The fulfillment of a promise to those who hear the call of Aphrodite's whisper.

— The End —

Author's Notes

As with my previous novel, *Black Hearts White Bones*, I apologize in advance for any mistakes associated with the historical and technical aspects of this story. Despite having conducted countless hours of research, a story this rich in nautical, aeronautical, and historical detail provides many opportunities to slip up. I believe I have kept such mistakes to a minimum. For those who love the history as much as the story, I offer the following notes for clarification and context.

Although several scenes in Aphrodite's Whisper take place on Silver Lake, Ocracoke's picturesque harbor didn't exist before its dredging in 1938. Prior to that time, it was a tidal basin known as Cockle Creek, essentially dividing the village into two sections. Because the harbor is now indelibly linked to the village, I used creative license to describe it as it exists today.

The scene where Superintendent Collins relates Ethan's heroic, single-handed rescue of seamen from the *Priscilla* is a true story. This incredible act of bravery was performed by Surfman Erasmus "Rasmus" Scarborough Midgett on August 18, 1899, while on routine beach patrol. The Secretary of the Treasury awarded Midgett the Gold Lifesaving Medal on October 18, 1899. The Coast Guard ranks the rescue among its top 10 of all time.

That African Americans could serve as lifesavers is one of the curious contradictions of Southern culture. While it is true they were paid less and were less likely to achieve higher ranks, they did indeed serve at interracial stations that became known as "checkerboard" crews. Most notable among them was Richard Etheridge, who, at the time of his promotion to Keeper of the Pea Island Lifesaving Station in early 1880, was one of eight African Americans serving as surfmen.

As a fictional character, Ethan Roberts obviously was not the first person to ride as a passenger on an airplane. That distinction belongs to Charles Furnas, a Dayton, Ohio mechanic who traveled, uninvited, to Kill Devil Hill on his own dime to help the Wright brothers. Unable to pay Furnas wages for his work, on May 14, 1908, Wilbur and Orville gave him the honor of becoming the first airplane passenger by alternately taking him up on two flights.

Readers familiar with the Outer Banks may have noted that I left off the "s" at the end of Kill Devil Hill instead of using "Hills." Before incorporation in 1953, the town was known by both variations of the spelling and by its most prominent physical feature – Big Kill Devil Hill.

There were only six people who witnessed the Wright brothers' first four flights, Surfmen Bob Westcott, John Daniels, Will Dough, and Adam Etheridge, young Nags Head waterman Johnny Moore, and lumber-buyer William Brinkley. While many accounts list only five people, I include Westcott because he observed the flights from the lifesaving station's lookout tower. Given the small number present at such a historic event, I kept Ethan's and Caelyn's involvement with the actual flight preparations to a minimum so as not to step too heavily on history.

Like the *Priscilla* rescue, Ethan's flaming of three observation balloons is an example of fact being as incredible as fiction. Frank "Arizona Balloon Buster" Luke was America's second-ranking ace during WWI and was posthumously awarded the Congressional Medal of Honor. During a 17-day span in September 1918 (only nine of which involved combat flying), Luke flew 10 missions comprising only 30 hours of flight time, shot down 14 enemy balloons (three during a single sortie) and four aircraft (seven according to some sources).

French fighter pilot Roland Garros is credited with having come up with the idea of using metal deflector plates to protect propellers from bullets fired from a fixed, forward-firing machine gun mounted on a Morane-Saulnier Type L.

For those who might complain that my depiction of Manfred von Richthofen's actions at the end of the story is too romanticized for war, I offer the circumstances of the baron's own demise to support such a scene. Fighter pilots of the day saw themselves as modern-day knights and adopted their own code of chivalry. After Australian Commonwealth Military Forces shot down and killed Richthofen on April 21, 1918, they gave him a full military funeral with an honor guard, six Royal Flying Corps pallbearers, and a 21-gun salute. A wreath placed on his grave read, "To Our Gallant and Worthy Foe."

Though the U.S. Coast Guard does have an official prayer, the Surfman's Prayer in this story is my creation.

Finally – and alas – the story that Caelyn tells Ethan about Aphrodite whispering to "her children on earth" is mythology of my own making. I only wish that it were true.

A PERSONAL REQUEST FROM THE AUTHOR

The success of independently published writers such as myself is almost totally dependent on reader reviews. If you enjoyed this novel and would like to see more of my stories make it to print, please post a review on GoodReads.com, Amazon.com/books, Kindle.com, Audible.com, or other book-related websites. And please be sure to tell your friends. Thank you.

www.ingramcontent.com/pod-product-compliance
Lightning Source LLC
Chambersburg PA
CBHW051203120726
47905CB00004B/964